Critical acclaim for Madeline Baker's previous bestsellers:

CHEYENNE SURRENDER

"This is a funny, witty, poignant, and delightful love story! Ms. Baker's fans will be more than satisfied!"

—*Romantic Times*

WARRIOR'S LADY

"Readers will be enchanted with *Warrior's Lady*, a magical fairy tale that is to be devoured again and again."

—*Romantic Times*

THE SPIRIT PATH

"Poignant, sensual, and wonderful....Madeline Baker fans will be enchanted!"

—*Romantic Times*

MIDNIGHT FIRE

"Once again, Madeline Baker proves that she has the Midas touch....A definite treasure!"

—*Romantic Times*

COMANCHE FLAME

"Another Baker triumph! Powerful, passionate, and action packed, it will keep readers on the edge of their seats!"

—*Romantic Times*

PRAIRIE HEAT

"A smoldering tale of revenge and passion as only Madeline Baker can write...without a doubt one of her best!"

—*Romantic Times*

MADELINE BAKER

**Winner of the *Romantic Times*
Reviewers' Choice Award
For Best Indian Series!**

**"Madeline Baker is synonymous with tender
Western romances!"
—*Romantic Times***

RECKLESS DESIRE

He's going to kiss me, Mary thought, and even as the idea crossed her mind, his lips were touching hers. Heat suffused Mary from head to foot as Cloud Walker's mouth crushed hers. His arms held her close, so close she could barely breathe. His body was trembling with desire, and she had no thought to resist.

She was breathless when he took his lips from hers.

"Mary." His desire for her was there in the throaty whisper of his voice as he murmured her name. She saw the love and the wanting in his eyes, and she swayed toward him. She had said no for too long. Tonight she would follow her heart....

RECKLESS DESIRE

MADELINE BAKER

LEISURE BOOKS NEW YORK CITY

For my son,
John,
while he's far away

A LEISURE BOOK®

Published by
Dorchester Publishing Co., Inc.
276 Fifth Avenue
New York, NY 10001

ISBN 0-8439-4591-5

The name "Leisure Books" and the stylized "L" with design are trademarks of Dorchester Publishing Co., Inc.

Printed in the United States of America.

Part One

1

1898

I felt the tears well in my eyes as I helped Mary pin her veil in place. My daughter, my only daughter, was getting married. Never had there been a more beautiful bride, of that I was certain. Our neighbor Ruth Tippitt had made Mary's wedding dress, and it was exquisite. Simple yet elegant, the gown was fashioned of white satin and lace. The collar was high, the sleeves were long and fitted, the skirt bell-shaped. The gossamer veil fell in graceful folds to the floor.

My Mary. A bride. She wore her long, dark brown hair loose, pulled away from her face with ivory combs. A faint touch of rouge brightened her cheeks. She had always been a lovely girl, but on this day, her wedding day, she was beautiful. Her gray eyes glowed with happiness, her mouth curved in a sweet smile.

Where had the years gone? Only yesterday she
had been a little girl, begging for a pony of her own,
babbling cheerfully as she helped me dust the house,
pouting because she couldn't always have her own
way, and now she was a grown woman, ready to place
her heart and her future into the keeping of the man
she loved.

Mary had always been a joy in my life. Sweet and
even-tempered, fun-loving and cheerful, she had never caused me a moment's trouble or worry. I had
named my daughter after my mother, who had been
the sweetest, kindest woman I had ever known. No
cross word had ever left my mother's lips. I never
heard her voice raised in anger or haste. She had been
kind to Shadow from the day I met him, showering
him with love and affection because he had no mother
of his own to care for him, understanding and accept-
ing him for who and what he was. Mary was like that
too. She never judged anyone, but simply accepted
people for what they were. She was generous and
soft-spoken, and had a genuine love for others.

There was a knock at the door and my father and
Rebecca stepped into the room. Pa looked fine in a
dark gray suit, white linen shirt, and shined-up black
boots. Rebecca looked pretty enough to be a bride
herself in a dress of pale pink silk.

"They're ready to start if you are, Hannah," Pa
said. With a sniff, he took Mary in his arms and gave
her a quick hug. "Be happy," he said gruffly. "If things
don't work out, don't be afraid to come home."

"Thanks, Grandpa," Mary said, kissing him on
the cheek.

Rebecca took Mary's hand in hers and gave it a squeeze. "You look beautiful, darling," she said, her eyes misty. "Just beautiful."

Mary nodded, and then we were alone again.

"Ready?" I asked.

"Ready," Mary replied, taking a last look into the floor-length mirror. "Nervous, but ready. How do I look?"

"Perfect."

We looked at each other for a moment, and then Mary gave me a hug. "I love you, nahkoa," she said tremulously. "Thank you for everything."

"I love you, too," I murmured. "Be happy."

"I will be," Mary said, her smile radiant. "I love Frank and he loves me. What could possibly change that?"

"Nothing, darling." I gave her a last, quick hug and left the room.

Blackie was waiting for me. My youngest son looked remarkably handsome in a dark suit and tie. His long black hair was neatly combed, his shoes were clean and polished. His eyes were a deep dark brown, his skin tanned from constant exposure to the sun. For a brief moment I studied his face, searching for some resemblance to Shadow, but except for the color of his hair, Blackie did not look like Shadow at all. And yet in my heart I knew that Blackie was Shadow's son, knew it without a doubt. Joshua Berdeen could never have fathered a child such as this. Never in a million years.

"Ready, nahkoa?" Blackie asked. He moved his shoulders and I knew he was uncomfortable wearing a suit and tie, but to please Mary he had agreed to wear it without a murmur.

"Ready," I answered.

Taking my arm, Blackie escorted me down the narrow aisle to the front pew. I sat down, smiling at my oldest son Hawk, my daughter-in-law Victoria, and my twin grandsons Jason and Jacob. The boys were seven months old now, and easily the most beautiful children ever born. They had black hair, dark blue eyes, tawny skin, and smiles to melt a grandmother's heart.

It didn't seem possible that I could be a grandmother. Grandmothers were elderly and frail, with gray hair, spectacles, and wrinkles. I didn't fit into that category yet, but then, I was only thirty-nine years old, young for a grandmother.

I gazed around the church. A profusion of wild roses and daisies added a splash of color to the altar and filled the early-morning air with a sweet fragrance. A long white runner covered the center aisle, and large white satin bows had been tied to the pews.

I nodded to several of our friends and neighbors who had come to share this joyous occasion with us. Fred and Myrtle Brown were sitting a few rows back. Fred's hair had turned completely gray now, but his green eyes were still jolly, and I saw that he was wearing his plaid vest, as usual. Myrtle had grown even plumper in the years I had known her. Her curly brown hair was touched with gray. Their son Jeremy sat between them. He was a handsome boy, more than a little vain about his blond good looks. Several of the young ladies in the church turned to stare at him from time to time, their eyes openly adoring.

Ruth Tippitt sat with Helen and Porter Sprague. Ruth's husband, George, was not well and rarely left their house now. Helen nodded in my direction, and I smiled at her. We had not always been friends with Helen and Porter. Although they had been the first people we had met when we moved to Bear Valley in the summer of 1885, we had not hit it off too well. Their daughter Nelda had made a rather rude remark about Indians, and Pa had asked the Spragues to leave our house. After that, Helen and Porter had tried everything in their power to make sure we weren't welcome in the valley, but then Shadow saved Nelda Sprague's life, and after that nothing was too good for Shadow or his family.

Nelda had been a rather homely child, but she had developed into a pretty young woman. She had her mother's red hair and her father's brown eyes, and a lovely figure. She was sweet on Henry Smythe, but Henry had a crush on the blacksmith's daughter Fancy. Young love, I mused, never ran smooth.

Glancing across the aisle, I saw Clancy Turner and his wife Nadine. They were sitting close together holding hands. Clancy and Nadine ran our local newspaper. It had started out as a one-page paper that carried only local news and recipes, but over the years it had expanded, and now Clancy ran a six-page newspaper that came out twice a week.

I saw Mary Crowley and her husband, Jed. Mary was pregnant again, and I wondered if she was ever going to stop having babies. She had nine children; the oldest was twelve, the youngest was two. Secretly, I envied Mary Crowley. I had always wanted a large family, but, unlike Mary, I had trouble getting pregnant, and now I was getting too old.

I felt a warm sense of home and belonging as I gazed at the people around me. How good of them to be here, I thought, to want to share this moment with us.

The measured strains of the Wedding March filled the air. Turning, I saw Mary walking down the aisle, her hand on her father's arm. Like Blackie, Shadow wore a dark suit and tie. Like Blackie, he was uncomfortable. But he wore it for Mary. This was her day, and it must be perfect in every detail.

My heart fluttered as my gaze lingered on Shadow. He was so handsome, so dear. His hair was long and thick, as black as night. His skin was the color of old copper, still smooth and unlined though he was forty-two years old. He smiled at me, his ebony eyes warm with love, as he walked our only daughter down the aisle.

I didn't hear the solemn words that made Mary and Frank husband and wife. Instead, I was remembering my own wedding day, hearing again the sweet, longed-for words that had made me Shadow's wife. He had worn a dark suit and tie on that day, as well. Our wedding had been lovely, everything I had ever dreamed of. Shadow had promised that we would be wed in the white man's way when I was free of Joshua Berdeen, and he had kept his promise. I had assumed we would have a quiet ceremony at home with just our family present, but we had been married in church. I had worn a white satin gown and matching slippers and a floor-length veil. There had been flowers and music and white satin bows on the pews. Everyone in the valley had been invited. Hand in hand, Shadow and I had stood before the altar. Tears of joy had welled in my eyes as we said our vows, and then the Reverend Thorsen had spoken the solemn, beautiful words that made me Shadow's lawfully wedded wife. No words had ever been sweeter or more welcome. I remembered how tenderly Shadow had made love to me that night, his hands and lips gentle, filled with promise and desire. How carefully he had aroused me, as though I were a tender virgin ignorant in the ways of men, until I was on fire for him.

Shadow took my hand in his as Frank kissed Mary. His dark eyes looked deep into mine, and I felt the force of his love wash over me, thrilling me down to my toes. Squeezing Shadow's hand, I offered a silent prayer to Man Above, hoping that Mary would find the same lasting happiness with Frank that I had found with the man standing at my side.

Pa took pictures after the wedding. He had sent away to Rochester, New York, and bought a Kodak camera for ten dollars. It was a remarkable invention, and Pa was as excited as a child with a new toy. He took numerous pictures, mostly of Mary and Frank and our family. Shadow refused to have his picture taken and no amount of coaxing could make him change his mind. I had never had my picture taken before, and I could hardly wait to see the results. Pa said the man at the drug store would develop the negatives in a special dark room he had built in the back of the store.

Later we had cake and punch at our house, and all the valley people came to help us celebrate Mary's wedding day. Frank's parents, Leland and Mattie Smythe, were old friends of ours. They had been one of the first families to move into Bear Valley. They had eight mighty handsome sons: Abel, Benjamin, Cabel, David, Ethan, Frank, Gene and Henry.

"Hannah, she's a lovely bride," Mattie Smythe said, giving my arm an affectionate squeeze. "Frank is lucky to get her."

"They're both lucky," I said, smiling. "I'm sorry Abel and Ethan couldn't be here."

Mattie nodded. Abel had moved to San Francisco several years ago. Ethan was a lawyer back in St. Louis.

"Abel would have been here," Mattie remarked, "but Carolyn is in the family way, you know. She's too far along to make such a long trip, and Abel didn't want to leave her home alone, this being their first child and all. Ethan is tied up on a case defending a man accused of murdering seven people. Ethan said he's certain the man is as guilty as sin, but that he's entitled to a fair trial just like everyone else."

I nodded, then turned away as several of our other guests crowded around to offer their congratulations.

The reception was a huge success. Mary and Frank received many lovely gifts, as well as a tidy sum of money, and then, too soon, they were ready to leave. I gave my daughter a hug, trying not to cry. She was a woman now, married, with a life of her own to live. She was no longer my little girl. Frank was her life now. He would be the one to soothe her hurts and share her joys. He would be the one she would run to for comfort, the one who would hear her innermost hopes and dreams and fears.

I watched my new son-in-law as he said his good-byes. He was a tall, handsome young man with dark brown hair and brown eyes. I had known Frank since he was a boy and he seemed like a fine man, steady and reliable. I was certain they would be happy together, but only time would tell.

Smiling through my tears, I stepped away from Mary so she could bid her father good-bye.

"Neyho," Mary murmured, and then hurled herself into her father's arms. She stood there for a long time, her arms tight around Shadow's waist, her face buried in his shoulder, and then she stood on tiptoe and gave him a kiss on the cheek. "I love you," she said, blinking back a tear. "Take good care of yourself and nahkoa."

Shadow nodded. His emotions, always under control, were very near the surface today. Mary was his only daughter and he loved her dearly. He had always been protective of her, concerned for her health and happiness.

Shadow took my hand as Mary and Frank climbed into the buggy and drove away. They would take the buggy as far as Steel's Crossing, then catch the train for Chicago. Frank had applied for a job at one of the banks there. Mary was excited by the prospect of living in the East, of dining in fine restaurants and going to the theater. She was eager to see what life was like away from Bear Valley, and I couldn't blame her. It was only natural that she should want to see more of the world. Bear Valley was a thriving community. We had a telegraph office, a newspaper, a bank, a small restaurant, a saloon, a schoolhouse, two churches, a mercantile store, a blacksmith, a dentist, and a doctor. And yet we were still just a small Western town, crude and more than a little wild by Eastern standards.

I watched Mary until she was out of sight. Once I too had dreamed of living in the East, of wearing stylish clothes, of eating off fine china and crystal by candlelight in a fancy restaurant, of going to the theater and spending an evening on the town. But no more. I was where I belonged, and I had no regrets.

I glanced up as Shadow squeezed my hand. "Do you think she'll be all right?" I asked. "She's so young."

"She is nineteen," Shadow replied. "Old enough to know what she wants."

"I hope he'll be good to her."

"He had better be," Shadow said gravely.

The house seemed empty that evening as I moved from room to room tidying up. I lingered in Mary's room, remembering the day she had been born.

I had gone into labor early that morning. Flower Woman had been there to help me, but I wanted only Shadow. He had been somewhat reluctant to help with the birth of our child. It was not something a warrior of the People was expected to do. Childbirth was best left to squaws and midwives. But when he saw how desperately I wanted him with me, how badly I needed his strength and love, he sat beside me, my hands clasped in his, through the long hours of labor. I had tried to be brave and strong like the Cheyenne women, but the pains had been so hard I could not hold back my tears. And then, cutting through the pain, came Shadow's voice, deep and resonant and filled with compassion. He talked to me for hours, telling me things I had not known, things I had never suspected. He told me of his mother, Morning Dove, who had died when he was only six years old. His memories of her were vague images of a graceful woman with long black hair and warm black eyes, a voice that was low and soft, arms that had held him tight. She had died of smallpox, and he told me of how he had always felt a little left out because he had grown up without a mother to love him or scold him. He told me of the thrill of the buffalo hunt, of riding alongside a herd on a fast pony with the dust churning and the cries of the other warriors rising above the thunder of many cloven hooves. He talked of riding to battle, heart pounding and blood running hot in your veins. You did not think of death once the battle began, Shadow had told me, his eyes bright with the memory, you thought only of defeating the enemy, of counting coup and gathering honors on the field of battle. He had told me of the time he killed his first man, a Pawnee warrior. He had felt sick at first, awed by the speed with which a man's life could be snuffed out. And then he had been filled with exhilaration. He had killed an enemy of the People, and it was a cause for rejoicing and celebration, not a time for sorrow.

I had listened to Shadow's voice, letting the sound surround me like loving arms as I grasped his hands; strong, capable hands that could take a man's life— hands that had shown me nothing but kindness and tenderness and love. I had gazed into Shadow's eyes, loving him with all my heart, as our daughter made her way into the world . . . and now she was grown and gone. How had the years gotten away so fast?

I left Mary's room as I heard Blackie's voice calling my name.

"Nahkoa, nahkoa!" He burst into the parlor, a wolf cub clutched in his arms. "Look, nahkoa," he said, thrusting the cub toward me. "I found him near the river."

I shook my head. Blackie was still wearing his good suit. This morning it had been clean, but now it was covered with grass stains and dirt. His shoes were muddy, his hands and face streaked with grime. It was in me to scold him, but the words wouldn't come. He was my last child, my baby. How could I scold him when he was smiling up at me, his dark eyes alight with excitement as the cub licked his face.

"Better give him something to eat," I said. "I'll see if I can find a box to put him in."

With a joyful nod, Blackie headed for the kitchen. I could hear him talking to the cub as he poured some milk into a bowl.

I stared after my son. Since the day he could walk, Blackie had been bringing stray animals home. Snakes and frogs, raccoons and possums, a skunk, a spotted fawn, countless birds and squirrels, a baby fox. And now a wolf cub. My Blackie, child of the woods and water. He seemed to have a natural affinity for all of God's wild creatures.

Shadow was shaking his head in wonder when I went out to the barn to find a box.

"So," I said, smiling, "you've seen our latest addition to the family."

"Yes," Shadow said wryly. "Perhaps we should open a zoo."

I laughed, my spirits rising as Shadow pulled me into his arms. My body molded itself to his as I lifted my face for his kiss, and then I wasn't laughing any more, for Shadow's mouth claimed mine in a kiss that took my breath away and left my knees weak and my legs rubbery.

"Hannah." His voice, deep and husky, caressed me even as his hands kneaded my back, then slid down to cup my buttocks.

I nodded at the unspoken question in his eyes. Effortlessly Shadow lifted me in his arms and carried me up the wooden ladder to the loft and there, in a bed of sweet-smelling hay, we made love.

My desire for my husband had never dimmed, and as he undressed I marveled anew that the sight of his body still had the power to excite me, that I still found his lovemaking thrilling and wonderful. My eyes moved lovingly over his face and form and found no flaw. He was tall, dark-skinned, and handsome. My fingers traced the powerful muscles that rippled in his arms and legs as he stretched out beside me. His stomach was still hard and flat, his chest broad and strong.

Shadow gasped as my wandering hand traveled leisurely down his belly to settle on his inner thigh, and I laughed softly, pleased by his response to my touch. Straddling his thighs, I let my hands roam over his body, my fingers tracing the scars on his chest. I remembered the day of the Sun Dance, how he had stood beside Hawk while Eagle-That-Soars-in-the-Sky slashed their flesh and inserted the skewers under the skin. I had marveled that Shadow and Hawk could endure such pain without a murmur, that they had possessed the strength and courage to dance around the Sun Dance pole for hours without food or water to sustain them, until the skewers had torn free of their flesh, releasing them from the sacred pole. The Sun Dance ritual was the most sacred of the Cheyenne traditions, one that few white people ever really understood. Shadow had been the epitome of what a Cheyenne warrior should be that day—tall and strong, firm in his beliefs, brave, haughty, perhaps, because he was one of the People.

I was filled with tenderness as I leaned forward, my bare breasts brushing against his chest as I kissed him. Shadow's arms went around me, drawing me closer still, until our bodies were one.

Shadow was not a young warrior anymore, but a man in his prime, and I gloried in his touch as he possessed me, satisfying my desire even as he satisfied my need to be a part of him. Now, for this moment, I was complete. I let out a long sigh as his life spilled into me, my whole body slowly relaxing as waves of pure pleasure engulfed me. How I loved him, this wonderful man who had been a part of my life for almost thirty years.

2

I went to church with Victoria the following morning. Hawk and Shadow never attended church services with us. I understood how Shadow felt, and I never tried to persuade him to accompany me although I would have loved to have him there beside me. Sometimes he rode along with me into town, then spent a quiet hour near the river while I went to church. But this day he stayed at home, and Blackie stayed with him.

Victoria and the twins were ready when I stopped by to pick them up. Marriage had agreed with Vickie, I thought. She was more attractive than ever, though she looked a trifle unhappy just now.

"What is it?" I asked as she settled onto the seat beside me, a baby in each arm.

"Nothing," she answered petulantly.

"Did you and Hawk have an argument?"

"No, not really, but he makes me so mad. I asked him to go to church with us, just as I do every week, and he refused, just as he does every week."

I nodded, wondering if I should try to make her understand, or if I should just keep my mouth shut. I didn't want to be a meddling mother-in-law.

"It wouldn't hurt him to go to church with me once in a while," Victoria went on. "It's only for an hour."

"That's true," I agreed. "But to Hawk, it's an hour wasted. He doesn't believe in the white man's god. Hawk and Shadow worship Maheo, and I don't think anything will ever change that."

"I know," Victoria said with a sigh of resignation. "And I don't want to change him, not really. But it just seems as though he could do it for me. I gave up a lot for him."

That was true enough. Victoria had given up a lovely home, an education in the East, and a lot more to marry Hawk. Her parents had deserted her when they discovered she was pregnant and that Hawk was the father. Bitter and ashamed, Horace and Lydia Bannerman had sold their home and left Bear Valley, apparently for good, leaving their daughter behind to get along as best she could.

"Have you ever heard from your parents, Vickie?" I asked.

"No," she replied softly, but I heard the hurt in her voice. I had never understood the Bannermans. I could not imagine leaving my only child when she needed me most, yet that was what the Bannermans had done.

I glanced at my two grandsons, cradled in

Victoria's arms. They were lovely boys, sweet of disposition. I supposed that Horace and Lydia Bannerman would have been ashamed of Jason and Jacob because they were a quarter Cheyenne, but I thought they were wonderful.

Victoria's spirits picked up when we reached the church. She had many friends in the valley, and they all clustered around her, eager to fuss over the twins, eager to chat and make plans for the church social to be held the following month.

We saw Pa and Rebecca at church. As usual, we all sat together, taking turns holding the boys when they got restless. Sunday was my favorite day of the week, a day to rest and worship, a day to take life easy. Usually Hawk and Victoria came by for a visit; sometimes we went to their house. Occasionally Shadow and I went to visit the Smythes or the Browns or the Tippitts. One Sunday a month, our whole family got together for dinner at Pa's house.

I smiled as Jacob crawled into my lap and made himself comfortable, then turned my attention to what the minister was saying. We had a new preacher in the valley now. The Reverend Thorsen had passed away shortly after Hawk and Victoria were married. Our new minister was a man in his early fifties. He had gray hair, long sideburns, and a closely-cropped gray beard. He was a widower, rather nice-looking, with regular features and light brown eyes. His name was Thomas Edward Brighton, and he preached fire and brimstone at his Sunday services. No one ever dozed off during one of his sermons, for he had a voice like thunder. Two of the widow women in Bear Valley had their eye on the Reverend Brighton, and it was a source of amusement to the people in the valley to watch Leona and Claire primp and flirt, trying to catch his eye. Thus far the reverend had avoided becoming entangled with either one, though it was noted that he was gaining a few pounds due to the many dinners they invited him to, and the numerous cakes and pies that were delivered to the parsonage in their efforts to outdo each other.

As the reverend's sermon came to an end, the choir stood to sing. I thought about what Victoria had said earlier and I glanced around the church. Most of the married women had their husbands by their sides; whether the husbands wanted to be there or not, I couldn't tell. But when I compared the men in the congregation to the man who waited for me at home, I knew I wouldn't have traded places with any of the women present. Let them have their civilized men clad in store-bought suits and ties, men who ran grocery stores and banks and newspapers. I had a man at home who was a warrior, a man who had fought for me, a man who had risked his life to protect our family from harm.

I said as much to Victoria on our way home from church.

"Would you trade Hawk for any of those men at church today?" I asked.

"Heavens, no," Vickie said, laughing as she hugged her sons. "Hawk is worth a dozen of those men."

"Exactly," I agreed. "Can you imagine being married to an old fusspot like George Williams, or a penny-pinching grouch like Harvey White?"

"No," Victoria said, laughing all the harder. "And what about that old stick-in-the-mud, Clarence Flagg?"

I laughed, too, though my conscience bothered me a little at poking fun at my neighbors. They were all nice men in their way, honest and hard-working, but they could never compare to Hawk or Shadow.

Victoria was relaxed and happy when I dropped her off at home. She asked me to come in for tea, but I was eager to go home to Shadow.

Hawk came to help Victoria and the twins down from the buggy, and we chatted for a few minutes about the weather and how big the boys were getting, and then I bade them good-bye and clucked to the team.

"Thanks, Hannah," Victoria called as I pulled out of the yard.

I waved and smiled at her, glad that she was Hawk's wife. I couldn't have been more pleased with my daughter-in-law if I had picked her out myself.

That night, lying in Shadow's arms, I told him about Victoria's wish that Hawk would attend church with her.

"I can understand how she feels," I remarked, snuggling closer to Shadow's side. "But I think she'll be all right now."

"Does it bother you that I do not attend the white man's church and worship your god?" Shadow asked.

"No. I know you worship Maheo, and though you don't think so, I believe that God and Maheo are the same being." I kissed Shadow's cheek. "It would be nice to have you there beside me, though."

"Why did you not tell me this sooner?"

"I don't know. It's not important."

"If you want me to go with you, I will go."

Was there ever such a man? My heart swelled with love as I kissed him again.

"It isn't necessary," I murmured. "I know you like to worship Man Above in your own way. I've never asked you to change for me. I'm not asking now."

Shadow smiled at me, his dark eyes moving over my face like a caress. "I know. I think that is why I love you so much."

"Show me," I whispered. My hand stroked his chest and flat belly, then slid down to his hard, muscular thigh.

Shadow groaned low in his throat as he grabbed me and gave me a fierce hug, crushing my breasts against his chest. His mouth possessed mine as his hands stroked my back, then slid around to caress my breasts.

"Hannah, I think you have bewitched me," he murmured, his voice close to my ear. "I can never get enough of you."

Ah, sweet words to hear. I closed my eyes, surrendering myself completely to the man who was my husband, thrilling to his touch, to the sound of his voice, low and husky with desire, as he whispered, "Nemehotatse, Hannah. Nemehotatse, forever."

"Nemehotatse," I replied, barely able to speak as our bodies became one. "I love you, too, forever."

3

The first rays of dawn were lighting the eastern sky when Hawk left the house and walked a short distance to the narrow stream that watered their property. Standing near the water's edge, he raised his arms toward the vast blue-gray sky and began to pray, pleading with Maheo to protect his family from harm, to bless his sons with health and strength, to smile on Victoria, who was pregnant again.

Some twenty minutes later, he finished his prayer. Stepping out of his buckskins, he walked into the stream to bathe. His solitary prayer and bath afterward were a daily ritual that he never missed, no matter what the weather.

Floating on his back, he thought of Victoria. He had not meant to get her pregnant again so soon. The twins kept her busy from dawn until dark, and though she rarely complained, he wondered if she were truly pleased to be having another child so soon. It was all his fault. He had vowed not to touch her until the twins were weaned, as was the custom among the Cheyenne. But he loved her so much. It was impossible to be with her every day, to see her and kiss her and hear her sweet voice, and not make love to her. Her body had changed since the birth of the twins. It was rounder, fuller, more feminine. He had not been able to keep his hands off her, and now she was pregnant again.

Emerging from the water, he slipped into his clothes and padded barefoot to the barn where he fed and watered the stock. Returning to the house, he saw that Victoria was in the kitchen preparing his breakfast. The twins were sitting on a blanket on the floor, playing with some brightly colored blocks that Leland Smythe had carved for them.

Victoria smiled as Hawk came up behind her and slipped his arms around her waist. "Good morning," she said cheerfully, and giggled as his tongue tickled her neck.

"Good morning," Hawk replied. He gave her a squeeze, then stooped to cuddle one child and then the other. My sons, he thought proudly. They had the look of the People in the color of their hair and skin, and Hawk was glad. He was proud to be Cheyenne, proud of his Indian heritage.

They shared a pleasant breakfast, then Hawk went outside to check on the five horses that were corralled in a small box canyon not far from the house. They were all mares ready to foal, and as he slipped through the fence, he saw that two of the mares had given birth the night before.

The horses whickered softly as he walked among them. They had all been broken to saddle and were accustomed to his presence. Approaching the mares that had foaled, he checked the afterbirth to make sure it had all been expelled, then checked the foals, a filly and a colt. Both were reddish-brown with spotted rumps. His own stallion had sired both foals.

After making certain the mares and foals were in good condition, he checked the pasture to make certain there was enough grass, and then left the canyon to check on the four yearlings corralled behind the barn.

With the stock taken care of, he threw a bridle on his stallion, fetched his rifle from the house, gave Victoria a lingering kiss, and then rode into the woods in search of a deer.

Bear Valley had grown considerably in the last few years, he mused, but the woods remained virtually unchanged. Tall trees reached toward the sky, their branches so thick in some places that they blocked out the sun. It was quiet within the forest, dark and primeval. A chipmunk skittered across his path, a gray squirrel scolded him from the safety of a tree limb, a blue jay shrilled raucously as it flew past his head.

Lost in thought, Hawk rode deeper into the forest until, without realizing it, he was at Rabbit's Head Rock. Reining his horse to a halt, he gazed out at the vast sea of yellow grass that stretched as far as the eye could see. Once the Sioux and the Cheyenne and the Arapahoe had roamed the endless prairie. Once the buffalo had darkened the earth like a curly brown blanket. But now all was quiet. The Indians languished on the reservation; the buffalo were nearly extinct.

He glanced at the huge gray rock. His mother and father had met near Rabbit's Head Rock almost thirty years ago. Even now, they sometimes came to this place to be alone.

Hawk grinned, remembering the time he and Victoria had sat against the rock, hugging and kissing, until Mercy Tillman showed up. Mercy had been a wild girl, rumored to have slept with most of the men in the valley. When she got pregnant, she had accused Hawk of being the father, certain everyone would believe he was guilty because he was a half-breed. There had been a confrontation at the Tillman shack, with Shadow and Hawk insisting that Hawk was innocent and Mercy Tillman's father Morgus arguing that Hawk was guilty as hell, and that Shadow had probably been sweet on Mercy as well. A fight had erupted between Shadow and Morgus, and when it looked as if Shadow might lose, Hawk had reached for Tillman's rifle, but Mercy got it first. They had struggled over the gun, and then it had gone off. The bullet hit Morgus, killing him instantly. To this day, Hawk didn't know who had pulled the trigger, nor did he care. He would gladly have killed Morgus and a dozen like him to save his father's life. Mercy had left Bear Valley shortly thereafter. He wondered, without really caring, what had happened to her.

With a sigh, he reined his stud around and headed for home, his eyes searching the underbrush for game. He was nearly out of the woods when he saw a big buck. Lifting his rifle, he took careful aim and fired.

The slug found its target and the deer dropped to the ground.

With ease Hawk placed the buck over the stallion's withers, vaulted onto the horse's back, and headed home, eager to see Victoria and his sons.

Victoria sighed wearily as she put her sons down for a nap. No matter how hard she worked, there was always more to do. Dishes, diapers, baking, mending, ironing, preparing meals, they all took such a lot of time and effort, and it seemed she never caught up. And now there was another baby on the way. She was glad to be having Hawk's child, proud to be his wife, but she wished she could put this child off another year or two. How would she manage three small children, a husband, and a house?

Picking up her mending basket, she sat down in a chair near the window and began to mend one of Hawk's shirts. Just once, she'd like to have nothing to do. Just once.

Resting her head against the back of the chair, she closed her eyes. She wished her mother lived nearby. It would be so nice to be able to go to her mother for help. But her parents had left Bear Valley when they discovered she was pregnant with Hawk's child. Pregnant and not married. Pregnant by a halfbreed. They had left the valley and never returned. Never even sent word as to their whereabouts, or wrote to ask if she was well. She knew she could go to Hawk's mother for help, but she was too proud to ask, too proud to admit that raising two sons and keeping a house was almost more than she could handle.

For a brief moment, she thought wistfully of the

home she had shared with her parents. Their house had been the biggest and nicest in all Bear Valley. She'd had a room of her own decorated in pastel pink and pale green, lovely clothes with matching hats and shoes, delicate underwear. Anything she had ever desired had been hers simply for the asking. *A fur muff, daddy, please,* and he had bought it for her. A pretty china doll. A silk parasol. Blue satin dancing slippers. Colorful ribbons for her hair. She had been pampered and petted all her life until she married Hawk . . .

Hawk was so wonderful, so handsome. Strong, yet gentle. Proud, but kind. Firm, yet tender. Many of the young women in the valley looked at him with longing, secretly envying Victoria because she had won his heart. He was different, exciting, forbidden. A few of the families in the valley refused to accept him because he was a half-breed, but most of the valley people accepted him for the fine man he was, just as they had learned to accept Shadow.

Victoria smiled. Hawk and Shadow were much alike in both looks and temperament. She recalled the night they had told Hawk's parents that she was pregnant. Hannah and Shadow had been sympathetic and understanding. They had not yelled at her or thought she was bad. Why couldn't her own parents have been like that? Her mother had burst into tears, sobbing hysterically that the family name had been ruined forever. Her father had pulled a gun on Hawk and ordered him out of the house. When Hawk was gone, her father had ordered her to pack her bags. *"You'll be on the first train headed east!"* he had threatened. But she had refused. For the first time in her life, Victoria had stood up to her father. Horace Bannerman had turned purple with rage. *"How can you be so ungrateful after all we've done for you?"* he had shouted. *"We've given you everything you've ever wanted and this is how you repay us? By sneaking off with that dirty half-breed like a damn squaw! Get out of my house, you harlot!"*

Victoria shook her head with the memory. Hawk's family had welcomed her into their home with open arms, and they had been kindness itself ever since. Why couldn't her own parents have been forgiving and understanding? Why had they left her, frightened and alone? She thought of Jason and Jacob and knew that no matter what mistakes they might one day make, she would never turn her back on them. Never.

With a sigh, she opened her eyes and resumed mending Hawk's shirt. She was a big girl now. She didn't need her mother and father to lean on anymore. Hannah had managed to raise three children and keep house in circumstances far worse than those Victoria now found herself in. Hannah had given birth to Mary in the wilderness with no doctor available, no midwife to help her. She had lived in a wickiup, cooked over an open fire, worn clothes of deerskin. She had grown all their fruits and vegetables, or harvested those that grew wild. She had skinned wild game, ridden to war with Shadow.

Victoria gazed at her surroundings. She had a house with four stout walls and a good roof, furniture that was comfortable if not elegant, clothes to wear, food to eat, two beautiful children. There was a doctor in town if she got sick. There were friends to talk to, a church where she could worship, stores to shop in. And there was Hawk to love. What more could she ask of life than what she already had?

She ran to the door when he came home, her blue eyes warm with love as she lifted her face for his kiss. No matter what hardships they might face, no matter what the future held, she would never be sorry she had married Hawk.

She was happier that night than she had been in weeks. She sang as she prepared dinner, hummed softly as she nursed her sons. How sweet they were, how dear. They were a part of her love for Hawk and his for her, tangible proof of their devotion. Smiling, she kissed each child, marveling anew at how small they were, how soft their skin was. She had not had much to do with babies until she had her own, and everything they did charmed her.

Later, she and Hawk sat side by side before the hearth, each holding a baby. They laughed, beaming with pride as the boys cooed and smiled at them.

Lying in Hawk's arms in bed that night, Victoria was blissfully happy. She loved being in his arms, loved the touch of his hands sliding along her flesh, the way his lips teased her own before claiming her mouth in a fiery kiss that sent sparks clear down to her toes.

Her hands played over his back and chest, delighting in the way his muscles moved beneath her fingertips. He was so strong, so much bigger than she was. She had always been a little afraid of very big men, but she had never been afraid of Hawk. He had a gentleness, a goodness, that few people ever bothered to discover.

She thrust her hips upward, suddenly anxious for him to possess her, wanting to be a part of him, to feel that he was a part of her.

Victoria's enthusiasm fired Hawk's desire and his arms crushed her close. Her breasts were soft and warm against his chest, her lips sweeter than nectar as he kissed her, his tongue savoring the taste of her.

She had blossomed since the twins were born. Her breasts were fuller, her hips a little rounder. Her figure was no longer girlish but that of a woman, and he loved every silken inch, loved the way she made little purring sounds as he claimed her for his own.

Her fingers kneaded his back, her nails raking the skin, then sliding along his shoulders to trace the muscles in his arms. Fire trailed in the wake of her touch. Closing his eyes, Hawk breathed in her scent, finding it warm and womanly and exciting.

He whispered in her ear, telling her that he loved her, extolling the beauty of her face and figure, and then she was whispering back, pouring out her love in a torrent of words even as his seed spilled into her.

Sated, they fell asleep in each other's arms.

Victoria was humming cheerfully as she dusted the mantlepiece. It was a lovely day, and she was filled with a sense of peace and contentment. Hawk was outside, chopping wood. Jason and Jacob were sleeping peacefully in their beds, a cherry pie was cooling in the kitchen window. She was about to lay her dust rag aside when she heard a knock at the front door.

Probably Hannah, Vickie thought. She ran a hand through her hair and smoothed her skirt as she went to open the door.

For a moment, Victoria could only stand there, staring at the woman who had knocked at the door. She opened her mouth to speak, but no words would come.

Lydia Bannerman licked her lips nervously. "Good afternoon, Victoria," she said, her words stilted. "May I come in?"

"Mama," Victoria breathed. "What are you doing here?"

Lydia Bannerman smiled tentatively. "Couldn't we discuss it inside?"

"Of course," Victoria said, stepping aside. "Come in."

Victoria led the way to the small sofa that stood before the hearth and sat down heavily, unable to believe that her mother was actually sitting down beside her. She glanced nervously around the parlor, experiencing a moment of real distress. Her mother would not see the simple beauty in the room. All she would see was the crude furniture and a lack of fine paintings and art objects like those that had graced the Bannermans' home years ago.

"How are you, Victoria?" Lydia asked, her voice strained but polite.

"Fine. And you?" They were talking to each other like strangers, Victoria thought, and in a way that's what they were.

Lydia looked away, giving Victoria a chance to study her mother. Lydia's auburn hair, once worn piled high atop her head like a crown, was pulled away from her face and gathered in a tight knot at the nape of her neck. Victoria was surprised to see how gray her mother's hair had become. There were dark shadows under Lydia's violet eyes, deep lines of worry around her mouth. Her dress, while clean, had been mended several times near the hem. Victoria's expression showed her astonishment. Her mother had never worn a dress that was less than perfect.

Lydia cleared her throat. "Victoria, I . . . this is very hard for me to say."

Vickie frowned. "What is it, Mother?"

"Your father and I treated you abominably," Lydia said in a rush. "I know I have no right to expect you to forgive me, but I . . . I need your forgiveness and your . . ." Lydia's face turned a bright pink. "And your charity."

"Charity?" Victoria repeated, confused. "What are you talking about?"

"Oh, Victoria, your father's dead and I have no money and nowhere else to go."

"Daddy's dead?" Victoria said, her voice suddenly childlike. How could it be possible? Her father had always been so big and strong. She remembered watching him work in the forge back East when she was a child. His arms had bulged with muscle when he shaped iron into wagon wheels or horseshoes. Sometimes he had entered contests with other blacksmiths, and he had always won. Why, he had never been sick a day in his life.

"Yes," Lydia said. "He made some very bad investments before he passed away, Vickie. I had to sell everything we owned. Even my wedding ring. I have nothing left. Nothing at all except a daughter who hates me." The last part was said in a very small voice.

"I don't hate you," Victoria said. "Not anymore."

"Oh, Victoria," Lydia Bannerman murmured, and burst into tears.

Victoria gazed at her mother's bowed head. This was the woman who had refused to give her blessing when Victoria decided to marry Hawk, the woman who had turned her back on her pregnant daughter and left town. Suddenly it all seemed long ago and unimportant. Horace Bannerman was dead and Lydia was alone.

After a moment, Victoria put her arms around her mother, and that was how Hawk found them some minutes later. He had been chopping wood for over an hour and he was tired and sweaty when he stepped into the parlor looking for Victoria.

Lydia Bannerman's head jerked up when she saw Hawk, her eyes registering her disapproval as she took in his buckskin pants and sweat-sheened torso.

Hawk flushed beneath his mother-in-law's scornful glance, suddenly conscious of the fact that he was covered with sweat and dirt and not wearing a shirt. He looked at Victoria, his expression vaguely accusing as he waited for an explanation as to why Lydia Bannerman was sitting in their parlor, weeping.

"Hawk," Victoria said. "I'm sorry your lunch isn't ready yet. My mother came to . . ." Victoria's voice trailed off. She wasn't sure why her mother was there. The news of her father's death could have been sent in a letter. "Why have you come here, Mother?"

"I need a place to stay," Lydia Bannerman answered, avoiding her son-in-law's gaze. "I was hoping you could take me in."

Disbelief washed across Hawk's features. Where

did Lydia Bannerman find the nerve to come here and ask Victoria for help when she and her husband had walked out and left her homeless and alone?

He began to shake his head, but Victoria quickly jumped to her feet and went to stand in front of him.

"Please, Hawk. She has nowhere else to go. My Daddy's dead, and Mama hasn't any money or anyone else to turn to."

"I do not want her here," Hawk said in a quiet voice. "She does not approve of me. She will never forgive you for marrying a half-breed, or accept her grandchildren for what they are."

"I wouldn't turn your mother away," Victoria said evenly.

Hawk let out a long sigh. "You are right, Victoria. She can stay as long as she wishes. But I think it will only cause trouble for us."

In the days that followed, Lydia stayed out of Hawk's way as much as possible. She knew her son-in-law did not approve of her, but he was unfailingly polite in her presence.

The one thing Hawk was wrong about was how Lydia felt about her grandsons. One look at them and she was completely captivated. She might not approve of Indians, might not approve of Hawk as a son-in-law, but she found no fault in the twins.

It was in the nursery that Hawk and Lydia found themselves alone together for the first time. Usually Victoria was present, acting as a buffer between them, keeping Lydia and Hawk on their best behavior. For a moment, Hawk and Lydia made small talk about the twins, and then, out of the blue, Hawk asked what had been uppermost in his mind ever since Lydia came to stay.

"How could you do it?" he asked in a hard voice. "How could you leave her like that?"

"I . . . I didn't want to," Lydia said, wringing her hands together. "Horace sold the house, and I had no choice but to go with him. He was my husband."

"You never wrote her. Not once."

"I wanted to, but Horace wouldn't let me. He was so angry, so ashamed because Victoria had married a . . ." Lydia bit down on her lower lip, afraid to say the word in the face of Hawk's anger.

"Half-breed," Hawk said harshly. "Go ahead, say it. It's what I am."

"Hawk, please—"

"I've seen she-wolves that are better mothers than you," Hawk said derisively.

"You must let me explain. I wanted to write to Victoria, honestly I did, but Horace got furious whenever I mentioned it. I thought of writing to Victoria secretly, but I knew she would answer my letters and then her father would know I had gone against his wishes. Later, when Horace got over his anger, he wanted to come back to Bear Valley, but he couldn't swallow his pride. He just couldn't admit he'd been wrong. His guilt over the way he had treated Victoria ate him up. I'm certain that's what killed him."

"He deserved exactly what he got," Hawk said coldly, and left the room, wondering how much longer he could stand to have Lydia Bannerman as a guest in his house.

4

I was stunned when Hawk told me Lydia Bannerman was staying with them. How did the woman have the nerve to show her face in Bear Valley after the despicable way she had treated her daughter?

Hawk was obviously upset about the situation at home. Lydia was trying hard to be nice, he said, but he could tell just by looking at her that her opinion of him had not changed over the years. She was crazy about her grandsons, though, apparently willing to forgive them for having a half-breed for a father. The atmosphere in their home was strained and uncomfortable, Hawk said, and he began spending more and more time at our place.

I ran into Lydia Bannerman at the mercantile

store about a week after she arrived. She had aged dreadfully since I had seen her last. Her auburn hair was turning gray, her face was lined.

We stared at each other for a full minute without speaking. Finally, with as much good grace as I could muster, I said, "Good afternoon, Lydia."

I could see by her expression that she had expected me to cut her dead. "Good afternoon, Hannah," she replied. "It's nice to see you again. You're looking well."

"Thank you. I'm . . . I'm sorry about Horace."

Lydia nodded, suddenly close to tears. "Life is so uncertain," she lamented. "One day I had a home and a husband, and the next I was penniless and all alone."

"I'm sure things will get better, with time."

Lydia Bannerman shook her head. "I don't see how they can," she said with a woebegone expression. "I know Hawk and Victoria don't like having me in their home, but I had nowhere else to go."

I felt an unwanted surge of compassion for the woman standing before me. Lydia had treated her daughter shamefully, but I could not help feeling sorry for her. Her husband was dead, she was apparently without money or friends, and Victoria had obviously not welcomed Lydia back into her life with open arms. But then, who could blame her?

At dinner that evening, I told Shadow of my meeting with Lydia Bannerman. He had no sympathy for her at all.

"She made her bed," he said coldly. "Let her lie in it." He flashed me a sardonic smile. "Wasn't that what

Horace told Victoria when she asked for help?"

"Yes. But you should see Lydia. She looks so unhappy, so forlorn. I feel sorry for her."

Shadow shook his head, his eyes wary. "You are not thinking of inviting her to stay here, are you?"

"Well, I was. Just for a little while."

"I would rather you did not."

I let the matter drop, for the moment. I knew how Shadow felt about Lydia Bannerman, but I also knew he had a soft heart. Sooner or later, he would relent.

As it turned out, we didn't have to feel sorry for Lydia very long. Two months after she returned to Bear Valley, she surprised the whole town by marrying the Reverend Thomas Brighton.

"I may go to church one day after all," Shadow remarked, grinning, when he heard the news, "just to see Lydia Bannerman playing the parson's wife!"

Hawk and Victoria were overjoyed with Lydia's marriage, not only because she seemed so happy with the reverend, but because it got her out of their house and into a home of her own.

I had supposed, now that Victoria and Lydia had been reconciled, that I would see less of my daughter-in-law and my grandsons, but it wasn't so. Victoria called on her mother once a week, taking the children to visit, and she occasionally invited Lydia and the Reverend Brighton over to her house for dinner, but Hawk and Victoria continued to spend a good deal of time at our place, and I was always the first one she called on to look after the twins. Hawk and his family came over for dinner at least once a week, and I marveled at how fast Jason and Jacob were growing. At nine months they were already trying to walk and talk, and their sweet smiles warmed me through and through. How precious they were.

I smiled happily as I served dinner to my family one evening. Hawk and Shadow were talking about the big July 4th picnic. Pa was kidding Shadow about being too old to race against young men like Hawk and the Smythe boys, and Shadow was boasting that he wasn't getting older, only better. Rebecca and Victoria, each holding a twin, shook their heads as they listened to the men banter back and forth. Blackie was trying to feed a baby bird he had found in the woods earlier in the day.

I was a woman content as I sat down at the table beside Shadow.

"Pa, would you please bless the food?" I asked, having to practically shout to be heard.

"What? Oh, yes, of course." Bowing his head, Pa blessed the food, and then asked the Lord to bless all those gathered at the table, amen.

As soon as the prayer was over, the men began talking about the race again. I remembered the harvest festival years ago when Shadow and Hawk had first raced against each other and Shadow had let Hawk win so our son would look good in Victoria's eyes. How long ago that seemed.

"What horse are you going to ride?" I asked my husband. "Smoke is getting too old to race."

Shadow winked at me. "Heyoka is not too old."

Heyoka had been sired by Smoke out of one of

Shadow's favorite mares. Shadow had been training the three-year-old colt for the last year, breaking the animal to the feel of a hackamore, the pressure of the reins, the weight of a man on its back. Shadow rarely used a bit on his horses, never used spurs. Heyoka was a beautiful horse, all black except for the spotted white blanket on his rump. He was quick and responsive, and Shadow was very proud of him.

I glanced at Hawk. "And will you ride the blue roan?"

Hawk nodded. The blue roan had also been sired by Smoke. He was eight years old now, and in excellent condition.

"When can I race?" Blackie asked, putting the baby bird back in its box.

"Perhaps next year," Shadow said. "Tomorrow we will go out to the pasture and you may pick a horse that will be yours alone."

Blackie's face lit up like a Christmas tree. He had a horse already, of course, but it was an older mare, not a horse fit for racing.

"I already know the one I want," Blackie said excitedly. "She's in the south pasture, the brown mare with the blaze face."

Shadow nodded. "A wise choice, naha. We will start breaking her to ride tomorrow."

Dinner was soon over and the men retired to the parlor while Rebecca and I cleared the table and did the dishes. Victoria took the twins into the bedroom to clean them up and get them ready for bed.

"I don't know anyone who appreciates a good

horse race as much as your father," Rebecca said. "Every year he gets worse. I'm surprised he doesn't want to ride in the race himself."

"Pa was never much for riding," I said. "Who do you think he'll bet on, Shadow or Hawk?"

"Both," Rebecca said. "He never can decide between them, so he just bets on them both. And since either Hawk or Shadow has won every year, your father never really loses."

I laughed at that, and we began to talk about other things. Rebecca mentioned that her daughter Beth was expecting her first baby. Beth had married a wealthy young man in June of 1896. Her husband, Jason Chatsworth, was from Pennsylvania, and that was where they made their home. Beth and Jason had met at a church social and it had been love at first sight.

"The baby's due the first of November," Rebecca said. "Beth is very excited."

"Are you hoping for a boy or a girl?"

"Oh, a girl, I think. We have lots of boys in the family, what with Hawk and Blackie and the twins. I think a little girl would be nice for a change. Beth said the Chatsworths are hoping for a boy to carry on the family name."

I nodded. Such things were important to some people.

"I'm trying to talk your father into going back East so we can be there when the baby arrives," Rebecca went on. "But you know how your father is. He hates to leave the ranch."

"But he'll do it for you," I said confidently. "All

you have to do is nag him a little, and the next thing you know, the two of you will be on a train bound for Pennsylvania."

"That's true," Rebecca said, her eyes twinkling merrily. "Sam's always given me anything I ever asked for." Rebecca smiled at me. "I'm a lucky woman."

"We're both lucky," I said, returning her smile. "Very lucky indeed."

July 4th bloomed bright and clear and hot. The sky was a brilliant blue, the sun like molten gold, as we drove to the church for the picnic. Blackie chattered excitedly the whole way, waving to his friends as he pulled up near the churchyard. It looked as if the whole town had turned out. There were people everywhere: women in colorful cotton dresses and wide-brimmed sunbonnets, men in white shirts and denim pants and high-heeled cowboy boots, children running and laughing, dodging between tables and people.

Heyoka pranced back and forth on the end of his tether, his ears flicking forward and back with excitement.

"He knows something's up," I remarked to Shadow. "Do you think he'll give you any trouble? He's never been around this many people before."

Shadow glanced at me, one black eyebrow arched upward. "Are you worried about me?" he asked, amused.

"Of course not. What is there to worry about?"

"Nothing."

Shadow smiled at me and my heart began to

pound a little faster. How handsome he was, and how I loved him!

We found a shady place and spread a blanket on the ground. Pa and Rebecca and Victoria and Hawk arrived a few moments later and spread their blankets next to ours, and we all ate together, stuffing ourselves with cold ham and fried chicken, potato salad and baked beans, fresh biscuits and honey. Rebecca had made a three-layer chocolate cake, Pa's favorite, for dessert. Victoria had made a deep-dish apple pie, and I had made cherry tarts.

Pa groaned as he sat back and loosened his belt. "I think I ate too much," he complained.

"Well, it's your own fault," Rebecca scolded. "You've eaten practically everything in sight." She shook her head ruefully. "And two pieces of cake! Shame on you."

"Is it my fault you women are such good cooks?" Pa lamented.

"No," Rebecca retorted, grinning, "but it is your fault you don't have a shred of will power."

Pa nodded sadly. "True, true."

We were relaxing after lunch, waiting for the games to start, when one of the valley girls came by looking for Blackie.

"He's playing down by the river," I told her, and after she thanked me and ran off, I looked at Shadow. "Who is that, and what does she want with our son?"

Shadow laughed, amused by my indignant tone. "There are too many people in the valley now," he said, shrugging. "I no longer recognize them all."

"She's a cute little thing," Rebecca remarked.

"Yes," I agreed glumly. "Too cute."

"Her name is Monica Sullivan," Victoria said. "She's fourteen years old. She watches the twins for me sometimes."

"Fourteen," I groaned. "Good Lord, an older woman."

Pa laughed at the expression on my face. "He's growing up, Hannah. You can't stop him, any more than I could stop you. Why, next thing you know, he'll be getting married."

"Blackie, married!" I could hardly speak the words. He was my baby, the last child in the nest. I never thought of Blackie as getting older. Somehow he was still a little boy in my eyes. Why, he still brought stray animals home. I had long ago lost count of the number of birds, squirrels, deer, foxes, possums, raccoons, skunks, dogs, and cats he had brought home over the years.

"He is already thirteen," Shadow reminded me. "In the old days, he would be learning to be a warrior."

"A warrior!" I wailed. "Why, he spends more time with his pets than he does with people."

Shadow inclined his head toward the river. Looking in that direction, I saw Blackie walking hand-in-hand with Monica Sullivan. She was a pretty little thing, I noticed glumly. Her hair was dark blond, her eyes were green fringed with long dark lashes. I felt like crying. My little boy, already holding hands with a girl!

"I was but twelve summers the day I first met

you," Shadow whispered so only I could hear. "That did not turn out so bad."

The thought did little to cheer me, but then I smiled as I remembered that day. So much had happened since then, yet I had only to close my eyes to summon Shadow's image to mind as he had looked that day at the river crossing back in the spring of 1868. I had been gathering wildflowers, going deeper and deeper into the woods until I found myself at Rabbit's Head Rock, a place I had been forbidden to go. It was there I met Shadow. Our life had come full circle, I mused. We had started in Bear Valley, and we would end here.

Lou Simpson picked up his fiddle and the strains of a lively polka filled the air. Shadow and I watched Jason and Jacob while Pa, Rebecca, Hawk, and Vickie went to dance. Hawk and Victoria made an enchanting couple. They smiled at each other as they twirled across the floor, and I thought how handsome Hawk looked in a light gray shirt, black twill pants, and moccasins. Victoria's face was flushed with pleasure, her lovely blue eyes shining with love and happiness as Hawk spun her around.

I saw Lydia Bannerman stroll by on her husband's arm, stopping here and there to chat with a member of the congregation. She waved at me, and I waved back. Lydia made the perfect preacher's wife, I thought. She had always liked to be in the center of things, and now she was one of the most important women in town. Most of the dances and socials were held at the church, and Lydia reigned supreme. As the minister's wife, she was privy to all the problems and secrets that came to the Reverend Brighton's attention, and many of the women came to Lydia with their problems, feeling more at ease discussing private matters with a woman instead of a man.

Yes, Lydia looked happy now. The dark shadows were gone from beneath her eyes and the tension lines had disappeared from her face. It was obvious she adored her husband, and I was glad that her life had turned out so well after all.

It was amazing how our little valley had grown over the years. Once I had known everyone by name, but now, looking around, I saw many people I did not recognize. Though we were still just a Western town without many modern conveniences, we were a thriving community. Many families on their way to Oregon or California passed through Bear Valley and decided to stay. I couldn't blame them, for it was a lovely place to live. Still, I was glad that our homestead was a good distance from town. I liked the feeling of solitude it gave us, liked being able to look out my front door and see only the river and the mountains and pine forest. I cherished the feeling of space around me, the sense of privacy that came from being the only family for miles around.

The afternoon passed quickly. There was a pie-eating contest, won by Gene Smythe, a potato-sack race, a baseball game. Ruth Tippitt won the blue ribbon for the prettiest quilt, Mattie Smythe won first place for the best apple pie. Carol Simpson won a prize for her strawberry preserves. As usual, the blacksmith won the arm-wrestling contest. Blackie and Monica Sullivan won the three-legged race.

I studied my son more closely than usual as the day wore on. Shadow was right. Blackie *was* growing up. As I watched him share a slice of chocolate cake with Monica, I caught a glimpse of the man he would become: kind, considerate, affable, slow to anger and quick to forgive.

Except for Shadow, no man in the valley could match Hawk's riding skills, and he easily won the bronc-riding contest and the bull-riding contest. Victoria cheered loudly, her face beaming with pride as the judge awarded Hawk an enormous blue ribbon. I glanced at Shadow, standing beside me, and frowned at the melancholy expression on his face. What was he thinking?

"Is anything wrong?" I asked, touching his arm.

"No. I was just thinking how quickly the years have gone by."

I nodded. They had passed quickly. It seemed like only yesterday that Hawk was riding a horse made of wood, and now he was a grown man, with a wife and children of his own. Mary was away in Chicago with her husband, and Blackie looked as though he was well on his way to being in love.

I was feeling suddenly melancholy myself when Shadow gave my hand a squeeze. "I did not intend for you to grow sad," he chided. "Nothing lives long but the rocks and the mountains."

"And my love for you," I said, smiling. "Shouldn't you be getting ready for the big race?"

Shadow nodded, and we walked hand-in-hand to where Heyoka was tethered to our wagon. As usual, Shadow would ride bareback, and after brushing the stallion, he slipped a bridle over the horse's head and vaulted lightly onto its back.

We had left Jason and Jacob with Rebecca, and now I followed Shadow to the starting line. There were sixteen horses in the race. I recognized Gene and Henry Smythe and Jeremy Brown among the riders.

A few minutes later, Hawk rode up on the blue roan. Like Shadow, Hawk rode bareback. He made a handsome sight, sitting straight and tall, easily controlling the roan as it pranced nervously beneath him.

I glanced at Shadow, saw the excitement dancing in his dark eyes as he waited for the race to begin. Heyoka stood quiet, his nostrils flared, his eyes wide, his foxlike ears constantly twitching back and forth.

Pa, Victoria, and Rebecca came to stand beside me. One of the Simpson girls was taking care of the twins so Victoria could watch the race.

The horses were all at the starting line now. Sheriff Bill Lancaster raised his gun and the riders leaned forward, hands tight upon the reins as they waited for the signal to begin. Lancaster fired his pistol and sixteen horses surged forward, their hooves churning up a great cloud of yellow dust.

It was a long race, plotted for speed and endurance. From the churchyard, the riders would head past the schoolhouse to the far end of town where they would cross the river, then follow the narrow trail along the river back toward town. Crossing the river again, they would round a sharp bend in the road and finish back at the churchyard.

The horses were bunched as they headed past the schoolhouse toward the edge of town. As they neared the river crossing, I could see that Hawk, Shadow, and Jeremy Brown had pulled ahead. Heyoka and the blue roan plunged into the water without losing a stride, but Jeremy Brown's big black gelding hesitated for a moment, and Gene Smythe rushed past him. Reaching the far side of the river, Gene's horse lost its footing in the mud and went to its knees. Jeremy Brown gave a victory shout as his horse leaped up the bank and back into third place. The other riders all made it safely across the river, lashing their mounts in an effort to catch Shadow and Hawk.

Heyoka and the blue roan were running neck and neck along the narrow river trail. My hand went to my heart as they approached a large log that lay across the trail. Heyoka and the blue cleared the obstacle effortlessly and I wished I could capture that moment forever. It would have made a beautiful picture, the horses rising gracefully into the air, heads high, forelegs tucked under, the riders leaning over their horses' necks, their faces intent.

The air was filled with yells and cheers as the townspeople hollered for their favorites. Pa was yelling so loud I thought his lungs would burst. One time he shouted for Shadow, the next for Hawk. Victoria had her hands clasped together, and I heard her murmur, "Faster, Hawk, faster!" Rebecca's clear brown eyes were shining with excitement. In my heart I knew she was cheering for Shadow. Once, the thought would have made me jealous, but no more.

For a short time the riders were out of sight behind a stand of timber, and then we saw them again. Shadow was in the lead, with Hawk close behind. The remainder of the riders were strung out behind them. Jeremy Brown was still in third place, Gene Smythe in fourth. I couldn't make out the others.

My heart swelled with pride as I watched my husband and my son. They rode superbly, their bodies in perfect rhythm with their horses. There were no better horsemen in all the world than the Cheyenne, I thought. Not even the Comanche could beat them, though they came close, I admitted, and then smiled. I was a bit prejudiced, after all.

As they splashed through the river, Shadow lifted one hand over his head and cut loose with the Cheyenne victory cry. The sound, long, ululating and loud, filled my soul with such joy I could not contain it, and the thrill of it poured out of me in an exuberant shout of my own as I ran forward to meet Shadow.

He did not slow down as he thundered toward me. I heard several people gasp as Shadow leaned over Heyoka's side, reached out one long arm, and grabbed me around the waist. With ease he swung me onto Heyoka's back, and then we were racing away from the churchyard.

I laughed as the wind stung my cheeks, remembering a day long ago when Shadow had swept me onto his horse's back. I had been young and frightened that day, but I was not frightened now, only tingling with anticipation as he guided Heyoka into the pine forest that grew thick along the edge of the river.

Pulling the lathered stallion to a halt, Shadow swung me to the ground, kissed me soundly on the mouth, and then began to dry the horse with a handful of grass.

With a wry grin, I sat down on the ground to wait. First things first, I mused, and watched as Shadow dried Heyoka, then walked the horse until it was cool.

"My turn now?" I asked as he tethered the stallion to a tree a short distance away.

"Yes," he replied, smiling roguishly. "Do you mind the wait?"

"No. I would wait for you forever."

"Would you?"

"Longer than forever. You look very handsome today."

"Only today?" he teased, sitting down beside me.

"Every day, you conceited oaf." I smiled up at him. "You didn't let Hawk win this time," I remarked, recalling the day when Shadow had held Smoke back so Hawk could win the race.

"I wanted Hawk to look good in his woman's eyes that day," Shadow said, his hand reaching out to stroke my cheek. "Today I wanted to look good in the eyes of my own woman."

"Oh, Shadow," I sighed. "Sometimes you say the most wonderfully romantic things."

"And will you reward me for being wonderful?" he asked, laughing softly as he began to unfasten the bodice of my dress.

"Only name your prize," I murmured. "Prize!" I exclaimed, pulling away. "You forgot to pick up your trophy."

"Later," Shadow said, slipping my dress over my shoulders and unlacing my chemise. "Much later."

And so we made love deep in the heart of the pine forest where we had first met. It was here that Shadow had first made love to me so many years ago. Our love was stronger now, deeper, richer, forged into an unbreakable bond by the happiness we had shared, the sorrows we had known.

Shadow slipped my chemise down, his fingers trailing lightly over my skin. Bending, he kissed my eyes, my cheeks, my mouth, let his lips slide down to nibble my neck and shoulders. There was fire in his touch, and I reached out to stroke his arms, then tugged at his shirt until he yanked it over his head and removed his trousers, then pulled my dress down over my ankles and tossed it in a heap beside his own clothes. My fingers explored his hard-muscled body, loving his quick response to my touch, the way he whispered my name, his voice low and deep, husky with yearning. I knew every inch of Shadow's flesh, as he knew mine, yet our love was ever new. His breath was hot upon my face, his hands impatient as they aroused me. Sometimes Shadow made love to me tenderly, prolonging each kiss and caress, taking me to the very brink of fulfillment again and again before he satisfied the longing he had created. At other times he was quick, impatient, possessive, satisfying his own needs before meeting mine. Today he was a warrior and I was his woman. We were wild and uncivilized as we made love deep in the heart of the sun-dappled forest, a man and a woman with no other thought but to quench the fiery passion that blazed between us as flesh met flesh. For this moment, there was no one else in the world, only the two of us, hearts and souls and flesh melded together as we soared to the skies.

5

Hawk smiled at Victoria as he helped her from the wagon. She looked enchanting in a blue print dress and perky straw bonnet.

"I will not be long," he promised. "I have to stop at the blacksmith to get some harness repaired, and then I am going to the feed store to pick up some grain. I will meet you back here in one hour. Will you be done by then?"

"Yes." Victoria smiled as Hawk bestowed a quick kiss upon her cheek before vaulting onto the wagon seat and turning the team toward the other end of town where the blacksmith shop was located.

It was nice to look forward to a pleasant hour in town to shop and visit with friends, Vickie thought. Her mother was sitting with the twins at home, and there was nothing she enjoyed more. It had taken a little time, but Victoria had managed to bury all her old hurts in the past where they belonged, and if she did not feel as warm and loving toward her own mother as she did toward Hannah, at least she and Lydia were friends again.

Her first stop was the mercantile store where she left her shopping list to be filled. Moving on down the street, she stopped in at Myers Millinery Shoppe to try on a hat she saw in the window. It was a wondrous creation of white lace, pink ribbons, and blue and white flowers. She gasped at the price. Three dollars and fifty cents! It was probably too expensive, yet she could not help admiring herself in the looking glass for a moment or two before placing the hat back on the shelf.

Leaving the millinery shop, she paused to chat with Ruth Tippitt and Myrtle Brown, who were also doing their weekly shopping. When Ruth and Myrtle asked Victoria to join them for an ice cream at the soda shop, she readily agreed. She enjoyed Ruth's crisp wit and Myrtle's dry sense of humor.

Hawk took longer than he had planned at the blacksmith, and by the time he went to the feed store, he was a good half-hour late in meeting Victoria.

He was driving down Bear Valley's main street toward the mercantile store when he saw Vickie. She was standing on the boardwalk near Brewster's Pharmacy talking to a tall man with curly blond hair.

As he drew nearer, Hawk saw that the man was wearing a twin brace of pistols, and that Victoria's face was bright red.

Drawing the team to a halt, Hawk overheard the man say in a coaxing tone, "Come on, honey, let me buy you something cool to drink. You're much too pretty to be standing out here all by your lonesome waiting for a man that may not show up."

Relief washed across Victoria's face when she saw Hawk pull up next to the store. "I'm no longer alone," she said, clutching her packages to her breast. "My husband is here."

Lyman Carter swung around, his pale green eyes meeting Hawk's. "You don't mean that redskin?" he asked disdainfully.

"Yes, I do," Victoria answered proudly. "Please excuse me."

The stranger shook his head in dismay. "How'd a pretty little gal like you get tangled up with a breed?"

"That's none of your business," Victoria retorted. "Now, please excuse me." Lifting her skirts, she started to walk around Lyman Carter toward the stairs.

Hawk clenched his hands at his sides. He longed to smash his fists into the stranger's face, but he knew Vickie would be angry if he caused any trouble in town.

"Hold on now," the stranger said, and reaching out, he grabbed Victoria by the arm, his fingers digging into her soft flesh.

"Let her go," Hawk said, biting off each word.

"You gonna make me?" Carter challenged.

"If I have to."

Lyman Carter grinned wolfishly, his narrowed eyes sweeping over Hawk and taking note of the fact that the half-breed was not carrying a gun.

Victoria's heart was hammering wildly in her breast as she glanced from Hawk to the stranger. She had never seen the man before. She had been waiting for Hawk when the stranger walked up to her and began talking to her, asking about the town, repeatedly complimenting her on the color of her hair and the beauty of her azure eyes, trying to persuade her to let him buy her a drink. When she told him she was a married woman, he had just laughed and said it didn't matter. He wasn't proposing marriage, just a good time.

Now she tried to twist out of his grasp, but his hand gripped her arm like a vise. She looked helplessly at Hawk, knowing there was going to be a fight.

Hawk's black eyes were glinting savagely as he dropped the reins and stood up in the wagon. "Let her go."

Carter paid no attention. Instead, he jerked Victoria closer to him. She was a lovely young woman, and he had a hankering to kiss her just once.

The packages in Victoria's arm tumbled to the ground as she tried to push the stranger away.

"Just one little kiss," Carter said. "One kiss and I'll let you go."

Hawk's anger exploded as the man's hand stroked Victoria's cheek. With a wild cry of rage, he leaped from the wagon. Taking the stairs two at a time, he grabbed the man by the arm and swung him around, his knotted right fist driving into the stranger's face.

Lyman Carter dropped Victoria's arm and tumbled down the steps. Hawk was on the man before he hit the ground, his fists lashing out at the man's face and throat. Blood washed over Hawk's hands and he gloried in it. Blood, he thought exultantly. His enemy's blood!

Lyman Carter began to fight back and the two men thrashed back and forth in the dusty street, grappling and gouging.

Victoria stood on the top step, her face pale, as she watched Hawk strike the stranger again and again. Both men were bleeding from a dozen cuts. The sound of Hawk's fists striking the stranger's flesh made her sick to her stomach and she glanced away. It was then she noticed that a crowd had gathered on the boardwalk behind her. She felt her cheeks grow hot as she recognized several of her neighbors standing nearby, watching and cheering while her husband traded blows with that dreadful man. How would she ever hold her head up in town again?

There was a loud gasp from the crowd, and when Victoria glanced back into the street, the stranger lay sprawled in the dust. Hawk's knife was sticking out of his chest.

Victoria could not take her eyes from the knife, or from the blood that stained the man's shirt front. So much blood. A man was dead, she thought dully, killed by her husband's hand. She stared at the knife and she seemed to hear her father's voice pounding in her head. *"He's nothing but a damned savage!"* her father had yelled at her over the dinner table. *"A damned savage, Victoria! And that's all he'll ever be!"*

Victoria shook the voice from her mind. Murmuring Hawk's name, she started toward him, and then the world went dark and she felt herself falling, falling, into a deep black void. Her father's voice followed her into the pit. *"A savage, Victoria, a savage—"*

Myrtle Brown's scream drew Hawk's attention from the body that lay crumpled at his feet. Looking up, he saw Victoria tumbling down the stairs in front of Brewster's.

"Vickie!" He gasped her name as he started toward her.

"Hold it," warned a voice from behind, and Hawk came to an abrupt halt as he felt the barrel of a gun jabbed against his spine. "Put your hands up real slow, and don't move."

"My wife—" Hawk began, and Sheriff Bill Lancaster jabbed the gun barrel into his back again.

"Get those hands up! Mrs. Brown is looking after your woman."

Hawk stood motionless, his hands clenched at his sides. All the color drained from his face as Myrtle Brown called for a doctor.

"Let's go," Lancaster said.

"Go where?" Hawk asked dazedly, his gaze riveted on Victoria's inert form.

"To the jailhouse. I'm arresting you for killing that there stranger."

"You're arresting me?" Hawk exclaimed. "I killed him in self-defense. He was reaching for his gun."

"I saw the whole thing," Lancaster replied. "And you never gave him a chance to reach for anything."

"At least wait until the doctor comes," Hawk pleaded. "I can't leave my wife lying there in the street."

"Mrs. Brown will look after her until Doc Henderson arrives."

"Dammit, sheriff, I won't try to get away. I give you my word. Just let me make sure Victoria is all right."

The sheriff snorted derisively. "Trust you? I didn't trust you redskins back in '77, and I sure as hell don't trust you now. Move it!"

It was in Hawk's mind to argue, but the pressure of the sheriff's gun against his back changed his mind. With a last look at Victoria's still form, Hawk turned and walked down the street toward the jail. Minutes later, he was locked inside one of the tiny cells in the cellblock adjacent to the sheriff's office.

Rage boiled inside Hawk's brain as he began to pace the narrow cell. He had done nothing wrong, yet here he was, locked up like some wild animal because he had defended his woman. Locked up because he was a half-breed. He slammed his fist against the wall, his anger growing as he remembered all the derogatory remarks he had heard through the years.

He remembered when he was just a boy and the schoolteacher at the fort had insisted he take a white name. He could clearly remember the night, soon after they had moved into Bear Valley when he was seven years old, when the Spragues had come to call and Nelda had asked Mary why Hawk's skin was so dark. Mary had given the girl a withering look as she explained that Hawk was an Indian, and she was, too.

"*I wouldn't brag about it if I were you,*" Nelda Sprague had replied scornfully. "*Everybody knows Indians are no good.*"

He vividly recalled the night Horace Bannerman had caught him kissing Victoria, remembered how the man had struck him across the face. "*Come on, you dirty half-breed,*" Horace Bannerman had challenged. "*I'll teach you to lay hands on a decent white woman!*" The word "half-breed" had sounded in his ears like thunder.

He thought of the way people in Bear Valley had looked at him when he married Vickie. Those who knew him had accepted their marriage pretty well, but others had looked at him with contempt, as if he weren't good enough to marry a white woman.

And maybe he wasn't good enough for her, he thought bleakly. But he loved her. Lord, how he loved her—and now she was lying in the street, unconscious, because of him.

Time dragged as he paced the tiny cell, restless and impatient. He had never been confined in a small space before, and he felt as if the walls were closing in on him. Four long strides carried him from one end of the cell to the other. Four strides carried him back.

An hour passed. Two. And still he paced. His thoughts were erratic, jumping from worry over Vickie to concern for what his father would think when he learned his oldest son was in jail for murder. His father. How could he face him? Yet he knew his father would have done the same thing in the same situation.

Pausing, Hawk stared blankly at the wall. His father had once killed a white man who had defiled his mother. He had heard the story many times, listening with awe as his mother told of being captured by the soldiers, how a corporal named Stockton had forced himself on her even though she was heavy with child, how his father had stealthily entered the tent where his mother was being held prisoner and hacked the white man to pieces.

Hawk whirled around as the door to the cellblock swung open and Victoria's best friend, Jenny Lee McCall, walked toward him. She stopped at his cell, her face grave.

"What is it?" Hawk asked hoarsely. "She isn't—?"

"No," Jenny Lee said quickly. "She's going to be fine, Hawk, just fine."

The tension drained out of Hawk's body.

Jenny Lee licked her lips. How was she going to tell Hawk the rest? She had always liked Hawk. He was a nice-looking young man. Before he married Vickie, she had daydreamed that he might some day call on her, but that was all in the past now. "Hawk?"

His eyes sought hers, the breath trapped in his lungs as he waited for her to speak.

"She lost the baby," Jenny Lee said sympathetically. "I'm sorry."

Hawk nodded slowly, a great sadness welling within him. He had regretted getting Vickie pregnant again so soon, but he had wanted the child. Their child. Vickie had been hoping for a girl . . .

"Hawk, is there anything I can do?"

"My father. Tell him what happened."

"I will. Anything else?"

"Vickie's mother is staying with my sons. Ask her if she can stay until Victoria gets better."

"I will. Hawk, try not to worry. I'll stay with Vickie and the twins if her mother can't."

Hawk nodded. "You are a good friend."

"I've got to go now."

Hawk nodded again. "Thank you for coming," he murmured.

Hawk stood in the middle of the cell for a long time after Jenny Lee had gone, staring into space. His child was dead before it had lived. Grief welled in his heart and he threw back his head and loosed a long, bitter cry.

And then he lifted his arms above his head and began to pray.

6

I could not believe my ears as Jenny Lee McCall
poured out her story in a flood of words and tears.
There had been a fight. Hawk had killed a man.
Victoria had miscarried. Hawk was in jail.

I glanced at Shadow, too stunned to speak.

Shadow did not waste time asking questions. He
thanked Jenny Lee for coming, escorted her to the
door, and reached for his buckskin jacket.

"Let us go," he said. Handing me my bonnet, he
took me by the arm and propelled me out of the house.

Moments later we were headed for town.

Sheriff Bill Lancaster was reluctant to let us see
Hawk, but one look at Shadow's face stifled the
lawman's objections and he let us into the cellblock

after first making sure that Shadow was not concealing a weapon.

Hawk's face lit up when he first saw us, and then his expression turned to one of shame.

"Are you all right?" I asked anxiously. His face was swollen, his mouth cut, his nose bloody. I made a mental note to insist that he be allowed to clean up.

"I am all right," Hawk answered.

"What happened?" Shadow asked.

Hawk let out a long breath and then told his story, how the stranger had accosted Vickie and put his hands on her, refusing to let her go. A fight had ensued, the man had reached for his gun, and Hawk had stabbed him.

I went cold all over as Hawk finished his story. We had many friends in Bear Valley. The Indian wars had been over for years. And yet I knew there were many people who would believe that Hawk was guilty of killing the man in cold blood simply because he was part Indian.

"I killed him in self-defense," Hawk said, his eyes pleading with us to believe him. "But the sheriff does not believe me. He said he saw the whole fight and that I killed the stranger in cold blood."

"I believe you," Shadow said. "Do not worry."

"Have you seen Vickie?" Hawk asked anxiously. "Is she all right?"

"We haven't seen her yet," I replied. "We wanted to see you first. Don't worry about Victoria. We'll take her home and care for her if Lydia doesn't feel she can handle it."

Hawk nodded, and then he looked at Shadow. "I am going crazy in here, neyho," he said, quiet desperation in his voice.

Shadow nodded, his dark eyes filling with compassion and understanding.

Hawk gripped the bars in both hands, his knuckles going white. "I would rather be dead than have to stay in prison."

Shadow nodded again. "Do not worry, naha. I will not let that happen."

Hope flared in Hawk's eyes, and then he let out a long sigh. "Tell Vickie I am sorry for what happened. Tell her I love her."

"I will tell her," Shadow said. "We will stop by again before we go home."

Outside, we walked hand in hand toward the doctor's office. I glanced at Shadow, started to speak, and then changed my mind.

"What is it, Hannah?" Shadow asked.

"You told Hawk not to worry, that you wouldn't let him stay in jail."

"Yes."

"You don't mean to try and break him out, do you?"

Shadow did not answer for a long moment, and then he said, "Our people die if they are confined in prison for a long time. We were not meant to live inside four walls, but to live wild and free. It is better for a warrior to be dead than in prison. I will not let Hawk die a little bit each day."

"Shadow . . ."

"I have been in prison, Hannah," he said, his

voice bitter with the memory. "I will not let that happen to Hawk. We will wait and see what kind of justice the white man has for an Indian."

"And if a jury finds Hawk guilty?"

"Then I will do what must be done."

I didn't argue. I knew that Shadow would do what he had to do, and nothing I could say would stop him. Jenny Lee had said there were many people on the street who had seen the fight between Hawk and the stranger. Surely someone had seen Lyman Carter reach for his gun. Surely that someone would come forward at the trial, if not before.

Dr. Henderson smiled as he ushered us down a whitewashed hallway to a small green room. Victoria was in bed, her face pale. There were dark smudges under her eyes.

"Don't stay too long," the doctor cautioned. "She needs her rest."

"Will she be all right?" I asked.

Dr. Henderson nodded confidently. "To be sure, to be sure. She's young and healthy. A few days of complete bed rest and she'll be back on her feet."

I nodded, and the doctor left the room, closing the door behind him.

"Vickie?"

Her eyelids fluttered open and I could see she had been crying.

"How are you feeling, Victoria?" I asked.

"Empty," she said. "How's Hawk? Have you seen him?"

"Yes. He's fine. He sends his love."

"I lost the baby," she said, and two large tears

welled in her eyes. "Oh, Hannah, it was awful! I've never seen Hawk so angry, and then he killed that man and there was blood everywhere."

She was sobbing now, reliving the horror of the moment. I started toward her, but Shadow reached her side first. Bending, he took Vickie in his arms and held her while she cried.

"Do not think about it," Shadow said, his voice soft and soothing. "It is over now. Everything will be all right."

"How can it be?" Victoria cried, her blue eyes frantic with worry. "Jenny Lee said they're going to hang Hawk for killing that awful man. What am I going to do?"

"Nothing," Shadow said. "You are going to stay in bed for as long as the doctor says. Then you are going home to take care of your sons. They will not hang Hawk."

Victoria blinked back her tears, her eyes intent on Shadow's face.

"They will not hang him," Shadow said again. "You must trust me and do as I say."

Victoria nodded. She had always admired and respected Shadow, and if he said everything would be all right, then everything would be all right.

Slowly, Shadow lowered her back onto the bed. "Sleep now. We will be back to see you tomorrow."

Like an obedient child, Victoria closed her eyes. Shadow took my hand and we left the room.

"Shadow, I'm afraid."

"Have I ever failed you before?"

"No."

"I will not fail you now. Do not worry, Hannah."

I nodded. I, too, admired and respected Shadow. He always knew what to do and how to do it.

We stopped at the jail to tell Hawk that Vickie was doing fine and that the doctor said there was nothing to be concerned about.

"Do not do anything foolish," Shadow warned Hawk as we prepared to leave. "I will take care of everything."

Hawk grinned wryly. "Do you read my mind, neyho?"

"No. But I remember the thoughts that went through my mind when I was in the stockade at Fort Apache. I remember thinking that I would do anything to get out. I see that same desperation in your eyes now. And I tell you again, do not do anything foolish."

"I understand, neyho."

"Good. I will send Blackie over to your place to look after your stock until you are home again."

"Tell him to keep an eye on the wall-eyed mare. She is due to foal soon, and she usually needs help."

Shadow nodded. "We will see you again tomorrow."

"Can I bring you anything?" I asked.

"A change of clothing," Hawk said, glancing at his blood-stained shirt. "And one of your apple pies."

"You'll have them," I promised.

It was hard, leaving my son in jail. I knew how he must hate being locked up, how desperately he needed to see Victoria, to know for himself that she was going to be all right. I prayed that he would listen to Shadow and not do anything foolish. To try to escape would only make him look guilty.

When we got home, Shadow sent Blackie over to stay at Hawk's place. Blackie was ecstatic at the thought of helping the mares foal, though he was less enthusiastic about staying in the house with Lydia.

Our place seemed very empty with Blackie gone, and I thought how sad it was that my children had to grow up and leave home. When they were young, I had thought they would always be there. Now Hawk and Mary had homes of their own, and soon Blackie would be grown and gone as well.

I glanced at Shadow. He was sitting on the edge of the hearth mending a bridle. The lamplight cast his profile in bronze, and I marveled at how handsome he was, this man who was my whole life.

A little fear began to niggle at the back of my mind as I thought about Shadow's promise to Hawk. I knew that Shadow would not let them hang our son, nor would he let Hawk languish in prison. Closing my eyes, I sent an urgent prayer to God and Maheo, begging them for help. Our lives would be turned upside down if Shadow were forced to break Hawk out of jail. My husband and my son would be fugitives, and our lives in Bear Valley would be over. What would I do then? Where would we go?

I remembered how it had been when Shadow and I were being hunted by the soldiers after Little Big Horn, how awful it had been to be constantly running and hiding, always afraid, always tired and hungry. I did not want to live like that again, and even as I thought about it, I knew it was impossible. I could not drag Blackie across the countryside, running and hiding. I could not endanger my youngest son's life. And what of Victoria? She was too fragile to endure such a life. Not only that, she had two young sons to consider.

I had been mending one of Shadow's shirts, and now I laid it aside and went to kneel beside him.

"Oh, Shadow," I murmured.

"I know," he said quietly. Laying the bridle on the floor, he stroked my hair. I loved the touch of his hand, and I closed my eyes as I rested my head in his lap. We sat there for a long time, content to be quietly close, both wondering what the outcome of the trial would be and how it would affect our lives in Bear Valley.

"Long life and happiness," Shadow said after a while. "That was what the hawks promised. Remember?"

"I remember."

"Tomorrow I am going into the hills. I will be gone most of the day."

"What about Hawk?"

"Tell him I will see him sometime tomorrow."

7

He rose just before dawn. Slipping out of bed, he pulled on an old pair of buckskin trousers and a pair of moccasins and padded noiselessly out of the bedroom, through the dark house, and out the front door. At the corral, he threw a bridle over Smoke's head, swung aboard the stallion's bare back, and headed for the hills.

As he rode eastward, the sun climbed above the horizon, splashing the sky with an ever-changing palette of colors: gray to lavendar, pink to rose, each color growing brighter until the whole sky seemed to be on fire with the birth of a new day.

Shadow rode at an easy, ground-covering lope, enjoying the feel of the wind in his face, the movement of the horse beneath him, the fragrance of earth and grass that filled his nostrils.

Reaching the hills some time later, Shadow urged the stallion up the steep slope until he came to a place where the ground leveled out. Reining Smoke to a halt, he dismounted.

For a long moment he stood staring into the distance, remembering days long past. Gazing down the corridors of time, he saw Hannah as she had been as a young girl. She was there at Rabbit's Head Rock that sunny day they had first met, a skinny little girl with flaming red hair and expressive gray eyes, a handful of wildflowers clutched in her hands. He saw himself as a young boy, lonely for a mother's love and attention. It had been Hannah's mother, as much as Hannah herself, who had drawn him to the Kincaid house time and again. There was a feeling of love there, a sense of warmth and belonging, and he had soaked it up. It had been Hannah's mother, Mary, who had taught him to read and write the white man's language. She had been a wise woman, knowing that, while it was all right to teach him some things, it was best not to try to make a white man out of him.

Turning his gaze to the east, Shadow thought of his father, Black Owl, and of the other men in the tribe who had taught him the ways of a warrior. He thought of Crazy Horse and Sitting Bull and all the other great chiefs he had known: Gall, American Horse, Hump, Red Cloud. He thought of his best friend, Calf Running, who had been gunned down by a soldier; of Clyde Stewart and Barney McCall and the endless days he had spent as a sideshow attraction in a traveling tent show. And then he thought of his children, of helping Hannah bring Mary and Blackie into the world, of the Sun Dance he had shared with Hawk.

He recalled the battles he had been in, the men he had killed, and then he thought again of Hannah, always Hannah. She was his strength, woven tightly into the fabric of his life.

Abruptly he raised his arms toward heaven. "Hear me, Man Above," he prayed in a loud voice. "Give me strength and wisdom that I might be worthy of my woman, that I might find a way to help my son."

Drawing a small pouch from the waistband of his trousers, he poured a generous amount of tobacco into the palm of his hand, then sprinkled it to the four directions.

"Hear me, Man Above," he cried. "I have need of your help."

He stood there for over an hour, his arms upraised, his face turned toward the sun, his heart pouring out a prayer to Maheo.

The sun climbed higher in the sky, and sweat trickled down Shadow's arms and back and chest, and still he stood there, unmoving, his whole being focused on that which he desired.

Another hour passed, two, and he dropped to his knees, unmindful of the heat or the gnawing hunger in his belly.

The fourth hour came and went and still he did not move, only knelt there, his lips moving in prayer.

It was late in the afternoon when he heard a great

rushing of mighty wings. Hardly daring to hope, he turned his head to the left and let out a long sigh as two red-tailed hawks appeared in the sky, wheeling and diving in perfect unison until they hovered above his head.

"Be strong," the male hawk cried in a loud voice. "Be strong, and you will prevail over your enemies."

"Be brave," the female cried in a loud voice. "Be brave, and you will have nothing to fear."

Another rush of wings, and they were gone.

Utterly fatigued, Shadow slumped to the ground, his heart at peace.

He remained there for thirty minutes, his eyes closed, and then he mounted Smoke and rode down the hill toward town, and Hawk.

8

Shadow was gone when I woke up. Rising, I dressed quickly and went into the kitchen. After drinking a cup of hot chocolate, I began to make the pie I had promised Hawk.

While it baked, I tidied up the house, my eyes wandering to the front window several times in hopes of seeing Shadow. Where had he gone? Knowing him as I did, I was certain he had gone off alone to seek guidance from Man Above.

It was just after noon when I went into town. Hawk was pacing back and forth when I entered the cellblock, and my heart welled with sympathy for my son. I remembered the time I had visited Shadow in the stockade at Fort Apache in Arizona Territory. Conditions there had been much worse than those

Hawk found himself in now, but Hawk's eyes reflected the same quiet desperation I had once seen in Shadow's.

"I brought the pie," I said, forcing a note of cheer into my voice, "and a change of clothing."

Hawk nodded. "Have you heard anything?"

"The trial is set for Friday. It's only three days," I said. "That's not so long."

Hawk swore under his breath. "Every day behind these bars is like a year," he exclaimed angrily.

"I know." I slipped his clean clothes through the bars, and then the pie. "There's a cloth and a bar of soap wrapped inside your shirt."

"Thank you, nahkoa. I did not mean to shout at you."

"It's all right."

I spent an hour with Hawk. We didn't talk much. He asked about the twins and I told him that Lydia was staying with them, and that Blackie was looking after the stock. The mare hadn't foaled yet.

Leaving the jail, I went to visit Victoria. She was looking a little better, though her eyes were haunted and sad. I stayed with her until she fell asleep, and then I drove over to Pa's place.

Rebecca had persuaded Pa to go back East to visit Beth, but they had postponed their trip, neither of them wanting to leave until after Hawk's trial.

Pa ranted and raved about the injustice of it all. Arresting a man for protecting his wife. Who'd ever heard of such a thing?

It was a delight to see Pa's temper flare, I mused with a grin. He was a sight to behold when he was riled. As a girl, I had always said his temper matched the red in his moustache, and though his moustache was all gray now, his temper hadn't cooled a bit.

Rebecca let him carry on for several minutes, and then she laid her hand on his arm.

"Sam, that's enough," she said quietly, and Pa's tirade came to an abrupt halt. "Hannah, is there anything we can do?"

"No. Judge Roberts is hearing the case, and Whitley Monroe has been appointed to defend Hawk."

"Roberts!" Pa flared. "Clive Roberts is an Indian hater from way back, and that limp wrist Whitley Monroe won't lift a finger in Hawk's behalf."

"I know," I agreed morosely. "But what can we do? Shadow asked Judge Roberts for a postponement until we can get another lawyer, but he refused. The trial is set for this Friday."

"Damn," Pa muttered. "I wish we had time to get ahold of Ethan Smythe. I hear he's made himself quite a reputation as a defense lawyer back in St. Louie."

"So I've heard," I said. "But there isn't time." I chewed on my lower lip for a moment. "Pa . . ."

"I'm listening."

"I'm worried. Shadow promised Hawk that he wouldn't hang or go to jail."

Pa frowned. "What are you saying, girl?"

"Just what you think I am. If the jury finds Hawk guilty, Shadow's going to break him out of jail."

"Oh, no!" Rebecca gasped. "Hannah, you mustn't let him do such a thing."

I uttered a short laugh. "Me, stop Shadow? You know that's impossible."

Rebecca nodded. "I know. Once he puts his mind to something, he does it."

"There'll be hell to pay if Shadow crosses the law," Pa mused aloud. "Does he understand that?"

"Of course he understands, but he doesn't care. He made Hawk a promise, and he'll keep it or die trying."

It was dark when I got home. Worried and lonely, I paced the parlor floor, my ears listening for Shadow's footsteps. Ten times in as many minutes I went to the window and looked out, but saw only darkness.

Too upset to eat, I drank several cups of lukewarm coffee, then sank down in a corner of the couch, staring into the fireplace.

I had almost dozed off when I heard Shadow's step in the hall. Rising, I flew into his arms, lifting my face for his kiss. He was here. He was safe. For now, nothing else mattered.

I sought comfort in his arms that night, needing to feel his strength, not only physically but spiritually. I knew he had gone to commune with Maheo that afternoon and though he had not yet told me what had happened, I sensed that something significant had transpired between Shadow and his special spirits, the hawks.

Shadow made love to me tenderly that night. It was not passion that forged us together, not desire, but need. I found strength in his nearness, a sense of renewal and rebirth. Hawk had been born out of our love, and that same love would see us through the trying days ahead.

Later, our bodies still united, Shadow told me of his trip to the hills, of the thoughts that had drifted down the corridors of his mind, of the heat and the hunger, and of the hawks. I marveled at what he told me. Always, the hawks had been there when he needed them most, and I listened in awe as he related their words.

I was nearly asleep when I felt Shadow's lips brush my cheek, and far off in the distance I thought I heard the shrill cry of a red-tailed hawk calling for its mate.

9

Sheriff Bill Lancaster grinned wolfishly as he slid the breakfast tray under the bars.

"Two more days, redskin," he drawled. "Two more days and you'll be hanging higher than Haman."

Hawk stood near the cell door, his eyes filling with anger as the lawman continued to taunt him.

"Yep," Lancaster went on cheerfully, "just two more days and you'll get a taste of the white man's justice. They'll drop that rope around your neck, snug the knot under your ear, pull it tight, and let 'er rip. Probably break your neck nice and clean. Then again, it might not. Might be you'll kick and choke a minute or two before you finally strangle to death." Lancaster nodded. "I reckon everybody in town will turn out for the show. Maybe even that pretty little wife of yours."

Hawk clenched his fists at his sides as the sheriff mentioned Victoria. His whole body grew tense as the urge to kill swept over him.

"Yeah," Lancaster went on, "she's a pretty little thing. Who knows, I might even court her myself. Once you're out of the way, she'll need a man to look after her. It would surely pleasure me to show her what it's like to have a real man in her bed instead of a lousy stinking savage."

Rage drove all else from Hawk's mind as Lancaster spoke of bedding Victoria. With a wild cry, he lunged at the lawman, his right arm snaking through the bars to close around Lancaster's throat.

Bill Lancaster struggled violently, his hand groping for the gun holstered on his right hip. As the world began to go black, he drew the gun and fired.

The slug ripped into Hawk's left side, tearing into flesh and muscle, but Hawk kept hold of Lancaster until the lawman's eyes rolled back in his head and he went limp.

Realizing what he had done, Hawk released Lancaster and the sheriff fell heavily to the floor. For a moment Hawk did not move. He had killed the sheriff and now they would hang him for sure.

Reaching through the bars, he searched the sheriff's pockets, muttering a prayer of gratitude when he found the key to his cell. Unlocking the door, he stepped outside. Grabbing Lancaster's gun, he hurried out of the jail, unmindful of the blood dripping down his side.

Lancaster's horse was standing hipshot at the

hitch rail and Hawk swung into the saddle, grunting with pain. The initial numbness was wearing off now and the wound throbbed steadily.

People were pouring out of the stores located near the jail, drawn by the sound of the gunshot. Ignoring the excited questions of those nearest him, Hawk lashed the horse with the end of the reins. Behind him, someone yelled, "Stop! Stop or I'll shoot!" but Hawk did not slow down or look back.

He rode hard, heading for the hills where he had gone to seek his vision. He pushed the horse to the limits of its endurance, knowing he had to put as much distance as possible between himself and the posse that was certain to follow.

Damn! What had he done? Why had he let Lancaster goad him into violence? Now he would be a hunted man for as long as he lived. He couldn't go home. He couldn't go to his father or grandfather for help. The law would expect him to turn to his family for help, and they would be there, waiting for him to show up.

He rode hard until he was about a hundred yards from the hills. There, he slid off the horse and slapped the animal hard on the rump, sending it back to town. His only hope was to cover his trail and lie low for a while. Perhaps, in time, he could make his way to the reservation and hide out. Perhaps he could find a way to get word to Vickie and his parents. Perhaps.

Light-headed and weak from loss of blood, he ripped a strip of material from his shirt and wrapped it around his middle and then, using all the skill his father had taught him long ago, he walked toward the hills, laboriously erasing all sign of his passing as he went along.

Sweat dripped into his eyes and trickled down his back as he began to climb upward. Thorn bushes snagged his clothes and scratched his face and arms. The constant movement sent little stabs of pain shooting along his side, and when he touched the makeshift bandage swathed around his middle, he felt the warm stickiness of blood seeping through the cloth. And still he kept climbing, his teeth gritted against the pain. He had to get away, to hide. No one would believe he hadn't meant to kill Lancaster. No one would understand the deep-seated hatred the lawman had aroused when he talked of bedding Victoria.

White men, Hawk thought bitterly. They had robbed the Indian of his homeland, of his way of life, of his freedom. On the reservation, they tried to turn the Indians into imitation white men. The government insisted the warriors cut their hair and raise cattle. They forced the children to go to school and learn the white man's tongue and the white man's ways. The Cheyenne and the Sioux were forbidden to practice their religion, and the Sun Dance, the most sacred ritual of all, had to be performed in secret, as though it were a thing of shame.

He had lived with whites all his life, and only now did he truly begin to hate them. He thought of Lancaster laying hands on Victoria, and the thought made him physically ill.

He climbed for what seemed like hours before he

reached a small cave recessed deep in the side of the hill. Erasing the last of his tracks, he dropped to his hands and knees and crawled into the narrow cavern, praying that it was empty. The cave smelled faintly of animal excrement, but it was an old smell. Crawling toward the back of the cave, Hawk closed his eyes and surrendered to the darkness hovering all around him.

10

I threw a worried glance at Shadow as he pulled the team to a halt before the jail. A crowd was gathered outside and everyone was talking rapidly, gesturing toward the end of town. I caught Hawk's name and felt a tremor of fear start in the pit of my stomach. Something had happened to Hawk!

Shadow helped me to the ground and we elbowed our way through the crowd toward the door of the Sheriff's Office. Phil Tompkins, one of Lancaster's deputies, blocked our way.

"What has happened?" Shadow asked.

"That kid of yourn escaped from jail," Tompkins said brusquely. "Nearly killed Bill Lancaster doing it."

"Oh, no," I murmured.

"Where is the sheriff now?" Shadow demanded.

"Inside. The doc's with him."

"I want to talk to him."

"Maybe later."

"Now," Shadow said, and pushed past Tompkins.

I followed Shadow into the sheriff's office. Bill Lancaster was sitting in the black leather chair behind his desk. He looked pale, and his throat was bruised and discolored, but he did not appear to be badly hurt.

"You'll be all right," Dr. Henderson was saying. "Throat'll be sore for a day or two, but no permanent damage has been done."

Closing his bag with a flourish, the doctor tipped his hat in my direction and left the office.

Lancaster glared at Shadow. "Get the hell out of here," he rasped. "I've had all the trouble I want with your family for one day."

"What happened?" Shadow asked.

Lancaster shrugged. "I got too close to that boy of yours and he grabbed me. Nearly strangled me to death."

Shadow took a step toward Lancaster. "Hannah, shut the door."

Wordlessly I did as I had been told.

Lancaster glanced at the closed door, and then at Shadow. "Now wait a minute—"

"I want to know what happened," Shadow said. He took his knife from his belt and studied the blade. "Everything that happened."

Lancaster shrugged. "I took the kid his breakfast and he went crazy."

"What did you say to him?"

"Nothing. I didn't say nothing." Lancaster's words came out in a rush.

Shadow closed the distance between himself and

the sheriff until they were only a foot apart. Shadow ran the edge of the blade over his thumb. The knife was razor sharp and a thin line of red trailed in the wake of the blade.

Lancaster swallowed hard as he glanced from the blood on Shadow's thumb to the menace lurking in Shadow's eyes.

"What did you say to him?" Shadow asked again.

"I . . ." Bill Lancaster looked at me, his eyes pleading for help. A thin layer of sweat had formed on his brow and along his upper lip.

"I would answer my husband's question if I were you," I told the sheriff coldly. "He can be very impatient sometimes."

Lancaster swore softly. Then, his eyes fixed on the floor, he said, "I was giving the boy a bad time, I guess. I . . . I was kidding him about the hanging, about how he'd die kicking at the end of a rope."

Kicking at the end of a rope. The years fell away and I could hear Corporal Hopkins taunting Shadow as we rode toward Fort Apache. "*Best get used to that rope, redskin,* he had called, tugging on the noose around Shadow's neck, "*cause you're gonna swing high and dry when we reach the fort. Yessir, I seen lots of Injuns dancing at the end of a rope. Ain't a purty sight, no sir. Sometimes a man's neck don't break just right, and he strangles kinda slow like, eyes bulgin' and feet kickin'. That's how you'll go, Injun, if I get to tie the knot.*"

I shuddered at the memory. Lately my dreams had been haunted by nightmares of Hawk climbing the stairs to the gallows, his head high, his black eyes blazing defiantly. In my dreams I saw the heavy rope circle his neck, saw the knot drawn tight under his ear. I would wake, sobbing, as the trapdoor yawned open at his feet.

Shadow's hand tightened around the hilt of the knife in his hand, his knuckles going white with the strain. "You bastard," he hissed. "What else did you say to him?"

"I . . ." Lancaster coughed nervously. I had seen braver men than the sheriff cower before the awful fury in Shadow's eyes and I could not blame the lawman for being afraid.

"Go on," Shadow demanded.

"I mentioned his wife, how pretty she was. I said . . . I said maybe I'd court her after . . ."

A low growl erupted from Shadow's throat as he drove the point of his knife into the top of Lancaster's desk, then grabbed Lancaster by the shirt front and hauled him to his feet.

I had not seen my husband in a killing rage for many years, but I knew that Sheriff Bill Lancaster was as close to death as he had ever been.

"You sonofabitch," Shadow growled, his voice low and taut with menace. "I am surprised Hawk did not break your neck."

Lancaster's face was gray, his eyes white with terror.

"I want your promise," Shadow said.

Lancaster nodded, fear strangling his voice so he could not speak. I knew that at that moment the sheriff would have readily promised Shadow anything he desired.

"I am going out to find my son," Shadow said quietly. "I am going to bring him back here to stand trial for the murder of Lyman Carter. You will not press charges against Hawk for attacking you. You will not speak to him again, nor will you send a posse after him. I will find Hawk myself."

"You got till ten tomorrow morning," Lancaster agreed reluctantly, and Shadow released him. The sheriff dropped back into his chair. Pulling a handkerchief from his back pocket, he mopped the sweat from his face and neck.

"Shadow, how will you find him?" I asked.

"I think I know where to look."

"This is going to look bad when he goes to trial," I said, frowning. "People will say he ran because he's guilty."

"If he does not come back to stand trial, he will have to run for the rest of his life."

Shadow was right, and I knew it. Yet I was certain that Hawk would never get a fair trial now, not here.

Shadow swore softly, and I looked at him askance.

"Look," he said, pointing at the floor near the door to the cellblock.

It was blood. I glanced at Lancaster, but he was not bleeding.

"Tell me," Shadow said, his eyes riveted on the lawman's face.

"He's hurt," the sheriff admitted reluctantly. "I don't know how bad. I think I may have shot him just before I passed out."

"If my son is dead, you are dead," Shadow said flatly. "Hannah, go home."

"Be careful," I said.

Shadow nodded. He gave me a quick kiss, and then he was gone.

When I left the sheriff's office, there was still a crowd gathered outside. An angry crowd. Several men stood near Deputy Tompkins.

"We should get a posse together," one of the men said in a loud voice. "If Lancaster hasn't got the balls for it, I do!"

"Damn redskins," growled another. "I knew you couldn't trust 'em."

Their voices died away as I walked down the steps and climbed into our buggy. A few of the people in the crowd had the decency to look embarrassed.

Fred Brown, a longtime resident of Bear Valley and an old friend, came to stand beside the buggy.

"We're with you," he said loudly enough for all to hear. "If you need anything, come and see us."

"That goes for my family, too," Leland Smythe added, coming to stand beside Fred Brown. "We're family now, and we're behind you all the way."

"Thank you," I said. "Thank you both."

Holding my head high, I clucked to the team and drove out of town. Only then did I let the tears flow. Hawk was hurt, perhaps badly hurt, and I was unable to help. Only Shadow could help our son now. Closing my eyes, I offered a quick prayer to all the gods, both red and white, begging them to watch over my son and bring him safely home.

I stopped at Hawk's place on the way home. Blackie came running out to meet me.

"It's a colt!" he cried, throwing his arms around

my waist. "Black as midnight, nahkoa. Wait until you see him."

"I'm sure he's beautiful," I replied, trying to smile. "And I'll be down to see him in a few minutes, but first I have to see Vickie."

Blackie nodded. He gave me a quick kiss on the cheek and then ran off toward the pasture where the mares were kept.

Heavy-hearted, I knocked on the front door, dreading what must be said.

Lydia opened the door. She smiled at me as she invited me in. "Victoria's in bed," Lydia remarked, "but she's awake. I know she'll be glad to see you."

Victoria took the news of Hawk's escape better than I had expected. She cried, of course, when she heard he had been shot, and I could have wept again myself. First Hawk had been arrested for defending her, then she had lost her unborn child, and now this.

"Your father warned you not to marry him," Lydia murmured from the doorway.

Victoria turned angry eyes on her mother. "Don't you dare say a word against Hawk!" she warned. "Not a word! If you do, I'll never speak to you again."

"I'm sorry," Lydia said quickly. "Forgive me."

Victoria nodded, and Lydia left the room.

"What will happen now?" Vickie asked.

"Shadow has gone to find Hawk," I said, smiling reassuringly. "He'll find him if anyone can."

11

Shadow rode straight for the hills, certain that Hawk would seek shelter in one of the caves scattered across the hillside. Outside of town he crossed a single set of horse's tracks heading toward the hills. The horse had clearly been moving fast, and Shadow suspected the tracks belonged to his son.

It was late afternoon when he reached the hills. Dismounting, he checked the ground for a sign and discovered the tracks of a horse heading back to Bear Valley. The tracks were not as deep as they had been earlier, indicating that the horse was now riderless.

Leading his rented mount, Shadow began to climb the hill, his eyes darting from side to side as he continued to search for signs. He smiled faintly when he found none. Hawk had learned his lessons well.

Shadow continued to climb upward, oblivious of the spiked thorns that caught in his clothing and bloodied his arms. He had explored these hills often as a boy. It had been a favorite place of his, a haven when he wanted to be alone. Hawk had come here to seek his vision. Instinctively Shadow knew that Hawk had come here to hide.

There were several caves cut into the hillside. He checked inside three of them before he found Hawk. The cave his son had chosen was near the crest of the hill. It was a good hiding place, small and well-camouflaged by a tangled mass of catclaw. Few white men would have noticed it.

The snick of a Colt being cocked sounded loud in the stillness as Shadow stepped into the cavern.

"Do not shoot, naha," Shadow said quietly.

"Neyho." Hawk's voice was weak but filled with relief as he heard his father's voice.

Striking a match, Shadow lit the candle he had brought with him and walked toward the rear of the cave. Hawk was huddled against the wall. The cloth swathed around his middle was caked with blood, his face was pale and damp with sweat.

"I did not mean to kill him," Hawk blurted. "It was an accident."

"He is not dead," Shadow said, kneeling beside his son. "Do not talk now. I have brought food and water and medicine. When you are stronger, we will go back to town."

"No! I will never go back."

"You are a man and a warrior," Shadow remarked calmly. "I will not force you to return, but it is a thing you must do if you ever hope to live a decent life with Victoria and your sons. If you run now, they will hunt you down like a dog."

"Neyho—"

"You must trust me, Hawk. You must go back and stand trial."

"I can't," Hawk cried. "Lancaster will make certain they hang me now."

"Lancaster will do nothing."

Hawk studied his father's face, and then he smiled faintly. He did not know what had happened between the lawman and his father, but he could guess.

"You will not let them hang me?"

"No."

"You have always known what was best," Hawk admitted with a sigh. "I will do as you say."

Shadow nodded as he placed the candle on the ground. "Let me have a look at your side."

Cold sweat broke out across Hawk's brow as Shadow removed the bandage and probed the wound.

"The bullet is still inside," Shadow said. "It will have to come out."

Hawk nodded weakly. "You cut a bullet from my flesh once before, neyho. Do you remember?"

"I remember. You were just a boy then, but as brave as any warrior of the People."

"It was a bad day," Hawk rasped.

Shadow nodded. Pulling his knife from his belt, he disinfected it with carbolic he had gotten from the doctor. "Ready?"

"Ready." Hawk closed his eyes, his mind seeking escape in the past as he remembered the other time his father had cut a bullet from his flesh. He had been a boy of twelve then. He had run away from home and gone to the Pine Ridge Reservation to see Sitting Bull, and to learn more of the new Ghost Dance religion that was spreading like wildfire among the Indians. The whites had been afraid of the new religion, fearing it meant the Indians were preparing to return to the warpath. Frightened and uneasy, the Indian agent, McLaughlin, had decided to arrest Sitting Bull and put an end to the dancing. But Sitting Bull had resisted arrest and there had been a battle. Hawk had been wounded. Sitting Bull and fourteen others were killed.

Hawk felt the sweat break out on his body as his father probed his side for the slug, and he clenched his teeth against the pain, not wanting to cry out, not wanting to show weakness before his father, the bravest of all the men he had ever known.

"Do not be afraid to give voice to the pain," Shadow said softly. "There is no one to hear you but me, and I will not think less of you for it."

Stubbornly, Hawk shook his head. He was a warrior of the People. A warrior did not show pain.

Pride swelled in Shadow's heart as Hawk fought to control his pain. Truly his son was worthy of the name warrior.

In minutes, Shadow had dislodged the slug from Hawk's side. He poured a generous amount of disinfectant into the angry wound before wrapping it lightly in a strip of clean cloth. He gave Hawk a powder the doctor had prescribed for fever, then started a small fire. Returning to his horse, he retrieved a coffee pot and the provisions he had purchased before leaving town and prepared a light meal.

Hawk ate very little and soon fell asleep.

Shadow gazed at his son for a long moment before covering him with a blanket. He recalled Hawk's determination to be a warrior, how he had sought a vision and participated in the Sun Dance. In the old days, Hawk would have been a leader among the People, able to live the life he had been born to live.

Leaving the cave, Shadow watched the sun descend toward the distant mountains. The setting sun stained the sky a brilliant crimson, deep and red like the blood of his people.

As shadows stretched across the land, he stripped down to his loincloth and then, standing alone on the hillside, raised his arms toward heaven as he prayed to Maheo for strength and wisdom.

The years fell away as he prayed and he was a young warrior again, beseeching the gods for a vision to guide him through life. For three nights and four days he had lingered in his chosen place, fasting and praying for a sign as he offered tobacco to the four winds, to Man Above and Mother Earth. But only endless silence and the hot rays of the sun had answered his entreaties. And then, on the fourth day of his quest, the sun had risen in all her glory, splashing the sky with all the colors of the rainbow.

Perhaps it is a sign, he had thought dully. *Perhaps, on this, my last day, a vision will come.* How could he face his father if it did not?

For the space of three heartbeats, a great stillness had hung over the hilltop, as if the very earth were holding its breath. Then a wild rushing noise had filled his ears, and as he stared upward at the sun, it suddenly seemed to be falling toward him. In terror he had pressed himself against the damp ground, fearing certain destruction. And then the sun had split in half and out of the middle had flown two red-tailed hawks. In perfect unison they had soared through the air, wheeling and diving, moving with timeless grace, until they hovered above his head.

"Be brave," the male hawk had cried in a loud voice. "Be brave, and I will always be with you. You shall be swift as the hawk, wise as the owl."

"Be strong," the female hawk had cried in a loud voice. "Be strong, and I will always be with you. You shall be clever as the hawk, mighty as the eagle."

And then, with a rush of powerful wings, the two hawks had soared heavenward and disappeared into the sun. And from that time forward, he had been known among the People as Two Hawks Flying.

Shadow sighed as he lowered his arms. Always in times of crisis the hawks had been there. He could feel them now, their wings wrapping around him, warm and comforting like the arms of an old friend. Peace welled in his heart and he knew there was nothing to fear.

12

Shadow brought Hawk home just after sundown. My son looked far older than his years, weary in mind and body. I knew he dreaded going back to jail, knew how humiliating it was for him to be trapped behind iron bars.

"Who knows he's here?" I asked Shadow.

"No one. I wanted him to have a good meal and a decent night's sleep before he goes back to jail."

I wanted that, too, and while I prepared all Hawk's favorite things for dinner, Shadow went to pick up Victoria and the twins.

Hawk and Vickie were quiet at dinner. Hawk didn't have much of an appetite, and I knew he ate more to please me than because he was hungry. They sat on the sofa while I cleared the table and washed the dishes. My heart ached to see the two of them together. Vickie was still a little pale from the miscarriage, Hawk was weak from the bullet wound in his side, their future was uncertain. But the love in their eyes was still strong.

Hawk held his sons, playing with them for a while before they went to bed.

"Hannah," Shadow said, taking my hand. "Let us go for a walk. I think these two would like to be alone."

Hawk sent his father a grateful smile, and then Shadow and I left the house and walked down toward the river crossing.

"Do you think you can trust Lancaster to keep his mouth shut about what happened?" I asked.

"He will not talk," Shadow said confidently. "Of course, everyone knows that Hawk escaped. But as long as Lancaster refuses to press charges, nothing will be done about it."

"You know they're going to convict Hawk for killing Lyman Carter, don't you?"

Shadow nodded. "I think he will be found guilty, but it is a chance he must take."

"Shadow, I'm afraid."

"There is no need to fear. In my heart I know that all will be well."

"How can it be?" I cried, wanting to believe him, yet unable to see past the dangers that lay ahead. "If Hawk is convicted, you're planning to break him out of jail. You'll both be hunted men then, and we'll never be able to settle anywhere for fear of being arrested. I'm too old to spend the rest of my life running and hiding. And it wouldn't be fair to Blackie, expecting him to live like that."

"Hannah, Hannah." Shadow whispered my name as he drew me into his arms.

I rested my head against his chest. He was so strong, so certain everything would be all right. How could I doubt him?

"I envy you the courage you get from your hawks," I murmured. "I wish I had their strength to draw on."

Shadow's hands moved in my hair. "You are my strength, Hannah," he said fervently. "Have you not guessed that by now?"

"Truly?"

"Truly. The hawks have given me courage, and sometimes wisdom, but you are the source of my strength. You have always been there when I needed you."

"When have you ever needed me?" I asked, frowning. "It is I who have always turned to you for comfort."

Shadow shook his head. "No, Hannah. I have found strength when I needed it just in knowing that you loved me. Do you remember when your mother died and you thought your father had also been killed?"

I nodded. How could I forget?

"I knew how hard it was for you to accept me that night, to willingly join your life with mine when I was an Indian. But once you made the decision, I knew in my heart that we would be together forever. When I rode to battle against Custer, I carried your love with me. When our people were being hunted and killed, it was the strength of your love that kept me going, that gave me a reason for living when it would have been so much easier to give up, just as it is your love that makes each day worth living now."

What had I ever done to deserve such tender words, such love? My heart felt suddenly light and carefree. If Shadow believed that we had nothing to fear, then I would not be afraid. He had never been wrong before.

Pulling back a little, I gazed up at him, smiling provocatively.

Shadow grinned at me. "I have seen that look before," he remarked, chuckling softly. "Does it still mean the same thing?"

"Oh, definitely," I replied. Slipping my hand under his shirt, I stroked the solid flesh beneath. "Definitely."

He stood there, tall and proud, his breath coming faster and faster as I began to undress him. After all these years he still refused to wear anything but buckskins except on very special occasions. But I did not mind. He was all Indian, all man, all mine, and soon he stood naked before me, a wonderfully handsome man, his copper-hued skin dappled with moonlight.

I laughed softly as I saw the tangible evidence of his desire.

"Do I amuse you?" he asked huskily.

"Oh, yes," I answered happily. "It is most amusing to find a naked savage lurking in the dark." I sighed as his hand slid around my neck and his mouth claimed mine. I was breathless when he released me. "Amusing and satisfying," I murmured, pressing myself against him.

"And will you now amuse me?" Shadow asked. His voice was teasing, yet husky with longing.

I nodded, suddenly unable to speak. Slowly, my eyes never leaving his, I began to undress.

Shadow's eyes grew dark with desire as I stepped out of my shoes, stockings, and petticoat. As I began to unfasten my chemise, he growled, "White women wear too many clothes," and tore the remaining garments from my body until I stood naked before him.

His eyes swept over my body, their touch like a caress, and then he drew me close. Flesh met flesh, more pleasing to the senses than silk or satin. My breasts were flattened against Shadow's chest as he held me tighter. I gazed up into my husband's face, admiring the beauty I saw there. His hair, long and black as night, brushed my bare shoulders as he lowered his head and kissed me deeply, passionately, completely. With gentle hands he lowered me to the ground. I shivered as my back touched the damp grass. But then Shadow lowered his body over mine, warming me as no blanket ever could, and I forgot the cold and everything else but the wonder of his touch and the magic of his kiss. His hands roamed over my body like a man following a well-known path. We had made love countless times, yet I never tired of his touch, never wearied of his embrace.

Tonight, he was the master and I his willing slave.

His eyes were on fire when they met mine, his hands gentle yet demanding as they played upon my willing flesh, until my heart was singing a song only Shadow would ever hear.

We spent the night at the river crossing, loving and sleeping and loving again, until at last the sun climbed over the mountains and it was time to go home.

Hawk was ready to leave when we reached the house. Victoria had prepared breakfast for us and we ate a leisurely meal, no one speaking of what lay ahead.

After breakfast we drove Vickie and the boys home. Hawk kissed each of his sons, held Vickie in his arms one last time, and then we drove into town.

Lancaster was sitting on a crate in front of his office when we arrived. He was obviously surprised to see us, and I had the feeling that the sheriff had been hoping Hawk would try to make a run for it so he could have the pleasure of hunting him down.

"Right on time," Lancaster drawled, glancing at his pocket watch.

"I said I would have him here," Shadow said coldly.

Lancaster nodded. "So you did." Rising, he opened the jailhouse door and led the way into the cellblock.

Hawk hesitated a moment before entering the very cell he had fled only the day before. He threw a desperate glance at his father as Lancaster closed and locked the door behind him.

"It is only for another day, naha," Shadow reminded him. "Do not give up hope."

"We'll be back to see you tomorrow morning before the trial," I promised.

Hawk nodded. I could feel his eyes following us as we walked away.

13

He woke with the dawn, his stomach in knots, his body tense, his nerves on edge.

It was Friday.

Rising to his feet, he faced the east and lifted his arms above his head, his mouth moving in silent prayer to Man Above.

The hours he had spent in jail since his escape had been long and lonely. He had spent the time pacing the narrow confines of his cell, his mind in turmoil. He yearned to see Victoria and his sons. He longed to see the hills and the sky and the trees, to feel the earth beneath his feet and the sun on his face.

The day before, when they'd parted, Vickie had given him a long, passionate note telling him of her love and concern, and he had read it over and over, his finger lightly tracing her signature. She had wanted to visit him in jail this morning, had begged for his permission to do so, but he had forbidden it. He did not want his wife or his sons to see him behind bars, locked up like some wild beast. He did not want the people in town staring at Vickie, pitying her because she had married him.

He ran his hand through his hair and then rubbed the back of his neck. Damn Lyman Carter! Why hadn't the man left Victoria alone? Why had he started to draw his gun? What did his father plan to do if the law found him guilty of murder?

Hawk shook his head in discouragement. He loved his wife and children. He loved the land where they made their home. He did not want to leave, did not want to spend the rest of his life running, hiding from the law, sneaking around in the dead of night to see Vickie and the twins. He did not want to stay in jail.

Agitated, he drove his fist into the wall. Damn Carter! If only he could turn back the hands of time. If only he had not killed the man. And yet he was not sorry for killing Carter. The man had touched Victoria, and he had paid for it with his life.

Muttering an oath, Hawk began to pace his cell. He knew every crack and ridge in the floor, he mused bitterly, every inch of the walls and bars and ceiling.

Relax, he had to relax, yet he felt as if he were about to explode. He focused his thoughts on the lessons his father had taught him. A warrior is brave in the face of death. A warrior does not show fear before an enemy. A warrior practices patience. What cannot be changed must be endured.

He sat down on the edge of the cot. Closing his eyes, he recalled the Sun Dance he had participated in when he was sixteen. His special spirit, the yellow hawk, had promised him happiness so long as he remained true to the teachings of the People. He remembered the words his father had spoken to him shortly thereafter.

"If you are at peace with yourself, you need never be concerned with what other people think or say, for no one can destroy you except yourself."

Hawk found a measure of comfort in those words in the hours that followed.

At nine, Tompkins brought in Hawk's breakfast. "Enjoy it," the deputy said sardonically. "It might be your last."

Hawk took a deep breath, stifling the angry words that rose in his throat. Muttering an oath, he shoved the plate aside. His appetite was gone.

Stretching out on the lumpy cot, he closed his eyes and his thoughts drifted back in time. . . .

He was a little boy. They lived with Calf Running and Flower Woman and their son, Nachi, in a small nameless valley near the Sierra Madre Mountains. Hawk remembered that time as the only truly carefree period in his life. He remembered the nights around the campfire when his father and Calf Running took turns telling stories of the old days, the old ways. He remembered the day they had found a small herd of buffalo. He had gazed in awe at the great shaggy beasts, wishing he was old enough to hunt one down. He had watched with pride as his father rode alongside the herd and killed a buffalo cow with one well-placed arrow. No meat had ever tasted sweeter.

He had learned what fear was in that little valley. Geronimo had come seeking rest and shelter, and the Army had come seeking Geronimo. They had fled the valley, pursued by soldiers. Calf Running and his family had been killed that day.

They had lived on the Rosebud Reservation after that, and he had hated it. Then his mother had been hurt and his grandfather had taken Hawk and his mother to New York to find a doctor. He had hated the city. And then, after many hardships and unhappiness, his parents had been reunited and they had moved to Bear Valley. He had felt a curious oneness with the land, a feeling of belonging. It was here that his people had once roamed wild and free, here that the great herds of buffalo had grazed, here that the mighty warriors of his tribe had lived and fought and died. Sometimes at night he could feel their spirits calling to him, and he ached with the need to live in the old way, to hunt and fight and dance as his ancestors had done so long ago.

And then he had met Victoria and nothing else had mattered, only Vickie. His arms ached with the need to hold her, his hands yearned to caress her soft flesh, to stroke the silken mass of her red-gold hair.

With a low groan, he sat up. Then, too restless to remain still, he began to pace once more, his feet traveling the familiar path from one end of the cell to the other.

A few minutes before ten, Lancaster and Tompkins entered the cellblock. Lancaster unlocked the door to Hawk's cell, then covered him with a rifle while the deputy shackled Hawk's hands and feet.

"The judge is waiting," Lancaster announced curtly. He jerked a thumb toward the door. "Let's go."

14

The courtroom was small and square and packed with people. I saw Pa and Rebecca sitting near the door. Pa smiled at me reassuringly and gave me a wink that seemed to say, "Don't worry."

I took Shadow's arm as we took a place on the front row. Victoria sat between Shadow and Blackie, her face as pale as death. Her hands were trembling.

Inwardly I was also trembling. So much hinged on the outcome of this trial. I knew that Shadow had a gun concealed beneath his buckskin jacket. I had begged him to leave it at home, but he had refused. Hawk would not hang, Shadow had said adamantly, and he would not go back to jail.

A murmur of excited whispers went around the courtroom as Hawk entered the building. His hands and feet were shackled, and I could see the humiliation in my son's eyes as everyone present stared at him, wondering if he had indeed killed Lyman Carter in cold blood.

As I watched, Hawk lifted his head and squared his shoulders, his eyes filling with disdain. A warrior did not show fear in the presence of his enemies.

I glanced around the room. Hawk knew these people. He had talked with them and laughed with them, but now they were the enemy. I saw Hawk's eyes settle on Victoria, saw love soften the hard lines on his face as he gave her a ghost of a smile, then sat down in the chair the sheriff indicated.

Victoria smiled at Hawk, her eyes shining with unshed tears, and I knew she was willing him to feel her love and support.

I studied my son's face. I saw the desperation lurking behind his eyes, knew he was humiliated to be seen bound in chains. Was he afraid? I had never known him to be frightened of anything, but now his life was at stake and I was afraid for him. Very afraid.

Judge Roberts entered the courtroom, and everybody stood up until he was seated. The charges against Hawk were read aloud. He was being tried for killing the man known as Lyman Carter.

I glanced at the members of the jury. Twelve good men, men I had talked to and laughed with at parties, men who owned shops and farms. Men who had sons of their own.

The prosecuting attorney, Simon Thompson,

called Fred Brown as his first witness. Yes, Fred said, he had been at the mercantile store on the day in question. He had seen the confrontation between Hawk and Lyman Carter.

"Did you see Lyman Carter pull a gun?" Thompson asked.

Fred Brown threw an apologetic glance in Hawk's direction, then slowly shook his head. "No, sir," he said after a lengthy pause.

"Thank you, Mr. Brown," Thompson said. "That will be all."

Clancy Turner was the next witness. His testimony was much the same as Fred Brown's. He had seen Lyman Carter talking to Victoria, had seen Hawk drive up, and witnessed the ensuing scuffle. He shook his head when asked if he had seen Lyman Carter reach for a gun.

"No, sir," Turner said regretfully. "But if Hawk says that's the way it happened, then that's the way it happened."

Simon Thompson grinned good-naturedly. "Thank you, Mr. Turner. You may step down."

Six other witnesses were called to the stand, and they all told the same story. No one had seen Lyman Carter reach for a gun.

Hawk's face was strained and pale as the last witness took the stand. His hands were clenched into tight fists.

I glanced at the jury, and I could see that they believed Hawk was guilty. Surely, if Carter had reached for a gun, someone would have seen him.

I put my arm around Vickie's shoulders and gave her a squeeze. She was trembling, her eyes bright with unshed tears.

Simon Thompson dismissed the last witness, and Whitley Monroe stood up to present Hawk's defense. As Pa had predicted, Monroe hadn't lifted a finger in Hawk's behalf. His only defense was to put Hawk on the stand and have him tell his side of the story.

Hawk stood straight and tall as he swore to tell the truth and nothing but the truth. Then, in a voice devoid of emotion, he told what had happened. He had warned Lyman Carter to leave Victoria alone, and Carter had refused. Carter had laid his hands on Victoria, and Hawk had pulled him away and hit him. There had been a fight, Carter had reached for a gun, and Hawk had stabbed him.

I watched the jury as Hawk told his story, and I knew they would find him guilty.

Hawk knew it, too. He sent a long, pleading look in his father's direction, and Shadow nodded. My heart began to pound as Shadow reached inside his jacket, and I knew that our whole future would be determined by what happened in the next few minutes.

The judge dismissed Hawk from the witness stand, then admonished the jury to consider what had been said and reach the proper verdict.

Shadow was pulling his pistol from inside his jacket when Porter Sprague stood up.

"Your honor," he called. "I have something to say."

Judge Roberts frowned. "Have you been summoned as a witness?"

"No, your honor. No one ever talked to me or to my missus, here, but we were there. We saw the whole thing, and we'd like to be heard."

"This is most unusual," Judge Roberts muttered.

"Most unusual," Simon Thompson said, rising to his feet. "I feel I must object."

Judge Roberts nodded. "Objection sustained."

"Your honor," Porter Sprague called, striding toward the bench. "I know this is unusual and all, but this is a court of law, and I feel like the truth's been overlooked. I have something to say, and I'm asking you to hear me out."

"Very well," the judge allowed after a moment. "Take the stand and be sworn."

There was total silence in the courtroom as we waited for Porter to be sworn in. I glanced at Hawk. He was learning forward, his eyes riveted on Porter Sprague's face. I could feel Vickie trembling, could see the tension in Shadow's face as he waited to hear what Porter Sprague had to say.

"Proceed, Mr. Sprague," Judge Roberts directed.

Porter Sprague looked uncomfortable in the witness box, but he spoke loud and clear. He had seen and heard the whole thing. Lyman Carter had made a pass at Victoria, and when she rebuffed him, he had refused to leave her alone. Carter had laid hold on Victoria's arm, and when Hawk told him to let her go, he had refused. Hawk asked Carter a second time to let his wife alone, but Carter again refused and pulled

Victoria closer to him instead. Hawk grabbed Carter by the arm and there was a scuffle. Hawk was winning when the stranger reached for his gun. Hawk had had no choice but to defend himself.

The judge dismissed Porter from the stand, and Helen Sprague was sworn in. She told the same story as her husband, almost word for word.

The jury was out for only a few minutes, and when they returned, the verdict was not guilty. Never had any words been more welcome.

Twenty minutes later, the courtroom was empty save for our family and Helen and Porter Sprague.

Hawk took Victoria in his arms and held her so tight I was certain her ribs would break, but she didn't seem to mind. They stood together for a long time, oblivious to everyone else.

"Porter, Helen," I said, my voice thick with emotion. "How can we ever repay you?"

"No need," Porter said crisply. "Shadow saved Nelda's life, and we don't forget a kindness."

"I'm so glad you were there," I said, hugging Helen. "So glad you were willing to come forward in Hawk's behalf."

Helen and Porter exchanged a glance I could not fathom. I looked at Shadow and saw understanding flare in his dark eyes.

"You were not there," Shadow said slowly.

"No," Porter admitted. "Oh, we were in town that day, but we didn't see the fight."

"How did you know what happened?"

Porter shrugged. "I didn't think Hawk would get

much of a trial. Everyone knows Roberts hates Indians, and Whitley is about as incompetent as can be, so I nosed around a little and when I found out everyone thought Hawk was guilty, I went out to see Victoria. She was there. She saw everything. She told us what really happened that day and we memorized it."

"But that's perjury," I exclaimed.

"I don't call it perjury," Helen Sprague protested with righteous indignation. "I call it repaying a kindness. I've known Hawk since he was a boy, and I know he wouldn't kill a man without a darn good reason. We haven't always been close to your family, but my Nelda might not be alive today if it wasn't for Shadow. I couldn't sit by and let your child die when Shadow had saved mine."

"Oh, Helen," I wailed, and gave her another hug.

Porter grinned at Shadow. "So long, neighbor," he said jovially.

"So long. Neighbor," Shadow replied.

"I just can't believe it," I said, watching the Spragues leave the courthouse. "Who'd have thought Porter and Helen would lie for Hawk?"

Shadow shook his head. "It is hard to believe," he agreed, and then he smiled. "Let us go home."

Pa and Rebecca left for Steel's Crossing the next day. From there they would catch a train bound for the East. They would be gone until spring.

The day after Pa and Rebecca left for Pennsylvania, an Indian showed up at our front door. He was tall and strikingly handsome, with long, straight black hair, deep-set black eyes, and a faint scar on his left cheek. I guessed him to be in his mid-twenties.

"I have come to see Two Hawks Flying," he said in a low voice.

Two Hawks Flying. I had not heard that name in years. Most of the people in Bear Valley were ignorant of the fact that Shadow had once been a Cheyenne war chief; most of those who knew had forgotten about it over the years.

Two Hawks Flying. It was another name for another time. A name I had rarely used.

I nodded as I stepped away from the door. "Shadow," I called over my shoulder. "You have a visitor."

Shadow came to the door, one eyebrow arching in surprise when he saw the young man waiting for him. "How can I help you?"

"I am looking for Two Hawks Flying of the Cheyenne," the young man said.

Shadow nodded. "You have found him."

"I have left the reservation," our visitor said. "I have come here seeking work."

"Who sent you to me?"

"The grandson of Eagle-That-Soars-in-the-Sky."

"I see." Eagle-That-Soars-in-the-Sky had been the shaman who had come to Bear Valley to instruct Hawk in the Sun Dance ritual when Hawk was sixteen. "What kind of work are you looking for?" Shadow asked.

"Any kind. I am good with horses and cattle."

"You are Cheyenne?"

"Yes. My father was Tasunke Hinzi."

"I knew him well. How are you called?"

"The whites call me William, but my people call me Cloud Walker."

"Which name do you prefer?"

A trace of a smile touched the young man's lips. "Which do you think?"

Shadow grinned. "Cloud Walker it shall be."

Shadow looked at me then, and I nodded. If he wanted to hire the stranger, I had no objections.

"Very well," Shadow said. "You may sleep in the barn, or in the lodge behind our house."

"The lodge," Cloud Walker said quickly.

"Come," Shadow said, "I will show you the way."

I stood at the kitchen window watching the young man stow his few belongings inside our old lodge. We had brought it back home after Hawk and Victoria moved into their own house. It was a constant reminder of the old life, a vivid symbol to our neighbors that this had once been Indian land.

In the days that followed, Cloud Walker proved that he was indeed a good man with horses. He broke them to saddle and bridle much as Shadow did, gently and slowly, never pushing a young unbroken horse too hard, never demanding more out of the horse than the animal could give. He brushed and curried our horses with loving care, doctored the sick ones, assisted foaling mares. He became quick friends with Blackie, for the two shared a mutual love for all God's four-legged creatures.

I wondered that Cloud Walker was not married,

but I did not feel I had the right to pry into his private life. He was a quiet man, who seldom smiled and never laughed. I sensed he had experienced a tragedy in his life, and late one night we learned his story.

Shadow and Cloud Walker were sitting outside sharing a pipe after dinner. I sat inside near the window, mending a pair of Blackie's jeans. The window was open, and I could hear the men talking.

"How did you happen to come here?" Shadow asked.

"You are well-known on the reservation," Cloud Walker answered. "Often late at night the old men speak of Custer and the Greasy Grass and of the chiefs that fought in the battle. Your name is often mentioned. I was only a child then, of course, but I have often dreamed of what it must have been like that day."

"It was a good day for us," Shadow said, smiling with the memory. "A good day, and a bad day. I have often thought that the whites would not have hated our people quite so much if we had not killed Custer and all his men."

"Did you see Custer?"

"Yes, but I never got close to him."

"Some of the white men on the reservation say Custer was not killed that day. They believe he was taken alive and tortured by one of the Sioux tribes."

"No," Shadow said. "If the Sioux had captured Custer, the Cheyenne would have heard about it."

"My father was killed at the Greasy Grass," Cloud Walker remarked.

Shadow nodded. "Tasunke Hinzi was a brave warrior. He killed many of the bluecoats that day. Crazy Horse said your father was wounded many times, but he continued to fight until he was too weak to hold a weapon."

Cloud Walker nodded. He had heard the story many times.

The men were silent for a moment, and then Shadow asked, "Why did you leave the reservation?"

"My wife was pregnant, and she was ill. When her time came, I went to the shaman, but he could not help her. I have hated the whites all my life. Never have I gone to them for anything. But my woman was dying, and so I went to the Army doctor and asked him for help. He was playing poker with some of the officers. I told him my wife was very sick and in labor with our first child. He said not to worry, that first babies took a long time to be born and that he would come to our lodge in an hour or so. I begged him to come quickly, but he refused. An hour would be soon enough, he said.

"When I got back to my lodge, my wife was dead. She had given birth to the child, and bled to death, while I was gone. The baby was dead also. It was a boy.

"I could not stay on the reservation after that. I knew if I ever saw that doctor again, I would kill him with my bare hands. I left that night, and as I was wondering where to go, I remembered that the grandson of Eagle-That-Soars-in-the-Sky had once mentioned that you lived in Bear Valley, so I came to you."

The men fell silent again, and I brushed the tears from my eyes, determined to do everything in my power to make Cloud Walker's life happy. He was so young, and he had suffered a great loss. Impotent rage filled my heart as I thought of the doctor who had held a human life so cheaply that he had played cards while a young woman and her child died. I would not have blamed Cloud Walker if he had covered the man with honey and let the ants eat him alive. It would have been his fate in the old days, and he deserved it no less now.

I was immediately ashamed of my uncharitable thoughts. I had no right to judge the man.

Shadow and Cloud Walker soon became good friends. Cloud Walker especially enjoyed Shadow's stories of the old days. He was much like Hawk, I thought sadly, and wondered if they would ever be content to live in the white man's world. Sometimes, listening to Shadow reminisce about the old days, I saw a deep sadness in his ebony eyes and I knew that, even after all these years, my husband still yearned for his old way of life. I couldn't blame him. I too sometimes longed for the days when Shadow and I had lived with the Cheyenne, when we had snuggled together inside a cozy hide lodge, certain that the future held only happiness for the two of us. I missed seeing the curly-haired buffalo running across the plains, their shaggy heads lowered, their tails sticking straight up like flags. I missed the sound of the warriors chanting as they danced around the campfire, their copper-hued faces painted in celebration of a victory over an enemy. I yearned to hear the soft, rhythmic beat of the drums as the old men spun stories and tales of long ago, of the days before time began when Heammawihio created the earth and the sky and the People.

Cloud Walker caused quite a stir in Bear Valley. Until his arrival, Shadow had been the only full-blooded Indian in the valley, but the people were used to him. They bought his horses, talked with him in town, knew his family. But now Cloud Walker was here. He was a stranger, silent and withdrawn, unknown. The women studied him from the corners of their eyes, wondering, somewhat fearful. The men stared at him openly, unabashed in their curiosity, yet a little ill at ease in his presence. The Indian wars had been over for years, but memories were long. Many whites still thought of the Indians as an inferior race. They believed the women were lazy, without morals or ambition. They thought the men were wild, savage, hungry for blood and white women.

I knew that such beliefs were false, but old ways and old ideas died hard. The people in town knew nothing about Cloud Walker, and gossip spread like wildfire in the wind. He was a spy from the reservation, sent to scout our strengths and weaknesses. He was Shadow's illegitimate son from a past affair. He was an outlaw hiding out at our place. He was a renegade guilty of killing a man back on the reservation.

The rumors flew for several weeks, many of them so farfetched that they were laughable. Cloud Walker

never confirmed or denied any of them. He simply
went his own way, undisturbed, and eventually the
people in town began to accept him for what he was, an
unhappy young man who worked hard and wanted
only to be left alone.

Part Two

15

Mary was thrilled with life in Chicago, the second largest city in the nation. It was said that there were forty-five hundred millionaires in America; many of them lived along Chicago's lake front in lavish mansions that looked more like medieval castles than homes. Mary did not envy them, the rich and famous people who dwelled in such splendor, though she sometimes spent an idle moment wondering what it would be like to have a private steam yacht with a crew of fifty, or to own a private railroad car with her initials carved on the side.

No, she did not envy the wealthy people who inhabited those huge estates. She felt rich enough just owning a gramophone and a piano and a telephone. She had always loved music, and she played records by the hour, humming while she did her chores. The dusting and sweeping, mopping and polishing, cooking and mending all went by so much faster if she could listen to her favorite songs while she worked.

Once a week she took piano lessons from a robust German woman named Gretchen Mueller. Mary was a little intimidated by Mrs. Mueller, but she delighted in her own growing ability to read music and play the simple songs her teacher placed before her.

Bicycling was also something Mary enjoyed. Soon after their arrival in Chicago, Frank bought a tandem bicycle. Cycling was all the rage in Chicago, and Frank and Mary spent many a sunny Sunday afternoon riding with their friends. Mary often felt guilty as they pedaled through the park. Back home in Bear Valley, Sunday had been a day of worship and rest, a day to visit Grandpa and Rebecca. But Frank preferred cycling to sermons.

Yes, life was good. Frank had a well-paying job at the Chicago Bank and Trust; they had a lovely home on a quiet residential street. The house was Mary's pride and joy. It was such fun, having a home of her own. She spent her days redecorating. The master bedroom was done in varying shades of blue, the kitchen was painted a bright cheerful yellow, the parlor was a stark and fashionable white, the dining room a subdued green.

When Frank received a promotion to assistant manager, they went on a buying spree, outfitting themselves in stylish new clothes and their home in new furniture. It was such fun to wear the latest

fashions, to walk down a city street and know that
people were admiring her. Frank looked dashing in a
new Hart, Schaffner & Marx spring suit. Mary had
gasped at the price. Imagine, fifteen dollars for a suit of
clothes! They shopped for a new carriage at Sears &
Roebuck, and Frank found a shiny black one he liked
for thirty-eight dollars. He bought a flashy black
gelding to pull it.

Six weeks after they arrived in Chicago, Frank
was sent to New York on business, and he took Mary
with him. The city had changed since she had seen it
last some thirteen years ago. It was bigger, flashier,
noisier than ever.

Sitting in their lavishly appointed hotel room,
waiting for Frank to complete a business meeting,
Mary thumbed through a mail-order catalog, looking
for presents to send to her family. There were advertisements for a variety of goods and services: Reming-
ton Typewriters, Packers Tar Soap, Columbia
Phonographs, Williams' Jersey Cream Toilet Soap for
fifteen cents a bar, Lowney's Chocolate Bonbons for
sixty cents a pound, Hall's Hair Renewer, guaranteed
to "grow bountiful, beautiful hair," Salva cea, guaranteed to be good for bruises, contusions, earache, piles,
colds, rheumatism, chilblains, neuralgia, headache,
itching, chafing, coughs, and fever sores. Surely the
wonder cure of the century, Mary mused, and a
bargain at only twenty-five cents a box. She grinned as
she read an advertisement for Smith & Wesson revolv-
ers. "Protect your family," the ad said, "a sense of
security pervades the home which shelters a Smith
and Wesson revolver."

After much deliberation, she decided she would buy bonbons and toilet soap for Vickie and Rebecca, a new wool cloak for her mother, and a set of the Encyclopedia Brittanica for Blackie because she thought he would enjoy reading about animals and places he had never seen. She could not decide what to buy for her father and grandfather. They had plenty of guns, no need for a new suit. Perhaps Frank could give her an idea when he came home.

That night, Mary forgot all about gifts for the family as Frank took her to dinner at one of New York's finest restaurants. Mary felt quite elegant in a dress of pale blue striped velvet and black kid slippers. She wore her hair piled high atop her head, held in place with a pair of jeweled combs.

They had just been seated when there was a flurry of excitement near the door as people began to point and whisper. Turning in her chair, Mary saw James Buchanan Brady, better known as Diamond Jim, entering the restaurant. Jim Brady was quite a celebrity in New York City. He had driven the first horseless carriage in the city, tying up traffic for two hours. He was often seen in the company of J. P. Morgan, John "Bet a Million" Gates, James R. Keene, and Judge William H. Moore, all magnates of note in industry, business, and banking circles. Brady could frequently be seen in what had come to be called Peacock Alley at the Waldorf-Astoria. It was said that people came from all over the United States just to watch the most glamorous and notorious men and women of the time stroll by. Frank had told her that the Waldorf had been built on the corner of Fifth

Avenue and Thirty-fourth Street on the site of Mrs. Astor's old mansion.

There was nothing particularly attractive about Diamond Jim Brady, Mary thought to herself as the man took a seat at a specially reserved table. He was rather portly and not especially good-looking, but he had a good deal of charm and Mary could see that he was well liked by those around him. It was said he had a two-million-dollar collection of gems, though his main interest in life was rumored to be food, and as Mary listened to him order dinner, she believed it. He ordered two dozen oysters, half a dozen crabs, a double portion of soup, and terrapin, duck, steak, and all the trimmings, including a variety of desserts.

Mary glanced at Frank, her eyes alight with wonder. Imagine, they were in the same restaurant as Diamond Jim Brady. A short time later, Lillian Russell joined Diamond Jim at his table. Her entrance caused quite a stir as men craned their necks to get a glimpse of her. It was said that Diamond Jim was sweet on the actress, and they certainly gazed adoringly at one another, Mary thought, smiling.

"You look like a little girl on Christmas morning," Frank remarked, smiling indulgently at his bride.

"I feel like one, too," Mary said happily. "Who would ever have thought we'd actually be in New York City, eating in the same restaurant with famous people."

"Stick with me, Mary Smythe," Frank said exuberantly. "And one day you'll wear diamonds and rubies, too."

"Really, Frank?"

"You can count on it. I intend to be rich and famous myself one of these days. You just wait and see."

"You don't have to be rich and famous for me," Mary said softly. "I love you just the way you are."

"You'll love me more when I've made a name for myself," Frank promised. "Wait and see."

Mary had fun in New York. She spent her days shopping and sightseeing while Frank attended to business. At night they went out on the town. They saw Lillian Russell perform, and Mary laughed heartily at the antics of the comic opera star. In truth, she thought the actress was a little short on acting ability, but her singing was wonderful. Another night they saw Bob Fitzsimmons acting in a play called *The Honest Blacksmith*. Fitzsimmons had once been a blacksmith and during one scene he actually clanged away on an anvil, shaping horseshoes.

On Sunday they went bicycle riding in Central Park, and there, riding a bicycle built for three, were Diamond Jim Brady, Lillian Russell, and another man who Mary later learned was Diamond Jim's cycling adviser, Dick Barton. Mary was surprised and amused when she found that Mr. Barton carried a gallon of orange juice on his back in case Diamond Jim got thirsty.

Like the other cyclists in the park, Mary could not help gawking at Diamond Jim and his companions. Imagine, a bicycle built for three! How like Brady to be different, to have something bigger and better than anyone else.

Mary and Frank spent two weeks in New York,

and Mary loved every minute of it, but she was anxious to get back to her own home in Chicago, her own things.

In the days that followed, they made many friends in Chicago, for they were a young, attractive couple always ready for a good time. Some of Mary's new friends were quite wealthy, and while Frank seemed to fit right in with their new crowd, Mary often felt like a fish out of water. True, it was fun and exciting to mingle with their new friends, but Mary lacked some of the finer social graces that were inbred in the beautiful women she was now associating with.

And they were beautiful. They styled their hair in magnificent pompadours and wore crisp shirtwaists and long flowing skirts. They played golf and tennis with gusto and grace, making Mary feel clumsy and incompetent by comparison. They knew all the latest songs: "A Bicycle Built for Two," "She Is Only a Bird in a Gilded Cage," and "She Was Happy Till She Met You." The men sang songs they heard in the beer gardens, songs like "The Man on the Flying Trapeze" and "There Is a Tavern in the Town."

Mary's new friends had never known fear or hardship, nor could they imagine it. Life was meant to be fun and they pursued it religiously.

Sometimes Mary thought back to her life in Bear Valley, and it seemed like a dream from long ago. The parties and church dances and walks in the woods all seemed so childish compared to the fancy balls and midnight dinners and trips to the theater that made up her days now. She recalled her childhood, living on the reservation with her parents, being hungry and scared, and she knew that her new companions would never understand, and for that reason she never mentioned it.

She refused to get homesick for Bear Valley. After all, she loved the city, the skyscrapers, the parks, the electric trolley cars, the churches. Chicago was the home of the 22-story Masonic Temple, the tallest building in the world. Chicago. It was noisy and exciting and there were so many things to see and do, so many interesting places to go. Yes, she loved the city. And yet there were times when she was surrounded by noise and people that she longed for the quiet beauty of Bear Valley, for the sight of vast empty prairies and snow-capped mountains, for breathtaking sunrises and the quiet song of a bird.

But she did not dwell on those things too often. Frank was handsome and charming, and she sometimes felt a twinge of jealousy when he laughed and flirted with one of their lovely new friends. Frank assured her that all the little smiles and touches meant nothing. Everyone did it. It was expected. After all, he pointed out, didn't the men in their crowd flirt with her?

Frank's reminder made Mary blush. It was true. Many of the men in their circle of acquaintances did flirt with her, complimenting her, teasing her, making outrageous proposals and promises of undying love. She had little experience with such things and usually stammered and blushed like a schoolgirl. Still, it was flattering to have nice-looking men of good breeding flirt and laugh and tease her.

She had never thought much of her looks before,

but now, sitting at her dressing table as she prepared for bed, she realized she *was* attractive. Her hair was thick and long, a rich brown in color. Her mouth was well-shaped, her nose small and straight, her brows delicate and gently arched. Her eyes were her best feature. They were a clear gray, brimming with laughter and a zest for life.

She smiled as Frank came up behind her and placed his hands on her shoulders.

"Tired?" he asked.

"A little," Mary admitted. She closed her eyes as Frank began to massage the back of her neck. Gradually his hands moved to her shoulders and then around to her breasts and then, as she gave a little gasp, he picked her up and carried her to bed.

Later, Mary wondered if she would ever grow to enjoy Frank's lovemaking. She knew it was supposed to be pleasant. On the night before her wedding, her mother and Vickie had made a few veiled references to the joys a woman could find in the arms of her husband, hinting that the act of love could be beautiful and wonderful. Mary had not found it so. Her wedding night had not been what she had hoped for. Frank had been eager to bed her, and for Mary the act had been quick and unsatisfying, even a little embarrassing. Frank had seemed pleased, however, and he made love to her frequently. Mary enjoyed the closeness of being held in Frank's arms, but she never really enjoyed the act itself. It never occurred to her that Frank might be at fault; instead, she wondered if there were something wrong with her, some flaw that kept her from finding fulfillment in her husband's embrace.

As the days passed, Mary began to be troubled without knowing why. The people around her were always laughing and happy. They seemed to have no cares, no worries other than what to wear, what to buy, or what party to attend. The women were vivacious, the men charming, and yet they all seemed to be searching for some elusive magic that would bring them true and lasting happiness.

Sometimes Mary felt that she was searching for it, too. At first she bought a new dress or something for the house whenever she felt depressed, but new things soon lost their charm and the emptiness she felt inside remained.

In time she realized that it was her marriage to Frank that was lacking. She had hoped that she and Frank would have the same kind of marriage her parents had. She wanted to experience the same feelings of love and companionship and caring that her parents felt for one another, that sense of security and strength that was always there no matter what troubles came their way.

Because she wanted her marriage to succeed, Mary made every effort to please Frank. She prepared his favorite foods, entertained his friends, laughed at his jokes, wore her hair in the style he preferred. She learned to play golf because he enjoyed the game, even though she thought it somewhat silly and a waste of time.

One of Frank's friends began paying more attention than usual to Mary. His name was Robert Hellman. He was a man in his early thirties with light brown hair, blue eyes, and a trim moustache. He was quite wealthy, having made several shrewd investments in railroad stock.

At parties Robert invariably found his way to Mary's side, insisting politely on several dances. Sometimes he took her outside for a walk through the gardens, his hand at her elbow, his eyes seeking hers.

At first Mary tried to avoid Robert, but as Frank became more and more involved in other pursuits, Mary found Robert's attention soothing to her hurt pride. Perhaps her own husband no longer found her attractive or interesting, but Robert did.

They were at a birthday party several weeks later when Robert made his intentions known. The party was for one of Frank's wealthy clients, and it was the most lavish affair Mary had ever attended. She wore a white-on-white silk gown with a square neck and long, tight-fitting sleeves. Tiny seed pearls were sewn around the neck of the dress and woven into the design on the bodice. It was the most elegant gown Mary had ever owned, and she felt like a fairy princess as they entered the Singleton mansion. But, once inside, she felt like a moth in a garden of butterflies. The gowns the other women wore were breathtaking. Fine silks and satins adorned with glittering jewels. The women wore diamonds and emeralds around their necks, on their wrists, on their fingers, in their hair. The men wore finely tailored suits with silk cravats, gaudy diamond or sapphire stick pins, solid gold watch fobs and chains.

Mary felt overwhelmed at the sight of so much wealth, and totally out of her element. At dinner she was careful not to spill anything on her gown, or on the elegant French lace tablecloth. The food was excellent: tender roast pork, tiny squab in rich sauce, thick steaks, turkey with all the trimmings, four kinds of vegetables, three kinds of potatoes, a variety of salads, rolls, and hot biscuits.

Mary ate until she was stuffed, and all the while she was conscious of Robert sitting across from her, his eyes openly adoring.

There was a lull after dinner. The men adjourned to the parlor for brandy and cigars while the women went into the solarium for sherry, or went upstairs to freshen their makeup and gossip.

At ten the orchestra began to play. Mary danced the first waltz with Frank. He was having a wonderful time, she could tell, and seemed excited about a business deal he was on the verge of signing with one of the guests.

Mary danced several dances with other men, some who were familiar to her, some who were not. And then Robert came to claim her for a dance.

"You look ravishing this evening," he said as he waltzed her around the dance floor. "Your perfume is divine, and that dress makes you look like an angel."

"Thank you," Mary murmured.

"None of the women here tonight can hold a candle to your beauty," Robert went on, his arm drawing her closer.

Mary laughed self-consciously. "Oh, Robert, how you do run on."

"But it's true!" he declared passionately. "They're all painted and powdered like porcelain dolls, but your beauty is real and comes from inside."

"Robert," Mary protested, though inwardly she was pleased. It was nice to know that someone thought she was pretty. Frank had not even mentioned her new gown or commented on how she looked. Perhaps he was disappointed in her.

When the dance was over, Robert took Mary's arm and escorted her out the side door into the garden. It was a lovely night, warm and balmy. The scent of roses permeated the air with sweet perfume as they walked down a narrow garden path lit with colorful Japanese lanterns. Mary paused to admire a bush that was thick with dark red flowers.

"Aren't they lovely?" she mused. "They look like red velvet."

"Your beauty makes them look like weeds," Robert vowed, and pulling Mary into his arms, he kissed her deeply, passionately. She was so beautiful, so desirable, and she was wasted on that husband of hers. He had wanted to declare his feelings for her before, but he had cautioned himself to be patient. She was young and inexperienced. He did not want to frighten her.

Shocked, Mary twisted out of Robert's arms, her cheeks flaming with righteous indignation. "Robert! What's gotten into you?"

"I'm sorry, Mary," he said contritely. "Please forgive me."

"Very well," Mary replied, flustered. "Please don't let it happen again."

"I love you, Mary," Robert said fervently. "I

know you aren't happy with Frank. I've seen the way you look at him, and I know how he's hurting you, how often he leaves you alone."

Mary did not deny it. What was the point in lying? Everyone knew that Frank had a wandering eye, and though Mary was certain that Frank had never been physically unfaithful to her, it hurt to know he was looking at other women and finding them attractive.

"Leave him, Mary," Robert said. "Come away with me. I'll make you happy, I swear it."

"Robert, please don't say anymore. I'm a married woman and I love my husband. You should not be saying these things, and I should not be listening."

"Do you?" Robert asked in disbelief. "Do you really love him?"

"Yes." She spoke the word with assurance, yet deep inside she wondered if it were still true.

"Are you certain, Mary? I'm a wealthy man. I can give you anything you want, anything you need. I know we could be happy together if you'll give us a chance."

Mary shook her head. She was touched by Robert's declaration and she was fond of him, but she was a married woman. She had promised to be faithful to her husband. It was not an oath she had taken lightly.

"I'm sorry, Robert. You've been a good friend, but I don't think we should see each other any more. Good night."

Mary tried doubly hard to make her marriage work after that. She danced less with other men, she tried to be cheerful and understanding when Frank came home after a hard day at the office, she endeavored to persuade Frank to stay home more often, but all was in vain. Frank didn't want to stay home. He liked going out, liked being seen with important people. It was good for business, he said.

As the days passed, it became harder and harder to smile and pretend that everything was fine when it wasn't. When her two best friends, Christy and Stacey, came to call, it was hard to chat about the latest fashions and coiffures from Paris, or the new play at the theater, when her heart was breaking. Indeed, it seemed as if all the joy had gone out of life. Like champagne that had been left out too long, Mary felt dull and lifeless. She missed Robert. She had thought of him as a good friend, nothing more, and his vow of love had been unexpected and disturbing, putting an end to their friendship.

They had been married only five months when Mary began to suspect she was pregnant. Frank was disappointed when she told him the news. He liked going out every night, liked being carefree, able to run off to a party on a moment's notice. A baby would tie them down.

Mary was hurt by Frank's lack of enthusiasm. She was looking forward to having a baby. Indeed, she longed to have several.

As her pregnancy grew more advanced, she and Frank began to quarrel. He wanted to go out on the town and have a good time, but Mary was too self-conscious about her expanding girth. Most women did not go out much when they were expecting, preferring to remain closeted at home until the baby was born.

When Frank started going out alone, Mary felt as though she had been discarded and abandoned. It was his child she was carrying, after all. Why couldn't he stay home and keep her company?

She cried many bitter tears in the days ahead. She was lonely and unhappy and she began to wish they had never left Bear Valley. They had been happy there. Perhaps if they had not come to Chicago they would be happy still. Frank had changed since coming here. He was so caught up in the glamour and excitement of their new friends that he had little time for a pregnant wife who could not go out dancing all night long.

As time passed, Mary began to hear rumors that Frank was having an affair with the daughter of one of Chicago's wealthiest men. She refused to believe it. Frank might enjoy flirting, but he would never be disloyal to her. Women who were supposed to be her friends couldn't wait to tell her the latest bit of juicy gossip.

"I knew you'd want to know," they said.

Or, "I wouldn't dream of telling you this, but we're such good friends . . ."

Mary told herself over and over again that it was all a lie, until the morning she picked up the newspaper and saw a picture of her husband dancing with Caroline Sinclair at a fund-raising dinner in one of Chicago's swank nightclubs.

Mary stared at the picture for a long time, her heart aching with such pain she was certain it would shatter within her breast. It was not a particularly clear photograph, but Mary could see the way her husband was gazing into Caroline's eyes, the look of adoration on his face, the way his arm held her a little too close. This was no casual flirtation, Mary thought, no innocent friendship.

She cried all that day. Locked in her bedroom, she let the tears flow freely. Frank had been unfaithful to her. She had left her home and family to spend her life with him. She was carrying his child beneath her heart.

Fresh tears welled in her eyes and cascaded down her cheeks. How could he hold their marriage vows so cheaply? How could he hold her and say he loved her when he was seeing someone else? How would she ever trust him again?

She cried until she had no tears left, and then she sat on the edge of her bed, staring blankly out the window. She felt empty, numb, as if a part of her had died. Frank had been unfaithful to her. Frank loved someone else. Frank had lied to her.

She was quiet at dinner that night, hardly touching her food. Perhaps she had been mistaken. Perhaps she shouldn't say anything and the whole dreadful mess would just go away.

And then Frank said, oh so casually, that he was going to the club that night, and suddenly Mary found herself screeching at him, her hurt and anger rushing out in a torrent of hot words and bitter tears.

Frank did not deny her accusations. Kneeling beside her, he took her hands in his and begged for her understanding and forgiveness.

"It will never happen again, Mary, I swear it," Frank vowed. "I love you. I know I've hurt you terribly and I'm sorry. It was all a mistake. She doesn't mean anything to me, I swear it."

And because she loved him, Mary believed him.

Frank stayed home nights after that, and Mary was content. They read the latest novels together, played cards, occasionally had a few friends in for dinner.

Mary's child was born on June 3, 1899, at three o'clock in the morning. It was a girl, with straight black hair, tawny skin, and dark blue eyes that were almost black.

Frank stared at the baby, a look of dismay on his face. "It's Indian," he said flatly.

"I'm Indian," Mary said, cradling her daughter closer to her breast. "Had you forgotten?"

"No," Frank said quickly. "Of course not. But . . ."

"But you didn't think our children would look Cheyenne," Mary said coldly.

"I guess I never really thought about it."

"Don't you want to hold your daughter, Frank?"

He took a step backward as though she had suggested something repulsive. "Later," he said, still staring at the child. "Later."

Mary gazed out the window after Frank left the room. Her marriage was a failure. All her bright hopes and dreams for a happy life with Frank had disintegrated like a dandelion in the wind. Perhaps they had never been right for each other. Perhaps she should never have married Frank at all. And yet, back in Bear Valley, it had all seemed so right.

Suddenly homesick, Mary picked up her mother's last letter. She had received it shortly before Katherine was born.

"Dear Mary," the letter read, "It is so hard to believe a whole year has passed since you and Frank were married. The days do fly by, though I miss you very much. Blackie is growing taller each day, and though he is turning into quite a handsome young man, he is still bringing home every stray he finds. Just now we are nursing two squirrels, a black bird with a broken wing, an orphaned foal, and a fawn with an injured leg. And we have the usual assortment of dogs and cats underfoot.

"Jason and Jacob are thriving. They're already seventeen months old and as cute as can be. They keep Victoria busy day and night, but they are adorable. And so smart. I hope I have dozens of grandchildren to keep me company in my old age.

"Do write the minute your baby is born. Your father and I were delighted with your invitation to come for a visit. Expect us in the summer after foaling season is over. You know your father. He always likes to be on hand when the new foals are born."

Mary grinned. Her mother always liked to be there, too, she thought. There had been many a night when her mother and father had camped out in the barn or the pasture to keep an eye on a mare that was due to foal. Mary, too, had experienced the awe and excitement of watching a new life make its way into the world. It was a feeling beyond description, the wonder of seeing life renewing itself.

Smiling, she read on: "Rebecca's daughter, Beth, gave birth to a daughter last November. Pa said the

Chatsworths were a little disappointed that she didn't have a boy to carry on the family name, but Pa said Jason is thrilled with his little girl.

"Pa and Rebecca came home in March, happy to be back in Bear Valley after spending such a long time in the East. They were sorry to have missed you, but apparently you were in New York when they stopped by. Both send their love.

"We have a new man working with the horses. His name is Cloud Walker, and he's a Cheyenne. Your father likes him very much, as I do. He seems to be a fine young man.

"Do write when you can. We love hearing from you. Give our love to Frank, and do take care of yourself. Your father sends his love . . ."

Mary pressed the letter to her heart. If only she could go home. If only she could pour out her hurts to her mother, and feel the comfort of her father's arms about her. But she was a grown woman now, married with a child of her own. She could not go running home to mama anymore.

Picking up her pen, she wrote her mother a long letter, telling her about Katherine's birth and how beautiful she was. She mentioned the latest fashions, and how warm it was in the city, and described the new lamps she had bought for the parlor. She wrote that Frank was doing well in his business, and related how exciting it was to associate with so many rich and famous people. She wrote about everything she could think of, except what was troubling her most.

For the next two months Mary tried very hard to be a good wife. She was always agreeable, she always had a smile for Frank when he came home from work. She kept their house immaculate, prepared dinners that bordered on gourmet feasts, dressed with care. She went out with Frank whenever he asked her whether she wanted to or not.

Going out was the hardest part of all. The women she had thought were her friends rarely called on her any more and she felt uncomfortable in their presence. Somehow, the birth of her daughter had brought Mary's own mixed heritage to her friends' attention. The men looked at her differently, too, now that they knew she was half Cheyenne.

Mary didn't understand what had changed. She was the same person she had always been. What difference did it make that she was half Indian? She looked the same, she talked the same. But it did make a difference. The women looked at her with scorn, the men eyed her with lust instead of admiration.

One night, at a large birthday party, one of the guests began to do his version of an Indian war dance. The fact that the man was drunk did not lessen the embarrassment Mary felt when he dragged her out onto the dance floor with him.

"Come on, honey," he said, "show us how it's done on the reservation."

"Please let me go," Mary said, trying to dislodge her hand from his.

"Hey, don't get uppity on me," the man chided. "Just give us a little dance. Like this, honey," he said, and began whirling around the floor, whooping and hollering, until he passed out.

Mary had never been so humiliated in her life.

Gathering her dignity around her, she walked out of the room.

"Forget it," Frank said as he followed her out. "Gus didn't mean anything by it."

"Didn't he?"

"Hell, you have to expect that sort of thing. You are half Cheyenne. No sense being thin-skinned about it."

"Take me home, Frank."

"I'm not ready to go home," he replied, shrugging indifferently.

Mary didn't argue. Getting her wrap, she left the party and walked the two miles home. It was a long walk and the night was cool, but she didn't care. She could not face those people again.

There were other parties after that, other remarks, other jokes. Everyone expected her to be a good sport while they made fun of her people. Everyone knew that Indians were inferior. The men were lazy and drank too much; the women had no morals; the children were thieves. Everyone knew that.

Secretly, when she was alone, Mary wept bitter tears. Her marriage was a failure. Frank never made love to her anymore, he never looked at their daughter, even though the child was beautiful and good-natured. He had not even cared about giving the child a name.

"Call her whatever you want," he had said indifferently.

And so Mary had named her daughter Katherine, after her maternal grandmother.

When Katherine was three months old, Mary

admitted defeat. Her marriage was over and she wanted only to go back home.

On the last day of August, Mary asked Frank for a divorce. He refused. A divorce would cause a scandal, he said, and he couldn't afford a scandal just now. He was on the verge of another promotion at the bank.

Mary did not argue. Instead, she waited until Frank left for work the next day, then she packed her things, bought a ticket for Steel's Crossing, and boarded the train bound for home. The trip, which had once taken months by wagon, would take less than two weeks on the train.

Mary left Frank a short note advising him not to come after her, though in her heart she hoped he still cared enough to try to get her back.

"Just tell your friends I've gone home for a visit," Mary wrote. "That won't cause a scandal."

16

I could not have been more surprised when I opened the door and saw Mary standing there, a child cradled in her arms, a suitcase at her feet.

"Mary! Why didn't you tell me you were coming?" I threw my arms around her and hugged her, baby and all. "Where's Frank?"

"I've left him," Mary said.

I took Mary's bag inside, and a few minutes later we were sitting side by side on the sofa. She smiled up at me as she placed the baby in my arms. "This is Katherine," she said proudly.

My heart swelled with love as I gazed at my granddaughter. She was beautiful. Her hair was thick and black, her eyes a dark, dark blue, her skin a tawny brown. When she smiled up at me, I was hooked.

"She's lovely," I said, stroking the baby's downy cheek. "Just lovely." I looked at Mary and saw the sadness in her eyes. "Do you want to talk about it?"

Mary nodded, and I listened with growing dismay as she told me all that had happened in Chicago. I found it hard to believe that Frank Smythe had changed so much. He had always been a quiet young man, polite, kind, crazy about Mary, or so it had seemed. I had been so certain that they were right for each other, that they would find happiness together. What had gone wrong?

"I had to come home," Mary said. "You don't mind, do you?"

"Of course not. Your old room is waiting."

Shadow was furious when he heard about Frank. He threatened to go to Chicago and skin him alive, and I knew that, if Mary but said the word, Frank Smythe was as good as dead. My husband had lived as a civilized, law-abiding citizen for many years, but he was still a Cheyenne warrior at heart. Frank had shattered our daughter's life, and I knew that Shadow would not hesitate to make him pay, and pay dearly. But Mary did not want revenge, she wanted only to be left alone.

She spent the rest of the day in her room. Once, I heard her weeping softly. The sound tore at my heart.

Mary was quiet and withdrawn during the next few days. She spent most of her time with Katherine, nursing the child, singing lullabies, speaking to her softly in the Cheyenne tongue.

I wondered why she spoke to the baby in Cheyenne and remarked on it to Shadow.

"I think she is trying to understand her own heart," Shadow mused. "I think Frank hurt her deeply when he rejected the baby, and now Mary is confused about who she is and what she wants out of life." Shadow smiled at me, his eyes dark and sad. "Mary never had to deal with being a half-breed before. I think if she were a man she would go out into the hills and commune with her special spirit, but she is a woman, and so she must follow her heart."

During the next few weeks, I noticed that Cloud Walker could not keep his eyes off Mary. He rarely spoke to her, but his eyes followed her every move.

It was on a warm Tuesday morning that Cloud Walker and Mary first spoke to each other alone. Cloud Walker was breaking one of the young colts when Mary happened to walk by the corral. She paused, intrigued by the sight of the handsome young man astride a wildly bucking horse. Usually the horses were calm and easy to break, but every now and then Smoke sired a colt with a wild streak.

Mary smiled as the young spotted stallion dropped its head and began to crowhop from one end of the corral to the other. When that failed to dislodge the unwelcome burden on its back, it began sunfishing and swapping ends.

Cloud Walker let out a wild cry, his long black hair whipping around his face as the animal galloped toward the far end of the arena. Mary felt her heart drop as the horse headed straight for the corral fence. At the last possible moment, the colt swerved to the right and bucked, but Cloud Walker kept his seat, a broad smile lighting his face.

The horse let out a squeal of rage and then, abruptly, dropped to the ground. Cloud Walker jumped clear as the horse rolled on its side, but he was back in the saddle as soon as the horse scrambled to its feet.

The colt bucked a few more times and then, admitting defeat, it stood quietly in the center of the arena, head hanging, sides heaving. Cloud Walker spoke to the horse, stroking its leathered neck and flanks, before vaulting lightly to the ground.

"You looked like you were enjoying that," Mary remarked.

Cloud Walker turned to face her, his heart beating faster at the mere sight of her. She was a lovely creature. Dressed in a pink-flowered cotton dress, she was the picture of what a woman should be, neat and clean and beautiful. She had a trim waist despite having recently borne a child, and her curves were soft and feminine. Her hair was as brown as mother earth, her eyes were a lovely shade of gray, always a little sad, even now, when she was smiling at him.

"It is good to ride a fine horse," Cloud Walker said.

"He doesn't act like a fine horse," Mary remarked. "He acts more like a loco bronc than a saddle pony."

Cloud Walker grinned as he gave the colt an

affectionate pat on the neck. "He has a lot of spirit, this one, but he is not mean. Only young and confused."

Like me, Mary thought. She said, "My father is very pleased with you. He says you are one of the best horsemen he has ever seen, and he has seen many."

Cloud Walker smiled, pleased by Shadow's words of praise. "Your father is the best horseman I have ever seen. He rides like a young warrior. All the horses know him and trust him, and he knows each of them by name."

"He is wonderful, isn't he?" Mary agreed, her voice filled with love and pride.

Cloud Walker nodded. Two Hawks Flying was a good man, someone to admire and respect, someone to emulate.

"Are you going to stay with us long?" Mary asked.

"As long as your father will let me. I have nowhere else to go."

Mary detected a note of sadness in the young man's voice and she wondered what had happened in his past to cause him unhappiness.

She lingered at the corral, watching as Cloud Walker cooled the colt, then stripped off the saddle and rubbed the animal down. Cloud Walker's movements were quick and sure as he handled the colt, and she watched, fascinated, as his muscles bulged and relaxed beneath his faded blue work shirt.

Mary turned away, suddenly ashamed of the direction her thoughts were heading. She was a married woman. She had no right to be admiring another man, no right at all.

Mumbling a hurried good-bye, she returned to the house.

"He's a fine young man," I remarked as Mary entered the kitchen.

Mary nodded, and I saw the color rise in her cheeks.

"There's nothing wrong with being friendly," I said as I placed a pan of bread on the stove to rise. "Cloud Walker needs a friend, and I suspect you do, too."

"Why is he so sad?"

"His wife and baby died not too long ago. He came here looking for work. I imagine the reservation holds too many bad memories for him to stay."

"How awful for him," Mary murmured. She gazed out the window, her eyes going to the corral. Cloud Walker had brought a new horse into the arena. It was a leopard Appaloosa filly. Cloud Walker swung effortlessly into the saddle and began to put the animal through its paces, now walking, now trotting, now a slow lope around the corral. The filly was a lovely creature, docile and sweet-tempered, eager to please. Man and animal made a pleasing picture as they circled the corral.

"Cloud Walker reminds me of your father when he was young," I mused, smiling. "He sits a horse with the same lazy grace, almost as if he were a part of the animal."

Mary nodded absently, and I wondered what she was thinking. Then Katherine woke from her nap and

Blackie came in clamoring for something to eat, and Mary and I stopped admiring Cloud Walker's riding ability and went to look after our children.

It was a beautiful fall day when Mary took Katherine down by the river crossing. Spreading a blanket near the water's edge, she made the baby comfortable, then took off her shoes and stockings and dangled her feet in the cool water. It was peaceful there, quiet save for the baby's happy cooing and the occasional song of a bird.

Staring out at the distant mountains, she wondered what Frank was doing. Did he miss her at all? Did she really miss him? A year ago she had fancied herself very much in love with Frank Smythe. Now she wondered if it had just been an infatuation, a desire to be on her own, to run off to the big city and play house.

She thought of Hawk and Victoria. They were so happy together, so much in love. You had only to look at Vickie to see that she was a happy woman. She obviously adored Hawk, and he worshiped her. Seeing them together was almost painful. They were so much a part of each other, and she felt so alone.

Her father and mother, too, shared a love that was a rare and beautiful thing. Mary knew of the many trials and heartaches they had shared, the suffering and sadness they had endured, yet it had not tarnished their love but made it stronger and more rewarding.

She did not hear his footsteps, but she was suddenly aware that she was no longer alone. Glancing over her shoulder, Mary saw Cloud Walker striding toward her. Again she could not help admiring how tall and handsome he was. He wore a pair of faded blue jeans, a red shirt, and Cheyenne moccasins. She thought he looked perfect.

Cloud Walker smiled at Mary uncertainly as he drew near. "Do you want to be alone?" he asked.

"No." Mary gestured at the place beside her. "Please sit down."

For a moment they were silent. Mary was keenly aware of the man sitting beside her. She had thought Frank Smythe was tall, but Cloud Walker was taller. Frank was handsome, but Cloud Walker was more so, and he possessed an inner strength of character that Frank Smythe would never have.

She felt Cloud Walker's eyes on her face and she blushed. What was he thinking? Why had he come looking for her? She felt drawn to him, and wondered if he felt the same.

"Why did you leave Chicago?" Cloud Walker asked abruptly. "If it is none of my business, tell me so."

"I was unhappy there, so I came home."

"Why were you unhappy? Was your husband cruel?"

"Not physically. He didn't beat me or anything. I guess he just wasn't ready to settle down. He wanted to laugh and flirt with every girl he met. And when Katherine was born, he . . . he was ashamed."

"Because she looks Cheyenne?"

"Yes." Mary laughed bitterly. "I think he forgot that I am Cheyenne, too, even though I don't look it." She turned to face Cloud Walker. "I felt like a freak. When our friends discovered I was Indian, they looked at me differently. Some of them made jokes, and some were shocked to think they had invited a savage into their homes. I'm not ashamed of being Cheyenne. Should I be?"

"No. They should be ashamed. But there will always be white people who think they are better than the Indian. They hear stories of the old days, and they think we are all savages."

"Maybe we are."

Cloud Walker made a sound of disgust low in his throat. "Do not talk nonsense. Is your father a savage? Your brothers? I have seen the way your father cares for your mother, how he cherishes her. Does a savage behave like that? I have seen Hawk help those less fortunate than he. Does a savage do that? I have seen Blackie save countless animal lives and do many kind things for the old woman who lives alone at the edge of town. Do savages save lives and help others unselfishly? You are being foolish, Mary," he said, his voice gently chiding. "Do not let ignorant white people destroy your faith in yourself, in what you are."

Mary smiled, her heart flooding with gratitude for Cloud Walker's words of wisdom. He was right, of course. She *was* being foolish.

"My mother told me about your family," Mary said after a while. "I'm sorry."

Cloud Walker nodded. Time had eased his grief and taken the edge from his pain. Now, as he gazed into Mary's soft gray eyes, he knew he was ready to love again.

They spent the rest of the afternoon together,

talking of unimportant things, playing with Katherine, wading in the cold water. Cloud Walker felt as if his heart had come alive again. He had been dead inside for so long that it was almost painful to smile, to laugh out loud. He could not keep his eyes off Mary. Her smile was breathtaking, her laughter like the tinkling of the tiny silver bells that had once adorned his mother's lodge. He watched her play with Katherine, and his heart ached to be a part of a family again, to hold a child in his arms, to know the love of a woman who was his and his alone.

He was aware of Mary with every fiber of his being. When she looked at him, his blood pounded in his ears and all his senses came alive. Her voice was like music and he asked her many questions just to hear the sound of her voice. Once, their hands touched and it was like being kissed by the sun. He felt the heat explode through his whole body. Did she feel it, too? Was she aware of the magic between them? Did it please her?

Mary was indeed aware of the chemistry between them. She wondered if it was merely a physical attraction or the promise of something deeper and more meaningful, and then she shook her head, disgusted with herself for even thinking such a thing. She was a married woman with a child. But she could not help the way she felt, the way Cloud Walker made her feel. Just looking at him made her heart sing and her blood hum, and when his hand touched hers, it was like being reborn.

Later they sat side by side while Katherine slept.

Cloud Walker watched Mary fashion a wreath from
leaves and grass, admiring the way the sun danced in
her hair, the way she smiled when a butterfly alighted
on her shoulder. Somewhere deep in the back of his
mind he knew that only trouble could come of his
feelings for her. A wise man would leave before it was
too late, before his unspoken affection for her blossomed into something beyond control. But he knew he
would not leave. Though she would never be his, he
would stay, just to be near her.

My daughter was happier after that. I saw the
change in her eyes, heard it in her voice. The bitterness seemed to have melted from around her heart and
she sang cheerfully as she helped me around the
house. She spent time with Blackie, telling him about
the East, about the museums and the zoo and the
theater. Blackie listened intently, his eyes alight with
interest, but he never expressed any desire to visit the
East except to see the zoo. Imagine, live elephants and
lions and tigers so close you could almost reach out and
touch them. And camels and exotic birds and snakes.
Alligators and seals, monkeys and gorillas.

Blackie had a natural talent for healing, and the
town's veterinarian, Chester Cole, decided that such a
gift should not go to waste. He began to take Blackie
with him on his rounds. My son was in heaven. He
spent every weekend with Chester Cole, traveling
from farm to farm, assisting the doctor as he treated
wounds and aided in difficult deliveries. Blackie
learned how to recognize various diseases and how to

treat them. He learned new skills in the care of cuts and burns, how to give injections. Chester Cole was amazed at how quickly Blackie learned, but Shadow and I were not the least bit surprised. Blackie had been practicing to be a veterinarian ever since he could walk.

Pa and Rebecca were taking life easy. Pa was growing older and he had hired two young Texans to look after his herd. A boy in town had been hired to weed Rebecca's garden. Pa spent a good deal of his time reading. He had bought several dozen books while in Pennsylvania, including several volumes of Shakespeare and Dickens. Rebecca had taken up knitting. Ruth Tippitt had taught her the basics, and Rebecca was busily engaged in knitting a sweater and matching cap for Katherine.

Once a month on a Sunday we all went to Pa's house for dinner. Sometimes we sat around for hours reminiscing about the old days, remembering how it had been when there were just a few families in Bear Valley. Sometimes Pa talked about his past and the days he had spent with the old mountain man who had saved his life after his parents were killed by Indians.

Other times we tried to predict what the future would bring. The turn of the century was only a few months away and there were dire predictions that the world would come to an end on January first. Other would-be seers predicted terrible catastrophes: fires and floods, earthquakes and plagues. Pa dismissed them all as a lot of hogwash.

At first Cloud Walker had refused to accompany

us to Pa's house for our monthly get-togethers. He was not family and he felt as if he'd be intruding. It was Mary who finally persuaded Cloud Walker to go with us, and though he rarely spoke, we all enjoyed having him there, especially Mary.

"There's a romance brewing there or I miss my guess," Rebecca remarked to me one afternoon when we were alone. "You can practically feel the heat between them."

I nodded, though I had mixed emotions about Mary's budding relationship with Cloud Walker. I had nothing against Cloud Walker. He was a fine young man, hard-working, honest, reliable. But Mary was still Frank Smythe's wife, for better or worse. Frank had written Mary only one letter since she had moved back home, asking her, quite formally, to reconsider her decision and return to Chicago. Mary had written him a short note in reply, stating she was not ready to return to Chicago, or to him. I knew she was hurt because Frank had made no mention of loving her or missing her; nor had he asked after Katherine.

I watched Mary and Cloud Walker now. They were sitting on the sofa before the fireplace with Katherine between them. I could see that Cloud Walker was remembering his own lost child as he played with my granddaughter. Some hurts took a long time to heal. Some never did.

I thought wistfully of my own first child. It had been a boy, stillborn in the wilds of Arizona. I did not often think of him, but sometimes my heart ached for the child I had never seen, never held.

I shook the melancholy memories away as Shadow stood up. It was getting late, time to start for home.

I gave Rebecca a hug and kissed my father on the cheek. There was a strong bond of love in our family, and I knew that no matter what the future held, we could face it so long as we were together.

17

Katherine was asleep in her grandmother's arms when Mary left the house to go for a walk. It was good to be back in Bear Valley, good to be home. Since returning from Chicago, she had renewed several old friendships with girls she had grown up with. Most were sympathetic about her marital problems, declaring that Frank Smythe was a heel of the worst kind to turn his back on his wife and daughter. A few were philosophical about the whole thing. If it was meant to be, it would work out in time; if not, it was for the best.

Mary felt a sense of peace as she walked along. She belonged here. The land was in her blood, in her heart, and she realized she would never have been happy to stay in Chicago for very long. She had missed the plains, missed the vast blue vault of the sky overhead, missed the sight of the distant mountains towering in the west. And most of all she had missed her family. It was a joy to see her mother and father and brother every day, to feel their love. Perhaps if Frank had loved her as her father loved her mother, she would not have missed her family quite so much. Or maybe it was just that she had not really loved Frank, at least not the way a wife should love her husband.

Mary sighed heavily. Eventually she and Frank would either have to resolve their differences or end their marriage, but for now she was content to leave things as they were.

She paused as she realized she had made a wide loop around the house to the breaking pen. The corral was empty, and she felt a pang of disappointment. She couldn't admit it, not even to herself, but she knew she had hoped to find Cloud Walker here.

She was turning back toward the house when she saw him coming toward her. He was leading the spotted Appaloosa filly.

Cloud Walker's heart skipped a beat when he saw Mary standing near the corral. Was it possible she had been looking for him? Could he be that lucky? His eyes looked on her and were pleased. Each time he saw her, he was struck anew by her beauty. Today she was wearing a black riding skirt and a bright yellow shirtwaist. Her hair, drawn away from her face, was gathered at the nape of her neck with a perky white bow.

"Hello," she said, smiling shyly. "I was just out for a breath of fresh air."

Cloud Walker nodded as he returned her smile. "Would you like to go for a ride?"

"Yes, I'd like that."

Mary followed Cloud Walker to the barn and watched while he saddled the spotted filly for her, then bridled a raw-boned black gelding for himself. Her heart gave a queer little thump when he put his hands around her waist to help her mount. Their eyes met and held for a long moment. To Mary, it seemed as though time had lost its meaning. Her mouth went suddenly dry and her stomach felt as though a million butterflies were dancing inside.

Cloud Walker felt the blood singing in his veins and he knew if he held Mary much longer, he would do something rash.

"Ready?" he asked hoarsely.

Mary nodded, not trusting herself to speak.

Side by side they rode away from the barn and down toward the river. It was a lovely day, cool and clear. Fat powder-puff clouds drifted across the sky, like ships floating on the sea.

Mary studied Cloud Walker furtively as they rode along. He looked good on a horse, she mused. He rode without a saddle, his long legs straddling the horse with easy assurance. His hands were light on the reins, knowledgeable, expert. He wore a pair of tight blue jeans and a dark red shirt. Well-worn moccasins hugged his feet.

They rode in silence for some time. At the river Cloud Walker looked over at Mary. "Shall we cross?"

"If you like."

The spotted filly followed the gelding into the river, stepping daintily into the water like a woman who didn't want to get her feet wet. The horse was a pleasure to ride, Mary thought as she stroked the mare's sleek neck.

When they reached the far side of the river, Mary urged the filly into a lope, laughing with delight as the wind whipped through her hair and stung her cheeks. It felt so good to be riding again, to run free over the vast sunlit prairie. She heard Cloud Walker coming up behind her and she urged the leopard mare to go faster, her heart feeling light and carefree for the first time in months. It was wonderful to be alive on such a beautiful day.

Mary let the Appaloosa run until the animal began to tire, and then she drew rein beneath a tree whose leaves had turned from spring green to brilliant autumn colors of gold and red and rust.

In moments, Cloud Walker drew up beside her, his dark eyes glowing and happy.

"You ride well for a woman," he said.

"Thank you, sir," Mary replied saucily. "You ride well for a man."

Cloud Walker threw back his head and laughed out loud. It was the first time Mary had seen him laugh wholeheartedly, and she was amazed at how much more handsome he was when he looked happy. It was the first time she had seen him look genuinely amused, the first time the sadness had been gone from his eyes.

For a few moments they sat in the shade in companionable silence. Birds twittered in the treetops, a squirrel darted down the trunk and disappeared in the tall yellow grass. In the distance a skunk made its way across the prairie, its tail straight up, its nose testing the gentle breeze that ruffled the grass and sighed softly through the autumn leaves.

"My father came to my mother's rescue out here when they were kids," Mary remarked, gesturing toward a low ridge some twenty yards away. "My mother was riding with a friend when a bunch of young Cheyenne braves surrounded them. The Indians wanted to kill Joshua and take my mother prisoner, but then my father rode up and told the Indians to leave the white girl and her friend in peace. My mother said she was scared to death until my father arrived, and then she wasn't afraid anymore."

"Your father is greatly respected on the reservation," Cloud Walker replied. "When the old ones speak of the great chiefs, your father's name is always mentioned."

Mary nodded. "He was a great warrior. My mother has often told us stories of his bravery in battle, and how he led a band of renegade warriors in one last effort to be free after the battle at Little Big Horn. My mother rode with them and fought with them for a short time," Mary added proudly. "I don't think I would have had the courage to ride into battle with the men."

"You never know what you will do until the time comes," Cloud Walker said. "But I think you are very much like your mother. I think you would also ride to battle beside the man you loved."

"Maybe," Mary allowed dubiously. "I hope I never have to find out."

"Have you heard from your husband?"

"No."

Hope flared in Cloud Walker's heart. His feelings

for Mary were growing stronger with each passing day. Perhaps if Mary and her husband decided to end their marriage, he, Cloud Walker, would have a chance to win her heart. The mere thought filled him with exhilaration. What joy, to have Mary for his own! And then reality set in. He had nothing to offer Mary, nothing at all. In the old days, he might have kidnapped her and carried her off to his lodge in the Black Hills, but those days were gone. He was a man without a home of his own, with nothing of value to offer a woman.

"Shall we sit down for a while?" Mary asked. "It's pretty here."

Cloud Walker nodded. Vaulting lightly to the ground, he placed his hands around Mary's tiny waist and helped her from her horse. He held her for just a moment longer than necessary before he released her, and then he sat down beside her on the thick buffalo grass.

"How long are you going to stay in Bear Valley?" he asked.

"I don't know. I was hoping. . . . oh, never mind."

"You were hoping your husband would have come after you by now?" Cloud Walker guessed.

"Yes," Mary admitted ruefully. "But I don't think Frank is going to come after me."

"Do you still love him?"

"I don't know," Mary answered, shaking her head. "I wonder if I ever did."

"If he comes for you, will you go back to Chicago with him?"

"I don't know that either."

"I do not mean to pry," Cloud Walker said apologetically. "Forgive me."

"It's all right," Mary assured him. She picked up a large red-gold leaf and twirled it between her fingers. "I don't think Frank and I can ever be happy together now. He's ashamed of Katherine because she looks like my father's people. I can't live with a man who's ashamed of his own child, ashamed of me. I don't think Frank will ever be able to overcome that."

"Then he is a fool," Cloud Walker said quietly.

Mary felt her cheeks grow warm under Cloud Walker's lingering gaze. There was no mistaking the caring in his eyes, the longing in his voice. She did not move as Cloud Walker slowly leaned forward, his lips touching hers in a kiss as soft and light as butterfly wings. In spite of the gentleness of his kiss, it affected Mary like a bolt of lightning, sending wave after wave of heat pulsing through her. Breathless, she placed her fingertips to her lips, stunned by the unexpected surge of desire that Cloud Walker's kiss had ignited. Frank's touch had never filled her with such turbulent emotions. His kisses had never made her blood turn to fire, or caused her insides to flutter wildly. She was stunned by a sudden desire to throw herself into Cloud Walker's arms, to feel his hands on her breasts and thighs, to feel his body lying close to her own. The intensity of her longing for him left her feeling confused and uncertain and a little frightened. But want him she did. Desperately.

Cloud Walker's feelings were much the same as Mary's. His dark eyes moved over her face, enchanted by the way the sun danced in her windblown hair, and by the way her eyes met his, looking shy and sensual at the same time. He longed to take her in his arms, to taste the honey of her lips one more time, to bury himself in her womanly sweetness. He gazed at her, his desire almost painful in its intensity, and saw that she wanted him as well. But he did not touch her. She was a married woman, and he had no right to want her, no right to touch her.

They gazed at each other for a full minute, their eyes speaking words they dared not utter aloud. Mary's heart was beating so hard she wondered if she might die; was certain she would die if Cloud Walker did not take her in his arms and ease the terrible hunger his one innocent kiss had aroused in her. Now she knew what her mother had meant by the pleasure a woman could receive in her husband's arms. Only Cloud Walker was not her husband. Shame washed over Mary, but she didn't care. She would gladly sacrifice everything for an hour in Cloud Walker's arms, to experience again the joy of his touch.

Abruptly, Cloud Walker stood up. He could not sit beside her any longer. Another moment and he would sweep her into his arms and bring shame on them both.

"We should go," he said.

"Yes," Mary agreed, extending her hands. "Will you help me up?"

Cloud Walker hesitated briefly before he took Mary's hands in his and pulled her to her feet. And now they were standing only inches apart. Mary did not let go of Cloud Walker's hands. She could feel him trembling slightly and as she looked up into the depths of his eyes, she knew why he trembled. He wanted her, and he was afraid. Afraid of hurting her, afraid of ruining her reputation. Afraid of being rejected.

Shamelessly, impulsively, Mary swayed toward Cloud Walker, testing her power over him. Her breasts brushed against his chest, and that brief contact was like striking a match to dry prairie grass.

Cloud Walker groaned low in his throat as he murmured her name. Did she know what she was doing to him? He whispered her name again, his mind in turmoil as he prayed to Maheo for strength to resist the delightful creature standing before him. He was only a man, after all, and she was so near, so beautiful.

Knowing it was wrong, Mary lifted her face for his kiss. She had to feel his lips on hers one more time, had to know if her response would be the same or if she had only imagined the ecstasy she had felt because she needed so badly to feel loved. Placing her hands on Cloud Walker's shoulders, she stood on her tiptoes and pressed her lips to his. And the same sweet wanting washed over her again.

With a cry that was as much pain as pleasure, Cloud Walker swept Mary into his arms and drew her body close to his own as he kissed her hungrily, passionately. His desire for the woman in his arms was a throbbing ache in his loins, a sweet torture from which he dared not seek relief.

Mary pressed closer to Cloud Walker, loving the way her body seemed to fit to his. She could feel his desire for her rising against her belly, and it filled her with joy. She knew suddenly what her mother and Vickie had been trying to tell her.

"Mary." Cloud Walker murmured her name reverently as his lips moved across her face.

"I know," Mary replied. "I feel it too."

Bodies pressed close, they kissed again, all else forgotten but the wonder of the love blossoming between them. Mary had never seen Frank fully naked in the harsh light of day, nor had she cared to, but now she yearned to see all of Cloud Walker. Dimly she wondered why Cloud Walker had the power to arouse her with a mere kiss when Frank's caresses had not, but she did not dwell on the matter. She was too caught up in the wonder of the new feelings coursing through her. It was as if her whole body had suddenly come alive, every fiber and nerve attuned to the touch of Cloud Walker's hands and lips.

Cloud Walker's kiss deepened as Mary pressed herself against him. His tongue slipped over her lips and tasted the hidden nectar of her mouth. Mary responded with a quick intake of breath. The blood pounded in her ears, and she had the odd sensation that she was floating in time and space, adrift in a world of wonder such as she had never imagined existed. She longed for nothing more than to have it last forever.

The sound of hoofbeats reached Cloud Walker's ears. Reluctantly, guiltily, he released his hold on Mary and stepped away as Shadow rode up.

For a moment Shadow just sat there, his eyes easily reading the guilt and desire in Cloud Walker's expression and the bright flush of shame in his daughter's cheeks.

"Hello, neyho," Mary said quietly.

"Go home," Shadow ordered sternly.

"No," Mary answered, defying her father for the first time in her life.

Cloud Walker's heart began to pound as Shadow slid effortlessly to the ground and stood before him. Mary's father had every right to be angry, he thought, discouraged, and wondered if Shadow would order him to leave Bear Valley immediately. Despair filled Cloud Walker's heart at the thought. He had grown to love this place almost as much as he loved Mary.

"What are your intentions toward my daughter?" Shadow demanded, his eyes boring into Cloud Walker's.

"I love her," Cloud Walker answered, his voice clear and proud.

"She is married to another."

Cloud Walker slid a glance in Mary's direction before returning his gaze to Shadow's face. "The marriage cannot last. Surely you know how unhappy she is."

"She is still a married woman. You have no right to interfere in her life so long as she is bound to another."

"You have no right to judge me," Mary blurted, not daring to meet her father's eyes. "You took my mother when she belonged to another man."

Shadow studied his daughter's face and saw the determination in her eyes even though she did not look at him. This was the first time she had dared argue with him, the first time she had not meekly obeyed his command.

"That was different," Shadow said at last. "Your

mother and I had been married by Elk Dreamer long before she married Joshua Berdeen."

"That marriage was not legally binding," Mary retorted. "And you know it."

"I do not wish to argue about that now," Shadow said irritably. "Your mother was blackmailed into marrying Berdeen. No one forced you to marry Frank Smythe."

"I made a mistake," Mary said, meeting her father's eyes for the first time. "Must I pay for it the rest of my life?"

Shadow looked at Cloud Walker again. "You say you love my daughter. I forbid it."

"I cannot help the way I feel," Cloud Walker replied with a shake of his head. "She is kind and good and beautiful. She deserves a man who will treat her with love and respect, a man who will be proud of her, of what and who she is."

"And do you think you are that man?"

"Yes. I love her with all my heart."

Shadow looked skeptical. "You have only known each other for a short time."

"You said you knew, the minute you saw my mother, that she was the only woman for you," Mary argued boldly.

"Yes," Shadow remarked dryly. "But she was not a married woman at the time."

Cloud Walker took Mary's hand in his. "The feelings are the same," he insisted.

Shadow nodded. How well he remembered the fire Hannah had stirred in his blood that day he had seen her near the river crossing. She had been wearing an old blue gingham dress. Her hair, as red as flame, had fallen in loose waves about her slender shoulders. Her eyes, ever a warm and lovely shade of gray, had returned his gaze shyly. He had known from that moment that no other woman, red or white, would ever hold his heart.

Shadow smiled faintly with the memory. Even now, some twenty-four years later, he felt the same.

"Do not shame my daughter," Shadow warned, fixing Cloud Walker with a hard stare. "Do not lie to her, or make promises you cannot keep. She has been hurt enough."

Cloud Walker nodded, his heart soaring with hope. "You do not disapprove then?"

"No. I think perhaps Maheo sent you here to ease the pain in Mary's heart."

"I will never do anything to bring shame to you or your family," Cloud Walker vowed fervently.

Shadow nodded, his gaze moving from Cloud Walker's face to Mary's. "Come, let us go home."

They met at the river crossing the following night. Cloud Walker arrived first, and paced the river bank restlessly back and forth along the water's edge, his heart and his mind eager to see her again. He whirled around at the sound of her footsteps, his heart swelling with emotion as she made her way toward him. She wore a simple yellow cotton dress. A multicolored shawl was wrapped around her shoulders to turn away the cold.

"Mary."

She walked straight into his arms, her lips parting

slightly as she lifted her face for his kiss. Contentment washed over her as Cloud Walker's arms drew her near.

They stood together for a long time before Cloud Walker let Mary go. "We must talk," he said.

"I know."

"I love you," Cloud Walker said gravely. "I know it is wrong, that you belong to another, but I cannot fight the feelings in my heart."

"It is the same with me," Mary confessed. "What are we going to do?"

"I do not know. Among our people, a woman simply places her husband's belongings out of their lodge when she wishes to end their marriage."

"I wish it could be that easy for us," Mary said. "I asked Frank for a divorce before I left Chicago, but he said no."

"Then we must wait until he says yes," Cloud Walker remarked ruefully.

"My parents didn't wait," Mary muttered under her breath.

"We will not make our love shameful," Cloud Walker said resolutely. "We will not sneak around as though what we feel for each other is wrong. I am a warrior, and a warrior does not defile the woman he loves. I will never do anything to cause you shame or hurt."

Mary nodded. He was right, of course. They must wait until she was free from Frank. It would be the hardest thing she had ever done.

They were together often after that night, but always in the company of others. Cloud Walker had

vowed he would not touch Mary until he had a right to
do so, but he did not trust himself to be alone with her.
Good intentions often dissolved in the face of tempta-
tion, and Mary was all too tempting. He thought of her
constantly, dreamed of her at night, and in those
dreams he held her and loved her as he so longed to do.
In his dreams she came to him, warm and willing, and
he possessed her over and over again, never able to get
his fill.

Shadow said little about the relationship between
his daughter and Cloud Walker. He saw the heated
looks that passed between them, the little touches, the
secret smiles. They were much in love, he mused, but,
like Hannah, he wondered if any good would come of
it.

18

The cold breath of winter blew across the vast prairie. The trees, once bedecked with gloriously hued leaves of red and gold and orange, now stood bare beneath the cold gray sky. The river was often covered with a thin coat of ice. Blackie dug his sled out of the barn and spent hours riding down the snow-covered hills with his friends.

Our family spent a peaceful Thanksgiving at Pa's house. As I sat at a table that was nearly groaning beneath a load of food, I counted myself a lucky woman. Shadow sat at my left. As usual, he was clad in a buckskin shirt, pants, and moccasins. As usual, he looked handsome and virile, and as Pa asked a blessing on the food spread before us, I offered my own silent prayer of thanks to God for giving me a man like Shadow to love.

Hawk sat across from me. My son had changed since his arrest the year before. He was quieter now, more withdrawn. Victoria told me Hawk often rode alone into the hills to meditate. She said he only went to town when it was necessary, and that he was close-mouthed and aloof except around his family and a very few close friends.

Vickie sat on Hawk's right. Hawk had chosen well when he picked a wife. Victoria was a lovely young woman, a wonderful wife, a devoted mother. I loved her as though she were my own daughter.

Mary sat on Hawk's left, one of the twins on her lap, but she had eyes only for Cloud Walker. It was easy to see that Mary had fallen head over heels in love with the handsome young Cheyenne, and I worried about her. Mary was still Frank's wife, after all, and had no business looking at other men.

Blackie sat at my right, engaged in a lively conversation with Pa. Blackie was growing, changing. He was almost as tall as Shadow now, and more and more I was convinced that Blackie was indeed Shadow's son and not Joshua Berdeen's. With each passing year, Blackie looked more and more like Shadow.

Pa sat at the head of the table, Katherine cradled in one burly arm. Pa really had his hands full, I thought. He was talking to Blackie, trying to keep Katherine quiet, and eating all at the same time. I was terribly proud of my father. He was active in our community, holding a position on the town council and on the school board as well. He was a good husband, a wonderful father, a doting grandfather.

Rebecca sat at the opposite end of the table across from Pa. Jacob was perched on her lap, eating off her plate with his fingers. I watched her smile at Pa and I saw the love in her eyes as she gazed at her husband. I wondered if she had ever thought, when she agreed to marry Pa, that she would one day have a houseful of people under her roof.

And then there was Cloud Walker. He sat next to Mary, looking a trifle uncomfortable at celebrating a white man's holiday. I knew he was concerned about his position in our household. He was not really family, only a hired hand who happened to be very much in love with our daughter. Mary had again written to Frank asking for a divorce, but so far she had received no reply.

After we finished dinner with pie and coffee, the women did the dishes while the men sat in the parlor, talking about the weather and their plans for the new year.

Two days after Thanksgiving, Frank Smythe arrived in Bear Valley. He went first to see his parents. Leland and Mattie welcomed Frank home with open arms, assuring him that he could stay with them until he and Mary could work things out.

Later that same afternoon, Frank knocked at our front door. He had changed drastically from the young man who had left Bear Valley a little over a year ago. Frank had always been quiet and soft-spoken, a little

self-conscious. But no more. This was a new Frank
Smythe, and he looked prosperous and self-assured in
a dark blue suit, starched white shirt, black tie, and
highly polished black boots. A neatly folded silk
handkerchief was tucked into the pocket of his suit
coat.

"Good day, Mrs. Kincaid," Frank said politely. "Is
Mary here?"

"Yes, she is, Frank. Won't you come in?"

"Thank you."

Mary had been sitting on the sofa mending one of
Katherine's frocks. She stood up as Frank entered the
room. There was an awkward moment of silence as
Mary and Frank regarded each other.

"Excuse me," I said, and went into the kitchen. I
closed the door, but I could easily hear what was being
said.

"Sit down, won't you, Frank?" Mary invited in a
voice that was coolly polite. "How have you been?"

"Fine, Mary," Frank replied briskly. "I want you
to come home with me."

"Do you, Frank?" Mary asked tremulously.
"Why?"

I waited for Frank's answer, wondering if he knew
how bitter Mary was, wondering if he truly realized
how much he had hurt her.

"I don't need a reason," Frank answered irritably.
"You're my wife, and you belong with me."

"I don't want to go back to Chicago," Mary said,
and I marveled at how calm she sounded, how sure of
herself.

"Listen, Mary, I'm in line for a big promotion at

the bank. Vice president, if you will. Do you have any idea what that means?"

"Yes. It means more money and more prestige and less time for me."

"Is that what's bothering you?" Frank exclaimed. "Dammit, Mary, I worked hard every day."

"And played hard every night. I can't go back to that, Frank. I won't."

"What do you expect me to do? Give up a promising career with a future and bury myself here in Bear Valley?"

"I don't care what you do," Mary replied.

A knock at the door stilled Frank's reply, and then I heard Cloud Walker's voice. Knowing I shouldn't, I peeked through the door. Frank had stood up when Cloud Walker entered the room, and now the two men were eyeing each other warily, like dogs about to fight over a scrap of meat. I wondered if Mary had written Frank about Cloud Walker. It didn't seem likely.

Cloud Walker cleared his throat. "You have company," he said, his eyes dark with jealousy. "I will come back later."

Frank was facing my way and I saw his eyes narrow suspiciously at the look of affection that passed between Mary and Cloud Walker. If the look they exchanged wasn't evidence enough of their feelings for one another, Mary's guilty blush cinched it.

"So," Frank drawled after Cloud Walker left the house, "that's the reason you don't want to come home with me."

"I don't know what you mean," Mary replied haughtily.

Frank snorted. "Don't you? It's written all over that pretty little face of yours. You've found some buck to take my place. I might have known," he sneered. "Once a squaw, always a squaw."

The crack of Mary's hand striking Frank across the face was as loud and clear as a pistol shot. "Don't judge my morals by your own," Mary said angrily. "I have never been unfaithful to you."

"Never?" Frank questioned skeptically.

"Never."

"I guess he's never held you or kissed you, then," Frank scoffed.

Mary's silence was all the answer Frank needed.

"I guess we have nothing more to say to each other," Frank remarked bitterly.

"Don't you even want to see your daughter, Frank?" Mary asked quietly.

"No."

"That's one of the reasons I left you," Mary said sadly. "You don't love Katherine, and you don't love me. I wonder if you ever did."

"Good-bye, Mary," Frank said curtly.

"What about the divorce?"

"Forget it. I'm not making it easy for you, my dear wife. I swallowed my pride to come here and ask you to come home. I want you back, and I'm willing to wait until you're ready."

"I'll never come back," Mary said defiantly.

"And you'll never be free to marry that redskin, either," Frank said triumphantly.

I heard the door slam as Frank left the house. I

waited a minute, and then I went into the parlor. Mary was standing near the fireplace, staring at the door. Two large tears welled in her eyes and rolled down her cheeks.

"Mary?"

"Oh, nahkoa," she cried, and dissolved into tears.

I put my arms around her and held her as she cried. Few things in life could be so bitter or as painful as a marriage gone wrong.

"Oh, nahkoa," Mary sobbed brokenly. "What am I going to do?"

"I don't know, dear," I answered. "Are you sure you don't want to go back to Frank and try to work it out?"

"He never even said he loved me, or missed me. He couldn't even take a minute to see his own daughter. How can you expect me to go back to him?"

"You're his wife, Mary, remember? For better or worse, until death do you part."

"I know, but I just can't go back to him. You have no idea what it was like."

"I can guess." I patted Mary's shoulder lovingly. "This is a decision you must make on your own. I can't tell you what to do. I guess you'll just have to follow your heart. But, Mary, don't forget you have a daughter to consider as well. Whatever you decide will affect Katherine, too. I know you're hurt and unhappy just now, but don't do something in haste that you'll regret later."

"You mean Cloud Walker."

"Yes. I know he cares for you, and you seem to

care for him, but be very sure of your feelings before you go too far to turn back."

Mary smiled at me through her tears. "Is that the voice of experience speaking?" she asked, sniffling.

"Yes. Now go dry your eyes and wash your face. Crying never solved anything."

19

We didn't know just how bitter and vengeful Frank Smythe could be until a few days later. When we heard he had left Bear Valley, we all breathed a sigh of relief, little dreaming that he was not quite through with us yet.

On the Friday afternoon after Frank left Bear Valley, Hawk and Cloud Walker rode into town to pick up a wheel Hawk had left at the blacksmith for repairs. They stopped for a beer before beginning the journey back home, paying little attention to the four men who followed them out of town.

Hawk and Cloud Walker were on a long deserted stretch of road when the four men overtook them. Too late, Hawk reached for the rifle under the front seat of the wagon.

"I wouldn't," warned one of the men, and Hawk raised his hands above his head as the four men drew their guns.

"What do you want?" Hawk asked, glancing at the faces of the four men. "We do not have any cash, if that is what you are looking for."

"It isn't," the leader said. "There's a ravine about a mile south of here. You know the one I mean? Head that way. And don't try anything funny."

Hawk nodded, his stomach in knots as he drove the team toward the ravine. He glanced at Cloud Walker, who shrugged perplexedly. If the men didn't want money, what did they want?

At the ravine, Hawk reined the horses to a halt and set the brake, then sat there, his hands clenched at his sides, waiting to see what would happen next.

"Get down," the leader of the group ordered curtly. "Wes, tie that one up and stuff a gag in his mouth. Marv, you and Cliff hang onto the other one."

Hawk thought briefly of trying to make a break for it as the man called Wes walked purposefully toward him, but there seemed little point in it. There was no way he could outrun a bullet. He remained passive as his hands were tied tightly behind his back and a kerchief was jammed into his mouth.

Cloud Walker struggled briefly as Marv and Cliff grabbed his arms and dragged him from the wagon. A sudden premonition told him they were not interested in Hawk at all, and his mouth went dry as he watched the leader dismount and stride toward him.

"Hurry it up, Castrell," the man called Marv said impatiently. "Somebody's liable to come along."

"Shut up," Castrell rebuked mildly. He looked at

Cloud Walker, his yellow eyes thoughtful. "There's nothing personal in this," he told the young man as he pulled on a pair of leather gloves. "I'm just doing a job I was paid to do, that's all. Don't come looking for me when it's over, 'cause I'll be long gone outa the territory by the time you heal up. And if you should happen to find me, I'll have to kill you."

A cold sliver of fear wrapped around Cloud Walker's insides as Castrell flexed his fingers. "What is it you have been paid to do?"

"Just rough you up a little, that's all."

"Who has paid you to do such a thing?"

Castrell shook his head. "I didn't ask the gent's name and he didn't give it. I just took his money."

Cloud Walker's body went tense all over as Castrell drew back his fist. In the split second before the first blow landed, he wondered if Frank Smythe was the man who had paid Castrell.

Cloud Walker sucked in his breath when he saw the first blow coming. It landed in his midsection, driving the breath from his body, and was quickly followed by another and another. The two men holding Cloud Walker strengthened their grasp on his arms as he began to struggle. Castrell was grinning as he drove his fist into Cloud Walker's face. Blood gushed from the Indian's mouth as his lower lip split. The next blow sliced open his cheek.

Cloud Walker stared into Castrell's face, willing himself to stay silent as the man struck him again and again, the blows coming steadily, methodically. It was hard to breathe now, hard to think. There was nothing in the world but pain, a bright red haze of pain that gradually dulled into one long, steady ache. His head lolled forward and his legs grew weak. Time lost all meaning and it seemed as though he had been trapped between the two white men forever while Castrell's fists meted out blow after blow.

A vague thought of death entered his mind and he thought he might welcome it if it would bring relief from the jarring pain that exploded through his tortured flesh each time Castrell's fist smacked into him.

Hawk watched helplessly as the man called Castrell methodically dealt blow after blow to Cloud Walker's face and midsection. The man was good at his job, Hawk observed ruefully. His punches were hard, solid, and precise. There was a sharp crack as Castrell broke one of Cloud Walker's ribs.

The sound roused Hawk's anger, and each blow added fuel to the fire. Cloud Walker was nearly unconscious now, and Hawk knew he would have collapsed but for the two men holding him erect.

Rage suffused Hawk as he watched Castrell continue to strike Cloud Walker. Suddenly, with a low growl, he hurled himself at Castrell, driving his shoulder into the man's back and knocking him off his feet.

Castrell landed hard, rolled over once, and gained his feet. "Come on, Injun," he called, motioning for Hawk to come toward him.

Anger overrode good sense as Hawk hurled himself at Castrell a second time, his right foot lashing out at Castrell's side. Castrell sidestepped easily, his fist striking Hawk across the face, and as Hawk sprawled in the dirt, Castrell kicked him in the back, driving the breath from Hawk's body.

"Let's go," Castrell said to his companions, and

the four men mounted their horses and rode away without looking back.

Hawk sat up. For a moment, he did not move, just sat there until the pain in his back receded. Blood was trickling from the corner of his left eye. He glanced at Cloud Walker and saw that he was unconscious.

Hawk tried to free his hands, but the knot had been tied by an expert and the rope refused to give.

He glanced up at the sky. The sun was setting, and he weighed the wisdom of walking home for help, and decided against it. There were still wolves and coyotes in this part of Bear Valley, and though they rarely attacked a man, Cloud Walker would be defenseless against them in case of an attack.

Cloud Walker groaned softly as awareness returned. There was the taste of blood in his mouth. His nose was broken, and when he tried to sit up, he realized that a couple of ribs were broken as well. Each movement sent waves of pain shooting through him, and it was with a great deal of effort that he managed to untie Hawk's hands.

Removing the gag from his mouth, Hawk stood up. "Do not move," he told Cloud Walker. "I will get the wagon."

Cloud Walker nodded, and then passed out again.

I gazed at Cloud Walker, my stomach churning as Hawk placed him on Mary's bed.

"What happened?" I asked, glancing at the nasty cut near Hawk's left eye.

"Four men stopped us on our way from town," Hawk answered. "They tied me up, and then one of them beat Cloud Walker until he was unconscious. When I tried to interfere, the man hit me." Hawk touched the cut near his eye. "Do not worry about me. This is nothing."

"Why did they stop you? Why would they attack Cloud Walker?"

Hawk shook his head. "They said someone had paid them to do it. They claimed they did not know the man's name."

"Did you recognize any of the men?"

"No."

"There's something you're not telling me."

"I think Frank Smythe put them up to it."

"Frank!" I exclaimed in surprise. "Surely he wouldn't stoop to anything so low."

Hawk shrugged. "Maybe. Maybe not."

"There's no time to discuss it now. Does Mary know about this?"

"Not yet."

We heard Mary enter the house just then. She was laughing as she carried Katherine into the room. She came to an abrupt halt, the laughter dying on her lips, when she saw Cloud Walker lying on her bed, unconscious and bloody. The color drained from her face as she stared at him.

And then she lifted tormented eyes to my face. "He's not—"

"No," I said quickly. "Just badly hurt. I'll need your help."

Mary nodded woodenly. "Hawk, take Katherine out of here, will you, please?"

With a nod, Hawk took Katherine. "I am going to get Vickie," he said. "I will take Katherine with me."

For the next half hour, Mary and I focused all our attention on Cloud Walker. We washed the blood from his face, placed a cool cloth over his eyes, which were discolored and swollen. There was a large cut across his left cheek, his lower lip was split, his nose was broken. Removing his shirt, I saw that his torso was also badly bruised. He groaned when I touched his left side, and I guessed he had a couple of broken ribs.

"Who is it?" he rasped, struggling to sit up.

"It's me, Hannah," I said. "Lie still while I bandage your ribs."

"Where am I?" Cloud Walker asked.

"Home," Mary answered, taking his hand in hers.

"You should not be here, Mary," Cloud Walker said hoarsely. "I do not want you to see me like this."

"Don't be silly," Mary retorted, fighting back her tears. "I don't intend to leave your side until you're well again."

"Mary . . ."

"Save your breath," she said firmly. "I'm not leaving."

When we had done all we could, I sent Mary out of the room and then, in spite of Cloud Walker's vehement protests, I gave him a sponge bath and tucked him, naked but clean, into Mary's bed. Moments later he was asleep.

Hawk told his story to Shadow and Mary later that evening. "They said not to try to follow them, that they were leaving the territory," Hawk concluded, his dark eyes filled with anger. "They said it was nothing personal, just a job."

"You're not going after them, are you?" Vickie asked anxiously. "It will only cause more trouble."

"You do not expect me to let them get away with it, do you?" Hawk exclaimed. He looked at his father for help. "We are going after them, are we not?"

"I think it is Frank Smythe we should go after," Shadow replied quietly.

Mary stared at her father. "Frank? What has he got to do with this?"

"Hawk thinks Frank put those men up to it," I explained. "And your father agrees."

"Is that what you think, too?"

"I don't know. I don't like to think that Frank would do such a despicable thing, but he was mighty jealous when he left here. Jealousy can make a man do something he wouldn't ordinarily do."

"When do you want to leave?" Hawk asked Shadow.

"First light."

"No, Hawk!" Victoria cried, grabbing hold of his arm. "Please don't go. It will only cause more trouble."

"Vickie's right," Mary agreed. "Your going after Frank won't solve anything."

"We cannot let him get away with it," Hawk retorted angrily.

"Mary's right," I said. "What good will it do for the two of you to go all the way to Chicago to get Frank? And suppose you beat Frank up. What then? He'll come back here to get even with you and it will never end. Just let it go."

"No," Hawk said, and I knew he was spoiling for a fight. Any fight.

I looked to Shadow for help. "Please don't go. I haven't asked you for much, but I'm asking now. Let it end here before someone gets killed."

"Very well," Shadow said. "We will not go after Frank."

Hawk stood up, his face dark with anger. "Always the white man wins!" he cried bitterly, and stalked out of the house.

"I'm sorry," Victoria apologized. "Come along, Jason, Jacob, it's time to go home."

"Don't blame him for being angry, Vickie," I said as I walked her to the door. "You can't blame him for being bitter."

"I know," she said sadly. "Good night, Hannah."

While Shadow went out to check the stock, Mary and I went to look in on Cloud Walker. Tears filled Mary's eyes as she took Cloud Walker's hand in hers and gave it a squeeze. Cloud Walker's face was a swollen mass of cuts and bruises. I knew that each breath was causing him considerable pain.

"Can I get you anything?" Mary asked.

"Water," Cloud Walker rasped.

Mary poured him a drink from the carafe on her bedside table, lifted his head while he swallowed thirstily.

"I'll leave you two alone," I said.

"No, nahkoa," Mary said. "Don't go. I . . . Cloud Walker, I . . ." Mary glanced at me, her eyes pleading for help.

I knew intuitively what Mary wanted to say. She

wanted to tell Cloud Walker that they shouldn't see each other any more except in the most casual way. But she couldn't find the words.

"Not now, Mary," I admonished. "Good night, Cloud Walker. Try to get some sleep."

"Yes, good night," Mary added quickly, and followed me out of the room.

In the parlor, Mary sat down on the sofa, her hands folded in her lap. "Why did you stop me?"

"Your timing's all wrong," I said, sitting down beside her. "You'll only upset him if you tell him now."

"I can't see him anymore," Mary lamented. "What if Frank comes back?"

"You can't live in fear of that," I said. "At any rate, I don't think Frank Smythe will dare show his face in Bear Valley ever again."

"Oh, nahkoa," Mary wailed. "He might have been killed."

"But he wasn't. Even Frank wouldn't go that far. Now, get hold of yourself, Mary. Go wash your face and look after your daughter. Cloud Walker will be all right."

I smiled at Katherine, who had fallen asleep on the rug in front of the fireplace. "Why don't you and Katherine sleep in our room? Your father and I can sleep in the lodge."

"I don't want to put you out of your bed," Mary protested.

"It's all right. See you in the morning."

Wrapping a shawl around my shoulders, I stepped outside and closed the door behind me. Shadow was standing in the yard, his expression grim.

"We're going to sleep in the lodge until Cloud Walker is better," I said. "Do you mind?"

"No."

"What's wrong?"

"I do not think Hawk will forget what happened. I think he will try to follow those men."

"What makes you think that?"

Shadow grinned ruefully. "Because it is what I would have done twenty years ago."

I gazed into the darkness, my heart heavy within my breast because I knew that Shadow was right. I also knew that Shadow would not let Hawk go after those men alone.

"When are you leaving?"

"At first light," Shadow said, putting his arm around my shoulders. "Come, let us go to bed. We have not shared a lodge in a long time."

20

Mary sat at the window staring out into the darkness. She never should have come home, she thought unhappily. It was all her fault that Cloud Walker had been hurt. If she had stayed in Chicago with Frank, none of this would have happened.

Rising, she moved to her parents' bed and gazed down at her daughter. Katherine was sleeping peacefully, her thumb in her mouth.

With a sigh, Mary stepped out of the bedroom. Perhaps a cup of warm milk would help her sleep. She paused at the door of her room, frowning. Had she heard a groan? Concerned, she put her hand on the doorknob and turned it slowly.

"Who's there?" Cloud Walker's voice was low and edged with pain.

"It's me. Can I get you anything?"

"Water."

Mary moved quickly to his bedside and poured him a glass of water. Gently she lifted his head while he drank.

"Are you all right?" Mary asked. "Are you in much pain?"

"I am better, now that you are here."

"Don't say that," Mary admonished. "If it wasn't for me, this never would have happened."

"Do not blame yourself," Cloud Walker told her. "You could not have known this would happen. Your husband may have had nothing to do with it."

"He did," Mary said positively. "I know in my heart that Frank is responsible, and I'll never forgive him for it. Never."

"Mary." Cloud Walker held out his hand, wishing he could see her face.

Mary took Cloud Walker's hand in hers and held it to her breast. Tears filled her eyes as she gazed at his face. It was horribly bruised and puffy. His eyes were both swollen shut, and she was glad he could not see her tears.

"Mary, what are you thinking?"

"Nothing. Would you like some more water?"

"No."

"Can I get you anything else?"

"No."

"You should get some sleep."

"I am not tired. Why are you awake at this late hour?"

"I . . . Katherine woke me."

"We need no lies between us, Mary."

"I'm sorry. I was worried about you, and upset about Frank. I don't know what to do. I think maybe I'll go back to Chicago, after all. Katherine needs a father, and I can't stay here forever. It isn't fair to expect my parents to support us."

"Do not run away from me," Cloud Walker said, and, drawing her hand to his lips, he kissed her palm.

"I can't be responsible for something like this happening again," Mary cried, jerking her hand free. "What if he kills you next time? I can't have that on my conscience. I can't!"

"I would rather be dead than face the future without you," Cloud Walker said quietly. "Only Maheo can see tomorrow. Let us live each day as it comes."

"I don't want to live without you, either," Mary admitted.

Cloud Walker smiled as he held out his arms. With a little sigh of contentment, Mary leaned toward him, her lips lightly brushing his.

Somehow they would find a way to face the future together.

21

The first gray light of false dawn was lighting the sky when Hawk left the house. Victoria had begged him not to go, but he had refused to be swayed by her pleas. He was tired of letting the whites walk all over him, tired of cowing to their laws and prejudices. Cloud Walker had been cruelly beaten, and the four white men who were responsible were going to pay for it.

Saddling the blue roan, he rode out to the ravine and picked up their trail, his eyes easily reading the tracks left by their horses.

The four men did not expect to be followed, Hawk mused. He had no trouble at all following their trail. They were heading east, toward Steel's Crossing.

There was nothing but open prairie between the ravine and the town, plenty of places to hide four bodies where they would never be found.

Hawk followed the tracks until sundown and then, in the distance, he saw them. Four men sitting around a small campfire, drinking coffee and smoking long black cigars as though they hadn't a care in the world.

Drawing his rifle, Hawk rode toward them.

Shadow pushed Heyoka hard. The horses's drumming hooves seemed to cry, "hurry, hurry, hurry" as he followed Hawk's trail. He had to reach Hawk in time, had to stop him from doing something for which he would be sorry once he'd cooled off enough to think rationally. The white man's law would not look with favor on an Indian who killed four men simply because those four men had roughed up one Indian.

At sundown Shadow topped a small rise and there, as if frozen in time, he saw Hawk and the four white men. Hawk was standing with his legs spread, his rifle trained on the four men.

Castrell stood up then, a cup of coffee in one hand. "Take it easy, boy," he said affably. "Don't do anything you'll regret."

"I will not be sorry to kill you," Hawk replied. "It is better than you deserve."

"Dammit, boy, it was just a job. I told you that."

"You talk too much," Hawk said. Lifting his rifle to his shoulder, he sighted down the barrel.

"Hawk!"

Shadow's voice rang out in the heavy stillness.

"Do not try to stop me, neyho," Hawk said, not taking his eyes from Castrell.

"Do not be a fool," Shadow said. Dismounting, he went to stand beside Hawk. "What will you solve by killing these men? You said yourself they were doing a job they had been paid to do. If you want vengeance, why not find out who paid them?"

"I have asked this one," Hawk said, gesturing at Castrell. "He refuses to talk."

Shadow glanced at the three men still seated on the ground, and then he looked at Castrell, his eyes thoughtful.

"I will make you a deal," Shadow said to Castrell. "My son desires vengeance, and I wish to know who hired you. I think you and Hawk will fight. If you lose, you will tell my son who hired you. If you win, you can go your way. What say you?"

Castrell snorted derisively. "You must think I'm crazy. What's to stop you from killing me if I win?"

"I give you my word as a warrior that I will not touch you."

Castrell nodded. He had dealt with Indians in the past. Most of them were decent, honorable men.

"A fair fight," Shadow said. "I will hold your gunbelt, and those of your men."

Castrell nodded. A sharp word stilled the protests of his companions. Moments later, Hawk and Castrell stood across from each other. Castrell's men stood bunched together, their faces showing disapproval. Shadow stood across from them, their gunbelts slung over his shoulder, Hawk's rifle resting in the crook of his arm.

"Any time," Castrell told Hawk, and Hawk rushed toward him, his eagerness to draw blood making him careless. Castrell pivoted on his right heel, his fist catching Hawk along the side of the jaw as Hawk lunged past.

Shadow's face remained impassive as the two men came together in a rush. Hawk and Castrell were about the same size. Hawk was younger, Castrell had more experience. Castrell's men cheered loudly as Castrell drew first blood. Their cheers became more exuberant when it appeared that Castrell would win. And for a time it did seem as if the white man would win the fight. But then, as Hawk's rage cooled, he began to move more carefully, and the battle swung in his favor. Castrell was tiring now, and both men were bleeding from a profusion of cuts and lacerations. They came together in a vicious charge, fists lashing out, and then Hawk knocked Castrell off his feet and pinned him to the ground. His hands closed around the white man's throat, and for a moment every old hurt and slight Hawk had ever received burned in his brain, urging him to choke the life from the man struggling beneath him.

He remembered living at the San Carlos Reservation, being forced to stay in that horrid place because his father was Indian. Later they had moved to New York. He had been seven or eight then, and obliged to attend school. His teacher had refused to let him keep his Indian name. *"You're no longer a little savage running around on the reservation,"* Mr. Patten had said disdainfully. *"It is time you had a decent name like everyone else in class."*

He remembered going to his mother, his pride outraged because his teacher insisted he choose a white name. It was his mother who had suggested the name Hawk. Mr. Patten hadn't liked it much, but it *was* English.

And then there was Nelda Sprague, looking at him as though he were an inferior class of human because he was a half-breed. He recalled how Mary had told Nelda, in a proud tone, that the two of them were half Indian. Nelda's reply had been burned into Hawk's brain: *"Well, I wouldn't brag about it if I were you,"* she had replied scornfully. *"Everybody knows Indians are no good."* There had been so many times when people had looked down on him, judging him by the color of his skin, willing to think the worst of him because he was Cheyenne . . .

Abruptly he loosed his hold on Castrell and stood up. Killing the white man would not atone for the many abuses he had suffered in the past. It would only prove he was indeed a savage. Slowly he shook his head. Nothing could change the past, or restore the way of life that was gone forever.

He gazed out at the endless prairie, and it was as if all the old hates and hurts had never been. He glanced down at Castrell, who was sitting up massaging his throat, and he wondered why it had seemed so important to avenge himself on the man. Why was he here, his knuckles bruised, his nose and mouth bleeding, when he had a beautiful wife and two fine sons waiting for him at home?

He glanced up at the sky and there, drifting on the air currents, he saw a solitary hawk. For a moment he was transported back in time and he was fourteen again, alone in the hills to seek his vision. A yellow hawk had appeared to him, a hawk that had changed into a man with yellow hair. *"I am waiting for you,"* the hawk-man had said, and then it had turned around and walked away. And as it walked, it turned into a hawk again and disappeared into the sun. Shadow had interpreted the vision for him.

"In your heart, you are Cheyenne, but the day of the Indian is over. If you wish to survive in this land, you must do so as a white man. You may hold fast to our beliefs and to the qualities that make a man worthy to be a warrior and a Cheyenne, but you will not be able to live as an Indian. The man with the yellow hair is you, just as the hawk is you. The hawk-man is a symbol of your mixed blood."

With a last glance at Castrell, Hawk turned and swung aboard the blue roan. It was time to accept what the hawk had told him, time to admit that he was as much white as Indian, time to stop wishing for the past to return and accept the present. *"No one can destroy you except yourself,"* Shadow had told him long ago. Hawk knew now that his father had been right again. He had been so full of hate since his arrest for killing Lyman Carter, so filled with bitterness, that it had been eating him alive. But no more.

"Neyho," Hawk called cheerfully. "Let us go home. My woman is waiting for me, and it has been a long time since I gave her the attention she deserves."

"What of these men?" Shadow asked, perplexed by the sudden change in Hawk's attitude.

Hawk shrugged. "They are no longer of importance."

Shadow grinned at his son. He was not often surprised by what others did, but today he had been caught completely off-guard.

"Then let us go," Shadow said. Swinging up on Heyoka's bare back, he looked down at Castrell. "I would know the name of the man who paid you."

"Smythe," Castrell muttered. "Frank Smythe."

Shadow nodded. "Do not come to Bear Valley again," he warned. And dropping the gunbelts on the ground, he reined Heyoka into a rearing turn and rode after Hawk.

22

Victoria paced the house, anxiously wringing her hands. Hawk had gone out to kill four men in cold blood. She could not believe that the man she loved was capable of murder, and yet she had seen the look in his eye when he left the house just before dawn. His eyes, so dark and intense, had burned with a fierceness she had never seen before, and it frightened her. The fact that her husband was half Cheyenne had never bothered her, not been important. It was what he was, a part of him, and she accepted it, just as she accepted the color of his hair and eyes. It was what made him unique, a man apart. She had never thought of him as a savage, never understood why her parents had been so upset over her marriage. Now, for the first time, she had an inkling of what her father had meant when he had called Hawk a savage, for he had looked totally wild and uncivilized that morning.

She had begged him not to go, pleading, weeping, threatening to leave him if he walked out the door, but it had all been in vain.

"I am going," he had said curtly. "It is a thing I must do."

She had been afraid of him then, for the first time in her life. When he was ready to go, he had come to her, bending to kiss her good-bye, but she had turned away.

Now, abruptly it occurred to her that Hawk might be killed. She thought of all the awful things she had said to him, accusing him of not loving her, of caring more about his stupid honor than he did about his wife and children. A sob rose in her throat as she remembered how she had screamed at him and then refused to kiss him good-bye. What if he were killed? What if she never saw him again, never had a chance to apologize for the awful way she had treated him? How would she live with herself if he died, knowing that his last memory of her was of an angry wife who had behaved like a shrew? She hadn't even tried to understand how he felt.

If only he would come home, safe and unhurt. She would beg for his forgiveness, on her knees if necessary. Hawk was her whole life. She could not face the future without him by her side.

Hours passed, and her guilt grew, tormenting her until she was near tears. And then she heard the sound of hoofbeats in the yard.

"Hawk!" She breathed his name as she ran to the front door and flung it open.

And he was there, swinging down from his horse.

She gasped as he turned toward her. His face was badly bruised, one eye turning black, his lower lip swollen. There was blood on his shirt.

"Hawk!" She cried his name as she flew toward him, her feet hardly touching the ground.

"I am all right, Vickie," he said reassuringly.

"Your face—"

"I am all right. I got into a fight."

"With that man?"

"Yes."

"Is he . . . ?"

"No. I did not kill him."

Relief made her knees weak and she swayed against her husband. "Oh, thank God."

She clung to him as they walked into the house, her eyes never leaving his face. He was alive. Nothing else mattered.

They went into the kitchen and Victoria filled a bowl with warm water and bathed Hawk's face and hands. His knuckles were scraped and swollen, she noticed, and tried not to think about how they got that way.

"Does your eye hurt?" she asked anxiously.

"A little. I am all right, Vickie. Stop fussing over me and give me a kiss."

"Your mouth," she protested. "Your lip is cut."

He didn't waste time talking any more, but pulled her onto his lap and kissed her hungrily. He stroked her hair, liking the way the long strands curled around his fingers. He kissed her eyes and her cheeks, her nose and forehead and the slender curve of her throat before returning to her mouth. She was so sweet, and she tasted so good. Had he killed Castrell, he might have lost her forever.

"Hawk," Victoria protested as he stood up and carried her toward their bedroom. "It's the middle of the day."

Hawk smiled down at her. "Do you really mind?"

"No," she answered softly. "I want to."

His grin was a trifle smug as he stepped into their bedroom and closed the door.

Placing Vickie on the bed, Hawk closed the curtains, then stood there, just looking at her.

"Are you going to stand there gawking all day?" Victoria asked coyly. "The twins won't sleep forever."

Hawk laughed softly as he stretched out beside Vickie, his mouth claiming hers once more. What a charming little witch she was, wanton and yet shy, teasing one minute and surrendering the next.

Victoria returned Hawk's kiss, her mouth parting as his tongue slid across her lower lip. She loved his kisses, loved the way they made her feel, all warm and mushy inside, as if all her bones had turned to water. Loving him, touching him, it was all so wonderful that she sometimes felt guilty for being so happy. Her mother had warned her that the intimate side of marriage was something a woman had to endure for the sake of having children and to please her husband, or else he would visit prostitutes to satisfy his coarse needs and desires, but Vickie never "endured" Hawk's touch. Rather, she glorified in it, thrilling to his caresses, basking in the warmth of his love.

She sighed as he began to undress her, his hands moving slowly as they slid her dress over her shoulders. Bending, he kissed her neck, her shoulders and arms, his kisses butterfly light as they continued to fall over each newly exposed area of flesh. She shuddered with delight as his tongue flicked over her bare belly and breasts, and she began to unfasten his clothing, wanting to see him, to touch him as he was touching her.

"Vickie," he groaned. "You are so beautiful."

"You are—" she whispered, and choked back a sob when she saw the ugly bruises on his torso.

"What is it?" Hawk asked, frowning.

"You're hurt."

"It is nothing," he assured her.

"Hawk, I'm so sorry for this morning. I didn't mean those awful things I said. Please forgive me."

"There is nothing to forgive," Hawk said, kissing her cheek. "I was wrong, and I deserved just what I got." His arms drew her close. "I did not mean to frighten you. I swear it will never happen again."

She nodded, too close to tears to speak. He kissed her then, a fiercely passionate kiss that told her better than words how much he loved her. Their bodies strained together, flesh caressing flesh, until they became one and there was no more need for words . . .

Hawk was different in the days that followed. He was more relaxed, more at ease. Victoria had not realized before just how tense Hawk had been most of the time until the tension was gone. He smiled more readily now, and spent more time playing with his sons. They went into town more often, sometimes for no other reason than to have a soda at the drug store.

Victoria was stunned when Hawk suggested that they invite a few friends over for dinner, and even more surprised when he casually remarked that he thought he might go to church with her the following Sunday.

Hawk could be quite charming when he put his mind to it, and many of the young women in town began to understand why Victoria had married him. He was tall, dark, handsome, with a roguish smile that could melt a heart of stone.

Vickie was baking bread one afternoon when Hawk entered the kitchen whistling cheerfully. Turning, she let her mouth drop open in surprise, for there stood her husband in a new light blue shirt, black twill pants, and a black leather vest. The blue in his shirt perfectly complemented his dark eyes and hair, and she thought he was quite the most beautiful creature she had ever seen.

Hawk flushed a little under her openly admiring gaze. "What do you think?"

"You look wonderful." Vickie smiled up at him, her eyes twinkling merrily. "I see you kept your moccasins."

"Boots," Hawk said with a grimace. "I could never stand to wear them."

Vickie nodded. "But what's the occasion?"

"No occasion," Hawk replied with a shrug. "I just got tired of wearing buckskins all the time."

"I like your buckskins," Victoria said honestly. "But this is a nice change."

"I bought something for you, too," Hawk said, reaching into his shirt pocket. "I hope you like it."

With eager hands, Vickie unwrapped the small square package he offered her. Inside she found a lovely cameo on a delicate silver chain.

"It's lovely," she murmured. "Thank you, Hawk. Will you fasten the chain for me?"

His hands lightly caressed her neck as he fastened the chain. Bending, he kissed the top of her head, his hands squeezing her shoulders. "Ne-mehotatse, Vickie," he said quietly. "I love you. Forever."

"Forever," she repeated softly.

At church on Sunday, Victoria wondered if having Hawk there was such a good idea. Every unattached female in the building stared at Hawk. Of course, he *was* incredibly handsome, so she supposed she could not blame them for staring. But afterward, they all came by, ostensibly to say hello to Vickie and to admire the twins, but Vickie knew it was just an excuse to be near Hawk. Muriel Perkins was almost drooling, and Faye McKendrick just oozed with charm as she complimented Vickie on her dress, though her eyes never left Hawk's face.

Victoria was fuming as Hawk helped her into their carriage and then handed her the twins.

"Why are you scowling like that?" he asked, frowning.

"You know why," Victoria retorted.

"If I knew, I would not ask," Hawk said, his tone reasonable.

"It's you!" Vickie said, exasperated. "You're just too darned good-looking in that suit." She stamped her foot petulantly. "All those women drooling over you

Thrill to the most sensual, adventure-filled Historical Romances on the market today...

FROM  LEISURE BOOKS

As a home subscriber to the Leisure Historical Romance Book Club, you'll enjoy the best in today's BRAND-NEW Historical Romance fiction. For over twenty-five years, Leisure Books has brought you the award-winning, high-quality authors you know and love to read. Each Leisure Historical Romance will sweep you away to a world of high adventure...and intimate romance. Discover for yourself all the passion and excitement millions of readers thrill to each and every month.

SAVE AT LEAST $5.00 EACH TIME YOU BUY!

Each month, the Leisure Historical Romance Book Club brings you four brand-new titles from Leisure Books, America's foremost publisher of Historical Romances. EACH PACKAGE WILL SAVE YOU AT LEAST $5.00 FROM THE BOOKSTORE PRICE! And you'll never miss a new title with our convenient home delivery service.

Here's how we do it. Each package will carry a 10-DAY EXAMINATION privilege. At the end of that time, if you decide to keep your books, simply pay the low invoice price of $16.96 ($19.98 CANADA), no shipping or handling charges added.* HOME DELIVERY IS ALWAYS FREE.* With today's top Historical Romance novels selling for $5.99 and higher, our price SAVES YOU AT LEAST $5.00 with each shipment.

AND YOUR FIRST FOUR-BOOK SHIPMENT IS TOTALLY FREE!*

IT'S A BARGAIN YOU CAN'T BEAT! A Super $21.96 Value!

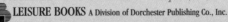 LEISURE BOOKS A Division of Dorchester Publishing Co., Inc.

GET YOUR 4 FREE* BOOKS NOW—
A $21.96 VALUE!

Mail the Free* Books
Certificate
Today!

4 FREE* BOOKS 🌸 A $21.96 VALUE

Free Books Certificate*

YES! I want to subscribe to the Leisure Historical Romance Book Club. Please send me my 4 FREE* BOOKS. Then, each month I'll receive the four newest Leisure Historical Romance selections to preview for 10 days. If I decide to keep them, I will pay the Special Member's Only discounted price of just $4.24 each, a total of $16.96 ($19.98 in Canada). This is a SAVINGS OF AT LEAST $5.00 off the bookstore price. There are no shipping, handling, or other charges.* There is no minimum number of books I must buy and I may cancel the program at any time. In any case, the 4 FREE* BOOKS are mine to keep—A BIG $21.96 Value!

*In Canada, add $7.95 US shipping and handling per order for first shipment. For all subsequent shipments to Canada the cost of membership in the Book Club is $19.98 US plus $7.95 US shipping and handling per order. All payments must be made in US dollars.

Name _____

Address _____

City _____

State _____ *Zip* _____

Telephone _____

Signature _____

If under 18, Parent or Guardian must sign. Terms, prices and conditions subject to change. Subscription subject to acceptance. Leisure Books reserves the right to reject any order or cancel any subscription.

Get Four Books Totally
F R E E* —
A $21.96 Value!

PLEASE RUSH
MY FOUR FREE*
BOOKS TO ME
RIGHT AWAY!

Leisure Historical Romance Book Club
P.O. Box 6613
Edison, NJ 08818-6613

AFFIX
STAMP
HERE

like they've never seen a man before. It was disgusting."

"Oh," Hawk said gravely. "It could not be that you are a tiny bit jealous?"

"Jealous? Me? Of course not."

"Good, because you have nothing to be jealous of."

"Don't I?"

"Vickie, you know there is no one else for me. Only you."

"I know," Victoria said, smiling sheepishly. "I'm sorry." It wasn't his fault he was so handsome, or that he looked so wonderful in a suit of dark gray broadcloth.

"I know how you can make it up to me," Hawk mused, flashing a roguish grin.

"Do you?" Vickie asked saucily.

"Yes, ma'am. And I will show you, just as soon as the twins go down for a nap."

And he did.

23

We all noticed the change in Hawk, and I saw that it wrought a change in Victoria as well. She smiled more often, and the worry that had often lurked in the depths of her clear azure eyes vanished as though it had never been. Women who had once gone out of their way to avoid my son began to find him charming, and men who had once looked at him suspiciously began to feel he could be trusted after all. Hawk, it seemed, could be quite captivating and friendly when it suited him.

"Are you sure you've told me everything that happened between Hawk and Castrell?" I asked Shadow. "Are you certain you didn't leave anything out?"

"I have told you everything," Shadow assured me.

"Then what caused the sudden change in our son?"

"I think that when he was on the brink of killing Castrell, our son came face to face with himself and he did not like what he saw."

"I don't understand."

"You cannot be a whole man when your heart is filled with hate. It eats away at you, and soon you hate yourself as well as everyone else. I think that for the first time in his life he accepted the fact that he is part white as well as Cheyenne, and that being half white does not make him less of a man, or less of a warrior."

"What are you going to do about Frank Smythe?"

Shadow shrugged. "I sent him a letter. I told him I knew what he had done, and that it would be wise for him to stay in Chicago. I told him that whatever was wrong with his marriage had nothing to do with Cloud Walker."

"Do you think Frank will heed your advice?"

Shadow smiled. "If he is wise, he will stay in Chicago. Personally, I hope he comes back to Bear Valley."

"Shadow, you wouldn't—"

"Kill him? No. I would just rough him up a little."

"Shadow!"

"I am only making a joke," he said. But I was not so sure.

All was peaceful in our home once more. Cloud Walker recovered rapidly, due in part to Mary's

devoted attention. She was at his side every minute
she could spare, talking to him, reading to him,
bringing him gourmet meals to tempt his appetite, as
well as the sweet treats he loved. She brought
Katherine in to visit him often, and the two became
good friends. Cloud Walker soon became Katherine's
favorite person besides her mother, and she laughed
and smiled for him more than for anyone else.

When Cloud Walker felt like getting out of bed,
Mary was there for him to lean on. They took many
short walks outside, for Cloud Walker could not long
abide being cooped up. Bundled in warm coats, wool
scarves, gloves, and hats, they strolled in the yard,
oblivious to the cold and the snow, lost in the warmth
of the love growing between them.

Mary fretted over what to give Cloud Walker for a
Christmas present, and I remarked that he could use a
new pair of moccasins, for his were badly worn.

The idea appealed to Mary, and she set out to
make him a pair. I helped her cut them out and
showed her how to stitch them together, and she spent
several hours sewing them, and then decorating them
with colored beads. When she was finished, they were
well-made and quite handsome. I knew Cloud Walker
would be pleased. It occurred to me that Shadow could
also use a new pair of moccasins, and so I spent part of
one morning cutting and sewing a pair for my husband.
Shadow refused to wear any other kind of footwear,
insisting that the shoes of the white man were stiff and
uncomfortable, and he was always in need of new
moccasins, for they wore out quickly. But these would

be special, and not for everyday. The hide I used for the upper part of the moccassins had been tanned and bleached until it was the color of cream. When the moccasins were stitched together, I decorated them with porcupine quills dyed red.

In mid-December Cloud Walker moved back into the Cheyenne lodge behind our house, but he spent a good deal of time with us. Katherine cooed and gurgled in his arms, and Mary's face glowed with that inner happiness that shines through when a woman is truly in love.

Frank continued to be stubborn about a divorce, and I knew it was hard for Mary and Cloud Walker to spend so much time together without being able to consummate their love. I often saw them standing close together under the trees, their arms linked around each other, and I wondered how much longer Mary could remain physically faithful to Frank Smythe. In a way, it seemed foolish to deny herself the joy of Cloud Walker's touch. I knew that in her heart, Mary had already betrayed her husband many times, and I thought that the Cheyenne had the right idea about divorce. Perhaps it wasn't moral or ethical according to the laws of the white man, but it was eminently more practical.

On Christmas Eve, we each picked one gift to exchange just before bedtime. Cloud Walker and Shadow were pleased with their new footwear, each declaring a perfect fit. I was delighted with Shadow's gift to me, a dainty silver locket on a fine silver chain.

Inside were pictures of Hawk and Victoria, and Mary and Blackie. Shadow refused to have his picture taken. It seemed strange that after so many years of living with my people he could still be superstitious, but on this one point he refused to budge, no matter how I pleaded. I argued that Geronimo had had his picture taken many times, that the old warrior even sold photographs of himself to earn money, but still Shadow refused, arguing stubbornly that he did not want his likeness captured inside the white man's black box.

"You will have to come outside for your present," Cloud Walker told Mary, so we all bundled up and trooped outside and there, tethered to the hitch rail, stood the leopard Appaloosa filly.

"For me?" Mary breathed in wonder.

Cloud Walker nodded. "She is my gift to you."

"Oh, Cloud Walker," Mary squealed in delight, and threw her arms around his neck.

"You said you'd never sell that mare," I whispered to Shadow as we went back into the house.

Shadow winked at me. "True, she no longer belongs to me, but she is still in the family. And when she is ready to be bred, I think Mary will want Smoke to be the sire."

"And you'll buy the foal."

"Perhaps," Shadow said, shrugging nonchalantly.

Later we sang Christmas carols and drank hot apple cider. We had bought Blackie a book on veterinary medicine, and he read it until he fell asleep.

Hawk and Victoria had gone to spend the evening with Vickie's mother and the Reverend Brighton. I missed having them at our place, but I couldn't blame Victoria for wanting to spend some time with her mother. Their relationship was growing closer and stronger, and I was glad. We would see Hawk and Vickie and the twins tomorrow at Pa's.

We had a lovely Christmas that year. Shadow surprised me with the best present of all by announcing that he was coming to church with us. I was certain he was only teasing me until he appeared in the parlor dressed in his dark suit and tie.

"Shall we go?" he asked, and taking my arm, he led me outside and helped me into the buggy. Cloud Walker was outside waiting for us. It seemed he, too, was going to church. He didn't own a suit, but he looked quite presentable in a pair of whipcord trousers and a white shirt. Cloud Walker helped Mary into the buggy, handed the baby to me, and teased Blackie about his slicked-back hair as he took a seat beside Mary.

"All set?" Shadow asked, glancing around.

"All set," we answered in unison, and he clucked to the team and we were on our way.

Our family caused quite a stir as we entered the chapel. Shadow had never attended church before and there was a great deal of nudging and whispering as we took a place near the back of the church. A few minutes later Hawk arrived, accompanied by Vickie and the twins. I looked at Shadow, and he grinned at me.

"Merry Christmas, Hannah," he said, smiling merrily. "Your whole family is here today."

I nodded, too overcome with emotion to speak.

"Are you pleased?"

"It's the best present I've ever had."

I felt my throat swell with tears as I gazed at each member of my family, and I had never been happier. The church had never looked more beautiful. The single stained-glass window behind the altar glowed with color as the sun came shining through, highlighting the picture of the Good Shepherd. The hymns we sang that day had never sounded sweeter, and the Christmas story touched me as never before.

I gazed at my two sons and my daughter, at my three lovely grandchildren, and felt my heart swell with love for my own children, and for the Virgin Mary's blessed son.

Shadow sat beside me, my hand enfolded in his, and when I looked up at him, my heart was so filled with love I thought it might burst.

"And she brought forth her firstborn son," the Reverend Brighton began, "and wrapped him in swaddling clothes and laid him in a manger; because there was no room for them in the inn. And there was in the same country shepherds abiding in the field, keeping watch over their flock by night. And, lo, the angel of the Lord came upon them, and the glory of the Lord shone round about them: and they were sore afraid. And the angel said unto them, Fear not: for behold, I bring you good tidings of great joy, which shall be to all people. For unto you is born this day in the city of David a Savior, which is Christ the Lord . . ."

After the service we spent a few minutes visiting

with our friends, wishing them all a Merry Christmas. Hawk, Shadow, and Cloud Walker stood together, looking a trifle uncomfortable as nearly the entire congregation came to greet them.

"Well, what did you think of it?" I asked Shadow on our way home.

Shadow shrugged. "It was . . . interesting."

"Interesting?"

Shadow nodded. "Perhaps someday I will read your Bible again. I think I would like to know more about the man called Jesus."

Smiling, I squeezed Shadow's arm. He had read our Bible many years ago when my mother was teaching him to read and write. Shadow had been a voracious reader back then. He had read everything he could lay his hands on: the labels on tin cans, old newspapers, my adventure books, a volume of Shakespeare that neither of us understood, my mother's cookbooks, and Pa's mail-order catalog. In the years since then, he had not had much time or inclination for reading. I made a mental note to make sure our family Bible was left on the nightstand that night, just in case Shadow felt the urge to read it.

At home we changed out of our church clothes and ate a leisurely lunch before getting ready to go to Pa's house.

Mary helped me clean up the kitchen while Shadow, Blackie, and Cloud Walker went out to check on the stock and hitch up the team.

It was fun having Mary home again. We laughed and talked as we did the dishes, trying to guess what we were getting for Christmas, remarking on the outrageous bonnet Lydia had worn to church, expressing our happiness at having the men attend church with us.

"I thought the roof was going to cave in," Mary mused, "the way everyone stared at neyho and Cloud Walker."

"Yes," I agreed. "This is one Christmas that the whole town will remember."

We sang Christmas carols on the way to Pa's house, laughing as our breath came out in great clouds of white vapor. The countryside was exquisite. The land and the trees were covered in pristine white, making the whole world look virginal and new.

Pa's house rang with happy laughter as our family got together. I had never seen so many presents in my life, and the parlor floor was littered with boxes and paper and brightly colored ribbons by the time all the gifts had been opened and admired: numerous toys for Katherine and the twins, a dainty gold watch for Victoria, a fur muff for Mary, a new shirt for Cloud Walker, a rifle for Hawk, a set of Charles Dickens for Rebecca, a skinning knife for Blackie, a rocking chair for Pa to relax in, a lovely blue shawl for me, a buckskin jacket for Shadow, and on and on. Katherine played happily with the wrappings, her gifts untouched.

"We could have given her empty boxes," Pa lamented good-naturedly. "Could have saved a heap of money."

The twins, now two years old, were into everything. They chased each other through the house, played hide-and-seek under the dining table, and generally made nuisances of themselves until Victoria put them down for a nap.

Vickie and I went into the kitchen to help Rebecca prepare dinner. The kitchen was fragrant with the heavenly aroma of baking turkey and mincemeat pie. I peeled potatoes while Vickie made gravy and Rebecca rolled out a mess of biscuits.

The twins woke up in time to eat and we laughed and talked around the dinner table between bites of turkey and sweet potatoes, beans, mashed potatoes, stuffing, and biscuits dripping with butter and honey.

After dinner we each took a turn at saying something nice about the person sitting next to them.

Pa declared Blackie was the best horse midwife he had ever seen. Rebecca pronounced Hawk the owner of the handsomest smile. Victoria said Shadow was the wisest man she had ever known. Cloud Walker said Mary was the best medicine a sick man could hope for. Shadow said I was the best wife a warrior could ever have. Blackie said Cloud Walker was almost as good with horses as his father.

"A high compliment indeed," Cloud Walker murmured, pleased.

Hawk said Vickie was the prettiest pregnant woman he had ever seen, and we all gasped at this unexpected piece of good news.

"When's the baby due?" Rebecca asked.

"August," Vickie replied, smiling at Hawk.

"We'll have to build a bigger house soon," Pa said

with a sigh. "We're outgrowing this one."

"I know," Rebecca said, grinning happily. "Isn't it wonderful?"

It was a lovely day. After pie and coffee, we gathered around the fireplace to sing Christmas carols. I stood beside Shadow, my arm around his waist, silently thanking God for the health and happiness that filled my father's house, and praying that the future would only bring more of the same.

24

January 1, 1900, blew in on the heels of a severe snowstorm that kept us all indoors. Blackie was content to sit on the sofa, his nose buried in his veterinary book. Cloud Walker and Mary sat on the floor in front of a cheery fire, dreaming the dreams that all young lovers dream. I sat at the opposite end of the sofa from Blackie, a pile of mending in my lap. And Shadow paced. He hated being cooped up in the house, and he prowled from room to room like a caged tiger, growling at everyone.

"How do you stand him?" Mary asked, grinning at me as Shadow stomped through the parlor on his way to the kitchen. "Doesn't he drive you crazy?"

"Sometimes," I admitted. "But he's always hated to be shut in, always abhorred small spaces."

It was shortly after noon when Shadow pulled on a heavy sheepskin jacket and went outside—to check on the stock, he said, but we all knew it was just an excuse to get out of the house.

I gazed out the window watching the snow fall. It was beautiful. As far as I could see, the earth was covered with a blanket of white. It was 1900, I thought. Imagine. I picked up a newspaper and thumbed through it. An article by Chauncey Depew, a man who had formerly been a railroad president and was now a junior United States Senator, was quoted as saying, "There is not a man here who does not feel 400 percent bigger in 1900 than he did in 1896, bigger intellectually, bigger patriotically, bigger in the breast from the fact that he is a citizen of a country that has become a world power for peace, for civilization, and for the expansion of its industries and the products of its labor."

In the same article, the Reverend Newell D. Hillis, pastor of Brooklyn's Plymouth Church, was quoted as saying, "Laws are becoming more just, rulers humane, music is becoming sweeter and books wiser; homes are happier, and the individual heart becoming at once more just and more gentle."

I frowned as I read that. There had been cries of outrage when President Roosevelt invited Booker T. Washington, the country's most famous Negro, to dine at the White House. Negroes were not allowed to vote. Of course, neither were Indians. I wondered if the Cheyenne cooped up on the reservation would find the laws more just, their homes happier, their rulers more humane. The changing times had done little to ease the misery of life on the reservation. Were we, indeed, more just and more gentle? There were still outlaws roaming the West. Butch Cassidy and the Wild Bunch were robbing trains. The Apache warrior, Geronimo, was still alive. I smiled as I thought of him. We had lived with Geronimo for a time, Shadow and I. It seemed so long ago that we had lived in an Apache wickiup deep in the wilds of the Sierra Madre mountains. So long ago. In 1894 Geronimo had been sent to Fort Sill, Oklahoma, where he attempted farming for a short time, but the Apaches had never been farmers and Geronimo began selling souvenir bows and arrows and pictures of himself to the tourists. It was sad, I thought, that a man who had once been a great leader had been reduced to selling trinkets, that a man who had once roamed the whole Southwest should be forced to spend his last days under the watchful eye of federal troops.

Turning the pages in the paper, I saw advertisements for various household goods and then, on the next page, a pen-and-ink sketch of a horseless carriage. It was a rather ugly contraption, I decided, said to be loud and dirty as it lumbered along coughing smoke and frightening horses and young children. A short paragraph beneath the picture stated there were twelve companies manufacturing automobiles of one kind or another, and it was predicted that the automobile would make the horse and buggy obsolete.

With a sigh I put the newspaper aside. I wasn't sure I cared for progress. Rising, I went to the closet and pulled out my long heavy coat, a scarf, and a pair of fur-lined gloves. Bundled up, I went outside to look for Shadow.

His tracks were clear in the snow and I followed them, taking long strides so I could place my feet in Shadow's footprints. The trail took me around the house and then to the barn. As I opened the heavy door, I heard Shadow's voice.

"Easy, girl," he was saying. "Easy now."

I smiled as I realized that one of the mares was foaling. She was a young mare who had been bred early and was giving birth several months before the other mares, who were due to deliver in the spring.

"How's she doing?" I asked.

"All right, I think. I cannot tell how long she has been in labor."

For the next hour we sat side by side watching the mare. Once, she scrambled to her feet and walked around for a few minutes; then, very slowly, she lowered herself to the ground again, her legs sticking straight out in front of her, her sides heaving.

"Poor thing," I murmured. "I know just how you feel."

When Shadow decided that the mare had been in labor too long, he washed his hands and forearms and then, while I watched in amazement, he reached inside the mare, his arm disappearing to the elbow.

"The foal is not in the right position," Shadow remarked, his brow furrowed. "I am going to try to turn it around."

I held my breath as Shadow attempted to turn the foal. The mare remained quiet, her ears flicking back and forth as Shadow murmured to her in soft Cheyenne.

"There!" Shadow exclaimed, and withdrew his hand.

Moments later, two tiny feet emerged, followed by a tiny black muzzle. Another push, and the foal was partly expelled. The mare rested a moment, then gave another push, and the foal was free of the birth canal. The mare whickered to her baby as she reached around to nuzzle it, and I marveled at the beautiful miracle of birth.

A few minutes later the mare scrambled to her feet, expelling the afterbirth. Later, Shadow would check the delicate membrane to make sure none of it had been left inside the mare to cause infection.

We laughed with delight as the newborn foal attempted to stand. It was a filly, solid black save for one white stocking on her left foreleg. The mare made soft encouraging noises as the filly tried to stand, and eventually the foal managed to get all four legs under herself at the same time and maintain her balance. Shadow dried the filly with a piece of soft toweling, and then the filly began to nurse.

Shadow put his arm around my shoulders as we stood there, basking in the joy of a new life.

"Blackie will be sorry he missed this," I mused. "We should have called him."

"No," Shadow said. "This was a moment for the two of us to share alone."

"Happy new year, my husband," I murmured.

"Happy new year, my woman," Shadow replied,

and bending down, he kissed me, a long lingering kiss that made me forget the cold and the snow and everything else but the joy I found in his arms.

Returning to the house, I saw that Blackie had fallen asleep over his book. Cloud Walker and Mary were wrapped in each other's arms, gazing rapturously into each other's eyes. So engrossed were they with each other that they were not even aware of our presence until Shadow noisily cleared his throat. Immediately the two young lovers drew apart. Cloud Walker met our eyes boldly, but Mary glanced away, her cheeks scarlet.

Cloud Walker gave Mary's shoulder a squeeze and then stood up. I could see by his expression that he was expecting a severe tongue-lashing from Shadow, or perhaps a well-deserved punch in the nose. Neither was forthcoming.

Instead, Shadow smiled at Cloud Walker, his expression one of understanding and compassion. "It is hard to be a warrior," Shadow said quietly. "Especially when one is young and his blood is on fire."

Cloud Walker nodded. Taking Mary's hand, he helped her to her feet. "I love Mary with all my heart," he said sincerely. "But I am not made of iron."

"I feel the same," Mary added proudly. "What are we going to do?"

"That is something the two of you must decide," Shadow answered with a shake of his head. "Cloud Walker is a grown man. You are a grown woman, with a child to think of. You must make your own decisions. Only remember, the decisions you make now will affect not only your lives, but the lives of those who love you and depend on you. What I would do, what I think you should do, may not be right for you."

"What would you do, neyho?" Mary persisted. "Please tell me. I need to know."

"I would take my happiness when and where I could find it," Shadow replied honestly. "But I do not have a young child to consider. And when I first took your mother, she did not have a husband waiting for her."

"Thank you, neyho," Mary said quietly. "Good night."

She walked Cloud Walker to the door and kissed him on the cheek. "Good night."

Cloud Walker nodded and left the house.

I put my arm around Shadow's waist as we watched Mary go to her room. "Do you think they'll wait?"

Shadow grinned wryly. "Do you?"

"No."

In February Mattie Smythe came to call. She was all aflutter when I opened the door, her face flushed, her eyes fever bright.

"Mattie, what is it?" I cried in alarm. "Are you all right?"

"We're going to Chicago!" Mattie exclaimed, waving a sheet of paper in my face. "Frank is rich! Oh, my, let me sit down. Here, read this."

My eyes quickly scanned the letter. Frank was indeed rich. He had made several prudent investments in some railroad stock and some oil stock, and both had paid off far beyond his wildest dreams. He was, in short, close to being a millionaire.

"Isn't it wonderful?" Mattie said. "He's buying a house for us next to the new one he's building for himself, and he wants all of us to come and live in Chicago. David is quitting his job at the mercantile so he can go with us. Oh, I just can't believe it! Oh, I almost forgot," Mattie said, digging into her skirt pocket. "Here's a letter for Mary. Well, I've got to go now. I've got so much to do. Give my love to the family."

Mary's letter read much the same as Mattie's. Frank was rich. He was building a mansion to rival that of the Vanderbilts and the Goulds, and he wanted Mary to share it with him.

Mary fretted over Frank's letter for days.

"I don't love Frank," she confided to me late one wintry evening. "Maybe I never did. I don't know. I think I just wanted to play house and Frank seemed to fit the role of dutiful husband. Oh, nahkoa, I'm so confused. Sometimes I think I should go back to Frank and make the best of it. He is Katherine's father, after all. But then I remember how he looked at her the day she was born, and how often he's been unfaithful to me, and I hate him. And then there's Cloud Walker. I love him, nahkoa, and I want to be with him always."

My heart ached for Mary. We talked far into the night, and in the morning Mary wrote to Frank, congratulating him on his success, but she made no mention of returning to Chicago.

A few days later Shadow brought home a Chicago newspaper. Frank's name was in the headlines in bold black print. The headline read: FRANK SMYTHE,

FORMER RESIDENT OF BEAR VALLEY, FINDS
SUCCESS IN CHICAGO

Below, next to his picture, was a long story on how
Frank had moved to Chicago and made his fortune.
The article went into detail about the mansion he was
building, and how he was bringing his parents to
Chicago to share his wealth. There was a brief paragraph stating that his wife, the former Mary Kincaid,
had returned to her hometown to care for her aged
mother, who was quite ill and in need of constant
attention.

"So that's how he explains Mary's extended ab-
sence," I exclaimed angrily. "She's home tending her
ailing mother! That cad. Why doesn't he just tell the
truth?"

Shadow laughed, his dark eyes glowing with
amusement. "Do not overtax yourself," he teased.
"Anger is not wise in one with ailing health."

"Oh, shut up!"

When Mary read the article, she just shook her
head. "I never knew Frank had so much pride. I guess
he just can't bear for anyone to think his marriage
could be in trouble."

"I can't imagine anyone believing that a wife
would stay away from her husband for so long without
at least going back for a visit," I muttered. "Aged
mother, indeed!"

News of Frank's good fortune spread throughout
the valley. There was a going-away party for the
Smythes in March, and practically everybody in Bear
Valley was invited. Mary refused to attend.

"I don't want everybody staring at me and wondering why Frank and I have separated," Mary explained. "And I especially don't want to listen to Mattie telling me my place is with my husband. Just give them my best and tell them I'll miss them."

A few days later a wire arrived at our house, the first we had ever received. It was for Cloud Walker and it carried sad news. His mother was ill, perhaps dying.

Cloud Walker began to pack immediately. His mother was all the family he had left.

"Is there anything I can do?" Mary asked.

"Yes," Cloud Walker answered hesitantly. "Come with me."

"To the reservation?"

Cloud Walker nodded. "I would like you to meet my mother. And I would like her to meet you."

Mary looked at me. "Is it all right?" she asked. "Would you mind watching Katherine while I'm gone?"

"Of course not. Come along, I'll help you pack."

25

They had been traveling most of the day. Mary, mounted on the leopard Apaloosa filly, rode behind Cloud Walker. He was riding a barrel-chested gray gelding he had borrowed from Shadow. The horse was big and raw-boned, and it picked its way through the snowdrifts with ease, leaving a trail that was easy for the filly to follow.

Mary's thoughts were mixed as they rode along. She was glad for a chance to be alone with Cloud Walker, yet a little afraid of what might happen between them. She was determined to remain physically faithful to Frank, yet she doubted her ability to do so for much longer. The attraction she felt for Cloud Walker grew stronger each day, as did the love she felt for him. He was such a good man, kind and caring, strong and reliable, with a deep sense of pride in who and what he was.

She gazed at his back, ramrod straight, and wondered if she was hoping, deep inside, that he would be able to crumble her resistance once they were alone together. Wasn't that why she had been so eager to accompany him? In her heart she knew it was, though she was loath to admit it even to herself.

With an effort she turned her thoughts from Cloud Walker and tried to imagine what his mother would be like. He had never mentioned that his mother was still alive, and Mary had assumed he was alone in the world. One thing she was not looking forward to was returning to the reservation. The short time she had spent on reservations as a child had been time enough.

At dusk Cloud Walker drew rein in the shelter of a tall bluff. Dismounting, he lifted Mary to the ground, then unsaddled their horses. Hobbling the mare and the gelding, he turned them loose to find what forage they could.

Mary cast about for something to say, but nothing came to mind. Picking up Cloud Walker's saddlebags, she began to rummage around inside for the cooking utensils. She was acutely aware of Cloud Walker standing behind her, and of the fact that they were alone out in the middle of the prairie. Quite alone.

Her hands were trembling as she laid a fire, filled the coffee pot with water from her canteen, and began to prepare dinner. Night came quickly, surrounding them in a cozy cocoon of darkness, with only the faint glow of their campfire for light.

"I hope you're hungry," Mary said, handing Cloud Walker a plate filled with meat and potatoes.

Cloud Walker nodded. His hand brushed Mary's as he took the plate she offered him, and the mere touch of her flesh on his caused his heart to pound. How could he be alone with her for three nights? Asking her to accompany him to the reservation had been a mistake, he could see that now. He could not ride with her, talk to her, sleep across the fire from her, and not touch her. He was only a man of flesh and blood, not a man of stone.

They ate in silence, the tension between them almost crackling. Mary kept her eyes on her plate, afraid to look up, afraid that Cloud Walker would see the desire that was surely shining in her eyes. She tried to think about Katherine, tried to remember that she was a married woman, but all she could think about was being out on the prairie alone with Cloud Walker.

When dinner was over, Cloud Walker rose quickly to his feet. "I am going to scout around," he said gruffly, and taking up his rifle, he left the campfire.

Mary breathed a sigh of relief when he was gone. She hurriedly washed and dried their few dishes, spread their bedrolls on either side of the campfire, then crawled into her blankets and closed her eyes, willing herself to sleep.

But sleep would not come. She tossed and turned for several minutes and then curled into a tight ball, determined to relax. She did not hear Cloud Walker return, but she knew instantly that he was there. From beneath the veil of her lashes she glanced across the

campfire, saw him remove his heavy buckskin shirt.
His skin was the color of dark bronze in the faint glow
of the dying fire, the muscles in his arms and chest
clearly outlined as he moved. His long black hair fell
over his shoulders.

Mary's mouth went dry as she watched him
stretch. How like a wild Cheyenne warrior he looked
in the afterglow of the fire. Never had he looked more
handsome, more virile, than he did now with the faint
light of the coals dancing over his face and the
darkness spread out behind him. A queer little tingle
started in the pit of her stomach as she watched him
take a last look around their camp before crawling
under his blankets. Her heart was beating so hard she
was surprised he could not hear it. When, at last, sleep
came, her dreams were filled with images of Cloud
Walker holding her, touching her, kissing her . . .

They rose early after a restless night. Mary
prepared a hasty breakfast while Cloud Walker watered the horses at a nearby stream. After breakfast,
Mary washed and dried the dishes and secured their
bedrolls while Cloud Walker saddled the horses.

Mary felt better when they were on the trail
again. The prairie spread before them for seemingly
endless miles, a vast white expanse of gently rolling
hills and stands of dense timber. Overhead the sky was
a clear bright blue.

In the old days the Indians would have been holed
up in the Black Hills, seeking shelter in the steep
canyons where the high walls blocked the cold winter
wind. Her mother had told her of the symbols and
pictures etched on the walls, drawn by various bands

to record their history or point the way to convenient campsites and waterholes. Mary had never seen the Black Hills, which were not hills at all but mountains, but her mother had told her of their beauty, of the elk and deer, bobcats and bears, mountain lions and golden eagles that made their home in the hills and canyons. She had a sudden yearning to see the sacred hills, to stand on ground where Indians had once lived, to see the land where her father had once roamed.

As the hours slipped by, Mary began to feel as if they were the only two people left in all the world. Once she saw a fox trotting across the trackless prairie, but that was the only sign of life she saw all that day.

At dusk Cloud Walker drew rein in a stand of timber and they made camp for the night. Mary was determined that they would not have to endure the awful silence of the night before.

"Tell me about your mother," she said after dinner. "What is she like?"

"Gentle," Cloud Walker answered, staring into the flames. "Gentle, but not weak. She raised me after my father died."

"What happened to your father?"

"He was killed at the Greasy Grass."

"My father was there, too," Mary remarked.

Cloud Walker nodded. "I wish I had been old enough to fight. I wish our people had never surrendered."

Mary smiled sympathetically. "You sound just like Hawk," Mary mused, "but it doesn't do any good to dwell on what can't be. My father taught me that. No one yearns for the old days as much as he does, but he doesn't waste time looking back. To survive, you have to go forward."

"It is easier for a woman."

"I guess so, though I don't understand why you men are all so eager to fight. War only brings death and heartache."

"So does life on the reservation," Cloud Walker retorted bitterly. "The Cheyenne are a proud people. Our men are brave and wise. They are not children, yet we are treated as though we cannot take care of ourselves. The Indian agent tells us what to do and what to wear. They are trying to turn us into white men. They take the children from the reservation and send them away to school. They cut their hair, and punish them if they speak the Cheyenne language. They want our men to be farmers, but we are not farmers. We are hunters. Our old people grow sick and die. Our young men drink too much firewater because it helps them forget they are no longer warriors."

Cloud Walker stared into the darkness. "Our people get sick, and no one cares. If that Army doctor had come just a little sooner, Prairie Grass Woman would still be alive, and my child with her. But he would not come, and now they are dead. Now my mother is ill. Perhaps she, too, is dead by now."

Mary's heart ached for the sadness in Cloud Walker's voice, for the naked hurt in his dark eyes. Rising, she walked around the fire and knelt beside him, her arm going around his shoulders in a gesture of comfort and understanding.

Slowly Cloud Walker turned to face her, and for a timeless moment their eyes met and held. And then, ever so slowly, his head moved toward hers.

He's going to kiss me, Mary thought, and even as the idea crossed her mind, his lips were touching hers. Heat suffused Mary from head to foot as Cloud Walker's mouth crushed hers. His arms held her close, so close she could scarcely breathe. His body was trembling with desire, and she had no thought to resist.

She was breathless when he took his lips from her.

"Mary." His desire for her was there in the throaty whisper of his voice as he murmured her name. She saw the love and the wanting in his eyes, and she swayed toward him. She had said no for too long. Tonight she would follow her heart.

Cloud Walker's pulse quickened as he realized that she wanted him as he wanted her. For the space of a heartbeat, neither one moved. And then, ever so slowly, Cloud Walker began to unfasten Mary's shirt. Mary's throat went dry as he slipped the soft flannel material from her shoulders. She shivered as the cool air touched her skin and Cloud Walker pulled her against him, letting his body heat warm her as he removed the rest of her clothing and then his own. In moments they were lying side by side, their bodies pressed together.

Mary was surprised by the desperate yearning that Cloud Walker's kisses aroused. Once, she had thought herself frigid because Frank's caresses had left her cold and unmoved, but now she was on fire. Her eager hands roamed over Cloud Walker's flesh, wanting to explore every inch, wanting to memorize every plane and hollow. His breath came hard and fast as her hands wandered over his body, and then it was his turn and Mary gasped with delight as his fingers danced over her breasts and belly and thighs. His lips kissed her face and breasts, his tongue stroked her belly until she cried out with sweet pain, begging him to possess her.

They came together in a rush of sweat-sheened flesh and breathless kisses, and Mary knew this was what she had been wanting ever since the first time she saw Cloud Walker. His whispered words of love washed over her, making her feel cherished and adored. She wrapped her arms around his neck, certain she would perish if he did not release the flood of desire raging within her. "Now," she urged, and shuddered with wanton delight as Cloud Walker's life poured into her, filling her with sweet warmth and a feeling of utter contentment.

Locked in each other's arms, they did not move for fear of breaking the magical spell between them. Mary had thought to feel ashamed, but she felt only peace, a sense of coming home after a long, dark journey in a foreign land. At last she was where she belonged.

Cloud Walker smiled down at her. "Am I not heavy?"

"Yes, very," Mary admitted. "But it is a wonderful burden."

Cloud Walker chuckled softly as he rolled onto his side, carrying Mary with him so that they lay facing each other, their bodies still united. Mary gazed into Cloud Walker's fathomless black eyes and knew that from that moment on her life would be forever entwined with his. Where he went, she would go. What he wanted, she would want.

"Ne-mehotatse," Cloud Walker murmured, and Mary knew she had never heard a more beautiful word.

"Ne-mehotatse," Mary replied softly.

With a sigh of contentment, Cloud Walker reached down and grabbed a blanket. Draping it over them, he kissed Mary lightly on the cheek. In moments they were asleep in each other's arms.

Mary could not stop smiling the next day. Every time she thought of how Cloud Walker had made love to her, she was filled with a warm glow. He loved her, and the very thought made her feel beautiful and desirable and wonderful. They could not seem to stop touching each other. Cloud Walker paused to rest the horses frequently, and each halt occasioned a kiss or a hug or a quick intimate caress. Mary secretly counted the hours until nightfall, eagerly anticipating another night in Cloud Walker's arms.

At bedtime her eagerness turned to shyness and she spread their bedrolls on opposite sides of the fire. Perhaps Cloud Walker was not as anxious as she to make love again. The thought hurt, but she did not want to seem too eager, too pushy, too possessive.

Cloud Walker frowned at her when he came back from watering the horses and saw their blankets spread so far apart.

"Have you tired of me already?" he mused, one black eyebrow arching upward.

"No," Mary said, finding it hard to speak. "I . . . I didn't know if you'd want to . . . if you wanted . . . me."

"Mary." Cloud Walker swept her into his arms, his mouth trailing fire as he kissed her eyelids, her cheeks, the tip of her nose, and finally her mouth.

Mary sighed as she relaxed in his arms. He wanted her. Oh, yes, he wanted her! The fact was evident in the way his arms crushed her close, in the passion of his kisses, and the warmth of his manhood pressing against her belly.

Without another word, Cloud Walker released her, but only long enough to move her bedroll next to his own. Then, lifting her in his arms, he carried her to their blankets and began to undress her. She was beautiful, he thought, so exquisitely beautiful. Her skin was smooth and unblemished, her breasts firm and perfect, her belly flat, her legs slim and nicely rounded. And her eyes—he had never thought to see another woman look at him like that, as though he were the most wonderful man in the world. Only a few months ago he had thought he had nothing to live for, and now Mary was here, loving him, giving him a reason to go on living. He thought briefly of Prairie Grass Woman and offered a silent prayer to Man Above for sending him two fine women to love.

That night they made love tenderly, leisurely, rapturously. Cloud Walker explored every inch of Mary's delectable body, marveling anew at her beauty. He reveled in the way she murmured his name as his seed poured into her, the way she shuddered with pleasure as his hands stroked her flesh, the way she responded to his touch, eager and trusting and unashamed.

It was only later, when she was asleep in his arms, her head pillowed on his shoulder, that he remembered she belonged to another man.

They reached the reservation just after noon the following day. The place was as dreary and depressing as Cloud Walker remembered. The warriors sat outside their lodges bundled in old buffalo robes or Army blankets, their faces devoid of welcome or curiosity as Cloud Walker rode toward his mother's lodge. A few young children stared at Mary, their black eyes wary and afraid. She was dressed like a white woman. Perhaps she had come to take them away from the reservation.

Dismounting, Cloud Walker helped Mary from her horse. Then, taking a deep breath, he entered his mother's lodge. Mary trailed after him.

The interior of the lodge was dark. There was no fire and it took Mary several moments before her eyes adjusted to the dark. She glanced around the lodge while Cloud Walker started a fire in the pit in the center of the floor. The lodge was small and virtually empty save for a buffalo-robe bed and a few cooking utensils. A small wicker basket held several items of clothing.

"Nahkoa," Cloud Walker murmured, taking his mother's hand in his. "I am here."

"Naha, is that you?" the old woman asked in a voice that was thin and weak.

"Yes, nahkoa. I have come to stay with you."

Tears filled the old woman's eyes as she gazed up at her son. "You will not have to stay long," she predicted. "Soon I will join your father in the world of spirits."

"Not too soon, nahkoa," Cloud Walker said, squeezing his mother's frail hand. "Here, I have brought someone to meet you." Cloud Walker motioned for Mary to come closer. "Nahkoa, this is Mary. She is the daughter of Two Hawks Flying. Mary, this is my mother, Singing Bird."

The old woman's eyes lit up at the mention of Two Hawks Flying. With an effort she sat up, her hand reaching for Mary's.

"So," the old woman said with a ghost of a smile. "You are the daughter of my old friend." She nodded to herself as though pleased. "Yes, you are truly his daughter. How is your father?"

"Very well, thank you."

Singing Bird nodded, and then she fell back on the robes. "I remember Two Hawks Flying well," she said wistfully. "I remember the day he rode off to the Greasy Grass with Tasunke Hinzi. Ai, that was a day to remember. We killed all the white eyes, just as Tatanka Yotanka had said we would. Ai, I remember how Two Hawks Flying rode at the head of our warriors, mounted on his big red stallion. And Crazy Horse was there, as well. 'Ho, brothers,' he cried. 'It is a good day to die.'" The old woman let out a long wail of grief. "My Tasunke Hinzi died that day."

"Rest now, nahkoa," Cloud Walker urged gently. "I will be here when you wake up."

Singing Bird nodded. Obediently she closed her eyes and was soon asleep.

"What a small world," Mary remarked. "Imagine, your mother knowing my father."

Cloud Walker smiled. "I grew up on stories of Crazy Horse and Sitting Bull and Two Hawks Flying. My mother never let me forget that the Cheyenne were a proud people."

"Tasunke Hinzi is a Sioux name," Mary said.

Cloud Walker nodded. "When my father was a young man, he saved the life of Sitting Bull, and Sitting Bull adopted him into the tribe and gave him a Sioux name. My father considered it a great honor, and so he kept the name the old chief had given him."

Mary smiled as she glanced at the old woman. "I think we grew up on many of the same stories. My father often spoke of Crazy Horse, of what a great chief he was. I wish I could have known him. He must have been a remarkable man."

"Yes. And now he's gone, like so many of our people."

Mary placed her hand on Cloud Walker's arm. "I love you," she murmured.

Cloud Walker placed his hand over Mary's. "That is just what I needed to hear," he said gruffly. "Come, let us go outside and get some fresh air. It smells like death in here."

Mary felt her spirits sag as they walked through the reservation. An air of hopelessness hung over the place. It was in the faces of the people they passed, in the eyes of the old men, in the wail of a woman as she mourned the death of her husband.

"Let's go back to your mother's lodge," Mary suggested. "I can't bear to see any more."

Cloud Walker said nothing, only took Mary's arm

and led her back to Singing Bird's lodge. His heart was filled with impotent rage as he pondered the way his people were forced to live. They were dressed in clothes that were worn and tattered. Their lodges were in need of repair, but there were no hides to repair them with. The few horses remaining to the Indians were thin and old. But, most depressing of all, the people had lost their will to survive. The men drank too much, trading what few items they owned for more firewater. The women were sluggish and dull-eyed. No longer did they sing and chatter as they did their chores. Even the children were subdued, their dark eyes sad and confused. Yes, the spirit had gone out of his people.

Cloud Walker's mother was still asleep when they entered the lodge. Her breathing was shallow and uneven, her face pale and waxy looking. Mary swallowed hard as she sat down on a folded blanket next to the firepit. Death was in the air.

Cloud Walker stood looking down at his mother. It would not be long before she walked the Hanging Road to the world of spirits.

That night Mary prepared dinner from the supplies they had brought with them. She made broth for Cloud Walker's mother, then watched, deeply moved, as Cloud Walker knelt at his mother's side and fed her.

After dinner Singing Bird reminisced about the old days when she had been a girl growing up in the Black Hills. She talked about Cloud Walker's father and how he had courted her for many moons, coming to her lodge late at night to play a flute, the notes soft and low and enticing. He had often followed her when she went to gather wood or to draw water from the river, hoping to catch her alone. She spoke of waiting for him in the evening, a big red courting blanket over her arm. It was a quaint custom, Mary thought. When a woman was courting, she would stand outside her lodge with a red blanket over her arm. If she looked with favor on the man who had come calling, she would hold out her arms, inviting him to stand beside her, and then she would cover them with the blanket. Mary smiled and thought how very romantic that would be, to stand close to the one you loved within the privacy of a warm red cocoon.

"When I was old enough to marry," Singing Bird went on, lost in the past, "Tasunke Hinzi brought my father three fine ponies and a fine buffalo robe. He was very handsome, your father, and very brave, and I was proud to be his wife. After he died, many men offered to take his place in my lodge, but I could not love them." She shook her head wistfully. "For me there could only be one man, my Tasunke Hinzi."

Talking had wearied her. Her eyelids fluttered down and she was asleep.

"They must have been very much in love," Mary murmured.

"Ai. When my father died, my mother hacked off her hair and cut off her little finger. She mourned him for over a year."

Mary's stomach churned as Cloud Walker talked of his mother's grief. She knew of the Cheyenne custom to self-inflict pain to express their grief, but she had never known anyone who had done it. Now, glancing at Singing Bird's right hand, she saw that the little finger had been cut off at the second knuckle.

Fighting the urge to vomit, Mary looked away. She had been raised to believe the traditions of her father's people, and most of them seemed beautiful and natural, but she was not sure she could accept self-mutilation. It seemed so barbaric, so pointless.

That night, lying in Cloud Walker's arms, Mary could not sleep. Being half Indian had never been particularly important to her before. Indeed, she had rarely given her mixed heritage much thought until Katherine was born. For perhaps the first time in her life, Mary had known what prejudice was. She had been shocked by Frank's attitude toward his daughter, hurt by the comments of women she had considered her friends. The word "breed" sounded ugly and demeaning when applied to Katherine, though the word had never bothered her before, not the way it had bothered Hawk. It had been difficult for her older brother. But then, Hawk had always been more Indian than white in his appearance and actions. He was proud of his Cheyenne blood, and he never let anyone forget it. Mary was proud, too, but she had accepted it as a part of her, like the color of her hair, never calling attention to it, never denying it. The people in Bear Valley had liked and accepted her, and she had liked them in return. Only in Chicago had she been subjected to ridicule and verbal abuse, and she had been hurt and surprised. The Indian wars had ended more than twenty years ago, yet most whites still thought of Indians as savages, as a people inferior to others.

Now, lying in Cloud Walker's arms, Mary felt the stirrings of a deeper, more meaningful pride in her race. Sleeping inside the lodge, her nostrils filling with the scent of smoke and herbs, she wondered what it would have been like to have been born thirty years ago when the Indians still roamed wild and free and the white men had not yet begun to covet the red man's land. She pictured herself living inside a conical hide lodge, wearing a fringed doeskin tunic and soft moccasins, tanning hides and caring for a husband. Would she have made a good Cheyenne wife? Could she have been happy living in a home of hide, spending long nights alone while her husband was out hunting with the other warriors, or riding off to war against some enemy tribe?

She glanced at Cloud Walker, sleeping peacefully beside her, and thought she would be able to endure anything so long as he was with her. She felt safe in his arms, safe and loved, and she knew she would rather spend the rest of her life in a crude hide lodge with Cloud Walker than share the finest mansion ever built with Frank Smythe.

Closing her eyes, Mary drifted off to sleep, and in her dreams she saw Cloud Walker riding across the plains astride a big black Appaloosa stallion. There were buffalo in her dreams, thousands and thousands of the great shaggy beasts. And wild horses. And a peaceful Cheyenne village laid out along the banks of the Powder River. But she had eyes only for Cloud Walker. He wore only a brief clout and fringed leggings; his long black hair, hanging to his waist, was adorned with a single black eagle feather. Her heart fluttered with excitement as he rode toward her, sweeping her into his arms. Together they rode across the vast sunlit prairie, their hearts beating as one. And then they were standing together before Eagle-That-Soars-in-the-Sky while the shaman spoke the solemn, beautiful words that made them man and wife. Her father was there, too, his face grave, looking tall and handsome in a buckskin shirt and leggings. Her mother stood beside Shadow, her gray eyes damp with tears of happiness. In her dream, Mary smiled as Eagle-That-Soars-in-the-Sky joined their hands together. They would live happily ever after . . .

A hoarse cry aroused Mary from a deep sleep. Opening her eyes, she stared at the hide walls and then, remembering where she was, she sat up, looking for Cloud Walker.

He was squatting beside his mother's bed, his head bowed. As Mary watched, he took a knife from his belt and slashed his forearms. Mary stared in horror as the blood dripped from the shallow cuts.

Singing Bird was dead.

After a long time, Cloud Walker stood up. Lifting his knife, he hacked off his long hair until it was only shoulder length. Only then did he notice that Mary was awake.

"She is dead," he said tonelessly.

"I'm sorry."

Cloud Walker nodded. "I wish to bury her according to our customs. I do not want the whites to put her in the ground. Will you help me?"

"Yes, of course."

"There is a needle and thread in that basket," he said, pointing to a small brown basket near the doorway. "Can you sew a blanket around her?"

Mary nodded.

"I am going out to find a horse to carry her."
Cloud Walker paused in the doorway. "Will you be all
right here alone?"

"Yes."

For the next half hour, Mary sewed a shroud for
Singing Bird. She tried not to think of the frail body
within the blanket's folds, tried not to remember that
the old woman had been alive only a short time ago.
When Cloud Walker returned, Mary had finished her
task.

"Let us go," Cloud Walker said. "It is early and
only a few of the people are awake. We must go before
the soldiers see us."

Nodding, Mary quickly pulled on her shoes and
gathered their gear together. Cloud Walker carried his
mother's body outside and draped it over the back of a
scrawny gray gelding. After helping Mary onto the
back of her horse, he swung up behind the blanket-
draped body of his mother and rode away from the
lodge toward a distant hill that was thick with timber.
Mary followed, leading Cloud Walker's mount.

It was late afternoon when they reached the hill.
Cloud Walker urged his horse steadily upward until he
found a large tree with several sturdy lower branches.
Dismounting, he lifted his mother's body from the
back of the gelding and placed it in the fork of the tree,
high enough off the ground to be safe from wolves and
coyotes.

Throwing back his head, he let out a long wail
that Mary recognized as the Cheyenne death song.
Then, drawing his knife, he dragged the edge of the

blade across his cheeks and chest.

"Hear me, Man Above," he cried. "Guide my mother's spirit safely across the sky to the afterworld."

Woodenly, he placed a small gourd of water at the foot of the tree, that she might have something to drink on her long journey. A small sack of corn meal was placed beside the water, that she might not hunger. A favorite shawl was folded at her feet to turn away the chill of the night. Lastly, Cloud Walker killed the scrawny gelding so that Singing Bird might have a horse to carry her on the long journey to the world of spirits.

Mary watched through eyes filled with tears. And as she wept, she seemed to feel the spirits of all her Indian ancestors gather around her, lending her strength and support for whatever lay ahead in the days to come.

Cloud Walker remained near his mother's body for nearly an hour, his arms raised in silent prayer.

Mary gazed at his face, as hard and unyielding as if it had been carved from stone. She looked at the blood drying on his face and arms and chest, and she knew suddenly why the Indians cut their hair and slashed their flesh. It was a way of expressing a grief that could not be put into words, a hope that, in causing themselves physical pain, they might find relief from the pain in their hearts.

They were quiet as they rode down the hill and away from the reservation. Mary felt as though she knew who and what she was for the first time in her life, and she wondered if she would ever have been truly happy with Frank. He would never understand who she was, what she was. How long would she have been able to stay in Chicago, away from the endless prairie, away from the land that was in her blood? She belonged here, in this place where her ancestors had lived and fought and died. This was where she wanted to be, where she wanted to raise her daughter.

Cloud Walker's thoughts were melancholy as they left the reservation far behind. Looking down the corridors of time, he recalled the days of his youth when Singing Bird had been a young woman. He had adored his mother. She had made much of his first kill, dressing the rabbit and serving it with a flourish. After his father died, she often told him stories of Tasunke Hinzi, of his bravery and cunning. Cloud Walker's only memories of his father were of what he had heard from his mother. She had been a remarkable woman, able to make life fun even when they were forced to live on the reservation. He had hated the reservation, hated the soldiers who patrolled the boundaries. Singing Bird had made up games and stories and refused to let him be discouraged. She was always certain that things would get better, always hopeful when they did not.

Cloud Walker smiled faintly as he pictured his parents together again at last, walking hand in hand in a sunny meadow in the world of spirits. Life and death were but two sides of the same hide, his mother had been fond of saying. Death was nothing to fear. It was simply birth into a new life, a life that would last forever.

Mary was somewhat surprised when Cloud Walker reached for her that night. She had not expected him to want to make love to her so soon after his mother's death, but he was eager for her touch. Their love was a symbol of life renewing itself, their union a token of hope for the future. Cloud Walker made love to Mary gently, tenderly, his hands warm and adoring, his eyes alight with an inner fire as his hands stroked her silken flesh. She was Woman, giver of life and comfort, and only in her arms could he find balm for his sorrow, relief from his pain. The warmth of her womanhood surrounded him and he emptied his life into her, praying that Maheo would bless them with a son.

26

Shadow and I were sitting in the kitchen playing poker when Mary came home. I had only to look at my daughter's face to know that she and Cloud Walker had finally shared the love they felt for one another. Glancing at Shadow, I saw that he was also aware of the step they had taken.

"Welcome home," I said, rising to give Mary a hug. "How was your trip?"

"Fine. But Cloud Walker's mother passed away while we were there."

"She was a good woman," Shadow remarked gravely. "I remember one time when the Pawnee attacked our village. Cloud Walker's father was away hunting, so Singing Bird picked up a war lance and his shield and defended their lodge. She killed a Pawnee warrior." Shadow smiled. "Tasunke Hinzi was sur-

269

prised to see his wife at the scalp dance the following night. He gave her a coup feather to wear in her hair." Shadow laughed. "He was proud, but a little upset that she had used his best lance and ruined his medicine. Finally he gave the lance to her for a souvenir and made himself another."

"I think I would have liked her," Mary said. "I wish I could have known her better." She ran a hand through her hair. "I need to wash up. Is Katherine asleep?"

"Yes, but she should be awake soon."

"Did she give you any trouble?"

"Goodness, no," I assured Mary. "That child is never any trouble. Dinner will be ready in about an hour, so you have time to take a nap if you need to."

"Thank you, nahkoa."

With a sigh, I sat down again. Mary gave Shadow a kiss on the cheek and then went to her room.

"Well," I said dryly, "we knew it was just a matter of time."

Shadow nodded. "I am surprised they managed to wait this long."

"It's hard to be young and in love," I murmured. "Remember?"

Shadow reached over and squeezed my hand, his smile warming my heart. "I remember. You did not mention Frank's letter."

"I know. I thought I'd wait until after dinner. I just know it's bad news."

Mary's face turned pale as she read Frank's letter. "He says he wants me back," Mary said tonelessly.

"He says he's sorry and wants to try again, and that if I refuse he'll take me to court for custody of Katherine. He says she's his daughter and he has a right to see her at least half the year."

"That bastard," Shadow said coldly.

"What am I going to do?" Mary asked. "You know he doesn't want Katherine. He doesn't care about her at all."

"He obviously wants you back quite badly," I mused, shaking my head. "Bad enough to blackmail you into coming home."

"It isn't fair," Mary exclaimed angrily. "I can't fight Frank in court. He's got money and position and a mansion! And friends in high places back in Chicago. He'll take Katherine away from me just for spite."

Shadow took Mary in his arms as she began to weep. "I think you should go back to Chicago," he suggested. "I think you and Frank need to talk. Perhaps you can work things out between you. If not, you will be no worse off than you are now."

"But I don't want to go back to Chicago," Mary wailed unhappily. "I want to stay here. I want to stay with Cloud Walker." Mary lifted her head and turned imploring eyes on her father. "I love him, neyho. I can't go back to Frank. I just can't."

"I think your father's right," I said. "Why don't you write Frank and tell him you'll come home when the snow melts? Maybe he'll change his mind between now and then."

Cloud Walker was furious when he heard about Frank Smythe's letter. He threatened to go to Chicago and cut out Frank's heart. He ranted and raved and stormed through the house, and when he finally calmed down, he admitted that the best thing for Mary to do was to go back to Chicago and try to convince Frank to give her a divorce.

Mary and Cloud Walker spent every spare moment together. They took Katherine for walks in the snow, they sat together on the sofa in the evening, quietly spinning dreams of a time when they could be together, just the three of them. Sometimes Mary and Cloud Walker took long rides along the river, sometimes they spent the night in Cloud Walker's lodge.

I did not judge my daughter, though my thoughts were divided. I did not like to think of her being unfaithful to her husband, yet I could not fault her for wanting to be with the man she loved. Love was such a fragile thing, so hard to find, so hard to hold.

Mary nestled in Cloud Walker's arms. It was cozy inside the lodge. A fire burned brightly, sending long orange shadows dancing across the lodgeskins.

She gazed at Cloud Walker's beloved face. This was to be their last night together before she left for Chicago, and she wanted it to be perfect, a night she could treasure the rest of her life. She closed her eyes as Cloud Walker lowered his head, his lips nuzzling her neck, the sensitive area just behind her ear, the curve of her cheek. Lifting her hand, she cupped the back of his neck, drawing him closer.

"Mary." He murmured her name as he kissed her forehead, her eyes, the tip of her nose.

"More," she whispered, and he slanted his mouth over hers, kissing her hungrily, his hands playing over her back and shoulders. Gently he carried her down to the ground, one hand molding her body to his so that they were touching from head to heel.

"Mary." His voice was low and husky, thick with emotion. "I cannot let you go."

"Please," Mary murmured, placing her hand over his mouth. "You promised we wouldn't speak of it tonight."

Cloud Walker placed his hand over hers and kissed her fingertips, his eyes silently begging her to stay.

"I have to go," Mary said, pleading with him to make it easy for her. "You know that."

Cloud Walker nodded. He *did* know. And he understood. But deep in the back of his mind, lurking in bitter shame, was the thought that if Katherine had never been born, Frank Smythe would have no hold over Mary. He banished the thought as soon as it surfaced, for he loved Mary's daughter dearly. But, oh, he loved Mary so much more.

Mary lifted her hand to his face, her heart swelling with tenderness as her fingers traced each hard line and angle from his straight black brows, down his hawklike nose, to the strong square jaw. He was so beautiful, and she loved him so much. He was everything she had ever dreamed of, everything she had hoped Frank would be, and wasn't.

"Love me," she begged, drawing his head down toward hers. "Love me now."

Cloud Walker needed no further urging. His arms tightened around her waist and his mouth slanted over hers. Mary gloried in his kiss. Reason told her it was wrong to let Cloud Walker love her when she belonged to another, but in her heart she knew it was right, and she returned his kisses passionately, desperately, knowing that these few precious moments would be their last. Her eyes moved softly over his face, loving the way his eyes burned with a fierce inner flame, reveling in his hard-muscled frame. He was every inch a male, rugged, virile, beautiful. How could she leave him? How could she go back to Chicago without knowing if she would ever feel Cloud Walker's arms around her again, ever feel his skin brushing against her own, his kisses branding her lips? How long would it be before she again experienced the ecstasy she found only in his arms?

They clung to each other, every touch and kiss bespeaking their love for each other. Cloud Walker yearned to beg Mary not to go back to Frank, but he bit off the words, knowing they would only cause her pain. His hands wandered over her flesh, delighting in her softness, the velvety texture of her flat belly. He knew every inch of her body as he knew his own. Her softness molded to his touch, her breath quickened as his lips moved over her face and breasts and belly, trailing fire, until she writhed beneath him. Her hands clutched his hard-muscled flesh, sliding down his arms. Her fingernails raked his back as she urged him on, her hips arching forward, enticing him.

And still he held back, wanting to prolong the moment, to savor this last night in her arms. Lifting himself on his elbows, he gazed down into her face. Her eyes were cloudy with passion, her lips slightly parted, her skin flushed and moist. The firelight cast golden shadows over her face and hair and his heart swelled with such love it was almost painful. Gently he kissed her forehead, her cheeks, the curve of her throat, until, unable to restrain his passion any longer, he thrust into her, making them one flesh. For this one moment she belonged to him, body and soul, in a way she would never belong to Frank Smythe. The thought gave Cloud Walker a bitter sense of satisfaction. Frank might be Mary's husband, but he would never have her heart or her love.

Cloud Walker held Mary all through the night, his eyes lingering on her face when she slept, his fingers threading through her hair, his lips brushing her cheek.

Mary woke just before dawn and they made love one last time, clinging to each other until, at last, it was time to part. There were tears in Mary's eyes when she left the lodge. She did not look back.

Later that afternoon Cloud Walker stood in the shadow of the barn watching as Mary and Katherine climbed into the buggy beside Hannah and Shadow. His eyes burned with unshed tears as the buggy pulled away from the house, his throat ached with the need to call her back, to beg her not to go. But he only stood there watching until she was out of sight.

It was hard to let Mary go, hard to watch Katherine board the train. Our house would be empty without them. We watched the train until it was out of sight, then Shadow gave me a comforting squeeze and we started for home.

In the days that followed, it got so that I hated to

pick up a newspaper, for Frank Smythe's name or picture seemed to appear in practically every issue. He had made several generous contributions to various charity organizations in the east, he was making speeches for Teddy Roosevelt, he was dedicating a new hospital wing. Only Carry Nation received more publicity than Frank. Armed with righteous zeal, Carry Nation had lead a group of women through Kansas in an antiliquor crusade, damaging or destroying many establishments that sold alcoholic beverages. Women all over America cheered her efforts to abolish Demon Rum.

Cloud Walker was subdued these days. He moped around the house for over a week, hardly eating, rarely speaking to anyone. He spent hours grooming Mary's leopard Appaloosa filly, currying the animal to within an inch of its life. I knew it made him feel closer to Mary, caring for something that had been hers. Once I found him in Mary's room just standing there staring out the window, his dark eyes filled with such pain my heart went out to him.

Cloud Walker haunted the post office in town, hoping for a letter from Mary, yet knowing she probably would not write. Mary had said that if Frank would not give her a divorce, she was going to do her best to make her marriage work for Katherine's sake. I knew that trying to be a good wife did not include sending love letters to someone back home.

Cloud Walker spent a lot of time with Shadow. The mares were foaling now, and the two men spent many nights sleeping in the barn or out in the pasture, wanting to be on hand when needed. Usually the mares had no trouble, but now and then a foal was born breech, or the mare died. Indeed, one of our older mares did die late that spring. It was left to Blackie to tend the orphan colt, a chore he loved.

Blackie moved the colt into a stall in the barn, and for the next few weeks our son spent most of his waking hours looking after the colt. The colt followed Blackie everywhere he went, tagging at his heels like a puppy. Blackie named the orphan foal Tag-Along, and it was a sight to see, watching our son and the young horse playing chase out in the pasture with the other mares and foals.

Blackie was growing and changing. He was doing well in school and had many friends in town, and Monica Sullivan openly adored him. She often found excuses to come to our house. Blackie did not seem overly interested in Monica as a girl, but he thought she was an okay friend because she wasn't afraid of spiders or snakes like other girls, and she liked frogs and rabbits. Too, she could sit a horse almost as well as Blackie.

Our son spent his weekends making rounds with Chester Cole, and when the veterinarian started to pay Blackie a small wage for his assistance, our son was in heaven. Imagine, being paid for doing something you loved! Blackie began saving the money he earned so he could go to college and study to become a veterinarian, and Pa told Blackie that he would match him dollar for dollar that he saved.

In mid-June the railroad came to Bear Valley. Shadow frowned as the first railroad car arrived amid a clatter of wheels and a cloud of black smoke. Civilization was here at last. The townspeople were thrilled. No longer would they have to make the long journey by horseback or carriage to Steel's Crossing to catch a train for the East. Now they could ride to the railroad station at the southern edge of the valley. No longer were we cut off from the rest of the world. No longer would supplies and goods ordered from the East have to be picked up at Steel's Crossing. Items ordered through the mail could be shipped directly to our town. It was cause for celebration, and Bear Valley threw a party to welcome the railroad.

It was quite a holiday. The school shut down, the saloons gave away free beer, the drug store offered free popcorn and root beer. There were speeches by the mayor, newly elected only a month ago, and by several of the railroad men who promised that the arrival of the iron horse would bring prosperity for everyone.

Pa nodded his head dubiously. It *would* be nice to be able to ship his cattle East, he opined, but he for one hated to see progress reach Bear Valley.

Shadow agreed. The railroad would bring more goods, but it would also bring more people. And it did. I could not believe how quickly Bear Valley grew. New buildings seem to spring up almost overnight. Tall buildings with balconies and latticework, false-fronted buildings with fancy scrollwork and shutters and lavish decorations. There was a new saloon, a new hotel, a new restaurant, three new stores, an ice cream parlor, and a Chinese laundry. Mr. Ling, owner of the laundry, drew as many curious stares as Shadow had once drawn. Even I could not help staring at him the first time I saw him. He was a remarkably tiny man, with a small goatee and a queue that hung past his waist. He wore long silk gowns embroidered with fans and dragons, and a shiny black skullcap. His wife was also very tiny. She too wore long silk gowns, and she always walked behind her husband when they went outside the shop. She was very quiet, but she had a warm smile and lovely dark eyes.

I saw a restlessness in Shadow in the days that followed the arrival of the railroad. Often I caught him gazing westward toward the vast prairie that stretched away for miles, the earth clean and unscarred, untouched by hoe or plow. Often he threw a bridle on Smoke and went for long rides alone. I knew, without asking, what he was thinking. And Cloud Walker confirmed my suspicions.

"He is feeling closed in," Cloud Walker remarked one day as Shadow rode away from our place toward the hills. "There are too many people now."

"I know," I said, smiling sadly. "Shadow will never be totally civilized. A part of him will always want to wander, to see land that is free and wild."

Cloud Walker nodded. "This is no way for a warrior to live," he said, gesturing at our house and the barn and corrals. "A warrior should live free, with only his horse, his woman, and his weapons."

"I'm afraid the day of the warrior is over," I said with a sigh. "And the day of the white man is here."

"Would you leave all this if Two Hawks Flying asked you to?"

"Leave?" I glanced at our home, at the trees and the corral and the horses frolicking in the distant pasture. "Has Shadow spoken to you of leaving?"

"No. But I think he thinks of it often."

I stared out at the prairie. It was beautiful now. The grass was a bright green, the sky a clear azure blue, the trees decked out with tender green leaves, the wildflowers in bloom. Yes, it was lovely now, but in winter it would become a cold and lonely place. If Shadow wanted to move on, would I want to go? Our home was snug and comfortable. I liked having neighbors nearby, liked having people around me, though I enjoyed my privacy, too. I liked being able to browse through Pendergast's Dry Goods Store for material and dresses, to be able to go into town when I ran out of sugar or salt or thread or bacon. I wasn't a young girl anymore, and the thought of starting over in a new place seemed more like work than another adventure.

And what about Hawk and Victoria? What about Blackie? He wanted to go to school and study to become a veterinarian. And what of Mary? And Cloud Walker? And my grandchildren? I could not leave Jacob and Jason. I wanted to be here, to see them grow up.

I thought about what Cloud Walker had said as I prepared dinner that night. Once, Shadow had discussed all his hopes and dreams with me. Why was he keeping this to himself? Was he afraid to tell me he wanted to move farther west? Was he afraid I wouldn't go with him? Or had he neglected to mention it because it was merely a passing fancy?

I caught Shadow watching me several times that evening, his dark eyes thoughtful. Once he started to say something, then changed his mind.

It wasn't until we were alone in our room that

night that he asked what was troubling me.

"You are," I admitted. "Why haven't you told me what's bothering *you*?"

Shadow frowned. "Nothing is bothering me."

"Don't lie to me," I said softly. "You've never lied to me."

"Hannah—"

"If you're not happy here, why haven't you told me? Why did I have to hear it from someone else?"

"Who has told you I am unhappy here?"

"Cloud Walker said you wanted to move on, to get away from Bear Valley."

"I never said that."

"But you've thought about it."

"Yes." Shadow gazed out the window. "It grows too crowded here to suit me. There are too many people, too much confusion. But I would not ask you to leave, Hannah. You spent too many years following me from place to place, living from day to day. Never knowing where your next meal was coming from. This is your home, our home. We will stay here."

"But you'd like to leave, wouldn't you?"

"Yes." His voice was low, filled with a deep yearning.

I turned away, unable to look at him, unable to face the unhappiness in his eyes. I had caught a wild creature when I married Shadow, I mused. I had caught him and gentled him, but he was still a wild creature under all the trappings of civilization, a wild creature who yearned to be free.

Shadow took me in his arms then and we did not discuss it any more that night. I clung to my husband, telling him with my kisses and my caresses that I loved him, needed him. Loved him. We made love desperately, our bodies straining to be close, closer, as if by the very force of our love we could solve all our problems and make them go away. My hands stroked Shadow's flesh, loving every hard-muscled inch, loving the way his skin felt beneath my hands and lips and against my flesh. His mouth nuzzled my breasts as his hands kneaded my back and thighs, and I wrapped my arms around his neck, drawing him closer as my hips arched upward to receive him. I was whole then, complete at last.

Later, when Shadow was sleeping peacefully beside me, the tears came.

Part Three

27

Mary took a deep breath as she stepped off the train. She spotted Frank immediately and forced herself to smile as he made his way toward her.

"Welcome home, Mary," Frank said, kissing her cheek. He glanced at the baby, sleeping peacefully in Mary's arms, and it was all he could do not to grimace with distaste. The girl was eleven months old now. Her hair was black, like her mother's, her skin was a deep tawny brown. When her eyelids fluttered open, he saw that her eyes were a dark blue-gray. He had never thought of Katherine as his daughter.

"How are you, Frank?" Mary asked.

"Fine, just fine." He motioned to one of the porters. "These two bags, please," he said curtly, and taking Mary by the arm, he led her to a shiny black carriage. A pair of matched gray geldings stood in the traces, a Negro in dark blue livery held the reins.

With a great show of affection, Frank helped Mary into the carriage, stepped in beside her, and closed the carriage door.

Mary leaned back in the plush green velvet seat. She had known that Frank was rich, but she had never given it much thought until now. He reeked of money. The carriage was new, obviously the best that money could buy. The horses were well-bred, so perfectly matched they might have been twins, though twin horses were rare. Frank's suit had been tailored especially for him, and it fit like a glove. His boots were of the finest Moroccan leather. A large diamond stickpin sparkled in his cravat.

He chatted amiably as they drove through town toward home, telling her about his parents' new house, about dining with Diamond Jim Brady, about the latest play he had financed. Oh, yes, and he had planned a party to welcome her home. Everyone who was anyone in Chicago had been invited.

Mary nodded and made all the proper replies, but inwardly she was wishing she had never left Bear Valley. As she looked around at the crowded city streets and saw the people bustling about, she was homesick for the peaceful beauty of the plains. Katherine jumped, startled, as a fire engine raced down the street, bells clanging wildly.

Mary gazed in awe at Frank's new home. It was bigger and more elegant than anything she had ever seen. It was two stories high and sat on an enormous piece of ground. The house was stark white, trimmed with dark blue shutters. A profusion of flowers bordered the long driveway that led up to the house. Acres of neatly manicured lawn surrounded the house.

Inside, the rooms were ornate, elaborately decorated in rich mahogany and dark maroon velvet. Thick carpets covered the floors. Heavy paper covered the walls. Crystal chandeliers hung from the high ceilings. Mary counted six bedrooms, a sitting room, a parlor, a conservatory, a large dining room, a spacious kitchen and pantry, a ballroom decorated with crystal and gilt-edged mirrors. There was a music room, a library filled with books, and a den stocked with a supply of good whiskey and Kentucky bourbon. A nursery, complete with a crib and rocking chair and a variety of toys, adjoined Mary's room.

"It's lovely, Frank," Mary murmured, a little overwhelmed by the luxury of her surroundings. "Just lovely."

Frank smiled, pleased. He had spared no expense in building this house. He was a wealthy man now, and he wanted everyone to know it.

After a tour of the house, Frank introduced Mary to the servants. There was Manly, the butler; Anna, the maid; Dulcie, the cook; Marta, the housekeeper; George, the valet, and Mrs. Anderson, the nanny Frank had hired to look after Katherine. In addition there were several men who worked outside, looking after the grounds and tending the horses.

It was going to take some getting used to, Mary thought, learning to order servants about and living in a mansion. But then, if Frank would just be understanding and reasonable, perhaps she wouldn't have to get used to it at all.

She squared her shoulders as they returned to the parlor. The sooner she said what needed to be said, the better.

"Frank, we need to talk."

Frank looked at Mary expectantly. He had seen the wonder in her eyes as he showed her the house, seen the realization dawn in her expression as she came to understand that her husband was a very wealthy man. Now, Frank thought smugly, now she'll realize this is where she belongs.

Frank smiled as he sat down on the sofa, patting the place beside him.

"Frank . . ."

He was looking at her expectantly, and Mary realized that what she had to say wasn't going to be as easy as she had hoped.

"Frank, I didn't come here for a reconciliation," she said in a rush, hoping to get the words out before she lost her nerve. "I came to try to persuade you to give me a divorce."

Frank Smythe stared at Mary, his eyes growing dark, his lips thinning with anger. "I don't want to discuss it," he said through clenched teeth.

Mary felt a tiny flutter of fear at the look on Frank's face, but then she thought of Cloud Walker, of how much she loved him, and new courage flowed through her veins.

"Please, Frank. You don't need me. Please let me go before we end up hating each other."

Frank stood up, his eyes as hard as flint. "I would

remind you to think of your daughter and what is best for her," he warned in an ominous tone. "Do I make myself clear?"

Mary held Katherine tighter. "Yes, Frank."

"Good. Now, why don't you go upstairs and rest awhile? My family is coming for dinner tonight. They wanted to welcome you home. Drinks are at seven."

"I'll be ready," Mary said dully.

Leaving the parlor, she walked upstairs to her room, her steps heavy with defeat. Placing Katherine on the bed, she slipped out of her traveling clothes and stretched out beside the little girl, who had fallen asleep.

Mary gazed lovingly into her daughter's face. There had to be a way to convince Frank to end their marriage so she and Katherine could go back to Bear Valley where they belonged. In the meantime, she would make the best of things for Katherine's sake, though it would not be easy living with Frank when it was Cloud Walker she longed for.

"Oh, Katherine," she murmured unhappily, "what am I going to do?"

Drawing her daughter close to her breast, Mary closed her eyes and drifted to sleep.

When she awoke, it was dark. Someone had laid out fresh underwear for her and lit a fire in the hearth to warm the room.

Rising, Mary felt a wave of panic engulf her when she saw that Katherine was gone. Heart pounding, she ran across the room and opened the door to the nursery. She breathed a sigh of relief when she saw Mrs. Anderson playing pat-a-cake with Katherine.

"Is anything wrong, ma'am?" the nanny asked.

"No, I . . . I just wanted to make sure Katherine was all right."

"She's fine, ma'am. We've become good friends, haven't we, darling?"

Mary smiled uncertainly. Katherine did seem happy with Mrs. Anderson.

"Best get dressed, ma'am," the nanny suggested. "Mr. Frank is expecting you downstairs in thirty minutes."

"Yes, thank you, Mrs. Anderson." Closing the door, Mary turned around to find Anna waiting for her.

The maid smiled. "I'm here to help you dress, ma'am," she said with a curtsey. "What will you wear tonight?"

"I don't know," Mary said. "I hadn't thought about it."

Anna walked to the armoire and opened the doors. Inside hung dozens of dresses in a wide variety of styles and colors—silks and satins for formal occasions, day dresses of muslin and linen and cotton. There were hats and shoes and gloves to match each dress.

"My, my," Mary murmured. Frank must have spent a fortune on clothes for her. But then, it was only fitting that she look the part of Frank Smythe's wife, and that meant she must dress with style and flare, as befitting the wife of a wealthy man.

Anna reached into the armoire and pulled out a simple yet elegant gown of pale blue satin. "This, perhaps?"

"Yes, that will do," Mary agreed listlessly. What difference did it make how she looked when Cloud Walker wasn't there to see her?

Anna helped her dress, then arranged her hair in a most becoming fashion. A bit of rouge came next, adding a touch of color to her face, and Anna pronounced that she was ready to greet her guests.

Looking into a mirror, Mary felt that she was looking at a stranger.

Mattie and Leland Smythe were waiting for her in the sitting room, along with David, Gene, and Henry.

Frank smiled benevolently as Mary entered the room. "You look lovely, darling," he said, crossing the room to bestow a kiss on her cheek.

"Thank you. How nice to see you all," Mary said, nodding to the Smythes.

"Don't you love this house?" Mattie gushed. "And wait until you see ours. It's not quite so grand as this one, but it's more than I ever dreamed of. Frank has been so generous." She beamed at her son, who basked openly in his mother's praise.

Mary nodded. "I'm sure your house is lovely."

"Oh, it is. You must come over tomorrow and let me show you around."

Mary nodded again, wishing that Mattie would stop carrying on about how wonderful Frank was.

Leland Smythe grinned at Frank, and then at Mattie. "I always knew Frank here would make something of himself, mother," he bragged. "He's going to be a big success, just like Abel and Benjamin and Cabel."

"And what do you boys want to do?" Mary asked, turning to David, Gene, and Henry.

David shrugged. "Frank's going to get me a job on the railroad."

"And I'm working at the Chicago Bank and Trust," Gene announced.

"And I'm not working at all," Henry said, grinning. "I'm going to college."

"That's wonderful," Mary said.

Mattie beamed at her sons. "David is getting married in December."

"Really?"

David nodded. "Yeah. I finally found a girl who would put up with me. She's a knockout, Mary, wait until you meet her."

They talked about David's wedding until Manly announced dinner, and then they all went into the dining room.

Mary was amazed at the amount of food placed before her. Soup and salad, two kinds of meat, three kinds of potatoes, four kinds of vegetables, bread and rolls and biscuits. Manly kept her wine glass filled, and by the end of the meal she was feeling slightly tipsy. Then came dessert, and a glass of sherry.

By bedtime Mary was light-headed and drowsy. Anna helped her undress for bed, and Mary was nearly asleep when Frank slid into bed beside her.

"Mary," he whispered. "Are you awake?"

"Yes," she murmured sleepily. "What's wrong?"

"Nothing, nothing at all."

Mary closed her eyes again, then gasped as she felt Frank's hands fondling her breasts.

"Not tonight, Frank," she protested. "I'm too tired."

"You don't have to do anything," Frank murmured huskily. "Just lie back and enjoy it."

"No, Frank, please."

"Don't ever tell me no," Frank warned in a voice suddenly hard and cold. "You're mine, and don't you ever forget it."

Mary started to protest, but some inner voice warned her to keep still. Frank was drunk and in a nasty mood. It would be foolish to argue with him now.

Closing her eyes, she surrendered to her husband's lovemaking, her whole being screaming in protest as he possessed her, violently taking what she had lovingly given to Cloud Walker.

Mary wept bitter tears after Frank left her bed to go to his own room. Was this what her life would be like now? No love, no affection, just a quick bedding to satisfy her husband's lust? She thought of the love and warmth in Cloud Walker's embrace, how he held her afterward, his arms and lips sweet and tender in the afterglow of the passion they had shared. Cloud Walker had made her feel loved and cherished. Frank made her feel as though she had been used and tossed aside.

She cried until she had no tears left, and then she fell asleep to dream of Cloud Walker.

The next few weeks were a mixture of ups and downs. It was pleasant, living in a big house and having a dozen people to attend her every need. She spent hours with Katherine, watching her daughter

learn and grow, smiling with pride as the child took
her first steps. She bought Katherine dolls and toys
and clothes, and delighted in watching her daughter's
eyes glow with excitement as she reached for colorful
balls and stuffed clowns and wooden horses.

There were parties and grand balls, and Mary
tried to have a good time. She wore beautiful clothes
and danced with handsome young men and drank
champagne and wine and pretended she was happily
married. But at night she could not pretend. Her
husband's caresses left her cold, and she dreaded the
nights he came to her bed. Sometimes she tried to
pretend it was Cloud Walker's mouth on hers, Cloud
Walker's hands stroking her breasts and thighs, but
Cloud Walker had been kind and gentle, considerate
of her likes and dislikes, sensitive to her needs and
desires. Frank was selfish, almost ruthless, in his
lovemaking, and she found it repulsive.

She turned her attention to charity work and
began to spend time with those in need. She donated
large sums of Frank's money to the local orphanage
and spent long hours with the children, making certain
the sick were cared for, that the children had clothes
and shoes and food on the table.

She went for long walks, she shopped in the finest
stores, she went bicycle riding in the park. She had tea
with Mattie Smythe. But no matter how she filled her
days, Frank was always there at night.

She was welcomed in the finest houses now, and
Mary thought it odd that her being half Indian had
ceased to be important now that Frank was rich. The

ladies in town bent over backward to make her feel welcome. They invited her to their teas and bazaars, included her in every party and social affair of the season, sought her advice about fashion, gushed over Katherine. Mary was always polite and agreeable. She returned their calls and invited them to her home, but all the while she was remembering how they had snubbed her before. And she knew she was accepted now only because Frank was in a position to help their husbands in their various occupations.

She had been back in Chicago for about five weeks when she began to feel nausea in the morning. At first she shrugged it off, thinking she might be catching the flu, but then, in a blinding flash of insight, she knew she was pregnant. Her joy at knowing that the baby had to be Cloud Walker's soon turned to anguish. How could she tell Frank?

And then, out of despair came a ray of hope. Frank would not want her when he learned she was carrying another man's child. Surely now he would give her the divorce she so desperately desired.

Frank Smythe swore under his breath when Mary told him the news. So she was pregnant and that Cheyenne buck was the father. His first impulse was to put his hands around her lovely little throat and strangle her. Bitch, he thought, lifting her skirts for that savage. . . . Jealousy followed anger. She had never been particularly interested in the intimate side of marriage. Perhaps he had treated her too gently. Perhaps she liked it rough. His rage grew as he thought of Mary submitting to another man, and then he laughed grimly. She submitted to her husband because it was her duty, because it was expected. She had not submitted to that damned savage, he thought bitterly. No, she had gone to him willingly enough. By damn, he would kill her.

But then the cool hand of caution overcame his anger. A divorce would not suit his plans at all. He would just swallow his pride and pass the brat off as his. Everyone knew that Mary was part Indian. No one would suspect that the child was not his.

Frank rubbed a hand across the back of his neck. Sometimes it seemed that his life was a mess. Lila was pestering him to divorce Mary and marry her, but the thought of divorce did not sit well with Frank. People of good breeding did not divorce each other. They simply put up a good front in public and went their separate ways in private. Lila was a beautiful woman and a veritable tiger in bed, virtually everything a man could want in a mistress, but he was not certain she could make the grade as the wife of a wealthy man. She was too crude, too earthy. Frank had high ambitions. He was well-liked in Chicago, respected in business, and it was in his mind to go into politics. That was where the power lay. But a man needed a good reputation for that. A lovely wife and children at his side. A clean bill of health, so to speak. Divorce always caused a certain amount of ugly gossip and speculation. Yes, the baby must appear to be his. After all, he thought with disgust, it could not look more Cheyenne than his own daughter.

Frank eyed Mary sternly. "No divorce," he said curtly. "Don't mention it again."

Mary stared at her husband in disbelief. Why was he being so stubborn? He didn't love her. He didn't love Katherine. Why wouldn't he let them go?

"Frank, please."

"I said don't mention it again. You are my wife, and you will remain my wife for as long as it pleases me. Perhaps in a few years when my reputation is solid enough to withstand the scandal, I might let you go, but not until then. Is that clear?"

"Yes, Frank, quite clear."

"Good." Frank smiled magnanimously. "It's almost time for dinner, my dear. We mustn't keep my family waiting."

With a nod, Mary left him and went to dress for dinner. Only in the privacy of her own bedroom did she let the tears flow.

She tried to run away the following week, and it was then she discovered that Frank had suspected she might try to go back to Bear Valley and had hired someone to keep an eye on her. She was standing in line to buy a ticket on the first train West when a tall man appeared at her side.

"Shall we go home, Mrs. Smythe?" the man said, taking her elbow.

"I don't want to go home just now," Mary said. She clutched Katherine to her breast, her nervousness transmitting itself to the baby, who began to cry.

"Mr. Smythe wants to see you at home," the man

said. "I don't think it would be wise to cause a scene, do you?"

There was nothing to do but go with him. At home, Mary railed at Frank.

"How dare you set a man to spy on me!" she raged angrily. "How dare you have me followed! I'm not your slave, Frank Smythe, I'm your wife, and I won't have someone following me everywhere I go."

"My pet, you are my wife," Frank replied coldly. "That makes you my property. Everything you do reflects on me. I will not have you running away every time I turn my back. I would remind you once again that if you do not behave yourself, I will give you the divorce you want so badly, but I will not let you keep Katherine. I will drag your name through the courts and have you branded an unfaithful wife and an unfit mother."

"You wouldn't dare."

"Indeed I would.

"And what about that mistress you keep on the side?" Mary flared, her voice bitter. "Lila, I believe her name is."

Frank shrugged. "A man is allowed an indiscretion now and then. Besides, I have enough money to hush up any scandal you might try to create."

Dismayed and discouraged, Mary turned on her heel and went to the nursery, but even playing with Katherine failed to lift her spirits. Why should she have to stay with Frank until he decided he no longer wanted her? she wondered bleakly. Oh, it was so unfair!

That night she wrote a long letter to her mother, pouring out her unhappiness, telling her how Frank had threatened to take Katherine away from her if she tried to leave him again. She begged her mother for help, signed the letter with love, and gave it to Manly to be posted with the other mail.

The next evening, Frank returned the letter to Mary. It had been opened.

"I think you might want to rewrite that," Frank suggested. His voice was mild, but there was a hard glint in his eyes.

Mary nodded. There was no point in arguing.

The following week, Frank announced his intention to run for the United States Senate, and Mary felt the chains growing tighter. Frank would never divorce her now. It wouldn't look good to the voters.

Another month went by, and Mary spent most of the time locked in her room or in the nursery playing with Katherine. She used her pregnancy to decline the invitations to parties and socials that came her way. It was a valid excuse and no one questioned it. Many ladies did not appear in public from the time they suspected they were in the family way until after the baby was born. Naturally, Frank did not let his wife's affliction keep him at home. He attended every social function, exuding charm and wit, lamenting the fact that his dear wife was indisposed.

Mary wrote another letter to her parents, advising them she was expecting another baby the first of January. She wrote about how big the house was, about how well Katherine was walking now, and how she had cut two teeth. She made no mention of Frank, or the fact that they now had separate bedrooms, other than to say he had decided to run for the Senate.

When she finished the letter, she handed it to Manly, unsealed.

It did not come back.

28

I frowned as I read Mary's letter for the second time. "There's something wrong," I remarked to Shadow. "Something she's not telling us."

"She is unhappy in Chicago," Shadow replied with a shrug. "She does not want to be there."

"It's more than that," I insisted. "Mary's letters have always been cheerful and spontaneous. This one sounds like . . . oh, I don't know, like she was afraid to say what she was really feeling. I think we should go to Chicago."

"Chicago!" Shadow exclaimed.

I grinned triumphantly. I had his attention now. "Yes, Chicago. I know how you hate cities, but I think Mary needs us."

Shadow frowned thoughtfully. "I think it would

be a waste of time. She is Frank's wife. She must do as he says."

I looked at Shadow, one eyebrow raised in consternation. "Aren't you the same man who was going to break his son out of jail if he didn't get a fair trial?"

Shadow's lips twitched slightly.

"The same man who defied the soldiers when they said *all* Indians must go to the reservation?" I went on. "The same man who made sure Hawk could participate in the Sun Dance even though it had been outlawed by the whites?"

Shadow was chuckling now.

I pressed my advantage. "The Shadow I used to know wouldn't let his daughter remain in an unhappy situation just because the law said it was the thing to do."

"Pack your bags, woman," Shadow said with mock ferocity. "We will leave first thing in the morning."

As it turned out, we made our plans for nothing.

Cloud Walker read Mary's letter twice, his face impassive. "I am going after her," he said, handing me the letter.

"There will be less trouble if Hannah and I go," Shadow remarked.

"Maybe," Cloud Walker said. "But she is my woman. I will go."

"Have you ever been in a big city before?" I asked.

Cloud Walker shook his head. "No. What difference does it make?"

"Maybe none," I said, "but it would be easier if we went along, to help with hotels and the like."

Cloud Walker shook his head stubbornly. "She is expecting a baby in January."

Shadow frowned. "What is your point?"

"It cannot be Frank Smythe's child."

I did some quick counting on my fingers. Cloud Walker was right. The baby could not be Frank's. I glanced at Shadow. "That's what she neglected to mention."

Shadow nodded. "Are you sure you want to go alone?" he asked Cloud Walker.

"Yes. I will leave in the morning."

I sat on the sofa, my heart heavy, after Cloud Walker left the house. Poor Mary, having to face Frank every day. I was sure he was making her life a hell on earth.

"There is nothing we can do now but wait," Shadow said. "Worrying will not help."

"I suppose you're not worried at all?"

Shadow grinned at me. "Perhaps a little."

"Do you think Cloud Walker will be all right?"

Shadow chuckled softly. "I think he will be fine. I am not so sure about Frank Smythe."

Cloud Walker boarded the train to Steel's Crossing early the following morning. It was his first train ride, and he had a moment of panic as the engine roared to life. It was a new experience, being carried along on a vehicle over which he had no control. Gradually he relaxed and began to enjoy the ride. The train was much faster than a horse. It would carry him quickly to Chicago, and Mary.

At Steel's Crossing he was disappointed to learn that the train for Chicago wouldn't leave until the following afternoon. At loose ends, he wandered through the town. It was much larger and more modern than Bear Valley. There was a daily newspaper, several banks, three restaurants, even a theater starring Vivian Dupre, "The Woman with the Velvet Voice." There were telephones in several establishments, and Cloud Walker wondered if Mary had a telephone.

He received a good many curious stares as he roamed from one end of the town to the other. Unlike the people of Bear Valley, the citizens of Steel's Crossing were unaccustomed to the sight of Indians prowling about. A few men made rude comments about Indians who thought they were as good as whites, but Cloud Walker let it pass. As much as he would have liked to show these smug whites what he thought of them, he knew that if he stepped out of line he would likely be arrested and thrown in jail, and trouble with the law was something he could not afford, not now when Mary needed him. He felt a sudden excitement as he thought of seeing Mary again. Mary, who was pregnant with his child.

That night he went to the finest restaurant in Steel's Crossing. At first he thought the owner would refuse to seat him, but the man showed Cloud Walker to a table in the far corner of the room. Cloud Walker ordered steak and potatoes. Then, carefully watching the people around him, he copied their behavior.

After dinner he went to hear Vivian Dupre. She did indeed have a voice like velvet, soft and smooth, but Cloud Walker hardly noticed. She was a striking woman, with long black hair and wide, expressive brown eyes. But it was her outfit that held Cloud Walker mesmerized. She was wearing just enough clothing to remain decent, if you could call a woman who exposed her arms, legs, and a good deal of cleavage decent.

Later he walked down the street, peering in store windows, marveling at the many luxuries and gadgets displayed. Growing weary, he walked to the outskirts of town and settled down on a patch of grass to spend the night. Lying there gazing up at the stars, he thought of Mary.

He had missed her as a man might miss an arm or a leg. He had been able to function. His life had not ended. But a vital part of himself had been missing ever since she left Bear Valley.

His eyes narrowed as he thought of Frank. If he had harmed Mary or Katherine, he would pay with his life.

Closing his eyes, Cloud Walker thought of Mary, only Mary, and in his dreams they lived happily ever after.

Just after noon Cloud Walker boarded the train that would take him to Chicago. Face impassive, he sat staring out the window watching the countryside fly by. The train went across land that had once known only the Indian and the buffalo, and he felt an old anger stir to life. The Army had driven the Sioux and the Cheyenne and the Arapahoe from the land so that settlers and pioneers could travel unmolested across the plains on their way to California and Arizona and Oregon. Miners had swarmed over the Black Hills in search of gold, polluting the streams and scaring away the game. The great herds of buffalo had been hunted to near extinction. Often hundreds of the big shaggy beasts had been slain for their hides alone. Now the land stretched away for endless miles, and as the train swept by, it seemed to Cloud Walker that he could hear the land weeping softly, mourning for the loss of the red man and the curly-haired buffalo.

A great sadness filled Cloud Walker's heart. No longer did the Cheyenne raise their lodges on the banks of the Powder and the Rosebud, no longer did the Sioux ride wild and free in the shadow of the sacred Black Hills. No longer did the squaws pick the wild roses that grew along the banks of the Rosebud River. Never again would the children play in the valley of the Little Big Horn. There was only stillness now, a great silence broken only by the churning wheels of the iron horse as it raced along the narrow twin ribbons of steel.

Cloud Walker arrived in Chicago on a late afternoon in July. He had no luggage, only a change of clothes wrapped in a blanket. He wore a pair of black trousers and a buckskin shirt, and the color of his skin and his long black hair instantly set him apart from the other men strolling along the sidewalk. Many people turned to gawk at him, their eyes registering surprise at seeing an Indian in their midst.

His first stop was at a livery barn where he rented a leggy bay gelding. Mounted, he felt more at home, and he rode down Chicago's main street taking in the sights and sounds and smells of the big city. He saw people with black skin and people with yellow skin, and he wondered why an Indian should cause such consternation when Negroes and Chinamen did not.

Eventually he found the Smythe mansion and he rode past at a slow walk, his eyes hardly able to take in such luxury. He tried to imagine Mary living in such a monstrous dwelling, but instead he saw her lying in his arms inside a snug lodge. The thought made his blood warm, and he rode to the end of the street and tethered his horse to a tree in a broad grassy expanse. On foot, he returned to Mary's house and took a position across the street, staying out of sight behind a large hedge. He stayed there for two hours, not moving. He saw Frank Smythe arrive home in a large black carriage; saw him leave again an hour later.

Cloud Walker lingered in the shadows until all the lights went out inside the house, and then he padded noiselessly across the road and made his way to the back of the house. It was no trouble at all to climb the fancy trellis to the second-floor veranda, and he sidled along, peering in windows, until he found Mary's room. She was in bed, her eyes closed, her dark brown hair framing her face like a silken cloud. Noiselessly he opened the bedroom window and crept inside.

On quiet feet he moved to her bedside and laid his hand over her mouth. Her eyelids flew open and fear shone in her eyes for an instant. Then she recognized him, and joy danced in her eyes and curved her mouth into a smile of welcome.

"Cloud Walker!" she exclaimed in a hushed whisper. "What are you doing here?"

"I have come to take you home."

"I missed you," Mary murmured. She reached out to stroke his cheek, to assure herself that he was really there and not just a dream. "I missed you so much."

"I know," Cloud Walker replied. "With me it was the same." He gazed at her intently. "Did he . . . did he hurt you?"

Mary hesitated before replying. "No."

"Do not lie to me."

"I don't want to talk about Frank," Mary said. "He didn't hurt me. Not in the way you mean."

"I would like to kill him," Cloud Walker rasped. "With my bare hands!"

"Don't talk that way, please," Mary begged. "It frightens me."

"Mary." His dark eyes grew warm and tender as he gazed at her lovely face. He wanted her so much, yet he was almost afraid to touch her, afraid his desire would rage out of control and he would do something to make her hate him or, worse, fear him.

Mary frowned up at him, her eyes searching his as she felt him tremble. "What is it?"

"I want you. Now. Always."

"I'm yours," Mary replied softly. "Now. Always."

Smiling provocatively, she drew the blankets aside and then, slowly and deliberately, began to unlace the ribbons that held her nightgown together. Her eyes never left his face as she slid the flimsy garment over her head and let it fall to the floor.

Cloud Walker's mouth went dry as he watched her. Never had she seemed more tempting, more desirable. Never had he wanted her more.

With a smile brimming with love, Mary reached up and tugged Cloud Walker's shirt. Wordlessly he shrugged out of his shirt, stripped off his pants and moccasins. Still, he hesitated. He had wanted her for so long, and now she was there, only inches away, offering herself to him. His eyes moved over her face, marveling anew at the quiet beauty he saw there. Her eyes, always so revealing, spoke volumes to him now.

"Mary."

Her face glowed with desire as she reached for his hand, drawing him down beside her on the bed. His arms slid around her, his hands stroking the smooth, silken flesh that was his, all his. He caressed her breasts, thrilling to the way they filled his palms, warm and alive. His fingers stroked the valley between her thighs, then moved lazily over her abdomen. His child rested there.

"It's not Frank's," Mary said.

"I know," he said tremulously. "My heart soars like a hawk." Whispering love words in her ear, he began to kiss her. "Maheo has answered my prayers."

He had thought to make love to her tenderly, gently, slowly, but Mary was on fire for his touch. Tonight she did not want tenderness, she wanted to be possessed, masterfully and powerfully. She needed his lips on hers, branding her as his, needed to yield to his strength, to blot out all memory of Frank. She offered herself to Cloud Walker heart and soul, knowing she was where she yearned to be, where she had always belonged.

Cloud Walker understood her need, and he made love to her fiercely, his hands and mouth telling her

with each caress and kiss that she belonged to him;
that she would never belong to another.

Their passion bound them together in a world
that was beautiful and tumultuous, and Mary felt a
deep sense of peace as Cloud Walker emptied his life
into her, a sense of knowing who she was and what she
wanted from life. She belonged to Cloud Walker now,
belonged to him in a way more binding than mere
words on a marriage certificate.

She knew they faced a difficult time ahead. Frank
might never give her a divorce. She might never be
able to marry Cloud Walker according to the laws of
man, but in her heart, Mary became Cloud Walker's
wife that night.

Mary woke abruptly. Had it all been a dream?
But no, Cloud Walker was lying beside her, his face
only inches from her own. He was here. He had come
to take her home. . . .

But she couldn't go home. Frank had threatened
to take Katherine from her if she tried to leave him
again, and she believed him. As much as she loved
Cloud Walker, she could not take a chance of losing
her daughter.

Pressing her hand to her mouth, she choked back
a sob of despair. Why did life have to be so cruel?

Cloud Walker's eyes opened and he smiled drows-
ily as he drew Mary closer and kissed her. "How long
will it take you to pack?"

Mary shook her head, her eyes filling with misery. "I can't go with you."

Cloud Walker's eyes narrowed. "Why not?"

"Frank. He'll take Katherine away from me. He can do it," she cried as Cloud Walker shook his head. "He has money and power and friends in high places."

Cloud Walker was about to argue with her when he heard footsteps in the hallway. Rolling over, he slid out of bed, grabbed his knife, and stood behind the door.

Mary licked her lips nervously as Frank opened the door and entered the room.

"Get dressed," Frank said curtly. "We've been invited to the mayor's house for breakfast. I would have told you about it last night, but . . ."

Frank's voice trailed off as the door closed behind him. Turning, he saw Cloud Walker standing across the room, knife in hand. "What the hell are you doing here?" Frank exclaimed, and then he snorted derisively as he glanced from Cloud Walker to Mary. "You little slut," he hissed. "Spreading your legs for that savage right here in my house. I ought to kill you."

Mary's face went white, but her eyes blazed with anger. "Slut, am I?" she shouted. "And where have you been, husband of mine?" she sneered. "And since we're speaking of sluts, how is Lila?"

Frank's face went purple with fury. In an instant he was across the room, his hand lashing out to strike Mary across the face.

Rage filled Cloud Walker as Mary let out a cry of pain. Throwing the knife aside, he hurled himself on Frank before he could strike Mary again, and the two men crashed to the floor. Cloud Walker's fists slammed into Frank Smythe's face, hammering blow after blow. Blood coated his hands as Frank's lower lip split, and

Cloud Walker knew an ancient sense of satisfaction as his enemy's blood warmed his hands.

"Cloud Walker, stop!" Mary cried. "You'll kill him!"

With an effort, Cloud Walker checked his temper. Rising, he backed away from Frank, who was barely conscious.

"Pack whatever you need and let us go," Cloud Walker told Mary.

She didn't argue, but quickly donned a long gray skirt and a simple white blouse. Grabbing a small valise, she packed a change of clothing and a few toilet articles.

"I'll get Katherine while you dress," she said. She hesitated at the door, her eyes darting from Frank to Cloud Walker. Frank groaned softly as he sat up, his hand rubbing his jaw.

Mary met Cloud Walker's eyes. "Will you be all right?"

Cloud Walker nodded. "Hurry."

Frank Smythe didn't move as he watched Cloud Walker dress. A cold fury burned in his brain, but caution warned him this was not the time to make his move.

"I should have let Castrell kill you," Frank muttered under his breath.

"Yes," Cloud Walker agreed. He shoved his knife into the waistband of his pants. "I am taking Mary home, and you will not try to stop us. If you do, I will peel the skin from your body an inch at a time and leave your carcass for the wolves."

Frank nodded. "Just get the hell out of my sight," he rasped.

Twenty minutes later, Mary and Cloud Walker left the Smythe mansion. Frank stood in the doorway watching them leave, and then he went to the telephone.

The first train west left in an hour. Cloud Walker purchased their tickets, then they went to a nearby cafe for breakfast. Mary could not take her eyes from Cloud Walker, could not believe he was here to take her home, that the nightmare with Frank was finally over. She smiled at Katherine, who was babbling happily as she ate from her plate and Cloud Walker's. Katherine had been overjoyed to see Cloud Walker again, and she had refused to leave his arms.

After breakfast they walked to the depot and boarded the train. Excitement fluttered in Mary's stomach as she took a seat by a window. Home. She was going home.

Cloud Walker sat beside her, his muscles tense, his jaw rigid. Frank Smythe was not the kind of man to give up something he wanted without a fight.

Mary laughed aloud as the train lurched into motion. "Home, Katherine," she exclaimed happily. "We're going home."

"Go home," Katherine said, and clapped her hands.

The motion of the train and the constant hum of the wheels on the track soon lulled Katherine to sleep. Mary, happy and content, rested her head on Cloud

Walker's shoulder and she too fell asleep.

They had stopped at a small town some sixty miles out of Chicago to take on mail and passengers when Frank Smythe and Harvey Castrell slid into the seat across from Cloud Walker. There was a .44 Colt in Castrell's hand. The barrel was aimed at Mary.

Cloud Walker's expression didn't change, though his whole body went rigid. He shook Mary gently. "Wake up."

Mary's eyes grew wide when she saw Frank and Castrell. Her hand tightened on Cloud Walker's arm.

"We're going to get up now," Frank said quietly. "All of us. We're going to get off the train, just like there was nothing wrong." He fixed Cloud Walker with a stern look. "If you try anything, anything at all, Castrell will kill her."

Cloud Walker nodded. Rising, he held Katherine close as he walked down the narrow aisle and stepped off the train. Mary followed, her insides quaking with fear.

Castrell went to rent a buggy while Frank kept an eye on Cloud Walker and Mary.

"Why, Frank?" Mary asked. "Why won't you let me go?"

"Shut up," Frank said mildly.

Castrell arrived a few minutes later. Pulling a length of rope from his back pocket, he tied Cloud Walker's hands behind his back and shoved him into the buggy. Mary followed, holding Katherine. Frank slid in beside her. Castrell drove the team.

Mary's heart slammed against her chest as her fear grew steadily worse. It was obvious that Frank

meant to kill Cloud Walker and dispose of the body
where it wouldn't be found. And it would never be
found out here, she thought, at least not for a long long
time. They were in the woods, going deeper and
deeper. Tall trees reached toward the sky, bushes and
shrubs grew profusely, their long branches making the
way difficult. There seemed to be no path, no trail that
would indicate people had passed this way recently. It
was a deserted stretch of country, populated by only a
handful of people who manned the train depot.

Cloud Walker kept his eyes on Frank. What did
the man have in mind? The answer burned in his brain
even as the question took shape. It was obvious that
Frank meant to kill him and take Mary back to
Chicago.

An icy calm settled over Cloud Walker as Castrell
reined the team to a halt. They were deep in the heart
of the forest now.

"Get out," Frank said.

Mary looked at Cloud Walker, her face as pale as
death, her eyes wide with fear.

"Do as he says," Cloud Walker said, his voice
betraying none of the apprehension he was feeling. "It
will be all right."

Clutching Katherine to her breast, Mary climbed
from the buggy, followed by Cloud Walker and Frank.
Castrell jumped from the driver's seat and came to
stand beside Frank.

"What are you going to do?" Mary's voice was a
hoarse whisper.

Frank grinned maliciously. "I'm going to castrate
that sonofabitch, and then I'm going to kill him. But

first I'm going to beat the hell out of him."

"No." Mary shook her head. "Please, Frank."

"'Please, Frank,'" he mocked. "It's too late for please, my dear."

Mary's heart filled with despair as Frank drove his fist into Cloud Walker's midsection. "Nobody takes what's mine," Frank growled, his fist smashing into Cloud Walker's face. "Nobody."

"Frank, stop!"

"Shut up, you slut!" Frank roared. "Or you'll be next."

Smythe hit Cloud Walker again, and Katherine began to cry. Choking back her own tears, Mary covered her daughter's eyes.

At last Frank stepped back. He rubbed his bruised knuckles, his eyes bright with satisfaction when he saw the damage he had done.

"Ready, Frank?" Castrell asked.

Frank nodded, and Castrell yanked Cloud Walker's trousers down around his ankles, then shoved him to the ground.

Mary felt the blood drain from her face as Harvey Castrell pulled a wicked-looking knife from his belt and handed it to Frank.

Cloud Walker began to struggle as best he could with his hands tied behind his back until Castrell jabbed the barrel of his Colt under his chin.

Frank knelt beside Cloud Walker, his lips pulled back in a venomous grin. "Spread 'em," he said curtly.

Cloud Walker was breathing heavily. Blood oozed from his nose and mouth and a dozen minor cuts, but he was hardly aware of the pain. His eyes glittered savagely as he glared at Frank Smythe. Sweat poured down his face as he eyed the skinning knife clutched in Frank's right hand. He could hear Mary sobbing, and he felt suddenly sorry that she would have to witness what was about to happen.

"Spread 'em," Frank said again. "When I get through with you, you'll never bed another white woman, or any other kind."

Cloud Walker closed his eyes, his jaw rigid, as he felt cold steel touch his genitals. It was going to happen, and there was nothing he could do about it. He was suddenly glad that Frank meant to kill him when it was over. Death would be better than living the rest of his life as half a man.

Mary watched what was happening, unable to believe her eyes, unable to believe that even Frank could be so cruel. She saw Cloud Walker flinch as Frank pressed the knife to his flesh, and she knew with awful certainty that Frank meant to do it. In an instant, she placed Katherine on the ground, scooped up a sturdy tree limb lying on the ground next to her foot, and ran forward.

"Mama!"

At Katherine's cry, Frank swung around. Muttering an oath, he dropped the knife and scrambled out of harm's way. Castrell was not quite so fast, and Mary struck him across the side of the head with the makeshift club. He fell sideways without a sound, knocked unconscious by the blow.

Katherine stared at her mother. Frightened by the violence she feared and did not understand, she started toward Cloud Walker. He would protect her.

Tossing the club away, Mary dropped to her knees and grabbed Castrell's gun from his holster. Scrambling around, she aimed the gun at Frank, felt her blood turn cold when she saw that Frank was smiling. There was a gun in his hand now, and the barrel was aimed at Cloud Walker.

"Tell him good-bye," Frank said. His voice was raw, his eyes filled with a lust for blood as his thumb drew the hammer to full cock.

There was no time to think. There was only time to act. She knew that Frank meant to kill Cloud Walker and that she had to stop him.

With a wordless cry, she squeezed the trigger. The bullet slammed into Frank's shoulder, numbing his arm so that he dropped the gun just as Katherine reached for Cloud Walker. The gun discharged as it hit the ground. The heavy .45 caliber slug passed through Katherine's body on an upward trajectory and came to rest just under Mary's right breast.

Mary let out an anguished scream as she saw her daughter collapse, and then she toppled to the ground.

Frank Smythe's face paled as his daughter fell, and he stared at her as if seeing her for the first time.

Rage pumped adrenalin into Cloud Walker's limbs as he watched Mary and Katherine fall. With a mighty effort, he burst his bonds.

"You bastard," Cloud Walker hissed, his hands reaching for Frank's throat.

Smythe recovered quickly. There was death in Cloud Walker's narrow-eyed gaze, and Frank dived for the gun he had dropped as he rolled out of harm's way, cursing as the movement sent a shaft of pain darting through his wounded shoulder.

Cloud Walker was moving, too, his hand grabbing the gun that had fallen from Mary's hand.

Two gunshots cracked in the stillness, and when the smoke cleared, Frank Smythe was dead.

Grief and anger warred in Cloud Walker's heart as he gazed down upon the man sprawled at his feet. This was the enemy, the man who had killed everything he loved. With a wild cry of pain and rage, he grabbed Castrell's knife and lifted Frank's scalp.

It was only then, as he stared at the grisly trophy in his hand, that his rage cooled and reality set in. Flinging the bloody scalp away, he knelt between Mary and Katherine, unmindful of the tears that dampened his cheeks. Katherine was dead, and Mary too. . . .

His heart quickened with unreasoning hope as Mary's body jerked spasmodically. She was alive! He moved quickly now. Using matches he found in Smythe's coat pocket, he lit a small fire. Wiping Frank's blood from the knife, he heated the blade in the fire to sterilize it, then let it cool. The bullet that was lodged in Mary's breast would have to be removed, and it would be easier to do it now while she was unconscious.

Cutting into Mary's tender flesh was the hardest thing he had ever done. She groaned, her face contorting with pain as he probed for the slug. Her eyes flew open as the tip of the blade located the bullet.

"Lie still," Cloud Walker said.

"What happened?"

"You've been hurt. Just lie still."

"Katherine. I want Katherine."

He could not speak, could not say the words that he knew would shatter her world.

Mary stared into Cloud Walker's eyes. His silence said it all, and she began to cry, great wracking sobs that came from the depths of her heart and soul. Her daughter was dead. So great was her pain at Katherine's death that she hardly felt the knife as it pried the slug from her flesh. She cried as Cloud Walker wiped the blood from the wound and then bandaged it with a strip of cloth torn from her petticoat.

She pushed him away when he would have gathered her into his arms. "No," she sobbed. "Leave me alone."

"Mary." The pain in his voice was only a little less acute than hers, but she did not hear it. Her daughter was dead and it was all his fault. If he hadn't come after her, Katherine would still be alive.

She wept until exhaustion claimed her.

Lifting Mary in his arms, Cloud Walker carried her deeper into the woods until he found a place beneath a tree that was smooth and carpeted with grass. Gently he placed her on the ground and covered her with his jacket. He sat beside her for several minutes, silently thanking Man Above that she was alive.

Sitting there, with the tension slowly draining out of him, he became aware of the aches and pains that Frank's beating had inflicted. Lifting a hand to his face, he grimaced as his fingers encountered bruised flesh. His left eye was swollen and sore.

He could hear the soft trickling of water rolling over stones some yards away. With a grunt, he stood up and made his way to the shallow stream where he washed the blood from his face and hands, and then took a long drink. The water was cold and sweet.

It was peaceful near the stream and he would have liked to stay there longer, but there were things to be done. Smythe had to be buried. Castrell would have to be taken care of. He thought briefly of killing the man, but enough blood had been shed for one day. And Katherine . . . tears stung his eyes as he thought of her running toward him, her arms outstretched, only to be killed by the same bullet that had wounded her mother.

When he reached the bodies, he saw that Castrell and one of the coach horses were gone, but there was no time to worry about Harvey Castrell. With any luck, he would die before he reached help.

Cloud Walker wrapped Katherine's body in several thick layers of moss, then wrapped her in Frank's coat and placed her inside the carriage. Dragging Frank's body into the woods, he used a flat piece of wood to dig a shallow grave and dumped the corpse into it.

Returning to the buggy, he unhitched the remaining horse and fashioned a crude bridle from a length of rein. Swinging aboard the animal's bare back, he rode to where he had left Mary. She was still asleep, her cheeks stained with her tears.

Riding to the train depot, he went to the small

store that supplied groceries to the local citizens and picked up a bottle of aspirin, iodine, bandages, enough food to last two or three days, and a couple of blankets.

The man in the mercantile store eyed Cloud Walker curiously. Indians were a rarity in these parts now.

"Somebody get hurt?" the man asked as he added up Cloud Walker's purchases.

"Hunting accident," Cloud Walker replied tersely.

"Hope it ain't serious," the man remarked. "Nearest doctor is forty miles east of here."

Cloud Walker grunted noncommittally, paid for his supplies, and left the store, which was the only building in town besides the telegraph office, a small restaurant, and a livery.

He stopped outside the telegraph office, intending to send a wire to Hannah and Shadow advising them of Katherine's death, but then changed his mind. There was no point in worrying them now, he thought bleakly, no point in breaking their hearts any sooner than necessary.

At the station depot he checked the departure schedule. The next train west was in five days.

His thoughts were troubled as he rode back to Mary. He had killed a white man, and they would surely hang him for that. No matter that Frank had intended to kill him, no matter that Frank had inadvertently killed Katherine and injured Mary. He had killed a white man who was rich and powerful.

He put the thought from his mind. He would

worry about it later. For now, he would focus all his energy on nursing Mary back to health and be glad that he would have these few days to spend alone with her before they returned to Bear Valley.

For Mary, the next few days passed in a haze of pain and grief. Waking, she was ever aware of Cloud Walker hovering at her side, his dark eyes haunted with grief and guilt. She knew that he would hold her and comfort her if she only said the word, but she could not seem to speak past the hard lump in her throat. She had let her love for Cloud Walker override everything else, and now Katherine had paid the price for her mother's lack of self-control. Katherine was dead, and nothing would ever be the same again.

She sought refuge in sleep, hiding from Cloud Walker's stricken gaze, hiding from her own hurt, her own guilt. But even her dreams betrayed her, and she relived the nightmare over and over again, waking in tears as she saw her daughter fall, heard her child's last anguished cry.

For three days she was wracked by pain and fever and guilt. Cloud Walker tended her wounds, changing the bandages often, insisting that she eat and drink even though she had no appetite. He held her close when the fever turned to chills, warming her body with his own. She saw the hurt in his eyes, and knew that he was suffering over Katherine's death almost as deeply as she, but she could not relent, could not reach out to bridge the awful gap that lay between them.

Four days after Katherine's death, Mary's fever broke. It was only then, as she lay staring at the sky, that she thought to ask about Frank.

"He's dead," Cloud Walker told her, his voice hard and flat.

"Dead?" Mary frowned. Had she killed him?

She looked at Cloud Walker and he shook his head.

"I killed him," he said. "He's buried in the woods."

"And Castrell?"

Cloud Walker shrugged. "I do not know. He took one of the horses and lit out."

Mary nodded, shocked by the wave of relief that washed through her. Frank would never hurt her again. He would not hurt Cloud Walker again, or threaten to take Katherine away from her . . . Katherine.

The fresh realization of her daughter's death stabbed at her heart.

"Mary." He ached for the pain he saw in her face.

"Take me home," she said, her voice empty of emotion. That was all she wanted now, to go home, to lay her head on her father's shoulder and pour out the pain that gripped her heart. It would be so good to see her mother again. Hannah, too, had lost a child. She would understand.

Cloud Walker settled Mary in the buggy, a blanket over her lap. "Are you comfortable?"

Mary nodded, and he turned away. Earlier he had taken Katherine's body from the carriage and placed it under the driver's seat where Mary could not see it.

At the station he carried Katherine's body to the baggage car. By luck there was a large empty crate inside, and the porter said he could place Katherine's body inside. Thanking the man for his kindness, he returned to the buggy for Mary. They found a seat in the last car, where there were no other passengers.

Mary sat at the window staring out. She felt numb, drained, empty of life. The wound in her breast ached a little, but it was as nothing compared to the ache in her heart. Why hadn't she stayed in Chicago? If only she had stayed with Frank where she belonged, her daughter would be alive today. Her arms ached to hold Katherine, to hear the child's happy laughter just once more, to see her sunny smile. . . .

"Mary."

Slowly she turned to face Cloud Walker. This was the man she loved. Why couldn't she feel anything for him?

"It was not your fault," Cloud Walker said, his voice filled with compassion and understanding. "Or mine. Do not go on blaming yourself, or me. It was an accident. There is no one to blame."

"An accident is when you spill a glass of milk," Mary replied bitterly. "My daughter is dead. Don't you understand? She's dead!" She jerked her hand away as he reached for her. "Don't touch me!" she screamed, tears washing down her cheeks. "Don't ever touch me again!"

"Mary." His voice was heavy with pain as he whispered her name. She was sobbing pathetically, her shoulders heaving with the force of her tears. Ignoring her protests, Cloud Walker gathered Mary into his arms and held her while she cried, and all the while he murmured to her, telling her that he loved her, that the pain would pass with time. When she wailed that it would not, he reminded her gently that he had lost a son not very long ago, and that the pain had indeed lessened.

"One day you will be able to remember Katherine and smile," Cloud Walker promised. "It will not be today, and not tomorrow. But one day." He placed his hand over her stomach. "Soon you will have another child to love," he reminded her. "Try to think of that, for now."

Mary gazed into Cloud Walker's face, seeing him, really seeing him, for the first time in days. His eyes were red-rimmed and deeply shadowed, as though he had not been sleeping well. There were long scabs on both his arms, and she knew he had gashed his flesh in his grief over Katherine's death. He too was suffering, she realized, suddenly ashamed of the way she had been treating him. She had been so wrapped up in her own grief that she had spared no thought for what Cloud Walker was feeling, for what he had been suffering. He had loved Katherine dearly. He had been the one who had washed the blood from the child's body and wrapped her in a shroud. It could not have been easy for him. None of it had been easy.

"I'm sorry," she whispered. "Sorry for the awful way I've treated you and the terrible things I said. Can you ever forgive me?"

Cloud Walker smiled for the first time in days. "There is nothing to forgive," he murmured, his voice thick with emotion. "I love you, Mary. I will always love you."

"Show me," she whispered, and closed her eyes as he pressed his lips to hers in a tender bestowal of affection.

The tears came then, but they were no longer tears of bitterness, but the gentle tears of a healing heart.

29

Victoria and I wept softly as we listened to Cloud Walker tell of Frank Smythe's treachery and Katherine's death. My heart ached for Mary. She had known so much unhappiness in her life, and now this.

"So," Shadow said. "What now?"

"He'll have to turn himself in," Vickie said. "What else can he do?"

All the color drained from Mary's face. "No!"

Cloud Walker's expression was bleak. "Victoria is right. Frank was too well-known to just disappear."

Shadow nodded. "That is true."

Hawk snorted. "What kind of trial do you think Cloud Walker will get? Certainly not a fair one, not in this town."

"There's not much law out here," Mary cried. "Why does anyone have to know? Please, Cloud Walker, don't leave me."

Cloud Walker ran a hand across his jaw. Hawk was right. He would never get a fair trial. Not here. Not anywhere. No one would believe he had killed Frank in self-defense. There were no witnesses. Only Harvey Castrell knew that Frank had intended to kill him, and Castrell wasn't likely to come forward in Cloud Walker's defense, even if they knew where to find him.

"If he doesn't turn himself in, it will only make him look like he has something to hide," Vickie said.

Mary went to stand beside Cloud Walker. "Please don't turn yourself in," she begged, her eyes huge in her pale face. "You're all I have left."

"Mary . . ."

"I don't want to live without you."

Cloud Walker shook his head helplessly. She looked so frail, so distraught. How could he leave her? Drawing Mary into his arms, he looked over her head toward Shadow.

Shadow shrugged. "I have no love for the white man, and no faith in his laws. But the decision must be yours. If it were me, I would wait to see what happens."

Cloud Walker nodded. He had no desire to spend time in jail, no reason to believe he would get a fair trial, or any trial at all.

"You won't go to the law then?" Mary asked hopefully.

"No. We will wait and see what happens," he said heavily and knew deep inside that it was a mistake.

Later, when Victoria and Mary were out of the room, Cloud Walker told us he had scalped Frank, a detail he had omitted earlier.

The thought sickened me, but Shadow nodded his approval. "About time someone took the bastard's hair," he muttered under his breath, and I saw Hawk smile.

We buried Katherine on a windswept hill under a tall pine tree. Cloud Walker held Mary while she cried, and I prayed that the two of them might find happiness together at last, for the price of their love had come high.

News of Mary's homecoming spread rapidly through the valley. Eyebrows were raised when people learned that she had left her husband for Cloud Walker. And when people discovered that Mary was pregnant, the rumors spread like wildfire. The gossips had a field day then, speculating on whether the baby was Frank's or Cloud Walker's.

Six weeks later, Mary and Cloud Walker were married by an old medicine man Shadow had summoned from the reservation. The wedding was held at the river crossing late at night, with only our family present. Mary wore a doeskin tunic I had made for her, Cloud Walker wore a pair of buckskin trousers and a fringed buckskin shirt. The rest of us also wore traditional Indian garb.

It was like taking a step back in time. Night Owl took Cloud Walker's hand in his and made a shallow incision in the palm of his right hand. Then, taking Mary's hand, he made a similar incision in her palm. His wrinkled face was grave as he joined their hands together. Solemnly he gazed from Mary to Cloud Walker, his deep-set black eyes as old as time.

"Now your blood runs together," he said in a quiet voice. "You are now two people, but one blood. What happens to one, happens to the other. When one feels joy, both will share it. When one feels pain, the other will know it. You will be a help to each other, nevermore to be alone, nevermore to be alone. Be kind to each other, and always remember that Maheo is with you."

Standing beside Shadow, I felt as if my own marriage vows had been renewed. As Cloud Walker tenderly kissed Mary, Shadow kissed me. And then Hawk kissed Victoria. We all laughed, our hearts filling with joy for the first time in weeks, as Jacob turned to Jason and kissed him soundly on the cheek.

Mary and Cloud Walker moved into the lodge behind our house so they could have a place of their own. I was sorry that Mary could not have a big wedding and a home of her own, but such a thing was out of the question until the matter of Frank's death was resolved.

Mary was suddenly, unaccountably shy as she followed Cloud Walker into the lodge. She watched as he touched a match to the kindling laid in the fire pit, and doubts began to fill her mind. What if this marriage didn't work either? She had been so sure she loved Frank, and look how that had turned out.

But then Cloud Walker came toward her, his dark eyes filled with tenderness, and all her misgivings vanished like smoke in a high wind. She must put the past and its tragedies behind her. Her heart swelled with such love it was almost painful as he took her in his arms and kissed her gently.

"Mary," he said huskily. "I cannot believe you are truly mine."

"Believe it," she whispered, and drawing his head down, she pressed her lips to his. A warm sense of belonging washed over her as her heart assured her that this was right. She didn't need a big wedding and a fancy dress, didn't need a white cake and champagne. Cloud Walker was her husband now. Her child would be born to its true father.

How tenderly they made love that night, heart speaking to heart and soul to soul. Mary let her eyes and hands roam over each precious inch of Cloud Walker's flesh, reveling in what she saw and felt, telling herself again and again that he was hers now, hers forever.

"I love you," Mary whispered.

"Ne-mehotatse," Cloud Walker replied, repeating the words in the Cheyenne tongue, and Mary was certain she had never heard a more beautiful phrase in all her life.

"Ne-mehotatse," she murmured tremulously, and Cloud Walker's smile warmed her to her soul. "I'll try to be a good wife," she promised.

"You are already a good wife," Cloud Walker said, nuzzling her breast.

"Is this all it takes to make you happy?" Mary teased.

Cloud Walker nodded, his hands stroking her hips and thighs as his tongue tickled her ear.

"I'll hold you to that," Mary vowed. "When the house is dirty and the kids are underfoot and there's no supper on the table, I'll just take you to bed and you'll have no complaints coming."

"Just one," Cloud Walker said, grinning. "You talk too much."

"Do I?"

"Yes," he said, and silenced her with a kiss.

He wanted her. Mary could feel the need in the tautness of his muscles, in the rasp of his breathing, in the press of his manhood against her belly. His desire sparked her own and she drew him close, her hands roaming over his flesh, her nails raking his back and shoulders as he possessed her. They moved together rhythmically, gracefully, like dancers, and Mary moaned softly as her own need for fulfillment soared upward. She strained toward him, feeling as though she would die if he did not give her that which she sought, and then it came, that sweet, sweet release that was so satisfying, so fleeting.

She closed her eyes, sighing with contentment as Cloud Walker shuddered convulsively, then lay still, his head pillowed on her shoulder.

For a time they did not move, then Cloud Walker rolled onto his side, taking Mary with him. She was soon asleep, but he remained awake for a long time, his face buried in the wealth of her hair, his hand cupping her breast. She was his wife now, his woman, and he would live and die for her.

Later, lying there beside her, he felt his child stir beneath his hand.

His child. Closing his eyes, he offered a silent prayer to Man Above, beseeching Him to bless the child with health and strength. And then, remembering Katherine and his own dead son, he prayed that the child might be blessed with a long and happy life.

I sat in the tub relaxing, my thoughts reliving Mary's wedding the night before. Mary had made a lovely bride, despite the hint of sadness that remained in her eyes. I understood the pain she felt at Katherine's loss. It was a hurt that would not heal quickly.

I was thinking of leaving the warmth of the tub when Shadow entered the room. I could feel him watching me and I was suddenly glad that Blackie had gone to spend the night with Hawk. Through the veil of my lashes I watched my husband pace back and forth, his eyes lingering on my water-covered body as I reclined in the tub.

I smiled as I saw the rising evidence of his desire. It wouldn't be long now, I mused with happy anticipation, and indeed, in a matter of moments Shadow had shucked his clothes and joined me in the bathtub. It was a tight fit, but we managed, and we spent a few pleasant moments cuddling in the tub.

"I pray Mary will find happiness now," I remarked.

Shadow nodded, his eyes wandering over my submerged flesh.

"I'm glad she's home again," I went on. "I like having our children close by."

"I like having you close by," Shadow remarked, and we began splashing each other. I was brushing my hair out of my face when I saw it, a single gray strand among the red.

"What is it?" Shadow asked, seeing my distressed expression.

"I'm getting old," I lamented. "Look. A gray hair."

Shadow started to laugh, but then, seeing that I was truly upset, he wrapped his arms around me instead.

"You will never be old, Hannah," he said sincerely. "You are young in spirit and young in heart. A gray hair cannot change that."

"But I don't want to get old," I said sadly. "I want to stay young and thin. I don't want you to be married to a wrinkled old crone with gray hair and sagging breasts."

"What of me?" Shadow asked, amused. "Do you think I am not growing older?"

"You don't look any older to me," I said, studying his face critically. "You're still tall and strong and handsome. Your hair is still black as sin. You hardly have a wrinkle. Oh, it isn't fair! Why do men get better looking as they get older? Women just get ugly and fat!"

He was laughing at me now, his dark eyes twinkling merrily. In spite of my protests, he dunked my head under the water to rinse the soap out, then lifted me from the tub and carried me dripping wet to our bedroom. For a moment he held me above the mattress; then, grinning roguishly, he dropped me. I landed on my back, my wet hair spraying water across the bedspread.

Still laughing, Shadow dropped down on top of me.

"What are you doing?" I asked irritably. "I turned to you for sympathy and you laugh at me."

"I am going to make love to you," Shadow said, his eyes glowing with amusement. "I am going to make love to you now, before you turn into a wrinkled old hag right before my eyes."

"And will you still make love to me when I'm a wrinkled old hag?"

"Yes," Shadow said gravely. "But I will close my eyes."

"Oh, you!" Grabbing a pillow from behind my head, I began to hit him with it. We tusseled on the bed for several minutes, wet flesh sliding deliciously against wet flesh as we wrestled in wild abandon. Then Shadow took my face in his hands and his mouth slanted across mine and all thought of fighting left my mind.

"Hannah, my sweet Hannah," Shadow murmured in my ear. "I will always love you. Skinny or fat, gray-headed or bald, young or old, you are my life, my heart. I cannot live without you." Drawing back a little, he gazed down at me, his beautiful black eyes warm and loving. "I want to grow old with you, to share every day that Maheo grants us."

I blinked back my tears as Shadow lowered his head toward mine and kissed me again, a kiss filled with love and promise that would last forever. I never worried about getting old again.

Mary knelt beside her daughter's grave, carefully arranging a bouquet of flowers. It was still hard to believe that Katherine lay sleeping in the ground, hard to accept the fact that her little girl was dead. She smiled through a mist of tears as she felt Cloud Walker's child stir within her womb, and her arms ached with the need to hold a baby again.

Sitting there, she bowed her head and prayed that this child would be strong and healthy. More than anything, she longed to give Cloud Walker a son. He rarely spoke of the little boy who had died, but she knew that the hurt had not healed completely. Perhaps this new child would help them both.

She knew he was there even before he spoke. It didn't seem at all strange that she could sense his presence. He was a part of her, after all.

"I am going into town," Cloud Walker said, squatting down on his heels beside her. "Come with me."

"I'd rather not."

"You cannot hide forever."

"I'm not hiding," Mary replied defensively. But, of course, she was. She was hiding from gossip and prying eyes. The townspeople's curiosity had been merciless ever since she'd returned from Chicago.

"We will have to face them sooner or later."

"Can't it wait until later?"

"No. I am not ashamed of our love."

Mary placed her hand in his. "Let's go and face them, then," she said, smiling bravely.

Mary was conscious of being stared at as they drove into town. Without being aware of it, she sat up a little straighter and placed her hand on Cloud Walker's arm.

It was Saturday and the streets were crowded with men, women and children who had come to town to shop and visit. There were half a dozen women gathered on the porch in front of the mercantile store and they all turned to stare at Mary and Cloud Walker as they drove by.

Cloud Walker drew the buggy to a halt at the feed store. "I will not be long," he said, then frowned as Mary alighted from the buggy. "Where are you going?"

"I need a few things from the mercantile store," Mary said. Head high, she marched down the street. She could hear the women talking about her as she climbed the stairs.

". . . some nerve, coming to town."

". . . left her husband for that Indian."

". . . I wonder who the father of that baby—"

"Good afternoon, ladies," Mary said loudly. She looked each of them in the eye. All the town's biggest gossips were present.

"Good afternoon," Ramona Claxton said stiffly, and the other ladies nodded in Mary's direction.

"Lovely day," Mary said.

"Yes, lovely," Donna Durning agreed.

"I couldn't help but overhear your remarks," Mary said, her mild tone belying the anger raging in her breast. "And since you're all determined to talk about me, I think you should know what you're talking about."

The women glanced at each other, their faces flushed with embarrassment. It was good to see them squirm, Mary thought uncharitably.

"In the first place," Mary went on boldly, "my marriage to Frank Smythe was a failure long before I met Cloud Walker. I don't wish to speak ill of Frank, but suffice it to say I had good and just cause for leaving him. You may believe it or not, but I tried very hard to make my marriage work, and I failed." Mary lifted her head a little higher. "I love Cloud Walker. He's a brave and honorable man. We have the same blood, the same heritage. I'm proud to be his woman, and proud to be carrying his child." She had not thought to let that slip, Mary thought in dismay, but it was out now. She granted them a cloying smile. "I know you'll be kind enough to tell everyone in town what I've said. Good day."

And with that, she swept past them into the store.

"Well, I never!" Donna Durning exclaimed.

"I think we've misjudged her," Muriel Harding remarked. "None of us know Mary very well, yet we were all willing to believe the worst."

"Nonsense," Carol Wilke retorted. "You heard her. She's carrying that Indian's child."

"He is terribly handsome," Muriel Harding mused. "Well, he is!" she insisted as the other women gaped at her.

"He's an Indian, Muriel," Ramona Clayton said derisively. "An *Indian!*"

"And here he comes," Carol Wilke said, lowering her voice.

Cloud Walker glanced up at the women standing on the porch and knew immediately that they had been talking about him. A guilty flush stained their cheeks, and they refused to meet his eyes. The thought of being the center of their gossip stirred his anger, and then he shrugged. You couldn't change human nature. People always feared or belittled what they didn't understand.

He flashed them his most beguiling smile. "Good afternoon, ladies," he said politely.

"Good afternoon," they chorused, and muttering hasty farewells to one another, they scattered like chickens before a fox.

Cloud Walker was laughing when Mary joined him. "What is it?" she asked. "What's so funny?"

"People," he said, lifting her into the buggy. "People can be very funny."

Mary frowned and then felt her cheeks grow hot as Cloud Walker kissed her soundly, right there in front of the mercantile store and about two dozen witnesses.

"That will give them all something to talk about," he said, and jumped into the buggy beside her.

They were smiling when they drove out of town.

The next day there was an item in the paper that gave the gossips still more to talk about. The story stated that Frank Smythe, prominent Chicago businessman, had been missing from his home for several weeks. There was speculation that he had left on a mysterious business trip, as well as the hint of foul play.

The following day, Hannah received a wire from Mattie Smythe asking if she had seen Frank and Mary.

"What are we going to do?" Mary asked, showing Cloud Walker the newspaper and the wire that evening.

"I do not know." The trouble he had foreseen was bearing down on them, he thought bleakly, and he was powerless to stop it. He would have to face the white man's law, or make a run for it. Either way, Mary would be lost to him.

Murmuring her name, he gathered her into his arms and held her tight, his lips moving in her hair. He wished he could tell her how much he loved her, how very dear and precious she was to him, but the words seemed inadequate. Instead, he cupped her face in his hands, his thumbs gently massaging her cheeks, his dark eyes gazing tenderly into hers. And then he kissed her with all the love and need in his heart.

Mary closed her eyes as Cloud Walker's lips brushed hers. Her stomach began to flutter and her whole body grew warm and tingly as Cloud Walker's hands moved slowly downward, caressing her arms and shoulders, then sliding down her ribcage to stroke her buttocks and thighs. Mary swayed against him, the newspaper dropping from her hand, everything else forgotten as she swayed against him, eager for his touch, for the fulfillment only he could offer.

With a low groan of desire, Cloud Walker carried her to their sleeping robes and there he made love to her, slowly, tenderly, his hands and lips trailing fire, his eyes dark with adoration as he kissed each silken inch of honeyed flesh.

"Ne-mehotatse, Mary," he murmured.

"Ne-mehotatse," she breathed softly, and then sighed as he cupped her breast in his hand, rubbing his thumb over the taut pink bud.

She felt his breath, warm upon her skin, as he began kissing her again, making it hard for her to breathe. She spread her hands across his chest, feeling the heat generated by his body. The present mingled with the spell of remembered passion, the one feeding on the other as his mouth slanted over hers. Her lips parted under the pressure of his kiss, her tongue meeting his, causing timeless sensations to swirl like liquid fire to the very center of her being, filling her with an age-old need that only he could satisfy. She closed her eyes as his life filled her with sweet warmth and contentment.

A gentle rap on the wall of the lodge roused Cloud Walker. Rising, he lifted the lodge flap to see Hawk standing outside.

"What is it?" Cloud Walker asked. But he knew. In the back of his mind, he knew.

"I was in town this evening. There is a man asking about you. He has the look of a lawman, though I did not see a badge."

Cloud Walker nodded. He had been expecting something like this for days.

"What are you going to do?" Hawk asked.

Cloud Walker shook his head. He could not bear

the thought of leaving Mary, could not give himself up
if it meant prison or the hangman.

"What is it?" Mary asked, pulling a blanket
around her and coming to stand beside Cloud Walker.
Her face turned ashen as Hawk explained.

"We've got to get out of here," Mary said urgent-
ly. "Now. Does neyho know about this?"

"Not yet," Hawk answered. "I came here first."

While they stood deciding what to do, the sound
of hoofbeats reverberated through the night. Mary
held her breath, her eyes and ears straining toward the
front of her parents' house as the horse came to a halt.

"We've got to go," she said, and began to dress.

"I will stall as long as I can," Hawk said. "Take my
horse."

Things were moving too fast, Cloud Walker
thought, but at Mary's urging, he quickly slipped on
his buckskins and they left the lodge. Mounting
Hawk's horse, they rode away from the house.

It was madness to run, Cloud Walker mused
bleakly. Winter was coming and Mary was pregnant.
But in his mind he could hear the sound of hoofbeats
coming from behind like the echo of doom.

"Hurry," Mary whispered, and Cloud Walker
urged the horse into a gallop, guiding the animal
through the darkness with the familiarity of a man
who knew the land as he knew his own name.

Cloud Walker reined the horse toward the river
crossing, felt Mary shiver as the cool spray kicked up
by the horse washed over them. When they cleared
the opposite bank, he urged the horse into a lope.

Mary clung to Cloud Walker, her eyes closed, her

face buried in his back. She shivered uncontrollably, chilled by the cold night air and by the fear that gripped her heart. Even in death, Frank would not let her go.

They rode for hours, now at a gallop, now at a walk to rest the horse. She knew, without asking, that Cloud Walker was heading for the Black Hills, one-time home of the Sioux and Cheyenne.

They traveled for days, hiding out when the sun rode the sky, traveling beneath the moon and the stars. It was eerie, crossing the endless prairie in the dark, never seeing another human being, listening to the coyotes serenade the night. She felt a new pride in her husband as they journeyed toward their destination, not only for his courage, but for his cunning. He had managed to steal a horse for her to ride, as well as a couple of blankets and a rifle. She had not asked where he managed to find such necessities.

At any other time she would have been appalled that her husband was stealing, but not now, not when it was a matter of life and death. She would have committed the thefts herself to save Cloud Walker.

She felt his eyes on her face, and she turned and smiled at him. He was worried about her, she knew, and she was careful never to complain about the cold or the long hours they spent in the saddle. She did not tell him how her back ached, or how utterly weary she was when they bedded down. Instead, she assured him that she was fine, just fine.

She marveled at his ability to find water and shelter, at his skill in finding game. They never wanted for food or water, and she never wanted for his love. Indeed, she had never felt so loved or so protected in her life. Whatever the future held, she was confident that Cloud Walker could handle it.

Cloud Walker drew his weary horse to a halt, his heart beating fast as he gazed at the steep gorge that was the entrance to Hell Canyon. Generations of his people had wintered here, finding shelter from the harsh winter of the plains.

Turning in the saddle, he smiled reassuringly at Mary. She had not complained once on their long journey, but he saw the weariness in her eyes, in the slight hollows of her cheeks, in the way she often pressed her hand to her back.

"We'll be there in a few minutes," he said, and Mary nodded, too tired to speak.

Cloud Walker sensed the spirits of his ancestors as he guided his horse through the gap between the high narrow walls. It was a rugged but beautiful land. Ponderosa pines and mountain cedars swayed in the night wind that blew softly through the canyon. A tiny creek bed meandered through the rugged landscape and rocks that littered the canyon floor. The cry of a coyote sounded from the cliffs. There were elk here, bobcats and black bears, mountain lions and eagles, deer and rabbits. They would not want for food.

Cloud Walker drew rein in the lee of a high canyon wall. In the moonlight he could barely make out the symbols and pictures that had been etched by his ancestors many years ago. The pictures recorded a part of their history, as well as showing the way to convenient campsites and water holes and buried caches of food and supplies. Later, perhaps he would explore some of the ancient campsites, but for now he needed to look after Mary.

With gentle hands he lifted her from her horse and stood her on the ground. When she started to unload their supplies, he caught her hand.

"I will do it. You sit down. Rest."

"I can do it," Mary protested. She did not want him to think she was weak, did not want to be a burden.

"I know, but I will do it."

She was too bone weary to argue. Eyes brimming with gratitude, she crawled under the covers he spread for her and was soon asleep.

Cloud Walker gazed at Mary, his dark eyes troubled. He had been wrong to bring her here. She had never lived in the wilderness, had never known hardship or deprivation. And she was pregnant. His eyes lingered on her swollen belly. His child rested there. How would Mary react when her time came and she had no woman to help her? He had delivered many mares, but never a woman. Would he know what to do? How would he live with himself if anything happened to Mary or the baby?

He shook such morbid thoughts from his mind. Unsaddling the horses, he turned them loose to forage in the canyon. He placed their supplies on a flat rock, then, using a large flat stone, he dug a firepit. Dry wood was plentiful and he soon had a small warm fire blazing brightly.

There was nothing else to be done until daylight. Sitting cross-legged on his blankets, he gazed at Mary, watching the firelight play in her hair, watching the shadow of the flames dance on the canyon wall. Almost, he could hear the voice of his ancestors. "Welcome home," they seemed to say.

30

It started with a fever and a sore throat, followed by weakness, an increased fever, and then the telltale sign—a tough, dirty gray membrane on the throat. It was a deadly disease and its name was diphtheria.

It spread through Bear Valley with astonishing speed, hitting nearly every family. Dr. Henderson turned the church into a hospital and worked there day and night, assisted by Chester Cole and Blackie and several women who had previous experience with nursing.

It was a terrible thing. Ruth Tippitt's husband died. Mary Crowley's baby died, and three days later two of her other children slipped away. Helen Sprague was one of the lucky ones; she developed a mild case and recovered, but that was rare.

I worried constantly that the disease would strike my grandchildren. I prayed day and night, beseeching the Lord to spare our little ones.

And day after day the number of crosses on our little hillside cemetery grew.

I was glad now that Mary and Cloud Walker were not here, that they would not be exposed to the dread disease. Not a day went by that I didn't think of my daughter, wondering where she was, if she was well and happy.

We had heard no more from the lawman who had come to our house in the dark of night. He had asked if we had seen Frank Smythe, if we knew of Cloud Walker's whereabouts. Shadow had replied that we hadn't seen Frank Smythe in months and that Cloud Walker was not in the house. The lawman had stared at Shadow for a long time, and then asked if he could search the house, and then had gone outside and searched the lodge and the barn. Finally he had ridden away toward the river crossing. Hawk had materialized out of the shadows after the lawman took his leave.

"They have gone," he had said quietly, and Shadow had nodded, his eyes gazing off into the distance across the river.

"Where would they go?" I had asked.

"Who can say?" Shadow had replied with a shrug. "There is a lot of country out there, hills and valleys where a man could hide and never be found."

Never be found. Those words haunted me. Mary and Cloud Walker could be killed and we would never know it.

But my immediate concern was for Blackie and the awful disease that was decimating Bear Valley's population. He came home at night bone weary. Sometimes he was too tired to eat and fell into bed still dressed. I worried about him continually, but he insisted that Dr. Henderson and Dr. Cole needed his help, and I couldn't keep him at home.

As the days went by, we heard of whole families succumbing to the disease. Daily Victoria swabbed the throats of the twins with iodine. She kept them inside the house, fed them well, made sure they got plenty of sleep. I don't know if that's what kept my grandsons healthy, or if it was the fact that we lived a good distance from town, but our family remained untouched.

The Reverend Brighton and Lydia worked long hours as well, comforting the sick, consoling the bereaved. Shadow refused to let me go into town to help, but I made large pots of soup and broth for the sick, and offered many prayers in their behalf.

And then Blackie got sick. He came home late one night complaining of a sore throat, and I knew that what I had been dreading all along had come to pass. My youngest son had diphtheria.

His fever rose moment by moment, or so it seemed, and I was in a constant state of fear. I bathed him with cool water, forced him to swallow as much liquid as he could hold, spooned the medicine into him that the doctor sent. Nothing seemed to help.

From the beginning, Blackie knew how sick he was. He had seen enough people die from the disease to know it was usually fatal.

"Do not be sad, nahkoa," he said late one night. It was difficult for him to speak, but he went doggedly on. "I am not afraid to die."

"I know you're not," I replied, blinking back my tears. "You've always been a brave young man."

"Not so brave as Hawk," Blackie remarked wistfully. "I do not think I would have courage enough to endure the Sun Dance, as he did."

"It doesn't matter."

"I think it matters to my father. Do you think he is disappointed in me?"

"I have never been disappointed in you," Shadow said as he stepped into the room. "You have always made my heart proud." Shadow smiled at his son. "In the old days you would have been a great shaman among the People. To be able to heal is better than being a warrior. Anyone can take a life. Only a few can restore it."

Blackie smiled faintly, pleased by his father's praise. And then his eyelids fluttered down and he was asleep.

Shadow took a seat beside Blackie's bed, his handsome face drawn and haggard, his dark eyes stained with tears. Blackie was our youngest, our baby. We had always spoiled him a little because he was our last.

I sat across from my husband, remembering the day our son had been born. Blackie's birth had been difficult and I had been alone in the house when my labor began. After several hours had passed, I knew something was wrong and began to be afraid. I pushed and strained, but the child would not come, and as I lay there, unable to expel the baby from my womb, I had imagined that death was all around me. I had seen him lurking in the dark corners of the room, watching me. I had been certain I was going to die, but then Shadow had come home. His voice had stilled my fears and he had delivered Blackie as competently as any doctor could have done. Our eyes had met as Shadow held the baby in his arms. Whose child was it? Shadow's, or Joshua Berdeen's? There was no way to be certain. *"It does not matter who fathered the child,"* Shadow had said as he placed my son in my arms. *"From this day forward, he will be my son, and I will be his father."*

I remembered the day Blackie had learned to ride a horse, his little legs clinging to the sides of one of one of our old mares, his chubby little hands grasping the reins as Shadow led the horse around the corral, eyes shining with pride.

Shadow had taught Blackie how to hunt and fish, how to read the signs of the seasons, to track, to speak the language of the People.

He had been such a sweet child, our Blackie. He had been but two years old when he brought home the first in a long line of injured animals. He had come into the kitchen that day with a small bird clutched to his chest. Together we had splinted the bird's broken wing. Blackie had fed it and cared for it with only a little help from me, and he had been overjoyed when the bird's wing healed and it flew away. He had always been such a happy child, always smiling and laughing, a joy to be around. He had seen beauty where others saw only ugliness, hope where others saw despair.

My memories brought tears to my eyes and I began to weep softly. I could not bear it if my son died. I had lost my firstborn son. Surely God would not take my baby.

Kneeling beside Blackie's bed, I began to pray, pleading with the Lord to spare my child, promising to try to lead a better life if only He would let Blackie live.

I fell asleep on my knees. When I awoke, it was almost dawn. Blackie was still asleep, his breathing shallow and uneven. He had kicked the covers off the bed and I replaced them, noting that his fever was still high.

Going into the kitchen, I filled the kettle with water, took a canister of herb tea from the cupboard. Blackie couldn't swallow anything solid, so I tried to get as much liquid into him as I could, even though it was painful for him to swallow.

Glancing out the window, I saw Shadow standing outside. He was naked save for loincloth and moccasins. His hair, long and black, fell to his waist. A single white eagle feather had been tied in his hair. There were streaks of black paint on his face and chest. His arms, bronze and thick with muscle, were lifted toward the sky in prayer. A small fire burned at his feet, and as I watched, he sprinkled a handful of sacred yellow pollen into the flame, and then raised his arms over his head again.

He was praying to Man Above in the old and ancient way, and I felt a shiver run down my spine as he called upon the gods of the Cheyenne. His voice, deep and filled with pleading, drifted through the half-open window.

"Hear me, Man Above, accept my offering and heal my son."

Again he sprinkled a handful of pollen into the fire, and this time the flames exploded upward like many-colored tongues licking at the sky. And then with great deliberation Shadow took a knife and raked the blade across his chest. A thin ribbon of red oozed from the shallow gash in his flesh.

"Hear me, Man Above," he cried again. "Accept my pain and heal my son."

A wordless cry erupted from Shadow's lips as he again raised his arms toward heaven, and at that moment the sun climbed over the distant mountains, splashing the clear skies with all the colors of the rainbow.

My breath caught in my throat at the scene before me. Shadow stood straight and tall, like a statue carved from bronze, and behind him the sky turned from red to orange to gold.

Shadow stood there for perhaps another twenty minutes, and I stood watching him, wanting to imprint his image on my mind forevermore.

Slowly Shadow lowered his arms. Turning his head, he saw me standing at the window. His eyes met mine, and I knew somehow that everything would be all right.

Miraculously, Blackie began to get better that very morning. By mid-afternoon his fever was dropping, and by the following day it was almost normal.

Never again did I doubt the power of prayer. In my heart I knew that my God and Shadow's were the same God, yet I could not help feeling that, in some mysterious way, our prayers had been stronger and more persuasive because they had been offered both to the God of the white man and that of the Indian.

Two weeks after the disease had run its course, everyone in the valley gathered at the church for a special memorial service. There were tears of sorrow for those who had passed away, and fervent prayers of thanksgiving for those who had been spared. I sat between Blackie and Shadow, my heart overflowing with gratitude. Hawk and Victoria were there too, the twins between them, and Pa and Rebecca.

It was the most spiritual service I had ever attended. The Reverend Brighton's sermon was lovely and inspiring. He offered consolation to the bereaved, assuring them that they would see their loved ones again, that those who had passed on were safe in the arms of God. They were not lost, only waiting in another sphere. And he spoke to those who had survived, admonishing them, lovingly, to cherish life and to spend it in service and love of others. He commended those who had labored in behalf of the sick, and stated that Dr. Henderson, Dr. Cole, and Blackie Kincaid were heroes in every sense of the word.

I could not have agreed more.

Following the service, we all went to Hawk's

house for dinner. Victoria and I were setting the table when her pains began. A few minutes later her water broke, and dinner was forgotten.

The men kept an eye on the twins while Rebecca and I sat with Victoria. Hawk paced the house restlessly, peering into the bedroom time after time to see how things were going. He held Vickie's hand when the contractions began to come harder, encouraging her to push, assuring her that he loved her, that everything would be all right.

After only three hours of relatively easy labor, my granddaughter entered the world. It was a tender moment when Hawk caught his daughter in his hands. Rebecca went out to announce the birth, while I washed the newest member of our family and wrapped the tiny infant in a blanket. Hawk was beaming with pride as he showed off his daughter to the rest of the family.

"She sure is small," Blackie remarked. "Cute, though."

"She's beautiful," Pa said. Gently he stroked the baby's downy cheek with one large, calloused finger. "Pretty as an angel."

"What are you going to name her?" Rebecca asked.

"Amanda Marie," Hawk said, smiling down at his daughter.

We all agreed it was a lovely name for a lovely child, and then we all left the bedroom so Vickie could nurse the baby and get some sleep.

In the parlor, Hawk produced a bottle of wine he had been saving for a special occasion, and we all toasted Amanda's birth and good health.

"I'm a happy man," Pa said jovially. He glanced around the room, his smile enormous. "I've got me a wonderful wife, a lovely daughter, a fine son-in-law, and enough grandkids and great-grandkids to make any man proud."

I gave my father a playful punch on the arm. "A fine son-in-law indeed," I teased. "I remember when you said you'd rather see me dead than married to an Indian."

Pa nodded ruefully. "Too true," he admitted. "But you could hardly blame me."

That was true, too. It had been Indians who had killed Pa's parents, a sister, and two brothers. Pa had been left for dead, and would likely have died of starvation and exposure if an old mountain man hadn't found him wandering around the charred remains of his family's wagon. Pa had stayed with the mountain man until he was sixteen, and then set out on his own.

Pa grinned at Shadow. "I hated all Indians for a lot of years for what they did to my family."

Shadow returned Pa's grin with one of his own. "I remember. But that was a long time ago."

Pa nodded. "Long ago," he agreed, smiling fondly at Shadow. "I know now that my girl couldn't have found a better husband anywhere, red or white. I'm proud to call you son." Pa smiled at each of us in turn. "Yessir," he said again. "I'm a happy man."

I woke from a sound sleep as Shadow slipped out of bed. Someone was banging on our front door, and I felt a cold chill tiptoe down my spine. Only trouble came knocking in the dark hours just before dawn. Good news could wait until morning.

I followed Shadow into the parlor, watched with trepidation as he reached for the rifle over the fireplace before he unlatched the front door.

Rebecca stood on the step in her nightgown and a robe. Her hair hung in a long braid over her shoulder. Her face was white and stained with tears.

"It's Sam," she said in a choked whisper.

My hand went to my throat. "Pa?"

"He's gone, Hannah," Rebecca said, and burst into tears.

Shadow placed an arm around Rebecca's shoulders and led her into the parlor. I lit a lamp and we sat on the sofa beside her, waiting for her tears to subside so she could speak.

Slowly Rebecca shook her head. "It was so sudden. We were in bed when he sat up complaining of a pain in his chest. I was going after the doctor when Sam called my name. When I reached his side, he was gone." Rebecca looked at me, her eyes welling with tears. "I didn't even have time to tell him how much I loved him."

I took Rebecca's hand in mine. "He knew that," I assured her. "Pa often said how glad he was that he found you, and how much he loved you." I choked back a sob. "We should be glad he went quick and didn't have to suffer. You know how Pa hated being sick in bed."

"Oh, Hannah," Rebecca wailed. "What will I do without him?"

I couldn't speak. Instead I put my arms around

her and we wept together, our tears mingling as we pressed our cheeks together.

I couldn't believe it. My father was gone. Once before I had thought my father was dead. It had been back in the spring of 1876. Our homestead had been attacked by Indians heading for a rendezvous with Crazy Horse and Sitting Bull at the Little Big Horn. My mother had been killed that day, and my father and I were facing certain death when Shadow arrived. He had bargained for our freedom with the attacking Indians, but the war leader had refused to let Pa go. I had not wanted to leave my father's side because I knew I would never see him again, but Pa had practically shoved me out the door to where Shadow waited to take me to safety.

In my mind's eye I could see Shadow as he had looked that day so long ago. I had not recognized him at first. His face and chest had been hideously streaked with broad slashes of vermillion. A single white eagle feather had adorned his long black hair. A black wolfskin clout had covered his loins; moccasins beaded in red and black had hugged his feet. It was only when he spoke that I had recognized him.

I had hated Shadow for the first and only time that fateful day, hated him because he was Indian, hated him because my mother was dead and my father was going to be killed and he couldn't do anything about it. And even as I had hated him, I loved him.

Looking at Shadow now, I knew that the love I had felt for him then was as nothing compared to the love we now shared. I remembered my surprise when we reached the Rosebud Reservation in the autumn of

1884 and found my father living there among the Indians. It had been like a miracle. I had thought my father long dead, yet there he was, alive and well, living with people he had once despised.

I looked into Rebecca's tear-stained face and knew there would be no miracles this time.

We sat there for a long time, too numb to speak. I remembered how I had adored my father when I had been a little girl. He had seemed bigger than life then, tall and strong and wise, able to solve all my problems with a hug and a kiss. Like all little girls, I had dreamed of marrying my father when I grew up. As I grew older, I longed to marry a man who possessed the same fine qualities I had admired in Pa.

"At least he got to see Amanda Marie," Rebecca said after a while.

"He lived a good life," Shadow remarked. "He was a man of honor. I was proud to know him, to be a part of his family." Shadow smiled down at me. "Do you remember the time my leg was infected and your father wanted to cut it off?"

I nodded. "I remember."

"Tell me," Rebecca said.

"It was just before the Indian wars started," I began. "There had been several raids on homesteads by the Sioux and Cheyenne. Shadow and I were going to run away and get married, but before he could come for me, a bunch of hotheaded Cheyenne warriors killed one of our neighbors and kidnapped his little girl. Shadow tried to persuade the young men not to fight, but they were determined, and when he realized he couldn't stop them, he left the village to warn us. Six white men found him riding alone, and they dragged him off his horse and did some terrible things to him. One of the men used a knife on Shadow's leg, and then they left him for dead. Shadow managed to make his way to our place and my mother treated his wounds, but the cut in his leg became badly infected. Pa wanted to amputate Shadow's leg before the infection spread any farther, but Shadow had made me promise not to let that happen. Pa was furious when Shadow refused to let Pa do what he felt was right."

Rebecca smiled a sad little smile. "He did have a temper, didn't he?"

"I'll say. Fortunately, we were able to get a Cheyenne medicine man to come to our house and he saved Shadow's leg."

A short time later Shadow made a pot of strong coffee and we sat up the rest of the night reminiscing about Pa, remembering the good times we had shared.

There were more tears in the morning when Blackie learned that his grandfather had passed away in the night. Shadow rode over to tell Hawk and Vickie the bad news and to bring them to our place.

Later, when the family was together, we all drove to Pa's house. Rebecca and I dressed Pa in his good Sunday suit and combed his hair, then Shadow and Hawk carried his body outside and placed it in the back of Pa's wagon and we took the body into town to the mortuary. The funeral was set for the following afternoon.

Nearly everyone in the valley turned out for Pa's

funeral. There weren't enough seats to accommodate the crowd of mourners and many had to stand outside the church.

Sitting through the funeral was one of the hardest things I had ever done. The Reverend Brighton delivered a glowing eulogy, extolling the many fine qualities of Samuel Obediah Kincaid, telling how Pa had been one of the first settlers in Bear Valley back in 1865, how he had lost his first homestead and his first wife during the Indian wars in 1875, and how he had come back to Bear Valley in the summer of 1885 to start again. The reverend praised Pa for being a wonderful family man, survived by his daughter and son-in-law, three grandchildren, three great-grandchildren, and his wife, Rebecca.

Rebecca leaned heavily on Shadow's arm as we made our way to the cemetery. I followed after them, my heart aching. Hawk walked beside me, his strong arm around my shoulders, his eyes damp with unshed tears.

When we returned home, the ladies of the valley came to call, each one bringing a covered dish, a salad, a dessert, a pitcher of cold lemonade, bread or biscuits or pies, until we had enough food in the house to feed our family for several days.

Blackie went to stay with Rebecca. I had tried to persuade Rebecca to stay with us for the next few days, but she wanted to go back to her own house. I guess she felt closer to Pa there.

The next few weeks were difficult. I thought of my father often, remembering the good times we had shared, the fun and laughter that had filled our house when I was a child.

I was surprised and dismayed when Rebecca came over to tell us she had decided to sell the house and move back East.

"There are too many memories here, Hannah," she said wistfully. "Everything reminds me of Sam." She choked back a sob. "I'm going to Philadelphia to be with Beth. I think I'd like to spend some time with my grandchild and my daughter." She gave me a half-smile, her eyes begging for my understanding. "I'll miss you, all of you, but I need to get away. I'll keep in touch."

Rebecca sold the house and the cattle to a young German couple with four children. Three days later, on a cloudy September morning, she boarded the train to make the long journey east.

I wept as we kissed good-bye. Long ago I had been sorely jealous of this woman, fearing that Shadow might care for her more than he cared for me. But once my foolish fears had been laid to rest, Rebecca and I had become good friends, and I knew I would miss her dreadfully.

31

Cloud Walker's steps were as quiet as the sunlight moving over the grass as he stalked the deer. He raised his rifle to his shoulder, then squeezed the trigger as the animal paused to test the wind. The gunshot echoed and re-echoed off the canyon walls, shattering the serenity of the morning.

Following ancient custom, he cut off a section of meat and left it behind to placate the deer's spirit. That done, he draped the carcass over his horse's withers and made his way back to the place that was now home.

Mary was waiting for him, her face wearing a smile of welcome. They had been in the canyon for over two months. The leaves were changing on the trees, the bright green turning to shades of red and rusty gold. The grass was turning yellow, the nights were growing longer, colder.

Mary had learned how to survive in the wilderness, and Cloud Walker had been her teacher. He had taught her how to butcher a deer, how to turn a green hide into a soft warm robe, how to prepare jerky and pemmican, how to make moccasins.

Once, Mary had wondered if she had the strength of character and courage to live as her mother had once lived. She knew now that she was worthy to be her mother's daughter. She could endure anything, anything but the loneliness that swept over her whenever Cloud Walker was away from her and she faced the long, quiet hours alone. It was like being the last person alive. Doubts and fears often crowded her mind then, making her wonder what she would do if something happened to Cloud Walker. Would she be able to find her way out of the canyon and back to Bear Valley? Her only other real fear concerned the birth of her child. She had thought to deliver the child at home, with her mother and Rebecca and Vickie to help her when the time came. Now she would have no one but Cloud Walker to rely on. There would be no woman present to soothe her fears, no doctor to call if the child were sickly, or if something went wrong during the birth itself.

She never mentioned her fears to Cloud Walker. Instead she assured him that there was nothing to worry about. She had given birth before and nothing had gone wrong. There was no reason to think this birth would be different from the first.

They worked side by side in companionable

silence as they butchered the deer. They would have venison steaks for dinner, and tomorrow Mary would dry the rest of the meat so they would have food for the coming winter. The hide would make a warm coat for Cloud Walker, similar to the one she had recently completed for herself.

Cloud Walker had erected a crude shelter. Branches formed the sides and roof. Mary had woven smaller branches and leaves together to thatch the roof and side walls. They had used mud from the creek to fill in the cracks.

It was a hard life, Mary mused as she stirred the fire and spitted the steaks. Just seeing to matters of food and survival took up most of the day. But the nights, ah, the nights when she lay beside Cloud Walker, secure in his arms and wrapped in his love, nights when he caressed her with his hands and lips, his murmured words of love pouring over her like gentle rain, at those times she counted the loss of her home and family in Bear Valley a small price to pay for Cloud Walker's life. She didn't miss having nice clothes then, didn't miss the bounty of her mother's table or the laughter of her friends. Things like hot water to wash in and clean sheets to sleep on did not tempt her when she saw Cloud Walker rising each morning from the stream where he bathed. Her eyes never tired of looking at him, her hands never grew weary of touching him. He was a warrior now in every sense of the word. He had discarded civilization as easily as he might discard a coat that no longer fit. Each day he became more Indian. He began to pray twice each day to Man Above. Whenever he killed an animal, he left a part of it behind, quietly thanking the beast for giving up its life that they might have food and clothing. When their ammunition began to dwindle, he fashioned a bow and arrows, using a deer tendon for the bowstring and eagle feathers to fletch the arrow shafts.

Together they had explored the canyon. Mary had marveled at the pictures left behind by ancient tribes. Once they found a cave depicted in one of the writings. Following the crude diagram, they had discovered a deep hollow in the rock. Inside were several shards of pottery, the remains of a large basket, and the whitened skull of a dog. Farther back in the cave they had found a large iron kettle, a rusted knife, and the horns of a buffalo. The kettle had come in handy. Mary had felt guilty taking it from the cave, though she could not say why.

After dinner they walked hand in hand to the creek to bathe. At first Mary had been shy about letting Cloud Walker see her naked while she was pregnant, afraid that he would be repulsed by her swollen breasts and distended belly.

"Do not hide from me," Cloud Walker had chided gently. "It is my child you carry, and my love as well." His hands had touched her belly reverently as his dark eyes gazed into her own. "You are more beautiful now than ever," he had whispered huskily, his lips brushing her forehead. "More beautiful than any woman I have ever known."

She had basked in his praise. She was not beautiful, she thought to herself. She was fat and ungainly. Her ankles were swollen, and her hands, too, and she moved with all the grace of a pregnant heifer, but she had accepted his compliment with a smile, his words warming her clear to her toes.

Now she stood naked before him as she washed her arms and legs, her eyes openly watching as he bathed. He was so beautiful it almost took her breath away. His skin glistened like wet copper, his hair was long and black, and his muscles rippled like silk as he moved.

He was aware of her gaze. She knew it by the way he grinned roguishly, and by the rising evidence of his desire as her eyes moved over his broad shoulders and long legs.

"Be careful, woman," he warned sternly.

"Of what?" Mary replied with mock innocence.

"Shall I show you?"

"Show me what?" Mary asked, stifling a laugh. "I see nothing to fear."

With a wordless cry, Cloud Walker grabbed her and carried her into the water, his strong arms careful as they lowered her into the cold stream. With ease he avoided her flailing fists. Catching both her hands in one of his, he held her arms over her head while he straddled her hips.

"Beast," Mary said, trying to wriggle free. "Would you take advantage of a helpless woman?"

Fire blazed in Cloud Walker's eyes as he nodded. How beautiful she was with her hair swirling around her face and her breasts pouting at him. His eyes lingered on the swell of her belly and he tried to imagine his child curled inside, floating in liquid as its mother was floating in the stream.

Mary wriggled uncomfortably beneath him as her bare bottom made contact with a rock. Cloud Walker rose instantly, drawing her with him. Lifting her into his arms, he carried her from the stream to the grass beyond, and there, under the bold blue sky, he made love to her, telling her with each kiss and caress that he adored her.

Mary returned his love with all the passion in her soul, reveling in the touch of his damp skin against her own, the way his eyes devoured her, the way his voice murmured her name as he possessed her, carrying her far away to a place where there was only warmth and happiness and a feeling of endless peace. . . .

Mary sat in the sun, her face set in determined lines as she scraped the hair from a deer hide. It was hard work, and as her arms began to grow weary, she thought of the countless Indian women who had performed this same task so that their husbands and children might have warm clothing. It was a tiresome chore, turning a green hide into a piece of soft, workable cloth. How much easier to go to the store and purchase a length of cotton. And yet there was a certain sense of pride and accomplishment in working with her hands.

When the last bit of hair had been removed, she sat up, one hand pressing against her back. It was then, as she rose clumsily to her feet, that she saw the two men riding down the canyon toward her.

A sudden stab of fear made her heart begin to pound. She was alone. Cloud Walker had gone hunting earlier that day and might not be back for hours.

She watched with a growing sense of panic as the men reined their horses to a halt only a few feet from where she stood.

The two men stared at Mary, and then at each other. And then they grinned.

"Howdy, missy," the man nearest her said. He was tall and heavy-set, with a long nose, a wide mouth, and pale gray eyes set under shaggy brows.

"Hello," Mary said, her voice betraying none of the anxiety she was feeling.

"What are ya doing out here?" the second man asked. He was of medium height, with regular features and long blond hair.

"I live here," Mary replied. "With my husband."

The two men glanced around the crude shelter, noting the single horse grazing some distance away. They exchanged knowing grins.

"Your husband ta home?" the second man asked.

"He's asleep inside," Mary said. "Shall I wake him?"

The second man laughed softly. "Yeah. Why don't you do that?"

They had called her bluff. For a moment she stood frozen with fear, and then she remembered the rifle.

"I'll get him," she said quickly, and hurried into the hut. The rifle was heavy, cold in her hands, and she wondered if she would have the nerve to squeeze the trigger if it became necessary.

The two men looked surprised when she reappeared with a rifle in her hands.

"I think you should go now," Mary said.

"I think she's right, Charley," the first man said. "I think we'd better go."

Charley nodded. There was nothing more dangerous than a scared woman with a gun in her hands. And yet, she was a pretty woman. And he hadn't had a woman in a long time.

"How about fixing us some grub before we go?" Charley asked. "We ain't had a decent meal in a month of Sundays."

"I don't have any food to spare," Mary said, her grip tightening on the rifle.

"A cup of coffee, maybe? I got the fixings in my saddlebag."

Mary chewed on her lower lip uncertainly. It would never do to let them know she was afraid, and yet she did not trust the man called Charley. His gray eyes were hot when they looked at her, blazing with a lust he could not conceal.

"No," she said firmly. "Just ride on."

"Not until I get something to eat," Charley decided, and swung down from his horse.

Mary's mouth went dry. He was walking toward her, his hand outstretched to take the rifle. And she could not pull the trigger. Could not shoot him in cold blood.

"That's better," Charley said as she lowered the rifle. "Ross, get the coffee and that side of bacon out of the pack so she can fix us something to eat." Smiling smugly, Charley plucked the rifle from Mary's hand. "What's your name, honey?"

"Mary," she answered hoarsely.

Charley nodded, his eyes sweeping over her figure. "You appear to be expectin'," he mused.

"Yes, I am."

"Don't matter. How's about fixing that grub?"

She turned away, glad for something to do. She worked slowly, her mind racing. There was no mistaking the fact that Charley intended to rape her. She was sorry she hadn't shot him, but even now she knew she couldn't have killed him in cold blood. This was different from the time she had fired at Frank Smythe to save Cloud Walker's life.

She filled the coffee pot with water and placed it over the coals, sliced the bacon into a pan and set it over the fire. Sitting back, she slid the knife into the pocket of her skirt.

Ross produced some hard biscuits and a tin of peaches and the men sat cross-legged on the ground, eating and talking while Mary stood by the fire. Time and again her eyes searched the canyon, hoping for some sign of Cloud Walker's return.

"So," Charley said, rising to his feet. "Just what are you doing away out here?"

"My husband is wanted by the law," Mary said.

"That right?" Charley said, grinning. "So are we. Small world, ain't it?"

The man called Ross spit into the fire. "What did he do?"

"He killed a man," Mary said. Perhaps if they thought her husband was dangerous they would go away and leave her alone.

"Killed a man, did he?" Charley drawled. "Well, hell, I've killed one or two myself." His eyes strayed to the hut, and then back to Mary. "Go inside, honey," he said. "Ross, you keep an eye on things out here. I won't be long."

"Leave her alone, Charley," Ross Parker said.

"Can't you see she's in a family way?"

"I don't need to hear any of your preachin'," Charley retorted. "Just keep your eyes peeled and your mouth shut."

Muttering an oath, Ross Parker poured himself another cup of coffee. Charley Everest was a good man on the trail, but he was worse than a rutting buck whenever he saw a pretty woman. He felt a twinge of pity for the young woman as Charley grabbed her arm and dragged her into the hut, and then he shrugged. Charley wouldn't hurt the girl none, and as soon as he'd had her, they'd ride on.

He was draining the last of the coffee from his cup when he felt the prick of a knife behind his left ear.

"Do not move," Cloud Walker warned. With his free hand he slid the white man's Colt from its holster and shoved it into the waistband of his buckskins. "Put your hands behind your back."

Ross Parker did as he was told. There was something in the voice of the man behind him that warned him not to do anything foolish.

Cloud Walker quickly tied the man's hands together, then tapped the man on the back of the head with the butt of the Colt. Ross Parker fell to the ground without a sound.

Inside the hut, Mary faced the man who intended to rape her, her eyes white with fear as he advanced toward her. His desire made an obscene bulge in his trousers, and she knew she would rather die than let him touch her.

She uttered a wordless cry of revulsion when he reached out to grab her, and then she remembered the knife in her skirt pocket. The touch of the knife handle felt reassuring in her hand as she jerked it out of her pocket.

"Don't touch me," she warned.

Charley Everest laughed softly. "Wanna play rough, eh?" he drawled. "Well, that suits me just fine."

He was darting toward her as he spoke, one big hand closing on her wrist, his thumb squeezing hard until her hand went numb and the knife dropped harmlessly to the ground.

"Don't try anything like that again," he growled, and pushing her to the floor, he straddled her legs, his hands fumbling with his belt.

"No," Mary begged as he lifted her skirts. "Please—"

He lowered his head, his mouth crushing hers, stifling her pleas. Mary writhed beneath him, her arms flailing, and then she stopped struggling as her hand brushed the knife. Driven by fear, she grabbed the knife and plunged it into his side.

Charley Everest grunted with pain as the blade pierced his flesh. Sitting back on his heels, he stared at the blood leaking from his side.

Mary stared at Charley Everest in horror. She hadn't killed him, and now he would finish what he had started. A movement near the door caught her eye and she saw Cloud Walker enter the hut. Relief washed through her and she went suddenly limp.

Everest sensed the change, saw the hope flare in her eyes. Muttering an oath, he swung around. The sight of Cloud Walker's enraged face was the last thing he saw.

Mary looked away, her stomach churning with revulsion, as Cloud Walker pulled Charley to his feet and shot him. The noise of the gunshot was deafening inside the hut.

Cloud Walker tossed the gun away. Kneeling beside Mary, he drew her into his arms, his hands brushing her hair out of her face, his eyes searching hers.

"Did he touch you?"

"No."

Sweet relief coursed through Cloud Walker as he buried his face in her hair. Thank God he had returned when he did.

Held in the security of Cloud Walker's arms, Mary felt all the tension and fear drain out of her, and the tears came.

Cloud Walker held her while she wept, his voice murmuring to her, assuring her that he loved her, that he would never let anything hurt her, that he would never leave her alone for so long again.

When her tears subsided, he helped her to her feet. Bending, he lifted Charley's body and carried it outside.

Ross Parker's face went pale when he saw the big Indian dump Charley's body across the back of his horse.

"I never touched her," he said as Cloud Walker started toward him. "I swear it! Ask her if you don't believe me."

"Shut up, white man," Cloud Walker said curtly.

Ross nodded. A clammy sweat broke out across his forehead as he watched the Indian draw the knife from the sheath at his belt. *Damn you, Charley*, he thought in despair. *I always knew you'd get me killed.*

His breath caught in his throat as the Indian stood before him. Never had he seen such hatred in any man's eyes.

Cloud Walker made a sound of disgust low in his throat as he cut the white man's hands free. The man's fear was pathetic, so strong he could almost smell it.

"Take your friend and get out of here," Cloud Walker said. "Do not come back."

Ross Parker turned and ran for his horse. Vaulting into the saddle, he grabbed the reins of the other horse and rode swiftly out of the canyon, cursing the day he had met Charley Everest.

For the next few weeks, Cloud Walker never left Mary's side. He went with her when she gathered wood, he remained nearby when she bathed in the stream, he sat in the shade fashioning arrows or honing his knife while she prepared their meals.

He carried his rifle whenever they left their lodge to go for a walk or a swim. He had always been wary and alert, but he was more so now.

"You don't think that man will come back, do you?" Mary asked.

"No," Cloud Walker replied. But he continued to be watchful and cautious.

Winter came in a rush of rain and wind. Thunder rumbled in darkened skies, punctuated by brilliant shafts of lightning.

Mary snuggled closer to Cloud Walker, awed by the raw power of the storm that raged all around them, making her feel small and helpless. How would they survive out here all alone? What if they ran out of food? What if they got sick? They could die out here and no one would ever know.

"What is it?" Cloud Walker asked as she stirred restlessly in his arms.

"Nothing."

"Nothing?"

"Honest, I'm fine." How could she tell him she was afraid when it seemed he feared nothing at all?

Cloud Walker held Mary close, warming her with the heat of his body. He sensed her fears and could not fault her for being afraid. Always she had been surrounded by her family, secure in their love and in the knowledge that they would be there in times of need. Now they were alone, utterly and completely alone. No, he could not blame Mary for being afraid. He, too, had worried about the future, not for himself, but for Mary, knowing all too well that if anything happened to him, she would probably not survive on her own. It was a thought that haunted him more and more as the days went by.

The cold days of winter passed slowly. There were many days when they never left the shelter of the lodge. At those times they told each other stories of their childhood, or spun dreams of the future. They talked often of the baby growing under Mary's heart, wondering if it would be a boy or a girl, speculating on what the world would be like when their child reached adulthood.

On one blustery night, Cloud Walker told Mary how Heammawihio had created the earth. In the beginning, Cloud Walker said, there was nothing but water and sky. No grass. No trees. No mountains. No animals or people. Suddenly a Person appeared floating on the water. He was surrounded by birds and geese and swans and ducks and all the birds that can swim. After a long time, the Person grew tired of floating on the water and asked the birds to look for some earth. The big birds dove into the water, but they came up with nothing. One by one, all the birds tried until finally a small duck dove into the water and surfaced with a bit of mud in its bill. The Person was pleased and he took the mud and worked it in his fingers until it was dry, and as the Person worked the mud, it grew larger and larger, and when he had a handful, he sprinkled it over the water and made little piles of earth here and there. When the mud dried, the dust made land, and the Person sat back and watched it spread until there was solid land as far as he could see.

Mary clapped her hands when Cloud Walker finished the story. "Tell me another," she said, for Cloud Walker's stories took her mind off the wind and the rain and the vast emptiness that surrounded them.

He had started to tell of Child of the Waters when Mary gasped and doubled over.

"What is it?" Cloud Walker asked anxiously.

"The baby's coming," Mary said, groaning as another pain caught her unawares. She reached for his hand, holding on as though she would never let go.

Cloud Walker watched Mary anxiously as the minutes went by, certain he would rather face a charging grizzly than watch Mary writhe in pain as she labored to bring their child into the world. Between contractions, he talked to her, telling her how much he loved her, how much he needed her, assuring her that everything would be all right, sponging the sweat from her brow. When the pains came, he let her hold onto him, unmindful of the long scratches her nails gouged in his hands and arms.

Mary groaned as another contraction threatened to tear her apart. "I forgot how much it hurts," she gasped, her hands gripping his with surprising strength.

He could think of nothing to say in reply. Instead he squeezed her hand sympathetically, wishing he could bear the pain for her.

It was near dawn when Mary gave one last hoarse cry of pain and their child made its way into the world. Cloud Walker gazed at the new life in his hands. It was a boy, wrinkled and red and beautiful. He held the baby for several seconds before he realized the child wasn't breathing.

Mary sat up, her face as white as the snow that covered the plains. "Is it . . . ?"

Cloud Walker felt his heart go cold. Grasping the child by its ankles, he held the baby upside down and swatted the infant's backside. Nothing. He glanced at Mary, his own eyes mirroring the fear he read in hers as he swatted the baby's bottom again. And then again, harder.

"Maheo," he murmured helplessly. "Please."

One more swat on the baby's dimpled bottom, and

a lusty cry filled the air. Tears streamed down Mary's cheeks as Cloud Walker cut the cord and placed their son in her arms.

"I love you," Cloud Walker said, his voice husky with emotion. "Both of you."

"I love you," Mary replied wearily. "Thank you for a lovely son." She gazed into the child's eyes. "I think we'll call him Adam," she said. "Because he'll be the first of many."

"Adam," Cloud Walker repeated softly. "It is a good name."

Swallowing his own tears of joy, Cloud Walker disposed of the cord and afterbirth, washed the baby, and then Mary. He felt awkward as he wrapped his son in a blanket of soft rabbit fur, then placed the child in Mary's arms once more.

A son! he thought exultantly. *I have a son.*

In the days that followed, Cloud Walker thought often of taking Mary back to her family in Bear Valley. It had been foolish to take her away from home. Their child might have died. Mary could get sick, and there would be no one to help them. In Bear Valley, she had friends and family. There was a doctor available. Again and again he thought of his son. What if the child became ill? He was no medicine man, he knew nothing of healing. He did not mind risking his own life in the wilds of Hell Canyon, but he was no longer willing to risk the lives of his wife and child. Each day Mary became more precious to him, his son more dear.

He told Mary he was taking her back to Bear Valley in the spring, but she wouldn't hear of it.

Returning to civilization would put Cloud Walker's life
in danger, and she refused to discuss it. Her mother
and father had lived alone in the wilderness and
survived, and so could they.

Gradually winter gave way to spring. The sun
warmed the canyon. Trees put on new gowns of
emerald green, and flowers poked their heads above
the earth, faces lifting toward the sky.

It was on one such sunny day that Cloud Walker
took his bow and went hunting. Mary held their son to
her breast as Cloud Walker rode away. It was the first
time they had been separated in months. He had not
wanted to leave her alone, but she had assured him she
would be fine. At any rate, they needed the meat.

Humming softly, Mary spread a blanket in the
sun and placed the baby on it, smiling with pride as
Adam waved his tiny hands and feet in the air. He was
a beautiful child, with curly black hair and deep brown
eyes. Already he was smiling at her and making soft
cooing sounds that filled her heart with delight.

While the baby napped in the sun, Mary opened
the door to the lodge to air it out. Feeling suddenly
industrious, she carried their sleeping robes outside
and spread them over a bush. Using a leafy branch,
she swept the floor of the lodge, smoothing the dirt.
Laughter bubbled in her throat as she worked. Who
would have thought it possible to be so happy with so
little? She had no furniture, few clothes other than
those on her back, none of the luxuries she had once
known. Only shelter from the elements, the barest of
necessities to sustain life, a wonderful son, and a
husband she adored.

Peeking out of the lodge to check on Adam, she uttered a wordless cry of fear as she saw a mountain lion prowling through their camp, his nostrils twitching as he smelled the remains of the fish they had eaten the night before.

She froze, hoping the big cat would eat the fish heads and bones and leave. And it might have done just that if the baby hadn't awakened and begun whimpering softly.

The mountain lion's interest was immediately drawn to the squirming child and it padded silently toward the baby, its long pink tongue lolling out of the side of its mouth, its nostrils flared as it caught the scent of milk.

The baby screamed as the big cat's tongue swept across his face.

With a scream of her own, Mary ran from the lodge, the branch in her hands.

"Go away!" she cried, swinging the branch at the cat's head. "Go away!"

The mountain lion spun around with an angry growl, one huge paw batting at the branch. With ease it knocked the limb from Mary's grasp. She scrambled after the branch, felt the animal's claws rip into the back of her leg as her hands closed around the limb. The animal was on her now, its body pinning her to the ground, blotting everything from her gaze but the sight of yellow fangs.

"Oh, God, help me," she murmured, and closed her eyes as the cat's breath filled her nostrils.

She was trembling violently as fear and panic took hold of her mind, and then, more welcome than anything she had ever known, came the wild war cry of a Cheyenne warrior, followed by the hiss of an arrow cutting through the air.

She was sobbing when the big cat fell across her body. And then Cloud Walker was there, freeing her from the cat's weight, lifting her into his arms. His face, drained of color, was the last thing she saw before she fainted.

It was dark when she regained consciousness. Cloud Walker sat at her side, their son cradled in his arm.

"Is he all right?" Mary asked anxiously.

"Yes," Cloud Walker said. "Only hungry."

Relief washed through Mary as she took her son and placed him to her breast. He was so dear, so sweet. What would she have done if he had been killed?

Cloud Walker's eyes were fathomless as he watched Mary nurse their son. He would never forget the horror of riding into camp and seeing Mary struggling with the mountain lion, never forget the scream that had filled the air, sending him back to camp as fast as his horse would carry him. It had been a near thing. Had he been a minute later, she might have been killed, and their child, too.

He glanced at her leg. The cat's claws had ripped a long gash in her flesh. He had washed it out as best he could and bandaged it with a strip of cloth torn from Mary's petticoat.

"Tomorrow," he said flatly. "Tomorrow we will start for Bear Valley."

"No," Mary said, shaking her head. "We can't."

"Tomorrow," he repeated, and left the lodge.

Outside, he gazed up at the vast indigo sky. He did not want to leave this place. He felt at home here, safe, free of civilization. But he could no longer place Mary's life and the life of his son in jeopardy. It was time to go home. Time to face whatever the future held.

32

It took every bit of will power I possessed to be polite to the man standing at my door. It was the lawman again. Hayes, his name was. He came to our house regularly, checking to see if Cloud Walker had returned, searching our house and the lodge out back.

His presence infuriated Shadow, as did the "wanted" posters Hayes had distributed in town. The flyers contained a detailed description of Cloud Walker and stated he was wanted for questioning in connection with the disappearance of Frank Smythe. There was a one-hundred-dollar reward for Cloud Walker's capture or for information leading to his arrest.

Mary was in my thoughts constantly. Her baby would have been born by now and I often wondered if it was a boy or a girl, if mother and child were well.

Shadow did not say much, but I knew his thoughts were much the same as mine. He always assured me that Cloud Walker could take care of Mary, that there was nothing to worry about, but I often caught him gazing into the distance, his eyes haunted and sad as he wondered where his daughter was.

Once, I suggested he go out to find Mary and Cloud Walker, to see if they were well, but Shadow shook his head.

"Cloud Walker is a warrior. How would it look if I went after him as though he were a child?"

"I'm not worried about his pride," I had retorted. "I'm worried about my daughter." But I knew Shadow was right.

Mattie Smythe wrote frequently, begging for news. Had I heard from Frank? Had Mary said anything about where Frank might be? As time went by, the Smythes hired a private detective to look for Frank. In addition, they offered a reward of one thousand dollars to anyone who had news of their son's whereabouts.

I felt sorry for Mattie. I knew how awful it was, not knowing where your child was. I longed to write and tell her what had happened. It would be hard for her, knowing Frank was dead, but it would be better than not knowing anything at all.

Several times I sat down to write her, to tell her what had happened between Frank and Mary and Cloud Walker, but I couldn't ease Mattie's mind without admitting that Cloud Walker had killed Frank, and I knew that Mattie and Leland would never believe that Frank had been capable of the treachery

that had led to his death. They would believe that
Cloud Walker had killed Frank in cold blood.

I was glad when spring came. Our mares dropped
their foals and soon our pastures were burgeoning with
new life. Baby birds twittered in the treetops, one of
Blackie's strays produced thirteen puppies, three of
our cats had kittens. The deer, which were plentiful in
the woods, could often be seen down by the river early
in the morning, spotted fawns at their sides. Occasionally we saw a black bear looking for grubs and berries
near the edge of the woods. Two fat cubs frolicked
beside her.

I warned Blackie not to try to steal one of those
cubs from its mother, and when he seemed reluctant to
obey, I told him of the time, long ago, when I had
yearned to hold just such a cub, and how it had almost
proved fatal to the boy who had blithely gone after the
cub. Finally Blackie promised me he would leave the
bears alone, and I breathed a sigh of relief. I did not
like bears.

It was the first of April, and Shadow was plagued
with restlessness. I could see it in the depths of his
eyes, hear it in his voice. I had rarely known him to be
irritable, but he was downright cranky now, and
nothing seemed to please him. I knew he needed to get
away from our place, away from too many people and
too much civilization. In addition, I knew he was
worried about Mary, that he fretted over the fact that
he could not help her, and so I suggested he take a few
days off and go hunting. Some fresh venison would
taste good, I said.

And so it was that on a cool April morning Shadow

threw some supplies in his war bag, kissed me good-
bye, and rode off toward the distant mountains.

The house felt different with Shadow gone, and
though I had many chores to occupy my time, I still
missed him. It gave me an odd sense of loneliness to
know that he was gone, that he wasn't just out
checking on the stock or working in the barn, but away
from home.

Hawk and Victoria came over later that day.
Vickie and I made two apple pies and baked several
loaves of bread while Amanda Marie slept peacefully
before the hearth and the twins played outside with
Hawk.

The house seemed even emptier after Hawk and
his family went home. I kept busy far into the night,
cleaning and mending and ironing things that did not
need ironing simply because I dreaded going to bed
alone. I was sorry now that I had let Blackie spend the
night away from home.

Finally I ran out of things to do and went to bed,
but I couldn't sleep. Instead I gazed out the window
into the velvety darkness, wondering where Shadow
was and what he was doing. Was he happy out there on
the prairie all alone? Was he thinking of me as I was
thinking of him? It pleased me to think so.

Agitated because I couldn't sleep, I punched
Shadow's pillow, angry with myself for suggesting that
he go hunting, and more angry with him because he
had gone.

It was after midnight before I finally fell asleep.

33

They traveled as before, crossing the prairie by night and sleeping by day. Cloud Walker pushed the horses hard, for Mary's leg had become infected and nothing he did seemed to help. Mary did not complain, but he knew she was in pain. Her leg was red and swollen, and no matter how often he lanced the infection and drained the thick yellow pus from the wound, there was always more.

He had nothing to give her to combat the fever that grew steadily worse, stealing her strength, until she was too weak to ride alone.

He traveled now without resting at all, Mary held in one arm, his son cradled in the other. Now, when he would have welcomed help, there was none.

He paused periodically and placed his son to

Mary's breast, but the fever seemed to dry up her milk and the child fretted constantly. He gave Mary as much water as she could hold, sponging her fevered flesh as they rode across the plains.

The last two days he rode without stopping. Mary was barely conscious when he reached Steel's Crossing, his son too weak to cry.

Dismounting in front of the doctor's office, he pounded on the door with the toe of his boot until at last a gray-haired man clad in a long nightshirt opened the door.

Dr. Marvin J. Harley did not waste time asking questions. It took but one look at Mary and the child to know there was little time to waste.

"In here," the doctor said, and led the way through the house to his office in the back.

Cloud Walker placed Mary on a long, sheet-covered table, stood grim-faced as the doctor examined her leg.

"How bad is it?" Cloud Walker asked.

"Very bad," Dr. Harley replied. He glanced up at the Indian holding the baby in his arms. "That child looks like it needs some nourishment. Two doors down there's a woman just gave birth to a baby. She's got more milk than she needs. Tell her I sent you."

"My wife—"

"I'll look after her. There's nothing you can do here."

Cloud Walker nodded. Tenderly he brushed a wisp of hair from Mary's cheek, his dark eyes haunted with the thought that she might die and it would be all his fault. Swallowing hard, he left the doctor's office.

Melinda McBain felt a moment of panic when she

opened her front door and saw a buckskin-clad Indian standing on the porch, a baby cradled in one arm.

"Yes . . ." she said, taking a wary step backward. "Can I help you?"

"The doctor down the street said you might be able to help me."

"Help you?"

"My son needs milk. His mother is ill and cannot feed him."

Melinda glanced at the baby again, and then into Cloud Walker's eyes. "Of course," she said, her heart going out to the child and its sad-eyed father. "Come in."

Cloud Walker paced the McBain parlor restlessly, hardly aware of his surroundings. Melinda McBain had taken the baby into the bedroom to nurse him, and now all he could think of was Mary.

He whirled around as the bedroom door opened.

"He's asleep," Melinda McBain said, smiling. "I think he's going to be all right."

"Thank you," Cloud Walker said. "I can never repay you for what you've done."

"It isn't necessary. Why don't you leave him here for a day or two and let me take care of him?"

Cloud Walker shook his head. "I could not—"

"I'll take good care of him. He's going to need a lot of nourishment to get his strength back, and I . . ." she blushed prettily and looked away. "I have plenty of milk."

It was the perfect solution, but he did not like being indebted to this woman, or to anyone else. Still, his child's life was at stake and he had no one else to turn to.

"I will do as you say if you are sure it will be all right." Cloud Walker agreed reluctantly.

"Fine. Why don't you go see how your wife is doing, and then get some sleep?"

Cloud Walker nodded. Murmuring his thanks once more, he left the house, his steps hurried as he made his way back to the doctor's office.

It was then he saw the "wanted" poster tacked to the bulletin board on the front of the newspaper office next to the doctor's office. Cloud Walker's name was on the flyer in bold black type.

He let out a long breath, then hurried up the steps to the doctor's house. Dr. Harley smiled as he opened the door.

"She's going to be fine, just fine," he said, stepping back so Cloud Walker could enter the room.

"Can I see her?"

"Of course. She's asleep now. I had to give her a sedative so I could patch up her leg, but she'll be fine. All she needs now is a few days' rest."

Cloud Walker blinked back his tears as he gazed at Mary. Her face was pale, her eyes shadowed with pain and weariness. Her leg was bandaged from her knee to her ankle.

"You're welcome to spend the night here," the doctor offered. "I've got a spare room down the hall."

"No," Cloud Walker said with a shake of his head.

"Well, suit yourself. I'm going to bed. Did you find Mrs. McBain all right?"

"Yes. She was very kind."

"She is that," the doctor agreed. "Good night."

Cloud Walker gazed at Mary for a long time, his

hand gently stroking her hair, his heart filling with love and gratitude. She would be all right. Thank all the gods, red and white.

Leaving the doctor's office, he walked to the outskirts of town and there, in the stillness of the night, he lifted his arms and offered a silent prayer of thanks to the Great Spirit for sparing the life of his wife and child.

Later he walked through the darkness, his mind in turmoil. Mary would be better off without him, he thought bleakly. Shadow would look after her and the baby much better than he could. As long as he was a wanted man, he could not settle down in one place. And he could not keep Mary with him. The danger was too great. Next time she was hurt, they might not be so lucky.

And yet, how could he leave her? She was his life, his reason for living. Without her, he would as soon be dead.

At last, overcome by weariness and a sense of hopelessness, he stretched out under a tree and fell asleep.

The sun was high in the sky when he awoke, and with the dawn of a new day came a new resolve. He would send Shadow a wire advising him that Mary was in Steel's Crossing, and when Shadow arrived, he would bid Mary good-bye and ride out of her life.

Rising, he walked back to town, determined to act before he could change his mind. He was nearing the telegraph office when the town marshal fell into step beside him. He had been so preoccupied, he had not even been aware of the man's approach.

"Just keep walkin'," Marshal Dunhill said. He gave Cloud Walker a gentle nudge in the ribs with the barrel of his Colt. "The jail's at the end of the street."

Cloud Walker nodded, his steps slow as he walked toward the marshal's office. He was keenly aware of the gun barrel nestled against his ribs, and aware that once they reached the jail, his chances of escape would be virtually nonexistent.

Better to die of a bullet in the back than kicking at the end of a rope, he decided, and without warning, he dropped to his knees, grabbed the startled marshal by the ankles, and fell backward, pulling Dunhill with him.

Rolling catlike to his feet, Cloud Walker sprinted across the street. Dunhill gained his feet seconds later and fired three shots in Cloud Walker's direction.

Cloud Walker grunted as the last shot grazed his rib cage. Pressing a hand to his bleeding side, he ducked into an alley, vaulted over a six-foot fence, and took cover under a pile of wood and debris stacked against the fence.

Marshal Dunhill cursed under his breath as he followed the Indian into the alley. Where had the redskin gone? With his gun at the ready, he walked to the end of the alley. Nothing.

Dunhill grinned. The redskin had fled, but there might be something he wanted more than his freedom.

The marshal was smiling when he returned to his office.

Cloud Walker pressed a handful of dirt over the wound in his side to stem the bleeding. Closing his eyes, he settled down to wait out the day.

It was near midnight when he left his hiding place and made his way toward the doctor's house. He had to see Mary one more time, had to know that she was well before he left town.

He circled the doctor's house twice, his eyes wary as they probed the darkness for any sign that the place was being watched.

When he was certain there were no lawmen lurking in the shadows, he padded noiselessly toward the room where Mary was sleeping.

Slowly, carefully, he lifted the window and stepped into the room. He had no sooner set foot inside the building than he felt hard steel against his spine, and he knew he had walked into a trap. Someone lit a lamp and he saw that the bed was empty. Dunhill and three deputies grinned at him over their gunsights.

"We've been expectin' you," Dunhill said. "Hank, put the cuffs on him."

"Where is my wife?" Cloud Walker asked.

"She's sleeping in another room down the hall."

Cloud Walker nodded, his body growing tense as the deputy known as Hank cuffed his hands behind his back.

"Let's go," Dunhill said.

"Can I see her?"

"Doc gave her a sleeping draught. She won't wake up until tomorrow."

"I want to see her."

Dunhill shrugged. "Make it quick."

Cloud Walker followed the marshal down the hall and into a small room. Mary was asleep on a narrow bed. Her face was pale, her hair like a dark halo around her head. Her injured leg was propped up on a pillow.

Cloud Walker felt a twinge of guilt as he looked at her. She had been attacked by a mountain lion and nearly raped and it was all his fault. No doubt but what she would be better off without him.

"Let's go," Dunhill said impatiently, and Cloud Walker nodded. Bending, he brushed his lips across Mary's cheek before he followed the lawman out of the room.

At the jail, the marshal removed the handcuffs before ordering Cloud Walker into a cell. Cloud Walker fought down a growing sense of panic as he stared at the thick iron bars, felt his soul recoil in horror as the door closed behind him, trapping him within a cold steel cage.

Mary stared at the doctor in dismay, her mind reeling. Cloud Walker had been arrested. Her son was being cared for by a stranger.

"Another couple of days and you'll be back on your feet," Dr. Harley said. "Get as much rest as you can."

"I want to see my son," Mary said.

Marvin Harley smiled indulgently. "I'll have Mrs. McBain bring him by. He's doing just fine. You needn't worry."

Mary nodded, holding back her tears until the doctor left the room. Cloud Walker was in jail. She could not picture him locked behind bars. How he must hate it.

A short time later, Mrs. McBain brought Adam to her. Mary's heart swelled with love as she cradled her son in her arms once again. How she had missed him!

"He's a fine boy," Melinda McBain remarked as she watched Mary examine her son from head to foot. "Always hungry."

"I can't thank you enough for what you've done," Mary said sincerely. "Dr. Harley told me how kind you've been."

Melinda McBain made a gesture of dismissal. "It wasn't anything. I love children and Marvin knows it. He often sends me little ones who need temporary care, and I'm glad to have them."

They chatted amiably for twenty minutes or so, and then Melinda McBain took Adam and left Mary so she could rest.

But Mary could not sleep. She climbed out of bed and limped over to the window. Gazing out into the street, she saw the marshal's office at the far end of town, and felt tears well in her eyes as she pictured her husband locked inside. Cloud Walker, who hated small rooms and enclosed spaces, who loved the out of doors and vast sunlit prairies.

The doctor scolded her when he entered the room a few minutes later and found her out of bed. Clucking to her like a mother hen with one chick, he shooed her back into bed, then brought her a cup of tea.

"You've got to rest," he admonished. "You've been through a bad time."

"I feel fine," Mary said, though in truth her leg pained her considerably.

"I don't care if you feel like dancing," the doctor

replied briskly. "Don't you get out of that bed again until day after tomorrow."

"Very well," Mary promised. "Dr. Harley, would you do me a favor, please?"

"Of course."

"I want to send a wire to my family and let them know where I am."

34

Shadow had ridden a good thirty miles before he bedded down for the night. Now, lying on his back under a blanket of stars, he listened to the sounds of the night—the swoosh of an owl stalking its prey on silent wings of death, the melancholy lament of a lonely coyote baying at the moon, the squeaky song of a cricket, the deep-throated call of a bullfrog looking for a mate. It felt good to be alone, miles and miles from another living soul. Overhead the stars twinkled brightly on a bed of black velvet. Nearby Smoke stood grazing on a patch of thick buffalo grass.

Closing his eyes, he found himself thinking of Mary and Cloud Walker. He knew that Hannah worried about Mary constantly, and as much as he

longed to go after them to ascertain for himself that all
was well, he dared not interfere. Cloud Walker was a
warrior, strong, reliable, and capable of looking after
Mary. Probably they were somewhere in the Black
Hills, holed up in one of the many canyons where the
Sioux and Cheyenne had once sought refuge.

Being a fugitive was never easy, Shadow mused
ruefully. But he and Hannah had survived, and he was
confident that Mary and Cloud Walker could do the
same.

He rose with the dawn the following morning and
rode northeast, heading for the land that had once
belonged to the Sioux and the Cheyenne. It was a big
land filled with rolling hills and timber. Smoke moved
in an easy lope, his long strides covering the miles with
little effort. Shadow rode easily in the saddle, his mind
devoid of all thought as he enjoyed the beauty of the
country around him. He saw a small herd of white-
tailed deer, a prairie-dog town, a skunk, a family of
possums, a doe with a pair of twin fawns at her side, a
fat raccoon. But no buffalo. Not one.

At noon he drew the stallion to a halt beside a
clear stream. Dismounting, he chewed on a piece of
jerked beef, drank from the stream.

Resting in the shade of a tall pine, he closed his
eyes. Immediately Hannah's image danced before
him. Beautiful, lovable Hannah with hair like a flame
and eyes of soft dove gray. Hannah, who had charmed
him from the day they met. Hannah, who had loved
him and seduced him without shame, never caring that
he was an Indian, never asking him to be more or less
than he was. Sweet Hannah, who had sold herself to

Joshua Berdeen so that he, Shadow, might not hang. She had ridden the war trail at his side, enduring hunger and cold and heartache just to be with him. Brave, loyal Hannah. She had more courage than a whole war party of Cheyenne braves.

Sitting up, Shadow perused the countryside, his eyes loving the beauty of the land that had once belonged to his people. He had been born here, grown to manhood here, fought the Crow and the Pawnee and the white man here. Likely he would die here, his body returning to Mother Earth to nourish the land for those who would come after him.

Hannah. He could think of nothing else, and he wondered what it was that had driven him out into the vast lonely prairie when he had a woman waiting for him at home. A woman who loved him with all her heart.

Shadow grinned ruefully. He was forever telling Hawk that the past was over and gone, that it was foolish to yearn for that which could never be, yet here he sat, foolishly wishing for a life that had been gone for over twenty years while Hannah waited for him at home, alone. Hannah, who had a smile warmer than the summer sun; Hannah, whose beauty rivaled that of the earth itself.

Rising, he whistled for Smoke, smiling as the big Appaloosa stud trotted obediently toward him. Like all true warriors, Shadow appreciated a fine horse, and Smoke was one of the best, second only to the big red roan stallion he had ridden to battle at the Greasy Grass.

Shadow patted Smoke's neck affectionately. He

had trained the horse himself, breaking the animal to hand and heel and the sound of his voice. The stallion had speed and bottom. In the old days he would have been prized as a war horse.

Tightening the cinch, Shadow was about to swing into the saddle when a rustle in the underbrush caught his attention. Glancing over his shoulder, he felt his blood turn cold as he saw a huge silvertip rear up less than twenty feet away. The stallion snorted and rolled its eyes as it caught the scent of the bear, and as the grizzly dropped to all fours and lumbered toward them, the Appaloosa jerked the reins from Shadow's hand and bolted down the hillside.

Shadow swore softly as his hand moved toward the knife sheathed on his belt. The grizzly was close now, so close Shadow could smell the bear's foul breath as it sniffed the air. Shadow stood his ground, knowing that the worst thing he could do now was run, though all his instincts urged him to flee. But no man had ever outrun a grizzly.

He held his breath as the bear came to a halt a few feet away, felt his whole body tense as the grizzly suddenly reared up on its hind legs and walked forward, towering over Shadow, who quickly pulled his knife from its sheath. He jabbed the blade into the bear's stomach as the animal slapped him with one huge hairy forepaw. The blow sent Shadow reeling backward and he fell heavily to the ground, landing on his back with such force that it knocked the breath from his body.

The grizzly roared with pain and rage. Dropping

to all fours, it charged the fallen warrior. Shadow scrambled to his feet. Placing his knife between his teeth, he reached for the low-hanging branch of a nearby tree in an effort to escape, but the bear was too fast. One paw swiped through the air, knocking Shadow to the ground again, and then the bear was on him, sharp yellow teeth and razorlike claws ripping through skin and muscle.

Teeth clenched against the pain, Shadow fought against the panic rising within him. Fur filled his nose and mouth as the bear mauled him, and he stifled the scream of pain and fear that rumbled in his throat as the bear's claws ripped into his side.

"Maheo, help me," he gasped, and in that instant he knew that his only chance for survival was to play dead.

Letting his head loll back, he went suddenly limp, forcing himself to relax completely even though the bear's teeth were buried in his arm.

The bear sensed the change in the man immediately. Releasing her grasp on Shadow, she backed off, her nostrils sniffing the man's body. Shadow remained perfectly motionless, his eyes closed, his mouth slack. Rearing halfway up, the bear nudged Shadow with her forepaws. Limp as a rag doll, he rolled over several times before coming up hard against a rock.

The bear followed her prey, swatting him back and forth like a cat toying with a mouse. Once, her tongue washed across Shadow's face and he was certain he was about to be eaten alive, but she merely licked the sweat from his brow.

Lying there, pretending to be dead, Shadow lost track of the time. The sun was hot on his face, flies swarmed over his wounds, but he dared not move. Once, chancing a quick peek through slitted eyes, he saw the grizzly. She was sitting on her haunches a few feet away, licking the blood from her wounds.

Minutes passed, each one seeming like an hour. Now and then the bear nudged him with a paw, but he kept his eyes closed and tried not to breathe too deeply. He could feel the blood oozing from the many claw and teeth marks the bear had inflicted in his arms and back and chest. There was a large gash in his right side. The ground beneath him was wet with his blood.

Then blackness washed over him, pulling him down, down, into a dark tunnel that had no end . . .

He regained consciousness a layer at a time. Opening his eyes, he stared up at the sky. He was badly hurt. Perhaps he would die. But first he must see Hannah one more time, hear her voice whisper that she loved him, feel the warmth of her smile.

Scooping up a handful of dirt, he packed it over the wound in his side to stop the bleeding and then he began to drag himself toward home. Hand over hand, slow inch by slow inch, he went forward. Dirt clods and sharp stones scraped his flesh until his arms and legs and chest felt raw. And still he went stubbornly forward, refusing to give up, refusing to quit. Refusing to release his tenuous hold on life until he had seen Hannah one last time.

He didn't remember passing out, but when he

came to, it was dark. He knew a moment of apprehension as he sensed a presence near him. Had the grizzly come back to finish him off? The thought made his mouth go dry.

Warily he opened his eyes, smiled weakly as he saw Smoke standing near his head. The horse whickered softly, its nostrils flaring at the scent of blood.

"Easy, boy," Shadow rasped. "Easy, now."

Clenching his teeth against the pain of his wounds, he managed to sit up. Dizziness engulfed him and he felt himself slipping into oblivion again. Fighting off the urge to surrender to the peaceful darkness, he reached for the stallion's reins and pulled himself to his feet. The movement broke the scab over the gash in his side, and he knew he was bleeding again. With an effort he hung onto the stallion's mane and managed to make his way to the horse's side. For a long moment he just stood there, his forehead resting against the stallion's warm flank. His arms and back and side felt as if they were on fire.

Muttering an oath, he grasped hold of the saddle horn with both hands and pulled himself onto the stallion's back. Sitting there, trying to gather what strength he had left, he assessed the damage done by the bear. His shirt and pants were in shreds. There were several long gouges down his arms, a bloody furrow down the length of his right leg. His whole body seemed covered with dried blood and dirt save for the gash in his side, which continued to ooze bright red blood.

Feeling light-headed, he wrapped his right hand in the stallion's mane, wound the reins around the saddle horn. Then, laying his head against Smoke's neck, he murmured, "Home, boy. Take me home . . . to Hannah."

35

Something was wrong. I glanced around the yard, a clothespin in one hand, one of Blackie's cotton shirts in the other. Everything seemed peaceful and quiet. Victoria was nursing the baby in the shade of a tree some distance away; Hawk and the twins were wrestling. The sound of the twins' laughter filled the air as they tried to pin their father to the ground. Blackie had gone to a veterinary convention with Dr. Cole and would be gone for several weeks. Hawk and Vickie had come to me company for the day.

But something was wrong. The sun seemed to have lost its warmth and I felt a cold chill steal over me. Shivering, I dropped Blackie's shirt back into the wicker basket at my feet, let the clothespin fall, unnoticed, to the ground.

Something had happened to Shadow. I knew it as

surely as I knew the sun would set in the west.

"Hawk!" I called his name, the panic seeping into my voice.

He came on the run, his eyes darting about to find the cause of my alarm. Vickie followed him, the baby clutched to her breast.

"What is it, nahkoa?" Hawk asked. "What is wrong?"

"Something's happened to your father," I said, the certainty of it growing stronger with every passing moment.

Hawk frowned at me. "What are you saying?"

"Shadow," I said, near tears. "Something has happened to Shadow. I know it."

Hawk and Victoria exchanged worried glances.

"Vickie, stay with my mother until I get back," Hawk said. "I think I know where he would go."

Vickie didn't waste time arguing, but hurried into the house as Hawk ran to the barn to saddle a horse. I was too numb to be of much help. I could only pace the floor, my heart sending urgent prayers to God and Maheo while Vickie packed food and water for Hawk's journey.

Fifteen minutes later, Hawk rode away from the house mounted on Heyoka. I saw him stop once to check the ground for sign and then he was gone from sight.

"Did you pack bandages?" I asked Vickie.

"Yes."

"Disinfectant?"

"Yes."

"Oh, God," I murmured, "please let him be alive."

Tears glistened in Victoria's eyes. "You don't think he's dead?"

"I don't know. I only know something is wrong, terribly wrong. Oh, I wish I had gone with Hawk!"

The hours passed slowly. I couldn't concentrate on anything. I tried to wash the dishes, but the pots and silverware fell from my hands to the floor, and Vickie finished the job for me. I picked up one of Shadow's shirts to mend the cuff, then sat with it clutched in my hands, staring out the window.

Vickie put the children to bed, then came and sat beside me. I went to the window time and time again, my eyes scanning the horizon for some sign of the man I loved. I prayed constantly, pleading for Shadow's safety, hoping my feelings were wrong, that Shadow was unhurt. Yet even as I prayed, I knew he had been wounded, perhaps fatally, and I knew just as certainly that I would not want to go on living without him.

Once, Victoria reached out to squeeze my hand. I was glad of her presence, grateful that she didn't try to fill the silence with meaningless chatter, or try to persuade me that nothing was wrong.

Just after dark there was a knock at the door. It was Justin Edwards, the telegrapher from town. One look at his face told me it was bad news.

My hands were shaking as I took the telegram.

"Sorry," he muttered, and turned away.

"What is it?" Vickie asked, coming to stand beside me.

"Mary's in Steel's Crossing. Cloud Walker is in jail awaiting trial. She wants us to meet her there." I looked at Vickie helplessly. "I can't go, not now."

"She'll understand," Vickie said. "Here, sit down and write a reply. I'll take it into town."

Hawk rode hard all that night, heading northeast across the river toward the land that had once been home to the Sioux and Cheyenne. Heyoka seemed to sense the urgency of its rider, and the miles slipped away as the young stallion fairly flew over the ground.

Hawk's thoughts were centered on his father, and as he rode, he sent prayers to Maheo begging for his father's life. And as he prayed, he wondered what tragedy his mother had envisioned that had so filled her heart with despair.

As dawn brightened the sky, Hawk tried to imagine what life would be like without his father. Always Shadow had been there, a bulwark of strength and courage, doing what had to be done no matter what the cost to himself. Hawk recalled how badly he had wanted to participate in the ritual of the Sun Dance, and how his father had taken the proper steps when the time came so that Hawk might fulfill his dream.

He reined Heyoka to a halt, his narrowed eyes searching the horizon for some sign of movement. The stallion stood with its head down, its sides heaving and lathered with sweat. Hawk smiled ruefully as he patted the animal's neck. If his father were still alive, he would be very angry when he learned of the punishing ride Hawk had forced upon the stud.

Twenty minutes later, Hawk was on the move again.

It was just after midday when he saw Smoke

walking toward him. Hawk felt his heart quicken with fear when he saw his father slumped, unmoving, over the horse's neck.

Urging the weary Heyoka into a lope, Hawk quickly closed the distance between himself and his father. Dismounting, he lifted Shadow from the stud's back and placed him gently on the ground. Thank God, he was alive.

"Neyho?"

Shadow's eyes flickered open at the sound of Hawk's voice. "Hawk?"

"Yes, neyho."

"Take me home."

"Yes, neyho."

"Hurry."

Hawk nodded, unable to speak. There was a note of urgency in his father's voice, as though he realized he might not have much time left.

Uncorking his canteen, Hawk gave his father a drink of cool water. Then, working quickly, he tended his father's wounds as best he could.

"Grizzly," Shadow rasped.

Hawk nodded. Shadow's face and body were badly chewed up. Dead skin hung in shreds from his arms, legs, and torso.

"Hurry," Shadow said, his voice weak. With a sigh, he closed his eyes.

Hawk made no effort to stay his tears as he saw that his father was unconscious. Working quickly, he fashioned a travois from two sturdy saplings and Smoke's saddle blanket. He positioned the travois behind the patiently standing Smoke and attached it with a length of rope to the horse. Then he lifted his father and placed him gently on the blanket, lashing his unconscious form securely in place for the ride. Taking up Smoke's reins, Hawk swung onto Heyoka's back and started for home, pushing the horses as fast as he dared across the rough terrain.

Shadow did not regain consciousness on the long journey home.

My heart was in my throat when I saw Hawk ride up leading Smoke with Shadow on a travois behind.

"He is alive," Hawk assured me quickly. "He was attacked by a grizzly." Hawk laid his hand on my shoulder, his eyes dark with worry. "He is badly hurt," he said as he carried Shadow into the house and placed him on Mary's bed.

"Get Dr. Henderson," I said hoarsely. "Go quickly."

I gazed at Shadow, tears streaming down my cheeks. Victoria, sensing my need to be alone, took the twins into the parlor where they could play without disturbing me.

After what seemed like an eternity, Hawk and the doctor arrived. Shadow's eyes opened as the doctor began removing the bandages from his torso. He saw me and smiled weakly, and then he passed out again.

My throat ached with unshed tears as I removed Shadow's torn shirt and pants. My stomach churned at the sight of his mutilated flesh, even as I thanked God that he was still alive.

The next two hours were very long. I bathed Shadow's wounds and the doctor applied disinfectant.

Then, fighting back nausea, I watched as the doctor reopened the awful wound in Shadow's side, swabbed it out with alcohol and disinfectant, then sewed the ragged edges together. Shadow groaned softly as the needle darted in and out of his flesh, and I was reminded of another time long ago when I had watched my mother stitch Shadow's leg.

When the doctor finished with the gash in Shadow's side, he began to painstakingly remove the dirt from the numerous cuts and abrasions Shadow had received. I felt my stomach heave as the doctor cut away the dead flesh from Shadow's arms, legs, back, and chest.

Dr. Henderson looked at me, one eyebrow arching upward. "Are you all right, Mrs. Kincaid?" he asked in a worried tone. "You're not going to faint on me, are you?"

"No," I said. But I wasn't so sure.

When at last the doctor had done all he could, he handed me a dark brown bottle of ointment and several packets of medicinal powders.

"Apply that salve to his wounds when you change the bandages, and give him one dose of the powders every four hours," the doctor instructed. "He's lost a good deal of blood, so give him as much liquid as he'll hold." Dr. Henderson gave me a sympathetic smile. "We should know by tomorrow night. Try to get some rest."

Taking up his hat and black satchel, the doctor nodded to Hawk and Vickie, patted my shoulder, and left the house.

"I'll go and put on a fresh pot of tea," Victoria said.

She paused in the doorway. "Try not to worry, Hannah. I'm sure he'll be all right."

I sat by Shadow's side all that night, my eyes never leaving his beloved face. His cheeks were cut and scratched, his lower lip had been torn, his eyes were swollen, yet he had never looked more beautiful. He was alive and that was all that mattered. I prayed to God that he would stay that way.

And yet I was afraid, so afraid. He had lost so much blood. He looked pale and haggard. The bandages on his arms and legs and torso covered nearly every inch of his flesh. Occasionally a low groan of pain escaped his lips, and the sound was like a knife in my heart.

Shortly after midnight he began to toss restlessly. Sweat poured from his body, soaking the bedclothes. He mumbled in his sleep, speaking incoherently in Cheyenne and English. I wiped his face and body with a cool cloth and gave him several swallows of cool water, but he continued to thrash about. Once I heard him mention Calf Running's name, and then he cried out in a loud voice, "The Army has her, and I must get her back!"

He was lost in the past, I thought, and I clearly remembered the time when I had been a prisoner of the Army. It had been after the battle at the Little Big Horn. Shadow and seventy renegade warriors had refused to surrender, and the Army had been pursuing us relentlessly. Shadow's men and the soldiers had been engaged in a fierce battle when I was captured. I had been pregnant with our first child at the time, but the man who had captured me had not been repulsed

by my swollen belly. He had been trying to rape me
when Shadow made his way into the tent where I was
being held prisoner. He had dragged Stockton away
from me. Yes, I remembered that night as though it
had happened only yesterday. It was one of the few
times I had seen Shadow's savage side. Stockton's face
had gone fish-belly white when he saw the hatred
glittering in Shadow's cold black eyes. The white man
had opened his mouth to scream when he saw the knife
in Shadow's hand, but all that had emerged was a
hoarse cry of fear. And then Shadow hurled himself at
Stockton, hacking and stabbing with terrible fury until
what had once been a man was no more than a
grotesque pile of butchered meat. Shadow's hands had
looked as though they had been dipped in red dye
when he pulled the knife from Stockton's body for the
last time. His breath had come in short, hard gasps, as
if he had been running a great distance. Feeling my
shocked gaze, Shadow had turned to face me, and the
face of the enraged killer had been magically trans-
formed into the face of the man I loved . . .

Shadow, my defender and protector. He had
killed three men who had dared to touch me. First
Stockton, then an Arapahoe warrior who had sought to
take advantage of me when we were alone in one of
the war camps, and then Joshua Berdeen.

"Oh, Shadow," I wailed softly, and burying my
face in my hands, I began to cry.

I had been weeping for a long time when I felt a
hand moving in my hair. Sniffing back my tears, I
lifted my head to find Shadow watching me.

"Hannah." His voice was weak and tinged with

pain. "Do not weep for me," he chided with a gentle half-smile. "Long life and happiness. That was what the hawks promised. Remember?"

I nodded. "I remember."

Shadow's hand dropped to my shoulder, and I felt him tremble convulsively as the movement sent a fresh wave of pain through him.

"Lie still. Does it hurt terribly?"

He nodded, his hand squeezing my shoulder. Abruptly his eyelids fluttered down and his hand fell away from my shoulder.

"Shadow!" I screamed his name, fearing that he had died. Pressing my ear against his chest, I could hear the faint beat of his heart and I began to cry again.

"Don't die," I sobbed. "Please don't die. I'll leave Bear Valley if you want. We'll live anywhere you say, only please don't die."

Hawk heard my sobs and came to sit beside me, talking quietly of memories we had shared. It was comforting, having him there beside me, though I did not really hear what he said. I could think of nothing but Shadow, and how empty my life would be without him.

The next hours were awful. Shadow tossed and turned fretfully, his body wracked by chills and fever. I gave him the medicine the doctor had prescribed, willing my husband to get better, praying as I had never prayed before.

Shadow's condition was unchanged in the morning. I gave him another dose of the medicinal powders, applied the salve to his wounds. He would have several scars on his arms and legs if he lived, I thought, and choked back my tears.

News of Shadow's accident and Cloud Walker's arrest spread quickly through the valley. All that day our neighbors came to call, expressing their concern, offering help if we needed it, leaving casseroles and covered dishes for our family.

I refused to leave Shadow's side. I could not eat or sleep, could only sit there, feeling numb inside. I could not bear to see him in pain, to know he was hurting and there was nothing I could do about it. He had always been so strong, so indomitable, it didn't seem possible that he could be so near death. He had cheated it so many times in the past.

His fever grew worse as the day wore on, and he became delirious. Lying there, he refought old battles and relived the agony and the ecstasy of the Sun Dance. I saw him weep for the death of his father, heard his cry of pain when our first son was stillborn, heard his anguished wail when he thought I had been killed back on the reservation.

I wept for Shadow's pain. Taking his hand in mine, I began to talk to him, telling him of my love, telling him how desperately I needed him, begging him not to leave me alone.

Dr. Henderson came late in the afternoon. "Sorry I couldn't get here sooner," he said apologetically. "Mrs. Killmore went into labor this morning. It was a difficult birth. Twins. One of them didn't make it."

I was sorry for Mrs. Killmore's loss, but more concerned over the fate of my own husband. I hovered near the doctor as he removed the bandage from

Shadow's side. The wound was red and ugly. I watched in horror as the doctor withdrew a wicked-looking instrument from his bag. He poured alcohol over the wound, sterilized the scalpel, and then lanced the wound.

Bile rose in my throat as blood and thick yellow pus oozed from Shadow's side. I gazed at the doctor with alarm. Shadow had already lost so much blood. How could he afford to lose more?

Dr. Henderson kept draining the abscess until only bright red blood flowed from the wound. With deft but gentle hands he bandaged Shadow's side, took his temperature, checked his pulse and heartbeat.

"Doctor—" I began.

"It's up to him now," the doctor said, nodding at Shadow's inert form. "I've done all I can."

I don't remember showing the doctor to the door. I couldn't seem to think or feel anything.

Hawk and Vickie went home to get some rest and look after their place. They came by that night, their faces grave with concern. I hardly knew they were there. They spoke to me and I answered, but I was hardly aware of what was said. I could think of only Shadow.

Hawk brought me a cup of black coffee laced with brandy, and I drank it without question.

Vickie came to sit beside me for a while, her eyes red and swollen. We sat together holding hands. Once we knelt by Shadow's bedside to pray. At midnight Vickie urged me to go to bed.

"You need to rest," she said. "There's nothing you can do."

But I refused to leave my husband's side.

The long dark hours of the night passed slowly. I sat beside Shadow, and the quiet surrounded me, seeming ominous and loud. Was it my imagination, or was death lurking just outside the door?

Half-asleep, I remembered the first time I had seen Shadow. He had been a boy of twelve at the time, handsome and arrogant. We had become friends and he had taught me to hunt and fish and skin a deer. They were not pursuits I had cared for, but Shadow thought that girl things were foolish and a waste of time, and he had refused to do anything he considered silly or undignified, which meant just about everything I liked to do.

I recalled the day of my sixteenth birthday. I had not seen Shadow for a long time. We had met by the river and he had been even more handsome than I remembered. He had worn only moccasins and the briefest of deerskin clouts, and I had not been able to take my eyes away from him. His legs had been long and well-muscled from years of riding bareback; his belly had been hard and flat, as it was now, ridged with muscle. His shoulders had been broad. Two livid scars had marred his chest, proof that he had participated in the Sun Dance. A third scar had zigzagged down his right shoulder. Like a bird hypotized by a snake, I could not tear my eyes from him. I could only stare, awed by his proud carriage, completely mesmerized by his savage yet utterly fascinating appearance. We had not said much that day, nor had we spent a great deal of time together, yet I had known that our lives would be intertwined from that day forward.

I remembered riding the war trail at Shadow's side, remembered my horror at killing a man. The dead trooper's face had haunted my dreams for weeks. Shadow, always sensitive to my moods, had done his best to comfort me. Nights, when we were alone, he talked to me of his youth, telling me amusing tales of his people in an effort to cheer me. But it had been his touch, the strength of his arms and his love, that had brought solace to my troubled soul. Only in his embrace had I felt secure. Sometimes it had seemed as though the whole world had gone mad, and only Shadow and the love we shared had remained unchanged.

Memories. My whole life was filled with memories of Shadow.

At dawn I forced myself to stand up and move around. My body was stiff and sore from sitting for so long, and I suddenly felt old, so old. Going to the window, I gazed out into the distance. The sky was growing light, coming alive with glowing shades of red and gold and lavender as the sun gave birth to another new day. It was a magnificent sunrise, and as the colors slowly began to fade, I saw two red-tailed hawks soar across the clear blue sky, wheeling and diving in perfect unison until they disappeared into the sun.

"Hannah."

His voice reached out to me, more welcome than life itself. Turning, not daring to hope, I saw Shadow watching me. He looked pale and weak, but his eyes were clear, and I knew the worst was over.

Murmuring a fervent prayer of thanksgiving, I ran to his side and placed my hand over his brow. It was cool. The fever had broken at last.

Shadow cocked his head to one side. "You look awful," he said candidly.

"You look wonderful," I exclaimed jubilantly. "Are you hungry?"

"Starved."

It was the best news I had ever heard. I gave him a big kiss, then went into the kitchen and prepared a bowl of broth for Shadow and a thick sandwich for myself. Now that Shadow was going to be all right, I was famished.

Shadow had a second bowl of broth and a cup of coffee, and I ate another sandwich.

"Hannah." Shadow laid the bowl aside and took my hand in his. "You look like you haven't slept in days."

"I haven't," I admitted sheepishly. "I was too worried about you."

"Come, lie down beside me."

"I'm all right."

"Hannah." His voice was stern. "If you get sick, who will take care of me?"

"That's blackmail," I muttered, but I obediently crawled into bed beside him, my head nestled against his shoulder, my arm going around his waist. I was careful not to touch his wounded side. With a sigh of contentment, I closed my eyes.

I slept all that day and into the next.

Shadow's recovery was slow but steady. He had been badly hurt and had lost a great deal of blood, but he was strong and possessed a fighting spirit, and that stood him in good stead now. He slept much of the time during the first week. I rarely left his side. I had almost lost him, and I could not bear to be away from him for more than a few minutes at a time.

Shadow, too, was aware of how close to death he had been. When he was awake, his dark eyes lingered on my face. In sleep, he held my hand in his, refusing to let go.

"It was a near thing," Shadow mused one evening after dinner.

"Too near."

Shadow grinned at me. "It was a very big bear."

"Were you afraid?"

"Not of dying. Only that I might not see you again." Shadow studied my face, his expression thoughtful. "Would you really leave Bear Valley if I asked you to?"

"Why do you ask?"

"One night I felt myself slipping away, and while I hovered between this world and the next, I had a vision. I saw my mother and my father waiting for me. They were dressed in buckskins whiter than any I have ever seen. I could see trees and flowers and many miles of green grass. And buffalo. Hundreds and hundreds of buffalo, grazing in a meadow."

"It was just a dream," I said, but I felt a strange shiver inside as Shadow shook his head.

"It was not a dream. My mother smiled at me, her arms outstretched, and I knew that if I went to her, all the pain I was feeling would go away."

Shadow stared at me, his eyes filled with wonder. "But then I heard you calling my name, begging me not to go. I looked back, and I could see you kneeling beside my bed. You were crying, and I could hear you begging me not to die. You said you would leave Bear Valley and live anywhere I wanted."

My mouth went dry as Shadow finished speaking. Perhaps he *had* gone to that place between life and death. The thought filled me with a nameless fear.

"I told my mother that you were weeping for me," Shadow went on, "and she said I must go back, that my unborn son would need a father when he was born."

I gasped, my hand going to my stomach. I had suspected for some time that I might be pregnant, but I had shrugged it off. Then, when Shadow had been hurt, I had forgotten all about it.

"Are you pregnant, Hannah?"

"I think so."

Shadow smiled from ear to ear. "Another son!" he exclaimed, and then he grew serious once more. "Would you leave Bear Valley for me, Hannah?"

"If you wish."

Shadow grinned wryly. "I do not want to leave. I do not know what I went looking for out there on the plains. Perhaps I am growing old and feeble-minded. Out there, alone, I realized that everything I had ever desired was waiting for me here. I was about to start for home when *mato* attacked me." Shadow shook his head ruefully. "I knew I was looking death in the face and that if I panicked I would never see you again."

Shadow laughed softly. "It was hard not to run, but I knew that running was the wrong thing to do, so I played dead instead."

I let out a long sigh, glad the nightmare was over.

Shadow told his story many times in the days

ahead as our friends and neighbors came to visit and to wish him well. Fred Brown, Porter Sprague, and Clancy Turner came to call one afternoon, and they exchanged stories, real and doubtful, about grizzlies and the men they had attacked. The grizzly was indeed a fearsome beast, with no enemy but man. A charging grizzly was a terrible sight to behold. Ears flat, hair flat, they could cover fifty yards in three seconds, a remarkable speed for such a large animal. Grizzly bears possessed a keen sense of smell, feared nothing, and considered almost everything to be food. Weighing only sixteen ounces at birth, a full-grown bear could easily weigh over a thousand pounds. Little wonder that both animals and man stayed out of their way.

I listened in horror as Fred Brown related the story of mountain man Hugh Glass. It was said that Hugh Glass had run afoul of an enraged grizzly while traveling with a small party of trappers. He managed to kill the bear in the struggle, but when it was over, Hugh was more dead than alive. The leader of the expedition left two men to stay with the wounded man until he recovered or died, but the two men left with Glass were certain he would never recover from the awful wounds he had received, and they abandoned him, taking his rifle and ammunition and supplies. But Hugh Glass had survived. Alone in the wilderness, he lived on wild berries and roots. Unable to walk, he crawled toward Fort Kiowa, over a hundred miles away, determined to seek vengeance on the men who had left him for dead. Eventually he was found by a band of Indians, who tended his wounds until he recovered. The most amazing part of the story was that, when Glass found the two men who had deserted him, he forgave them. Few men were lucky enough to survive such a violent encounter with a grizzly. How thankful I was that Shadow had been one of the lucky ones.

With Shadow's life out of danger, my thoughts turned to Mary and Cloud Walker. Shadow urged me to go to Steel's Crossing to keep Mary company and get acquainted with our newest grandchild. It was tempting, but I could not leave Shadow. He was still bedridden and unable to care for himself, though he wouldn't admit it. Hawk thought about going to stay with Mary, but he had his hands full here just looking after his place and ours.

I wrote Mary daily, hoping she would understand why we couldn't be there, hoping she had the inner strength to meet whatever the future held.

36

Mary wept tears of joy as she read her mother's letter. Thank God, her father was out of danger and on the mend, though he was still weak and bedridden. He was a terrible patient, her mother said, and complained about everything except the pain as his wounds healed.

Laying the letter aside, Mary gazed out the window of her room at Mrs. Spencer's boardinghouse. So much had happened in such a short time. Cloud Walker had been questioned repeatedly about Frank's disappearance, but he had refused to say anything. With no evidence of foul play and no corpse, it had looked as though he might be released from jail, and then Harvey Castrell had been arrested for being drunk and disorderly in Lincoln County. The sheriff who arrested Castrell recognized him from an old "wanted" poster, and Castrell had been extradited to Steel's Crossing to stand trial for the murder of a local shopkeeper five years before.

Mattie and Leland Smythe had arrived at Steel's Crossing about the same time. The detective they had hired had gotten wind of Castrell's arrest and notified them that Castrell was in jail awaiting trial. Mattie and Leland had rushed to town to see if Castrell knew of Frank's whereabouts.

Mary had been visiting Cloud Walker when Mattie and Leland entered the cellblock. She could still recall the wolfish grin on Castrell's face as he told Leland and Mattie that Cloud Walker had taken Frank and himself into the wilds and killed Frank in cold blood, and that he himself had barely escaped with his life. He even told them where it had happened. He told the same story to the prosecuting attorney.

Mattie had burst into tears as she whirled on Mary. "This is all your fault!" she cried, her voice thick with loathing. "If you hadn't lusted after that savage, my Frank would still be alive."

Mattie was on the verge of hysteria when Leland put his arm around his wife's shoulders and led her out of the cellblock.

Mary spent every minute possible with Cloud Walker. Daily there were new lines of bitterness around his eyes and mouth. She sensed the tension mounting within him, lurking in the shadows of his calm exterior like a lion ready to strike. They spoke of Adam, of Shadow's brush with death, of everything but the coming trial.

On a sunny day in early May, Harvey Castrell was tried for murder and found guilty. He was sentenced to hang, but the sentence was to be delayed until he had testified at Cloud Walker's trial, which was set for the following week.

The day after Castrell's trial, the marshal received a wire saying that Frank Smythe's body had been found. A statement from a local doctor accompanied the wire, stating that Frank Smythe had been shot twice, once in the shoulder and once in the chest, and that he had been scalped.

"Scalped him, too, eh?" Castrell remarked. He was sitting on his cot with his back to the wall while he watched Cloud Walker pace his cell. "That's going to look bad in court."

Castrell grinned maliciously. "Looks like I'll have the last laugh after all," he mused. "After all, it's your word against mine, and I have nothing to lose by lying."

"I should have killed you when I had the chance," Cloud Walker rasped.

"Too true, too true," Castrell agreed. He laughed softly. "Going to the gallows won't be so bad knowing that you'll be right behind me."

Cloud Walker's face remained impassive, but inwardly he shuddered. Castrell was right. No jury was going to believe that he had killed Smythe in self-defense.

Cloud Walker's trial was set for May 15. Mary

tried to put on a brave face when she saw Cloud Walker the night before the trial. She kept her voice light as she talked about Adam, and how good it would be to get back to Bear Valley after the trial, and how anxious she was to have her parents see the baby. Cloud Walker's eyes never left her face. Each minute he spent with her was precious now, and he memorized each detail of her face and figure, wanting to carry her image with him into the next life.

Gradually Mary ran out of things to say and they stood together as close as they could with the iron bars between them.

"Well, hell," Castrell muttered. "Aren't you going to kiss her? Might be your last chance."

Cloud Walker swore under his breath. Damn the man! Wasn't it enough that his lies were going to kill any hope they had for a future? Did he have to spoil what little time he and Mary had left?

Mary felt the anger churning within her husband and she placed her hand on his cheek. "Please," she whispered. "Just ignore him."

Cloud Walker nodded. Reaching through the bars, he circled Mary's waist with one arm as he bent to place a kiss on her lips. Mary pressed closer to him, the bars digging into her flesh as she returned his kiss.

For one brief moment she forgot everything but the touch of Cloud Walker's lips on hers. And then the door to the cellblock swung open and the marshal informed her that visiting hours were over.

Reluctantly she followed the marshal out of the cellblock.

Cloud Walker didn't sleep that night. He paced

the narrow cell for hours, or stood at the tiny iron-barred window and stared out at the night. With the coming of dawn, he raised his arms above his head, his eyes lifted toward heaven, as he murmured a prayer for help.

Everyone in Steel's Crossing turned out for the trial, eager to hear the whole sordid story of Mary's love affair with an Indian that had led to murder.

Cloud Walker's face was an impassive mask when he entered the courtroom. He was dressed in buckskins. His hair, long and black, fell past his shoulders. The women in the crowd murmured to one another. He was terribly handsome. No wonder Mary Smythe had been tempted into his arms. He was tall and dark, virile, and oh, so masculine.

The men nodded as Cloud Walker took his seat. One look at that face, those unfathomable black eyes, and you knew the man was capable of killing.

There were several witnesses. Harvey Castrell's voice rang with sincerity as he told his story. Yes, he had been there the day Cloud Walker abducted Mary. Yes, Cloud Walker had taken Frank Smythe and himself into a deserted part of the country and shot Frank in cold blood. Castrell said he had been struck by Mary and then had played possum and seen the whole thing. He had been lucky to escape with his life.

The man at the train depot testified that he had seen Frank Smythe, Harvey Castrell, Cloud Walker, and Mary leave the train together.

The porter testified that he had seen Cloud Walker and Mary board the train several days later. No, he had not seen Mr. Smythe or Mr. Castrell.

A hush fell over the courtroom when Mary took the stand. Her eyes never left Cloud Walker's face as she told her story. Yes, she had married Frank Smythe, but they had been unhappy together and she had returned to Bear Valley. She had met Cloud Walker there and fallen in love with him. She told how Frank had blackmailed her into going back to Chicago, that he had refused to give her a divorce even when she told him she was pregnant with Cloud Walker's child. She told how Cloud Walker had come after her, how Frank had followed them and forced them to leave the train.

The spectators gasped when she related that Frank had threatened to castrate Cloud Walker and then kill him. She had tried to interfere. She had hit Castrell with a branch and grabbed his gun, intending to use it to make Frank go away, but Frank had a gun, too. She had shot Frank in the arm and he had dropped his weapon.

Mary's voice dropped to a whisper and her eyes filled with tears as she told how Frank's gun had gone off when it hit the ground, killing Katherine. That was all she remembered.

And then Cloud Walker took the stand. Why had he run away if he had nothing to hide? Why hadn't he gone to the law and confessed? Why had he scalped Frank Smythe?

He answered the questions in a voice that was hard and flat. He had run away because he was an Indian who had killed a white man, a very rich and powerful white man. He had not confessed because he knew that no one would believe he had killed Smythe in self-defense. And he had scalped Frank Smythe because it pleased him to do so.

In the same flat voice, he told his version of what had happened. It was the same as what Mary had said.

"Frank reached for his gun at the same time I reached for the one Mary had dropped," Cloud Walker said in conclusion. "My aim was better."

Mary looked at the faces of the jury as Cloud Walker finished his story. They didn't believe him. She knew it without doubt.

The marshal took Cloud Walker back to jail, leaving Castrell in the custody of one of his deputies as it didn't seem wise to let the two convicted men get close to each other.

Rising, Mary went to stand before Harvey Castrell.

"Why are you doing this?" she asked. "Why?"

"I don't know what the hell you're talking about," Castrell growled.

"Please tell the truth. Please don't let them hang my husband. You know he's innocent. You're the only one who can help us."

"I ain't in the helpin' business," Castrell retorted.

Tears streamed down Mary's cheeks. "I'll get down on my knees and beg if that's what you want," she cried. "Please, Mr. Castrell. I love him. Haven't you ever been in love?"

Harvey Castrell looked away. Of course he'd been in love. Once, a beautiful young woman had begged him to give up his outlaw life and settle down, but he had refused, and when he finally changed his mind it was too late. She had died, sad and alone.

"Please," Mary said again. "We have a son who needs a father."

Castrell looked deep into her eyes. "Deputy," he called to the man standing behind him. "Get the sheriff. I've got something I need to say."

37

I ran into the bedroom, tears of joy streaming down my face.

"They're coming home!" I cried, throwing my arms around Shadow's neck. "Cloud Walker's free and they're catching the next train home."

Disentangling himself from my grasp, Shadow took the wire from my hand. Harvey Castrell had changed his story at the last minute. He had seen the whole thing, and Cloud Walker had killed Frank Smythe in self-defense. Cloud Walker had been acquitted. Castrell's sentence had been carried out the next day.

Mary and Cloud Walker arrived on a sunny afternoon four days later. Shadow wasn't supposed to be out of bed yet, but he refused to stay home, and our whole family was there to welcome Mary and Cloud Walker home. Tears of joy flowed freely as we embraced each other. The whole ugly incident was over at last and Mary was back home where she belonged.

Mary and Cloud Walker immediately began making plans to build a home of their own. They chose a piece of land near our place and decided to get started on the building right away. Fred Brown and Porter Sprague and several of our other neighbors offered to help, and they began the following Saturday.

The house was about half done when Shadow had recovered enough to help. Daily I thanked God that my husband was his old self again. His face, that handsome rugged face I loved so well, healed without a scar. The lacerations and abrasions on his arms, legs, back, and chest left several long white scars, but I didn't care. He was alive and that was all that mattered.

With life back to normal, I had more time to dwell on my pregnancy. I was cross a good deal of the time, but Shadow was unfailingly patient and supportive. I had not planned to have another child. Much as I had always wanted a large family, I had always had trouble getting pregnant. I had assumed that Blackie would be my last child, and though I had hoped for more children when I was younger, I had resigned myself to three and been grateful that they were all healthy and happy.

Blackie and Shadow continued to humor me when I was cross and out of sorts. They took over many of my chores so I could rest, and that made me even more irritable. I wasn't an invalid, I was just pregnant. Pregnant and fat and unattractive.

Shadow found me crying in our room one day. He quickly came to my side, his eyes dark with worry at the sight of my tear-streaked face.

"What is it?" he asked anxiously.

"Nothing," I wailed. "Leave me alone."

"Hannah, what is wrong?"

"I'm fat. I look like a pregnant heifer. How can you stand the sight of me?"

Shadow chuckled, and the sound of his amusement angered me. He could laugh! He wasn't the one who was pregnant. He didn't have morning sickness. He hadn't lost his shape. The smell of cooking meat didn't make his stomach turn.

"Go away," I said petulantly. "Go away and leave me alone. This is all your fault."

"Hannah."

I was instantly contrite. His voice was filled with such love and compassion, how could I stay mad at him?

"I'm sorry," I mumbled.

"You are not fat," Shadow said quietly. "You are pregnant with my son. Our son. Are you sorry?"

"No, of course not."

"You know that I love you?"

"Yes."

"Then why are you unhappy?"

I shrugged my shoulders, ashamed to look at him because I had been acting like a spoiled child.

"We have been blessed, you and I," Shadow said, stroking my hair. "You have often said you wished for more children, and I have always longed for another son." Shadow smiled at me, his eyes dancing merrily. "Or even a daughter."

"I know. But I didn't want to be having children when I was too old to take care of them."

Shadow laughed, and I laughed with him. We had been blessed, and I put the blues behind me where they belonged and instead thanked God for the new life growing beneath my heart.

In October we received a letter from Rebecca. She was doing well. Her daughter, Beth, was expecting again. Twins, the doctor said. Rebecca sent her love to each of us and talked about a visit, perhaps in the spring.

When Thanksgiving came, our family had much to be grateful for. We were all happy and healthy, surrounded by those we held dear.

As I gazed at the people sitting around our table, I felt my heart swell with joy. Hawk was busily trying to get Jacob and Jason to eat the food on their plates, but the twins, now four years old, were more interested in throwing it at each other. They were handsome boys, full of mischief. Victoria shook her head at the twins, leaving them to Hawk while she nursed Amanda Marie.

Blackie only grew more handsome as time went on. He was a good boy, dependable, level-headed, witty, and ambitious. We all expected big things from Blackie.

And Shadow . . . he was cradling Mary's son in his arm, his dark eyes glowing with pride as he glanced around the table.

Our eyes met and held, and then we smiled at

each other. Truly, we had been blessed.

A month later, on the day before Christmas, our son was born. Mary and Victoria were there to help me, but I wanted only Shadow beside me.

"I'm too old to be having a baby," I gasped as a contraction knifed through me. "I'm a grandmother!"

Shadow laughed softly as he squeezed my hand. "You will never be old. Having a baby in the house will keep us young."

"Easy for you to say," I wailed. "You don't have to give birth, or get up in the middle of the night to take care of it. Oh, God, it hurts."

The laughter left Shadow's eyes and his brow grew lined with concern. "I would bear the pain for you if I could," he said in a ragged voice.

"I know you would." My nails raked his arms as the contractions came closer together. "Talk to me. It doesn't hurt so bad when you talk to me. Tell me about you."

"You know all there is to know," Shadow chided softly. "You have lived most of my life with me."

"Tell me," I begged.

He could not refuse, so he began to tell me of the day we had first met, of how he had felt when he saw me near Rabbit's Head Rock.

"You were just a child," Shadow said, his voice as soothing and gentle as sweet summer rain. "Just a skinny little girl child with a handful of wildflowers and a scared look on your face. You stood up to me, though," he said, smiling. "You even offered me a cookie."

"I offered you one," I panted. "And you ate them all."

"They were very good. Looking at you that day, I knew you would become a beautiful woman. It was hard for me to stop seeing you, but I had to learn the ways of a warrior, and so I went back to my people when the time came, determined to put you out of my heart and my mind forever." Shadow smiled. "Almost, I succeeded. I spent all my time learning how to be a Cheyenne warrior, and as I came of age I began to court a maiden in our village. You remember Bright Star? I think I might have married her if I had not ridden to the river crossing one warm summer day and seen you there. You were just fifteen at the time, but more lovely than any woman I have ever seen before or since. I went often to the river crossing after that, hoping to find you alone, but you were always with Orin. Or Joshua."

Shadow's voice grew hard and his eyes grew angry when he mentioned Joshua Berdeen's name.

"I knew you were too young to marry," Shadow went on, "so I went away with my people to our winter camp, determined to make you mine when I returned the following spring."

I smiled as Shadow paused in his story. How well I remembered those wonderful days before the Indian wars, when Shadow and I had courted and loved and laughed. There had been no misery or unhappiness for us then, no fears for the future, only our love and our hope for a long and happy life together.

I groaned as another contraction knifed through

me. Shadow squeezed my hands, his eyes filled with empathy.

"Hang onto me," he urged.

I nodded, my nails raking his arms as the pains came closer and harder.

I drew blood, but Shadow did not seem to feel the pain. He had always been so brave. I wished I had some of his strength, some of his courage, to buoy me up now. He had suffered so much pain in his lifetime, so much heartache, yet he had never turned bitter or cruel.

I remembered the abuse he had suffered at the hands of the men who had dragged him from town to town back East, billing Shadow as "Two Hawks Flying, the Last Fighting Chief of the Plains." Shadow had been mocked and whipped and humiliated. Joshua had left him in the wilderness to die of exposure or starvation, whichever came first. He had been wounded in battle many times, knifed and left for dead by settlers. Many times he had taken revenge on those who had caused him harm, many times he had killed those who had caused me pain, yet underneath it all he remained a man who was kind and gentle, filled with love for his family, for all of life.

I could not hold back a cry as the worst pain of all tore through me.

"Push, Hannah," Shadow urged softly, and within minutes, our son made his way into the world, and into Shadow's capable hands.

Reverently Shadow gazed at his son, then held the baby up for me to see. Our son was wrinkled and red and beautiful. My eyes filled with tears of joy as our son squirmed and began to cry.

Mary and Victoria came in then. Shadow cut the cord, Mary bathed and dressed the baby, and Vickie helped me expel the afterbirth, then helped me into a clean nightgown and changed the sheets on the bed.

When I was presentable, Hawk and Cloud Walker brought the twins in to see the baby. Everyone remarked on how adorable he was, how tiny, how perfect.

Blackie looked at me and grinned. "Thanks, nahkoa," he said, chuckling. "I always wanted a little brother." His chuckle turned to full-fledged laughter. "Will you give me a little sister next year?"

"Scoot," Mary said, shooing Blackie out of the room. "Don't even think such a thing."

Later, when Shadow and I were alone, he sat beside me while I nursed the baby. I basked in the love shining in my husband's eyes.

"What shall we name him?" I asked.

"You decide."

"I've always liked the name Daniel," I mused. "What would you think of Daniel Blue Hawk?"

Shadow grinned at me. "It is a fine name."

Our eyes met and held, and though Shadow did not speak, I could hear his voice whispering in my heart.

"Long life and happiness, Hannah," I could hear him say. "That is what the hawks have promised."

And I knew it was true.

Epilogue

Hannah and Shadow lived a long and happy life, just as the hawks had promised. They lived to see the automobile replace the horse, to see airplanes take to the sky, to see movies with sound. Many changes took place in their lifetime, but their love for one another never changed and never grew old.

Hawk and Victoria had four sons and three daughters. Hawk was elected sheriff of Bear Valley when Bill Lancaster resigned, and he spent the rest of his life upholding law and order. Hawk was a fair and compassionate lawman, for he had seen a prison cell from the inside and he knew that no matter how guilty a man appeared, there was always a chance that he was innocent.

Victoria was active in the women's rights movement and was the first woman in Bear Valley to vote in an election.

Mary and Cloud Walker had seven sons and two daughters. They never left Bear Valley, but spent their lives together raising blooded Appaloosa horses and beautiful dark-eyed children.

Blackie's love and concern for people and animals never faltered, and he went to college and became a veterinarian, just as he had always dreamed of doing.

Daniel Blue Hawk became a writer. His first novel chronicled the lives of his parents as related to him by his mother.

The story began: "I was nine years old the first time I saw the Cheyenne warrior who would one day be known as Two Hawks Flying . . ."

THE ANGEL & THE OUTLAW

MADELINE BAKER

Bestselling Author Of *Lakota Renegade*

An outlaw, a horse thief, a man killer, J.T. Cutter isn't surprised when he is strung up for his crimes. What amazes him is the heavenly being who grants him one year to change his wicked ways. Yet when he returns to his old life, he hopes to cram a whole lot of hell-raising into those twelve months no matter what the future holds.

But even as J.T. heads back down the trail to damnation, a sharp-tongued beauty is making other plans for him. With the body of a temptress and the heart of a saint, Brandy is the only woman who can save J.T. And no matter what it takes, she'll prove to him that the road to redemption can lead to rapturous bliss.

_3931-1 $5.99 US/$7.99 CAN

APACHE RUNAWAY

MADELINE BAKER

Ruthless and cunning, Ryder Fallon is a half-breed who can deal cards and death in the same breath. Yet when the Indians take him prisoner, he is in danger of being sent to the devil—until a green-eyed beauty named Jenny saves his life and opens his heart.

___4464-1 $5.99 US/$6.99 CAN

Dorchester Publishing Co., Inc.
P.O. Box 6640
Wayne, PA 19087-8640

Please add $1.75 for shipping and handling for the first book and $.50 for each book thereafter. NY, NYC, and PA residents, please add appropriate sales tax. No cash, stamps, or C.O.D.s. All orders shipped within 6 weeks via postal service book rate. Canadian orders require $2.00 extra postage and must be paid in U.S. dollars through a U.S. banking facility.

Name_____
Address_____
City_____State_____Zip_____
I have enclosed $_____ in payment for the checked book(s).
Payment <u>must</u> accompany all orders. ❏ Please send a free catalog.

A WANTED MAN.
AN INNOCENT WOMAN.
A WANTON LOVE!

Madeline Baker

When beautiful Rachel Halloran took Logan Tyree into her home, he was unconscious. A renegade Indian with a bullet wound in his side and a price on his head, he needed her help. But to Rachel he was nothing but trouble, a man whose dark sensuality made her long for forbidden pleasures; to her father he was the answer to a prayer, a gunslinger whose legendary skill could rid the ranch of a powerful enemy.

But Logan Tyree would answer to no man—and to no woman. If John Halloran wanted his services, he would have to pay dearly for them. And if Rachel wanted his loving, she would have to give up her innocence, her reputation, her very heart and soul.

__4085-9 $5.99 US/$6.99 CAN

MIDNIGHT FIRE

MADELINE BAKER

"Lovers of Indian Romance have a special place on their bookshelves for Madeline Baker!"
—*Romantic Times*

A half-breed who has no use for a frightened girl fleeing an unwanted wedding, Morgan thinks he wants only the money Carolyn Chandler offers him to guide her across the plains, but halfway between Galveston and Ogallala, where the burning prairie meets the endless night sky, he makes her his woman. There in the vast wilderness, Morgan swears to change his life path, to fulfill the challenge of his vision quest—anything to keep Carolyn's love.

_4056-5 $5.99 US/$6.99 CAN

Spirit's Song

MADELINE BAKER

She is a runaway wife, with a hefty reward posted for her return. And he is the best darn tracker in the territory. For the half-breed bounty hunter, it is an easy choice. His was a hard life, with little to show for it except his horse, his Colt, and his scars. The pampered, brown-eyed beauty will go back to her rich husband in San Francisco, and he will be ten thousand dollars richer. But somewhere along the trail out of the Black Hills everything changes. Now, he will give his life to protect her, to hold her forever in his embrace. Now the moonlight poetry of their loving reflects the fiery vision of the Sun Dance: She must be his spirit's song.

___4476-5 $5.99 US/$6.99 CAN

Dorchester Publishing Co., Inc.
P.O. Box 6640
Wayne, PA 19087-8640

Please add $1.75 for shipping and handling for the first book and $.50 for each book thereafter. NY, NYC, and PA residents, please add appropriate sales tax. No cash, stamps, or C.O.D.s. All orders shipped within 6 weeks via postal service book rate. Canadian orders require $2.00 extra postage and must be paid in U.S. dollars through a U.S. banking facility.

Name_____

Address_____

City_____State_____Zip_____

___ enclosed $_____ in payment for the checked book(s).

___ must accompany all orders. ❏ Please send a free catalog.

___ OUT OUR WEBSITE! www.dorchesterpub.com